Romantically Challenged

Romantically Challenged

BETH ORSOFF

NAL NEW AMERICAN LIBRARY

New American Library
Published by New American Library, a division of
Penguin Group (USA) Inc., 375 Hudson Street, New York, New York 10014, USA
Penguin Group (Canada), 90 Eglinton Avenue East, Suite 700, Toronto,
Ontario M4P 2Y3, Canada (a division of Pearson Penguin Canada Inc.)
Penguin Books Ltd., 80 Strand, London WC2R 0RL, England
Penguin Ireland, 25 St. Stephen's Green, Dublin 2,
Ireland (a division of Penguin Books Ltd.)
Penguin Group (Australia), 250 Camberwell Road, Camberwell, Victoria 3124,
Australia (a division of Pearson Australia Group Pty. Ltd.)
Penguin Books India Pvt. Ltd., 11 Community Centre, Panchsheel Park,
New Delhi - 110 017, India
Penguin Group (NZ), cnr Airborne and Rosedale Roads, Albany,
Auckland 1310, New Zealand (a division of Pearson New Zealand Ltd.)
Penguin Books (South Africa) (Pty.) Ltd., 24 Sturdee Avenue,

Rosebank, Johannesburg 2196, South Africa

Penguin Books Ltd., Registered Offices: 80 Strand, London WC2R 0RL, England

First published by New American Library,
a division of Penguin Group (USA) Inc.

First Printing, April 2006
10 9 8 7 6 5 4 3 2 1

REGISTERED TRADEMARK—MARCA REGISTRADAA

LIBRARY OF CONGRESS CATALOGING-IN-PUBLICATION DATA:
Orsoff, Beth.
   Romantically challenged/Beth Orsoff.
      p.   cm.
   ISBN 0-451-21774-8
   1. Dating (Social customs)—Fiction. 2. Women lawyers—Fiction. 3. Los Angeles
(Calif.)—Fiction. 4. Rejection (Psychology)—Fiction. I. Title.
   PS3615.R67R66 2006
   813'.6—dc22   2005029523

Printed in the United States of America

PUBLISHER'S NOTE
This is a work of fiction. Names, characters, places, and incidents either are the product of
the author's imagination or are used fictitiously, and any resemblance to actual persons, living or dead, business establishments, events, or locales is entirely coincidental.
   The publisher does not have any control over and does not assume any responsibility
for author or third-party Web sites or their content.

Acknowledgments

Thank you to my first readers—Patti Gandras Alperin, Erwin Chemerinsky, Susan Essex, Eileen Hale, Pam Kirsh, Susan and Evan Rubin, and Samantha Paynter Sandman—for their patience and honest feedback. Thank you to my parents for not freaking out when I told them I was quitting my day job to write a novel. Thank you to Rose Hilliard and Barbara Collins Rosenberg for helping me to bring Julie, and especially Joe, to life. And last but not least, thank you to my husband, Steve, the first reader of every draft, and my biggest fan.

CHAPTER 1

The Wedding from Hell

"**M**arry me," he said.

I looked down into his watery brown eyes. "You're drunk."

"No I'm not," was all he managed before he belched again, filling the air with the sour scent of stale beer. "If you turn me down you'll regret it. Maybe not today. Maybe not tomorrow, but soon and for the rest of your life."

It took me a few seconds to remember where I'd heard that sentiment before. "You can't propose to me with lines stolen from *Casablanca*. And besides, that's the speech Humphrey Bogart made to Ingrid Bergman to convince her *not* to marry him."

"Oh," was all he said before he closed his eyes and returned his head to the table, its resting spot for the previous half hour.

My cousin Sharon's reception was typical of large Jewish weddings. A two-hundred-plus formal affair where everyone was drunk and the over-forty crowd sambaed its way across the dance floor. I was one of nine bridesmaids. The only one without a date. Which was why I got stuck sitting next to Peter, the fourteen-year-old brother of the groom. He didn't have a date either. But at least he had a good excuse: He wasn't old enough to drive his girlfriend to the wedding.

Despite the company, I spent most of the evening hiding at my table. It was the only place where someone dressed in a polyester teal-green gown with shoulder pads big enough for a linebacker and more tulle than a tutu could blend in. But when the fourteen-year-old looked like he could vomit at any moment, I decided to take my chances with the rest of the room. Even interrogations by my relatives were better than being puked on.

I'd only made it ten feet from the table before I heard my name shouted from the dance floor. I turned toward the voice automatically and saw my mother's Aunt Rose waving at me. It was too late to run in the other direction. We'd made eye contact.

Aunt Rose's white-blond hair sparkled in the light from the chandelier as she shimmied across the room in her black sequin cocktail dress, my Uncle Ed in tow. "Julie, dear," she said, grabbing my hands, "where have you been? We've been looking for you all night."

Avoiding my family. "Just blending with the rest of the teal ballerinas," I said.

"Don't be ridiculous, dear, those dresses are beautiful. Aren't they, Ed?"

"Beautiful," Ed said, mopping his flushed face with his handkerchief.

"So tell us how you are, dear," Aunt Rose asked. "I don't think we've seen you since the last wedding. Whose was it again?"

"Madeline's."

"Right." She released my hands so she could use hers for emphasis. "Your poor Uncle Jerry, having to make two weddings back to back like that."

I nodded sympathetically. I'd hoped Sharon would wait until I'd at least found a date before she got married.

"Of course Joan is thrilled to have both of her daughters married. And both under thirty. How old are you now, dear?"

"Thirty-two," I said and forced a smile.

"Don't worry, dear. Your time will come."

"Julie's time better come soon or she's going to miss out." I recognized that snide voice even before I spun around in my matching teal heels, bringing me face-to-face with my sister, Deborah. Somehow she'd managed to sneak up on me from behind. Not an easy task for someone with forty-eight-inch hips.

"What are you talking about?" I said. "Women can have children in their forties. My clock isn't even ticking yet." I'd repeated this statistic so many times in the last year I was actually starting to believe it.

"That's if you want to have a baby alone," Deborah said and smirked. "If you want to get married first, you're going to have to do it by the time you're thirty-five."

"How would you know?" Deborah had gotten married right after college and had been popping out babies ever since. She was only four years older than me, but she already had three children.

"I read *Modern Woman*," she said, but quickly returned to offense. "There was a big article this month about all the single women over thirty-five who can't find husbands. Did you know there are ten million more single women over thirty-five than single men?" Deborah shifted toward Aunt Rose. "Apparently the few single men left think that once a woman hits thirty-five, all she wants to do is get married and have babies. They won't even date them anymore."

"You're making that up." At least I hoped she was.

"It's true, lawyer girl. Look it up."

Before I could tell Deborah that she was just jealous because

I was thin and had a career and she was fat and didn't, the band leader began a soulful rendition of "You Light Up My Life," and Deborah left to find her husband. It was their wedding song.

"Just ignore her, dear," Aunt Rose said when Deborah was out of hearing range. "Men love women who have careers." She leaned closer. "They think if a woman has her own money, she won't spend all of theirs."

I glanced back at my table and saw that the fourteen-year-old was now sprawled across both his chair and mine. If I didn't want to talk to any more relatives—and I didn't—I could think of only one place to go. I said good-bye to Aunt Rose and Uncle Ed and headed toward the ladies' room.

I hadn't even made it past the tail end of the conga line before I was spotted by my Uncle Jerry. He stumbled in my direction, bow tie undone, but every perfectly coiffed gray hair still glued in place, with help from his sister-in-law Maureen. Uncle Jerry was the host, so I felt obliged to stop.

"Hi, honey," Maureen said with her trademark phony niceness. "Are you having fun?"

"She better be," Uncle Jerry slurred. "Do you know what this wedding is costing me?"

"It's great, Uncle Jerry. Sharon looks beautiful." Thirty seconds of chitchat and I'd be on my way.

"I know," he said, and transferred his arm from Maureen's shoulder to mine. "I can't believe my baby is married. You know, after Madeline's wedding we all thought you would be next. I even bet on you."

Great, now I'm a racehorse.

"No, Jerry," Maureen said, "that was *two* weddings ago. Since Julie's boyfriend left her, she's been out of the running."

After equally uplifting conversations with another great-aunt and two distant cousins, I finally made it to the ladies' room. I sat in the cold marble stall and forced myself not to cry—otherwise my mascara would run and everyone would know I'd been crying, and that would be even worse than having to listen to all of my relatives tell me that they just couldn't believe a smart, attractive girl like me couldn't find a man.

With the exception of my mother's Aunt Rose, the older generation considered my being an attorney a liability rather than an asset. It meant I spent too much time on my career and not enough on the paramount task of looking for a husband.

After ten minutes of deep, cleansing breaths, I stood up to leave when I heard Maureen's fake laugh and another voice I didn't recognize. I hiked my dress up again and sat back down. A cold toilet seat was still better than another conversation with Maureen.

"Who was that woman you and Jerry were talking to?" the Other Voice asked.

"Which one?" Maureen replied. "Jerry was all over the place."

"The bridesmaid," the Other Voice said. "The short one with the dark hair and the big chest."

"That was Jerry's niece Julie. Sheila and Phil's daughter. I'll have to ask Jerry if she had a boob job. Those definitely weren't real."

Boob job? Hasn't anyone heard of the water bra?

"Is she here with anyone?" the Other Voice asked.

"No," Maureen said. "Why?"

"I was thinking she'd be perfect for my brother. He just broke up with his girlfriend and he goes for those cutesy types."

Why are the short girls always described as cute? Why are we never beautiful? Then I looked down at my teal green gown and realized in this outfit, I should be grateful for any compliment.

"I don't think your—" Someone chose that inopportune moment to flush the toilet, temporarily disrupting my eavesdropping. When the water stopped running, I heard Maureen say, "Her ex writes for that TV show *Legal Love.*"

"Which one is that?"

"The one on Friday nights about the female lawyers who are great at their jobs but can't find a decent husband."

"I saw that once. I thought it was good."

"It is." Maureen lowered her voice, but she still spoke loud enough for me to hear. "Supposedly the 'Ilene' character, the one whose boyfriend is cheating on her and she doesn't know it, is based on Julie."

That was it. I burst out of the stall and into the center of the ladies' room. "I'm not Ilene, I'm Susan. The one who goes out with all the studs and dumps them as soon as they fall in love with her."

Maureen stood frozen with her mouth open, her lipstick hovering two inches from her face. The Other Voice, a pale, mousy woman, gasped. The other two women, whom I thankfully didn't know, just stared at me.

I sprinted out the door before anyone had recovered enough to respond.

CHAPTER 2

There's Always Vodka

It only took a few seconds for my anger to dissolve into tears. Despite what I'd told Maureen, she was right. I was the one whose boyfriend was cheating on her and didn't know it. I couldn't rewrite history, but I could avoid my relatives and I definitely knew a way to dull the pain.

The hotel bar was perfect—dark and quiet and nearly empty. The only other patrons were a couple at a table near the windows and a middle-aged man sitting at the corner of the bar. I went to the opposite end and sat down.

The tall, dark-haired bartender put down the magazine he was reading and walked toward me. "Can I help you?"

"Stoli and 7-Up with lime."

"Are you okay?" he asked, watching me attempt to soak up my tears with the sleeve of my dress.

"Fine."

"You sure?"

"Yes," I said. "Thanks."

"You know the drinks at the wedding are free. These you have to pay for."

"Just bring me the drink, okay?"

He took the hint and returned a minute later. "Six-fifty," he said and set the glass down in front of me.

I opened my purse and realized I didn't have any money. Only a lipstick, a used tissue, and my room key. "Can I charge it to the room?"

"Sure." He handed me a check. "Just write down your room number and sign here."

I took my drink to an empty table near the door. The middle-aged man must've thought that was a sign that I wanted company.

"May I?" he asked in a thick Texas drawl. He had his hand on the chair across from me. That's when I noticed the cowboy boots and the silver belt buckle shaped like a horse.

What does a person have to do for a little alone time? "I'd really rather you didn't," I said.

He sat down anyway.

"Bill Engel." He extended his hand.

I shook it lamely. "Listen, Bill, no offense, I'm sure you're a great guy, but I'd really rather be alone right now."

"Come on now, missy. You can be alone anytime. This is your one and only opportunity to meet me. How many cowboys do you think there are in New Jersey?"

"I imagine not too many, but I'm really not interested." I didn't want to be rude, but I'd had enough socializing for one night. I picked up my drink and went back to my corner bar stool.

Cowboy Bill followed.

I drained my glass in two gulps and asked the bartender for another. When he placed the check on the counter, Cowboy Bill grabbed it.

"I'll get that."

"No." I yanked the check from his hand. "I can pay for my own drink." The last thing I wanted was for this guy to think I owed him something.

"Now why are you bein' like that?"

The alcohol hadn't kicked in yet and I could feel my anger boiling up to the surface. "If you don't leave me alone, I'll call the police."

"What do you think the police are gonna do? I haven't touched you." Like magic, the accent had disappeared.

"Then I'll sue you for harassment."

"What are you, one of those bitchy New York lady lawyers?"

"No, I'm one of those bitchy L.A. lady lawyers."

The bartender interrupted. "How about I call you a cab, Mr. Engel?"

"I don't need no cab," Cowboy Bill said. "I can hold my liquor." Then he swigged the rest of his beer, slammed it down on the counter, and stomped out.

"Thanks," I said to the bartender.

"No problem, little lady," he said with his own Texas twang.

I had to laugh. "What was up with that guy's accent? I've never met anyone from Texas who could turn it off and on like that before."

"He's not from Texas," the bartender said, "he's from Trenton. He just likes playing cowboy."

"Why?"

The bartender shrugged. "Too many *Big Country* weekends on TNT?"

We both laughed at that.

"Sorry about before," I said. "I'm just having a bad night."

"I figured," he said. "No one with a smile like yours could be all bad."

"Thanks," I mumbled into my drink while I fought back another grin. When I pulled my tattered tissue out of my purse and attempted to use it to blow my nose, the bartender reached under the counter and handed me a stack of cocktail napkins.

"Thanks," I said again while desperately trying to think of a witty follow-up. After ten seconds of silence I gave up and asked, "So how did you know I was with the wedding?"

"The dress." He nodded at it with his chin. "I don't know a woman alive that would wear one of those things voluntarily."

A guy with a fashion sense. He must be gay.

"And no," he added, "I'm not gay."

"I wasn't thinking that," I lied.

"Well most women would. I don't know anything about women's clothes, but I know every woman I've ever met hates bridesmaids' dresses."

"I'll drink to that," I said, and drained my second vodka and 7-Up. He poured me another. This one tasted mostly like vodka. I was starting to get that warm glow and I wanted it to last.

CHAPTER 3

Going Home

The next thing I remembered was answering my wake-up call at 9 a.m. The brunch was scheduled for 10 a.m. I could live without food. I rolled over and went back to sleep.

The phone rang again at 10:15.

"Where are you?" It was my mother's voice. "Everyone is asking for you."

"Tell them I don't feel well and I'm not coming," I said.

"Everyone will just think you're hungover," my mother said, clearly intending the accusation.

"Then tell them I'm hungover and I'm not coming."

"Fine," she said. "I'll make up an excuse. But your father wants to leave for the airport by noon, so make sure you're ready." Click. She hung up on me.

I lay on the bed with my head throbbing and tried to put the pieces back together. I was alone, on top of the covers, and still wearing my bridesmaid dress. That was a good sign. No pantyhose, but I vaguely remembered ripping those off in the bathroom earlier in the evening.

I still had my panties on, but my bra was missing. That was weird. I must've taken it off during the night. The last thing I remembered was talking to the cute bartender. I guessed (hoped) I must've just gotten drunk and come upstairs and passed out. If it was anything else, I'd hear about it sooner or later. I always did.

After four aspirin and three bottles of water, I felt well enough to shower and get dressed. When I'd finished, it was almost noon and I still hadn't packed, so I just threw everything from the dresser and the closet into my suitcase. I'd sort it all out when I got home.

At exactly twelve o'clock (my parents are punctual if nothing else), my dad knocked on my hotel room door. My mom had sent him upstairs to get me while she stayed downstairs in the lobby making all the requisite good-byes. Apparently, when you're married, one partner can fulfill all social obligations on behalf of both partners, thereby freeing up the other partner for the more mundane matters. No wonder single people are so busy. We have to handle everything ourselves.

♡ ♡ ♡

As soon as the valet closed my mom's car door, she turned her attention to me.

"So where were you last night?"

"With you and Dad at the wedding," I said. "Remember?"

"Don't be a smart-ass," my dad said, but smiled at me in the rearview mirror.

"We were looking for you," my mom said. "You missed a real scene. Peter, the groom's younger brother, was sneaking beer all night and passed out under the table. No one even knew he was gone until he woke up during the cake-cutting ceremony and started vomiting all over the table. The other groomsmen had to carry him out with an ice bucket under his chin."

I'd escaped just in time.

My mom continued, "Of course his parents were mortified. Sharon said she thought you were keeping an eye on him, but you were nowhere to be found."

"I wasn't his babysitter. I just sat next to him at the table."

"Where were you when they were cutting the cake?"

"I must've just left. I was tired, so I went upstairs a little early."

"Your sister said you got mad at her when she tried to talk to you. She told me you were yelling at Maureen too."

Thirty-six years old and Deborah was still tattling to mommy. "Mother, can we please not discuss this right now." I didn't like discussing my love life (or lack thereof) with my mother even when I wasn't hungover.

"Okay," my mother said. "All I'm saying is you can't get upset every time you go to a wedding."

"I don't get upset every time I go to a wedding," I said, trying to remain calm. "I get upset when everyone hounds me about getting married."

"Well, you know, dear"—here it comes—"you're not getting any younger. . . ." I mouthed the words along with her.

At this point my dad spoke for the second time that hour. "You know what the alternative to aging is don't you?"

My dad's favorite rhetorical question. I looked out the window and saw the first sign for Newark Airport. Only two miles ahead. Thank God.

CHAPTER 4

And So It Began

I was just happy to be on the plane. The airline could even lose my luggage and I wouldn't care. My weekend of humiliation was over, and I had five hours to read the new Scott Turow novel I'd started on the flight out. This time I had an aisle seat, and the woman on my other side already had her iPod on, so I was in the clear.

I was standing in line for the restroom when I heard, "Boy, this plane is crowded." I turned around and saw a skinny guy with a deeply receding hairline smiling down at me.

"It's summer," I said and turned forward again to watch the end of the *Seinfeld* rerun playing on the video monitor.

"Have you seen this one?" the skinny guy asked.

"Yeah," I said, "but it's funnier with the sound."

He nodded. "I'm John, by the way."

I introduced myself, and we continued with meaningless airplane chitchat until the restroom opened up.

I didn't see John when I returned to my seat, and happily went back to my book.

Five minutes later I heard, "So do you live in L.A.?"

John was standing in the aisle next to me. I held my place in my book with my finger. "Yeah," I said. "Do you?"

"I just moved there."

I nodded and went back to my book. I guarantee that if I was even remotely attracted to this man, he would not be talking to me. It was my cosmic karma: lucky finding parking, unlucky in love.

"Did you grow up out there?" he persisted.

"No," I said. "I'm originally from New Jersey. I moved out to L.A. ten years ago." Maybe if I don't ask him any questions in return, he'll figure out that I'm not interested.

"I'm from New York myself," he said.

I nodded. Would it be too rude if I read while he talked? I was still pondering this question when John sat down in the middle of the aisle. I, along with everyone else in the vicinity, just stared at him. Surely this had to violate some sort of airline regulation.

I glanced at the man sitting across the aisle. I was almost positive he was listening to every word, but he kept his eyes pinned to his crossword puzzle. The woman on my right took off her headphones. When I looked at her, she just smiled and pulled a magazine out from the seat pocket in front of her.

"So what kinds of things do you like to do in L.A.?" John asked.

Was this guy actually going to ask me out? Didn't he realize all of these people were listening? Apparently my weekend of humiliation was not quite over.

"Oh, the usual things," I said. "Movies, the beach, hanging out with my friends." Just pick one and get this over with!

"I like movies," he said. "Why don't I give you a call some-time and we can catch a movie together."

"Sure." I still wasn't interested, but I couldn't just reject the guy with everyone watching. It was too cruel. I'd blow him off later, in private.

"Why don't you give me your number," he said.

"I don't have a pen," I replied, hoping he didn't either.

Before he could respond, the guy across the aisle ripped off the corner of his crossword puzzle and handed it to John with his pen.

I knew he'd been listening.

♥ ♥ ♥

I waited in baggage claim for my suitcase and my friend Kait-lyn, who'd promised to pick me up. Kaitlyn would be easier to spot than my black luggage. With her mass of wavy red hair and her minimum four-inch heels, she always stood out in a crowd.

"So how was the weekend?" Kaitlyn asked. "I bet it wasn't as bad as you thought it would be."

"No," I said, "it was worse. And it's not over yet." I'd spotted John on the other side of the luggage carousel. He'd retrieved his bag and was scanning the crowd. I positioned Kaitlyn in front of me while I continued to search for my suitcase.

"Who are you avoiding?" she asked.

"Brown hair, blue jacket, dark green suit bag."

"I don't see him," she said.

"Good, maybe he left." I spotted my suitcase rolling down the chute and stepped out from behind Kaitlyn to retrieve it just as John rounded the carousel from the other side. He rolled his luggage cart over to where Kaitlyn and I were standing, not caring that he was blocking access for several people who were forced to maneuver around him.

"I've been looking for you," he said.

"Why?" I asked.

"I thought maybe I could give you a ride home."

"Actually, I have a ride." I introduced John to Kaitlyn.

He looked dejected for a moment, but quickly rebounded. "Then I'll give you a call this week. I thought we could do something Friday night."

This time no one but Kaitlyn was listening, so I didn't have to feel guilty. "I'm not sure I can make it Friday night."

"Then how about Saturday?"

"I know I have plans one night next weekend," I told him. "I'm just not sure which one."

"No problem," he said. "I'll take whichever night you're free."

Some people can't take a hint.

John walked us to the exit, then left to catch the shuttle to long-term parking. I followed Kaitlyn to her car in the short-term lot. I waited until we were buckled into her black Mustang convertible before I filled her in on the wedding and how I'd met John.

"I didn't think he was bad-looking," Kaitlyn said as she sped down the 405 Freeway. But Kaitlyn liked bald men. "At least you have a date for next weekend."

"I'm not going out with him."

"Why not?"

"Besides the fact that I'm not attracted to him, he's pushy and annoying."

"He just likes you," she said.

One of Kaitlyn's most irritating traits. She insists on seeing the good in everyone. "But I don't like him."

"You're just scared."

"No, I'm not."

"You haven't gone out with one guy since you and Scumbag broke up."

"Not true. I had lunch with that auto broker just last month."

"That wasn't a date. He was trying to sell you a car."

Kaitlyn was right about that. As soon as I told him I still had a year of payments left on my Acura, he asked the waitress for the check and never called again.

"It's been over a year, Julie. It's time."

"It's only been eleven months, and you know I spent most of that time working on the trial. I didn't even have time to sleep, let alone date."

"I know, I know." I was sure she was rolling her eyes behind her sunglasses. "All I'm saying is you need to get back out there."

"You should've been at the wedding."

CHAPTER 5

Monday Morning Depression

Even after a bad weekend, I still get Monday morning depression. It usually starts as an anxious feeling on Sunday evening, which moves into a mild unhappiness on Monday morning when the alarm clock rings, and blossoms into a full-blown depression the moment I pull into the office parking garage. My only consolation is that I know all of my co-workers are afflicted with the same disease.

I arrived at the office at 9:25 a.m., my usual time. Six years ago, when I'd started at Rosenthal & Leventhal right out of law school, I arrived at 9 a.m. But I quickly learned that any time I spent in the office prior to 9:30 was a waste. The Rosenthal of Rosenthal & Leventhal never arrived before 9:30.

A few of the firm's senior attorneys arrived at 9:29, but they'd already made partner, so they could afford to be bold. Occasionally my friend Simone, who occupies the office next to mine, would sneak in at 9:45 a.m. But she always called her secretary in advance and told her to turn on her lights and computer before Rosenthal arrived so he would think she'd just stepped out to the ladies' room when he made his morning lap around the office to check who was and wasn't in. My secretary Lucy, besides being completely incompetent, was also Rosenthal's stepdaughter, so I couldn't get away with anything.

After unlocking my own office door, turning on my own lights, and retrieving my own mail (this was one of Lucy's mysterious-illness Mondays), I followed my usual morning routine. I turned on my computer and checked voice mail while I waited for it to boot up, then I checked e-mail, snail mail, and skimmed *Variety* while occasionally admiring the view of the Santa Monica Mountains from my thirty-second-floor office window. By the time I finished, it was 10 a.m. Since this was Monday, and Rosenthal left the office every Monday morning for his weekly 11 a.m. appointment with his shrink two floors below us, that meant I only had to work for an hour before I got a break.

Simone walked into my office promptly at 11:02 for our Monday morning depression-reliever/bitch-about-our-jobs/weekend-catch-up session. She must've had a court appearance earlier that morning, because she was wearing her conservative (for her) outfit—black summer-weight wool Armani jacket with matching skirt that stopped short four inches above her knee, three-inch pumps that brought her 5'9" frame to a full six feet, and her long, silky-straight chestnut hair pulled back in a clip.

"I could think of a million places I'd rather be today than here," Simone said, flopping down in my guest chair.

"So could I, but Jersey wouldn't be one of them."

She sat up. "I almost forgot. How was the wedding?"

I gave her the highlights.

"Don't take this the wrong way," Simone said after I'd finished, "but I think your mother may be right."

First Kaitlyn and now Simone. What was this, a conspiracy? "Consider yourself my ex-friend."

"Just hear me out," she said. "Your sister was telling the truth about that article. I read it myself."

Before I could object to what I would've argued were the obvious flaws in the analysis, she put her hand up to stop me. "Assume for the sake of argument that the article is correct. That means you need to be married by the time you're thirty-five."

"You're supposing that I want to get married and have children."

"You know you do, so don't bother denying it."

"Not true," I said. Simone leaned back in the chair, folded her arms across her chest, and puckered her lips. "Okay, if you swear never to tell my mother, I'll admit that I really would like to get married someday. But I'm still undecided about the kids."

"Agreed," Simone said. "But since you haven't affirmatively decided *not* to have children, you'll want to keep your options open. Therefore, you'll need to get engaged by the time you're thirty-four so you can plan a nice wedding, or, in your case, so your mother can plan a nice wedding. And you'll want to know the guy for at least a year first, which means you'll have to meet your future husband when you're thirty-three."

"I'm already thirty-two."

"Plenty of time to find a husband," she said.

"Easy for you to say. You're engaged."

She stretched out her long, shapely legs. "Yes, but that's only because I did lots of dating first. It's really just a numbers game. You just haven't met enough men."

"Meeting men"—or at least ones I'm interested in—"isn't as easy for me as it is for you, Simone. I don't look like a model."

Greg, the other sixth-year associate in the firm and the only natural blond I know, leaned against the doorway to my office. "What is that I heard about models?" he asked.

"You were standing outside the door listening, weren't you?" Simone said.

"Of course not," Greg replied. "I was just walking by when I thought I heard you say some models were coming in and I wanted to offer my services—in case they needed an escort or something."

Simone stood up. "I don't know how your wife puts up with you."

"I'm sure she considers herself a very lucky woman," Greg said to Simone's back as she walked out. To which Simone responded by slamming her office door shut.

Someday I was going to figure out what made those two so combustible.

Greg sat down in the guest chair Simone had just vacated and put his feet up on the corner of my desk. It was a good thing I hadn't planned on getting any work done this morning.

"What's up, Greg?"

"Nothing much," he said. "I just wanted to tell you not to sell yourself short. If I were single, I'd go out with you."

"So you *were* listening."

"Yes," he said, "but you're missing the point."

"Which is?"

"That it's actually easier for women who look like you than for women who look like Simone."

This ought to be good. "How do you figure that?"

"Because you're approachable. A lot of guys don't ask out the beautiful women because they're afraid they'll get rejected."

I knew I wasn't a goddess, but I didn't need Greg to confirm it for me. "So what are you saying? Men ask out ugly women because they think the ugly ones are so desperate there's no way they'd turn them down?"

"No," he said. "What I'm saying is that a guy is a lot more likely to ask out a cute girl, like you for instance, rather than one who's knockdown gorgeous, because he thinks he actually has a chance with the cute one."

I wasn't sure which was worse, Greg's theory or my desperately wanting to believe it was true. "Are you serious?"

"Absolutely. I'm sure if you put yourself out there you won't have any trouble getting dates. You just need to get out more."

I was still skeptical.

"Trust me," he said, and flashed me his reptilian smile.

Before I could come up with a snappy response, the reminder window on my computer popped up. It was 11:50. Rosenthal's fifty-minute hour with his shrink was up, which meant that it was time for the rest of us to go back to work.

CHAPTER 6

The Scintillating Single Life

I felt guilty for wasting almost the whole morning, so I paid penance by spending the entire afternoon on the most boring task imaginable: reviewing documents. By six o'clock, I'd sifted through seven banker boxes, more than ten thousand sheets of paper, and I still hadn't found the smoking gun. Probably because there was none. There never was, except, of course, in the movies and on TV. But I was still required to look.

I was calculating the odds of getting caught if I snuck out early (less than 50 percent since Lucy wasn't there to flub my excuse) when my computer dinged and my e-mail message indicator popped up on the screen. It was from Rosenthal. My and the rest of the litigation attorneys' presence was required in the conference room at seven o'clock.

Simone and I groaned simultaneously. The long, narrow conference room table was covered with trays of sandwiches and bowls of salads. If Rosenthal was buying us all dinner, it meant he was planning on a late night.

Simone, Greg, and the other three litigators in the firm all went back to their respective offices to call their significant others. They wanted to warn them not to worry if they didn't arrive at their usual time.

I stayed in the conference room, alone. I didn't miss Scumbag, he was a liar and a cheat, but I did miss having someone to call. That's the worst part about being single. No one worries about you if you don't come home.

We ate all of the pastrami and half of the turkey and roast beef sandwiches, and finished off most of the Caesar salad. Rosenthal showed up twenty minutes later with a specially prepared high-protein, low-carb grilled salmon concoction, and we all had to breathe in the garlic fumes for ten minutes while he ate.

After picking his teeth at the table and checking his hair in the reflection from the empty foil container, Rosenthal was ready to begin. "I called this meeting to tell you all about the barnstorm I had on the way to work this morning."

Simone, who was seated across from me, inconspicuously drew the number one in the air. Rosenthal's first malapropism of the week. His record was five, but we were sure he could beat it.

"What we need," he continued, "is a client party."

That's a brainstorm?

"We could invite the clients to the Christmas party," Parker, the firm's most senior associate and designated scapegoat, suggested.

"No," Rosenthal said, and pressed his lips together before the words "you idiot" escaped. "We need to have one now. Something big and glitzy. We need to remind them that we're here, we're talented, and we're ready for their business. . . ."

Rosenthal droned on for at least another half hour before Parker excused himself to go the restroom. Five minutes later a greenish Greg followed, then an extremely pale Simone, then me.

We all waited together in the Cedars-Sinai Hospital Emergency Room. It didn't take us long to figure out we'd gotten food poisoning. Everyone but Rosenthal. He was the only one who hadn't eaten the tainted deli meat.

None of us wanted to go to the emergency room, but Rosenthal insisted. He wanted medical records for the lawsuit against the restaurant. He told us we could each keep whatever settlement he extracted for pain and suffering, but since he paid us for sick days, he was keeping the payment for lost wages himself. We weren't in any condition to argue with him.

I'd been lying on the table in Exam Room Two for what seemed like hours when my knight in white lab coat walked in. "So how are you feeling this evening, Ms. Burns?"

I lifted my head off the table and stared into his dark brown eyes. He was medium build, had light brown hair, and adorable dimples in both cheeks. I really wished I didn't smell like vomit.

"I've been better," I said, trying not to breathe on him.

I read his name tag while he examined me. D. COHEN, M.D.

"What's the *D* for?"

"David."

David Cohen. He had to be Jewish. I was about to look for a ring when I started to feel the bile rise in my throat. He must've recognized the signs, because he handed me a silver basin and told me the nurse would be right in.

I sucked on ice chips before I left, just in case I ran into Dr. David. But by the time I was released, he was gone. As were all of my co-workers. They'd all been picked up by their boyfriends, husbands, and wives. If it wasn't after eleven, I might've called Kaitlyn for a ride. Instead, I called myself a cab, picked up my car at the office, and drove myself home.

I walked into my dark apartment and turned on all the lights. I checked my answering machine—no messages. I flopped down on the couch and tried to tickle the Elmo doll that now lived with me instead of my niece Ashley. No response. His batteries were dead. I'd tickled him so much lately, I'd worn him out. I glanced over at the plant in the corner of my living room, the last remaining vestige of Scumbag. The once thriving minipalm was brown and withered. I was the only living being in the house.

That's when I decided. Cosmic karma be damned.

CHAPTER 7

A Whole New Me

The shot they'd given me at the hospital the night before had worked. I woke up the next morning feeling fine, but that was no reason not to take advantage of a bona fide sick day. Besides, I needed some free time to buy Elmo fresh batteries, pick up a new plant, and find my soul mate.

I left a voice mail at the office, shut off the alarm clock, and went back to sleep. My mother woke me an hour later.

"Are you okay?" She sounded genuinely concerned.

"Of course, Mom. What's wrong?"

"Your secretary called us this morning and told you had to go to the hospital last night."

I was going to kill Lucy. I spent the next ten minutes reassuring my mother that I wasn't going to die of food poisoning anytime in the near future and promised to "doctor myself up," whatever that meant. Then I called Lucy.

I didn't even wait for her perky voice to finish saying "Julie Burns' Office" before I interrupted with "Why did you call my mother and tell her I went to the hospital?"

"Because she's your emergency contact."

I imagined her innocent, freckled face and instantly felt guilty for wanting to strangle her, even though I still wanted to strangle her. "But there was no emergency. And how did you even know?"

"Greg told me this morning."

"Greg's in the office?"

"Of course."

"How about Simone?"

"She's here too. I think you and Parker are the only ones out."

Not a good association. I liked Parker, but I wanted to be made partner next year, not the new firm scapegoat.

"I'll be in at eleven."

"I thought you were sick?"

"I'm feeling better," I said and hung up. God knows what she'd tell Rosenthal. If she wasn't his stepdaughter, I would've replaced her ages ago, but I couldn't even get her transferred to another attorney. I'd tried, but Rosenthal wouldn't allow it. He told me she's my "pendant to bear."

♡ ♡ ♡

I called Kaitlyn from the car on my way to work. I was hoping she'd meet me for dinner and a soul mate searching strategy session. Her assistant told me she was out sick. Since it was one of those rare smog-free Los Angeles summer days, I tried her cell before finally reaching her at home. She greeted me by coughing in my ear.

"I guess that means you're not faking," I said.

"No," she coughed again. "You know I'd never do that."

That made one of us. "What's wrong?" I asked.

"Summer flu. It's been going around the office."

"Do you need anything? Food? Drugs? Entertainment?"

"No. I'll just lay here and pray for an early death."

"When's the last time you ate?"

After a loud nose-blowing she said, "I don't know. Last night maybe."

"I'll be there by eight."

♡ ♡ ♡

After work, I stopped at the grocery store for orange juice and a pint of Ben & Jerry's Chunky Monkey, then Jerry's Deli for some chicken noodle soup, and finally Blockbuster for a copy of *Out of Africa*, Kaitlyn's favorite movie. It wasn't the evening I'd envisioned, but Kaitlyn needed some TLC.

She answered the door in her short-sleeve cloud pajamas, her red hair flattened on one side of her head and puffed out three inches on the other. She laid on the living room couch while I set our plates on the coffee table. Kaitlyn had a kitchen table, but in the ten years I'd known her I'd never seen her use it for anything other than storage.

"Hallelujah," she said and threw up her gangly arms when I told her my decision.

"Calm down, I haven't found him yet." I was trying to soak up the soup she'd spilled on the coffee table before it reached her Persian rug. "I've just decided to look. The problem is, I don't know where."

"Singles bar," she suggested.

"Only someone who hasn't been on a date in four years would think you could find your soul mate in a singles bar." Kaitlyn had gone directly from her college sweetheart to her law school sweetheart to Billy, her first and only blind date. They'd been together ever since, although the last nine months had been long-distance.

"I know," she said, practically throwing her spoon at me. "The guy from the plane."

"Are you out of your mind!"

"I'm not saying he's necessarily The One, but you should at least get to know him before you rule him out."

"First, he never even called me and—"

"Yet," she said. "Did you check your messages today?"

"No, but—"

"No buts, go check your machine. And get me the ice cream while you're up."

I followed instructions and found a message from Plane Guy asking me to call him back. I hate it when Kaitlyn's right.

"Call him back and tell him you'll go out with him Friday night," Kaitlyn said through a mouthful of Chunky Monkey.

"But he can't be The One," I whined.

"Didn't your mother ever tell you Prince Charming might not come in the package you expect?"

"No, and even if she did, you know I never listen to my mother."

"Then listen to mine." Kaitlyn's mother was a psychologist and had been married three times, the last one when she was sixty. I had to give the woman credit. She had a career when most women didn't and she knew how to find a good man.

"I don't even know what that means."

"It means keep an open mind."

"I have an open mind."

"No you don't. Since Scumbag, you run every guy you meet through your mental checklist and if he fails in any category, no matter how minor, you immediately eliminate him."

"That's not true."

"Then why haven't you gone on a date in almost a year?"

"Because I find great parking spaces instead of great men. It's my karma. I have to find a way to reverse it. Maybe I should start valeting everywhere I go."

She rolled her eyes. "Finding your soul mate has nothing to do with parking and everything to do with your attitude."

"What's wrong with my attitude?"

"Why won't you go out with the guy from the plane?"

"Because he's annoying."

"See." (I didn't.) "You talked to him for a whole five minutes and you've already ruled him out."

"What are you saying? Prince Charming is disguising himself as an annoying skinny guy with a receding hairline?"

"I'm saying give him half a chance before you blow him off."

I was about to say no when I realized maybe Kaitlyn was right. Maybe Plane Guy was Prince Charming wrapped in annoying paper and I just had to open the package to find out. And if, as I suspected, he really was a frog, then I could prove Kaitlyn wrong. It was a win-win scenario.

"Fine," I said, "but if I have a terrible date it'll be on your conscience."

She took the spoon out of her mouth and gave me her most self-satisfied grin. "I can live with that."

CHAPTER 8

Prince Charming

The new, open-minded me reluctantly agreed to go out with John on Friday night. He called me Thursday night to work out the details.

"So what do you want to do tomorrow?" he asked.

"I don't know," I said. "How about dinner?"

"Dinner? That's so boring."

"Then how about a movie?"

After a few seconds of silence he said, "Nah, I don't feel like a movie."

"Okay. Then what *do* you feel like?"

"I don't know, I just moved here. You need to show me around."

Prince Charming was trying my patience. "That's fine, but you'll need to give me a hint about what you're looking for."

"Forget it. I'll come up with something and surprise you. I'll pick you up at eight."

I snuck out of work early Friday night so I would have time to shower, dress, and eat dinner before John arrived. I wasn't going to spend the entire evening hungry just because he thought dinner was boring. When I buzzed him upstairs at ten minutes to eight, I intended to chide him for being early, until I opened my front door.

"What are you wearing?" I said, despite it being quite obvious that he was wearing sweatpants and a torn T-shirt under his raincoat.

"My workout clothes," he said and held up his gym bag as an offer of proof.

"Why?" was all I could manage.

He walked into the living room, sat down on the couch, and put his sneakered feet up on my glass coffee table. "I joined a gym on Monday and they sent me a free guest pass. I thought we could go work out, then grab a coffee."

Maybe I'd been out of circulation too long, but when did working out become an acceptable first date activity?

"It's on Roberston," John continued. "Just a few blocks from here."

"I know the one," I said. "I used to belong there."

"Used to?" He took his feet off the coffee table and sat up. "What's wrong with the place?"

"Nothing, I just got really busy at work and let my membership lapse."

He relaxed back into the couch. "Good, then you can sign up again tonight with me as your referral. That way, I get the free gift. I think they told me it's a voucher for a health food restaurant. We can go there afterwards for dinner."

At this point, the close-minded Julie would've told him to get the hell out and never call again. But as the new open-minded Julie, I just said, "I wasn't planning on renewing my membership."

"Why not?"

"I've decided to join a new gym by my office."

That wasn't a total lie. I'd driven past the gym near my office a few weeks ago and had momentarily considered joining. I just hadn't thought about it since. Not that I didn't need to—I did. I'd gained six pounds since Scumbag left me, although I could only attribute three to the breakup. The other three could be directly traced back to last Christmas's cookie binge.

"Well, we don't need to go to dinner, you can still use my guest pass."

Lucky me.

I left John in the living room while I went into my bedroom to change. It took me ten minutes just to locate my sneakers. I found them buried in the back of my closet under an old black leather purse I hadn't used in years but couldn't part with and a jumble of dry cleaner's hangers.

By the time I'd peeled myself out of my black jeans (the only pair I still owned that didn't make me look fat) and pulled on my baggy sweatpants, I was starting to think maybe this hadn't been such a bad idea after all. John was definitely a cheapskate, but if we were only going to the gym it would be a short evening, and at least now I was comfortable.

"Which way is your car?" I asked John as we stood under the awning of my building waiting for the rain to let up.

"That way," he said, pointing toward the end of the street, "but I figured we'd walk."

"In the rain?" It was obvious John was new to Los Angeles. Los Angelenos don't walk anywhere. Ever. Especially not in the rain.

He pulled his car keys out of his pocket and said, "C'mon, I have an umbrella in the trunk."

"Do you have two?" I asked.

"It's a big one," he said. "We can both fit. It'll be romantic."

I could imagine strolling through an unexpected tropical rain shower, hand in hand with a gorgeous guy. My hair would be mussed, but my makeup would still be perfect, and my floral sundress would be clinging to me in all the right places. The guy would only be wearing Bermuda shorts. His muscular upper body would be glistening with a mixture of sweat and raindrops. He would be holding his soaking wet T-shirt over our heads in an ineffectual yet gentlemanly attempt to keep us dry. That would be romantic. Walking six blocks to the gym in a cold downpour with John the Annoying Cheapskate was not romantic.

John held the umbrella at an angle in his left hand. This succeeded in keeping the wind from blowing the rain directly into our faces, but also meant that he was the only one actually under the umbrella. By the time we reached the gym, my fingers were numb and the right side of my body was completely soaked. Except for a few wet spots at the bottom of his sweatpants, John was completely dry.

Luckily, the woman at the reception desk remembered me from the years when I had been a regular. She let me borrow shorts and a T-shirt from the lost-and-found box while she ran my clothes through the towel dryer.

I found John upstairs on a treadmill. He'd already started a slow jog.

I stepped onto the treadmill next to him. "I've never seen it this empty before. When I used to come here there were always at least five people ahead of me on the waiting list and tonight there's not even a line."

"Isn't it great?" he said. "I love to work out on Friday nights."

I just nodded. On the rare occasions when I'd even considered working out on a Friday night, Scumbag had always talked me out of it. He told me only losers without friends went to the gym on Friday nights. I decided to be nice and keep this opinion to myself. Instead, I asked John how his week had been and he started telling me about his job in marketing for a petrochemical company. I asked questions and nodded dutifully on the off-chance that my initial impression of him had been wrong and that he was actually a good catch. We were forty-five minutes into the date and so far he hadn't said or done anything to change my mind.

Abruptly, John asked, "Are you going to walk the whole time?"

I looked down at the timer on my treadmill. I'd only been walking for three and a half minutes. "I'm warming up," I said. "I haven't worked out in awhile."

"There's no point in working out if you're not going to raise your heart rate. If you're just going to walk at that pace, you might as well not even bother."

I increased the speed on my treadmill from 3.3 to 3.6 and immediately started to sweat. John seemed satisfied and went back to talking about himself. A few minutes later John pronounced that we'd warmed up enough and it was time to run.

"John, I haven't worked out in almost a year. I'm not running."

"Coward."

I should've bailed on him right then, but I took the bait. "I'm not a coward. I just don't want to hurt myself."

"You won't hurt yourself with a slow jog. It's the same as walking fast, only you burn more calories."

I was about to ask if he was implying that I looked like I needed to burn more calories, but stopped myself. I was afraid he might answer truthfully.

"C'mon," John said. "We'll only run for ten minutes, then we'll take a break and move on to the free weights."

Free weights? "I'll run for ten minutes, John, but then I'm done. You can finish your workout while I shower and change."

"Okay. I'm sure it takes you longer to get dressed anyway, so this way I won't have to wait."

John increased the speed on his treadmill to 6.5 and I increased mine to 4.2. I was breathing heavily, but I was still breathing. Six minutes into it I didn't think I could go on any longer, so I switched the display to countdown and started counting along with it. I only had a minute and thirty seconds to go when I noticed my shoelace had untied, but I didn't want to stop when I was so close to finishing.

The last time I looked at the clock I was down to fifty-three seconds. Then I was facedown on the treadmill.

"Julie, are you all right?" It was the woman from the reception desk. She was kneeling next to me. I read her name tag: TRACY. Then I looked up and saw John standing behind her. He didn't look nearly as concerned as Tracy did, but at least he'd stopped jogging.

I thought I was okay until I tried to move my left leg. My shoelace was still caught in the treadmill. Tracy removed my sneaker and untangled it from the machine. She'd had to cut the lace, but otherwise it was fine. It looked a lot better than I did.

I had a bump on my forehead the size of a plum and, according to John, similarly colored, and my left ankle was swollen to twice its normal size.

"I don't think it's broken," Tracy said, "but you really should get it x-rayed, just in case."

"Do you know where the hospital is?" Tracy asked John.

"No," he said. "I just moved here."

"I know where it is," I said to Tracy. "But you'll need to call us a cab. We walked over from my place."

"That's okay," John told her. "I'll run back and get the car."

That was the first acceptable thing he'd said all night.

Tracy helped me down the stairs and into the locker room. She brought me my dry clothes and waited for me while I changed. Then she helped me back to the lobby to wait for John.

"What kind of car does your boyfriend drive?" Tracy asked as she wiped a clear circle into the fogged-up glass entrance.

"I don't know," I said. "This is our first date."

"He took you to the gym on a first date?" Her incredulity was evident both from the sound of her voice and the look on her face.

"Thank you, it's nice to know I'm not the only one who thinks that's weird."

"Is he at least taking you to dinner afterward?"

"Only if I renew my membership and he gets the free gift certificate to the health food restaurant."

Tracy tried to stifle a laugh. "You can really pick 'em."

I gave her a half smile. "He picked me." But I won't make that mistake again. Even proving Kaitlyn wrong wasn't worth this.

We heard a horn honking and Tracy helped me out to John's car. John waited behind the wheel while Tracy maneuvered me into the passenger's seat. I made a mental note to myself to send Tracy a thank-you gift. I didn't need to make a mental note to lose John's phone number.

I directed him the four blocks to the Cedars-Sinai Hospital Emergency Room, where I was quickly becoming a regular.

"If I knew it was this close, I wouldn't have bothered with the car."

He'd just negated his one good deed.

Kaitlyn arrived at my house the next morning with a *grande*-sized Starbucks House Blend for her (she never went anywhere before noon without one) and a giant blueberry muffin for me. After taking off her shoes and promising me that this time she wouldn't spill her coffee, and if she did, she'd pay to have the furniture cleaned, she settled herself on my white futon.

"So how did you leave it?" she asked.

"You mean after he abandoned me in the emergency room because, unlike the gym, hospitals are packed on Friday nights, and he needed to go home and get his beauty rest before his seven a.m. tee time?"

Kaitlyn smiled sheepishly. "I guess he wasn't Prince Charming after all."

"No," I said, "he wasn't. And I'm finished with this open-minded stuff. I'm going back to my mental checklist. That way I can eliminate the losers before I waste an entire evening with them and end up on crutches."

"It wasn't a total waste. You got to see the Jewish doctor again."

Leave it to Kaitlyn to find the silver lining. "For five seconds in the hallway, with my hair in a ponytail, and no makeup."

"Yes, but he remembered you."

"As the girl who almost puked on him."

She leaned down to where I was sprawled on the carpet with an icepack on my ankle and patted the top of my head. "No, Jules, as the cute lawyer with the great smile whose phone number he wanted but stupidly forgot to get."

Only Kaitlyn would think that, and I loved her for it.

CHAPTER 9

Elmo Never Lies

It was an uneventful Friday night. But after my previous Friday night with Plane Guy, I was happy with uneventful. The swelling on my ankle had gone down, so I was off the crutches, and the plum on my forehead had shrunk and faded to a green grape. I'd met Kaitlyn for dinner at the Cheesecake Factory earlier in the evening and she swore that with makeup on and my hair combed forward, the bruise wasn't even noticeable.

By nine o'clock I was lying on the couch in my boxer shorts and T-shirt, searching for something good on TV. After I'd been around the dial twice, I gave up and started flipping through the magazines scattered across my coffee table. Satin pants were out, skinny heels were in, and men really didn't want to date women over thirty-five, at least according to *Modern Woman*.

Only three years left, or just one if I followed Simone's timetable. How did this happen? Thirty-two and I was practically an old maid. But wasn't being an old maid still better than dating—or, God forbid, being married to—someone like Plane Guy? I knew what my mother would say, but I wanted a second opinion.

I retrieved Tickle Me Elmo from his resting spot at the far end of the fouton and stared into his big, black eyes. I'd purchased him last December as a Hanukkah present for my niece, Ashley, but she already had one, so my sister Deborah mailed him back to me. I was supposed to exchange him for a Cookie Monster, but he looked so cute with that orange nose and those googly eyes that I just couldn't do it. Now Cookie Monster lives with Ashley and Elmo lives with me.

I propped Elmo on a throw pillow and asked him what I should do. I squeezed his right foot and he said, "Tickle Elmo again."

"Yes, Elmo, but should I keep dating? I mean, what's the point if they're all gonna be as bad as Plane Guy?" Then I squeezed Elmo's tummy.

"Elmo's not ticklish there."

Hmmm. "So you're telling me they won't all be as bad as Plane Guy?" I squeezed his left foot.

"Elmo's a little ticklish there."

A good sign. "Then you honestly believe my soul mate is out there and I'm not destined to spend the rest of my life lying on this couch watching television and tickling you?" I squeezed Elmo's right underarm.

"Elmo loves being tickled."

Uh-oh. That could be interpreted either way. I decided to give Elmo one last chance before I moved on to the Magic 8 Ball. "So what you're really saying is, I got off to a bad start with Plane Guy, but I just have to keep trying until I find The One?" I squeezed Elmo's left underarm and held my breath.

"That's it, that's it, that tickled Elmo the most," he cried and vibrated right off the couch.

I had my answer. Everyone knows Elmo never lies.

CHAPTER 10

It's Not a Party Without Rosenthal

The next night I tore myself away from Elmo and the Cary Grant marathon on AMC, donned my black Garfield & Macks pantsuit, and headed to Rosenthal's house for the firm's first-- ever client party. Mrs. Rosenthal met me at the door of the sprawling six-bedroom, Spanish-style house in Brentwood, a pricey westside suburb, and introduced herself. We'd met several times before, but she never remembered. I wasn't important enough to have a permanent notation in her mental date book.

Mrs. Rosenthal led me down the hallway, past the decorator-perfect formal living room, through the cavernous family room with state-of-the-art home-theater system, and out to the party in the backyard. It was nice to know that all of my hard work had paid off for someone, although I would've preferred that someone be me.

Mrs. Rosenthal pointed me in the direction of the bar and said, "Why don't you get yourself a cocktail, honey, and mingle."

I turned around to thank her, but she'd already moved on.

I waited at the bar for my vodka and 7-Up with lime and admired her handiwork. It really was impressive, especially since she'd pulled it together on such short notice. The theme was Casino Night and she'd created Vegas in L.A. under a huge white tent. She'd placed a roulette wheel in the center, ringed by poker and blackjack tables, flanked by double rows of slot machines on both sides. All that was missing was the chain-smokers and the busloads of senior citizens.

♡ ♡ ♡

I'd given my order to a female bartender, but it was a male bartender who handed me my drink. "Hi, there," he said.

I said hello back. He was cute, but almost certainly a wannabe. All of the waiters and bartenders in L.A. were wannabes—either actors, writers, directors, or some combination of the three. After six wasted years with Scumbag, I'd sworn off wannabes. This time around I was only going to date "be's."

"This outfit suits you much better than the last one," the bartender said.

"Excuse me?" I responded.

"You don't remember me, do you?"

I stared at him for a few seconds. He was about six-feet tall, with short hair a shade lighter than black, and blue eyes that practically glowed in the dark. I would remember someone with eyes like those. He looked a little familiar, but I couldn't place him.

"I'm sorry," I said, "you're going to have to give me a hint."

Before the bartender could respond, Rosenthal came up and put his arm around me. "C'mon," he said, steering me toward the center of the tent where the hundred-plus guests were congregated. "There's someone I want you to meet."

"Bruce, I was talking to someone."

"You can flirt with the bartender later. I want you to meet Mark Parsons. He's the general counsel for Rosebud Productions."

I knew the name. Rosebud was one of the largest independent production companies in Hollywood. Its last three films were big box-office hits, and it was riding high, for the moment at least.

"What do you want me to do?" I asked, although I already knew the answer. Rosenthal wanted me to flirt with Mark Parsons. It was the only reason he ever introduced the firm's female lawyers to clients.

♡ ♡ ♡

Mark Parsons looked like a younger version of Rosenthal. He was medium height and build, with dark, graying hair. I guessed he was in his mid-forties. He was standing next to a very tall, very pregnant blond woman who looked like she was in her mid-twenties.

Rosenthal put his hand on Mark's back. "This is Julia Burns," Rosenthal said, "one of our senior associates." Rosenthal was the only person besides my mother who ever called me Julia.

Mark Parsons introduced himself and the blonde standing next to him as his wife, Natasha. Rosenthal left us and I attempted to schmooze, but I'm just not that good at it. Mark dutifully answered all of my questions about Rosebud, their past successes, and what films they had in the pipeline, while scanning the room for faces he knew. Luckily, he found one at about the same time I ran out of things to say. Mark excused himself to greet someone else, leaving Natasha with me.

I was relieved, although I must've looked concerned, because Natasha said, "Don't worry, you did fine. He's just working the room."

I nodded. I wanted to bolt too, but I felt obligated to stay and chat with the wife of the person whose business I was supposed to be getting. I was sure Rosenthal would agree.

"So when are you due?" I asked her.

"Two more weeks," she said. "I wish it were sooner. I can't stand the bloating. I don't even recognize my ankles anymore."

I looked at her ankles. They were thinner than mine.

"Is this your first?" I asked.

"Yes," she said and rubbed her belly. "We'd been trying for years without success, but as soon as I quit my job, I got pregnant. It must've been the stress."

"Either you started trying when you were eighteen or you're older than you look." The words popped out of my mouth before I could stop them. I wanted to blame it on the vodka, but I'd only had one drink.

She just laughed. "Actually, I'm thirty-six."

Oops. Missed that one by a decade.

"I used to be a production executive at Rosebud," she continued. "That's how I met Mark. We've been married five years. Are you married?"

"No," I said, "still single."

"Dating anyone special?"

After my nosiness, I certainly couldn't object to hers. "Not at the moment. Right now I'm just looking."

"I know how that goes. I used to do a lot of dating before I met Mark. But after awhile you get tired of it."

I nodded. I'd only had one date and I was already tired of it.

"One night I was at a dinner party," she said, "and I must've been complaining to someone that I hadn't found the right guy yet. Then this older woman I'd never met before walked up to me and said, 'Honey, they're all the same, just pick one.' It turned out to be good advice. A year later I married Mark."

As if on cue, Mark returned. "C'mon baby," he said to her, "there's someone I want you to meet."

♡ ♡ ♡

I found Simone in line at the buffet. We helped ourselves to shrimp, crab legs, and assorted pastas, then weaved through the maze of guests until we found an empty table for two. Simone told me about the clients Rosenthal had foisted her upon, and I told her about Mark and Natasha.

After we ate, we played the slots until I lost all my chips, then we proceeded to the roulette table so Simone could lose all of hers. I didn't see Natasha for the rest of the night, but I couldn't get her story out of my head. Was that woman right? Were they really all the same? Should I stop looking for my soul mate and just pick one and be done? Finally, I asked Simone.

She paused as if giving serious consideration to my question, then said, "Yes, I do."

"Really?"

"No, of course not. And I cannot believe you're seriously considering marital advice from someone you don't know, who you just met at a party, who got that advice at a party from someone *she* didn't know."

"I didn't say I was taking it, I just wanted to know what you thought of it. Besides, I couldn't take it even if I wanted to. There's no one to pick from."

"You could always call Plane Guy."

"I'm not that desperate."

"How do you feel about blind dates?" she asked.

"I don't know, I've never had one. But it seems like it would be kind of awkward."

"It's just awkward for the first few minutes. Then it's like any other date. Sometimes better because you haven't met before, so you have lots of things to talk about. You're less likely to get those deadly lulls in the conversation."

That was a good point. I also didn't have any other prospects at the moment, so I said, "I guess it would be okay if the person setting us up was a friend of mine and knew my taste."

"Good," she said, "because there's someone I want you to meet. His name is Ken and he's a lawyer."

"Ugh, not a lawyer." I've always felt that two lawyers together would be a bad combination. You'd fight all the time, and since both your friends and coworkers would be lawyers, you'd have to spend your entire life surrounded by lawyers. That couldn't be a good thing.

"You need to get over your anti-lawyer attitude. There are tons of lawyers in this town. If you rule out all the lawyers and all the wannabes, there won't be anybody left."

"What about doctors?"

"I don't know any single doctors, do you?"

I thought of the handsome ER doctor who hadn't asked for my phone number. "Okay, what does he look like?"

"He's cute," she said. "He's about 5'8" or 5'9", brown hair, nice body."

"That's kind of short."

"What are you talking about? He's six inches taller than you."

"Every guy I've met since the third grade has been taller than me, but that doesn't mean I want to date them. I like tall guys."

Tall women just don't understand the short woman's dilemma. They think that as long as the man is taller than the woman when she's wearing heels, that the height requirement is satisfied. Tall women don't realize that if both parents are short, as mine are, their child is doomed to shrimpdom. A short woman has to marry someone tall just to give her future children a fighting chance.

"But I guess I could live with 5'9"," I said, "if he's really cute."

"Good, because I've already told him about you, and he's interested. I just wanted to check with you first before I gave him your number. Do you want me to have him call you at the office or at home?"

"The office." At least then if it didn't go well, I could have Lucy screen his calls.

CHAPTER 11

Blind Date Doesn't Mean Blind Date

I looked for the blue-eyed bartender before I left the party, but I couldn't find him. I thought about asking one of the other bartenders if they knew where he was, but decided against it. I didn't even know the guy's name. What was I going to say? What happened to the blue-eyed guy dressed like you who was here earlier? Besides, I was sure he was a wannabe, so there was really no point.

The following morning, mere seconds after Rosenthal left for his therapy session, Simone situated herself in my office.

"I gave Ken your number," she said. "He's going to call you this week."

I was still so consumed with Monday morning depression I'd forgotten I'd agreed to a blind date. "How do you know this guy again?"

"He's a friend of Todd's. They play basketball together."

Todd is Simone's stockbroker fiancé. He's loaded, but an arrogant jerk. Not that I would ever say that to Simone. She goes for that type. I myself go for the sensitive yet manly type. The kind of guy who likes romantic movies but can still fix the leak in your faucet. My type seems to be harder to find.

"But you've met him, right?" I asked.

"Once," she said. "At one of their games."

"For how long?"

"Stop worrying. I wouldn't set you up with a loser."

I hoped not, since it was too late to change my mind. "So how are the wedding plans coming?"

"A nightmare. We can't even agree on a date. I'm ready to elope, but Todd wants the big wedding. It's his first time."

This would be Simone's second wedding. Her first was when she was in her early twenties. She married a rock star named Roach from the Blind Alleys. The band was at its peak then, and she and Roach had one of those ridiculous five-hundred-person weddings at the Plaza Hotel in New York. The marriage lasted less than a year, but Simone received a nice settlement anyway. She says she doesn't care about money, but she always seems to end up with rich men.

"I'm surprised he cares," I said. I didn't think Todd was in touch with his feminine side.

"I think his mother's the one that cares. Since Todd's sister eloped and his brother has finally come out and admitted he's gay, his mother sees this as her last opportunity to plan a big wedding. Just like your mother."

"The difference is that my mother already planned a big wedding—for my sister."

"Yes, but that was a long time ago."

A ray of hope. "Then maybe all I need to do is remind her and she'll stop hounding me about getting married."

"You wish," she said.

And I did.

Ken called on Wednesday afternoon. He told me about his job as a bankruptcy attorney (a plus—he had a career, even if it was in law), his house in the Valley (a minus—nobody likes the Valley, not even the people who live there), and his dog (neutral—I would have to meet the dog and see if we got along). We clicked on the phone, so I had high hopes for the date.

Which meant that I woke up Saturday morning in a panic. Naturally, I called Kaitlyn.

"I have nothing to wear," I said without even saying hello. "I went through my entire closet this morning. All I have are work suits and jeans. No date outfits."

"What'd you wear on the last date?" she asked.

"Sweatpants."

"Oh, right. What time is he picking you up again?"

"Seven-thirty. I figure I need to be in the shower by six-thirty at the latest."

"It's only eleven. Meet me at Nordstroms in an hour. That will give us six hours to find you a cute date outfit, plus some new makeup, and maybe one or two pairs of shoes for me."

"I need new makeup too?"

"We can discuss it later. I'll see you in the shoe department in an hour."

When I arrived at noon, Kaitlyn was already trying on. In twenty minutes she'd purchased a pair of flats, a pair of heels, and was already debating between several handbags. She was my inspiration. I could spend all day shopping and still come home empty-handed. According to Kaitlyn, it was because I'm both particular and indecisive—a bad combination. I needed to work on that.

In two hours we'd scoured petites, contemporary, and individualist, but hadn't found a pair of black pants that made me look thin but didn't need to be shortened (since I had no time for alterations). We fanned out through the rest of the mall and finally ended up in Ann Taylor.

"They're perfect," Kaitlyn said when I'd tried on the fifth and final pair.

I pulled the tag out of the back to check the price. "I can't buy these, they're a size eight."

"So?"

"So I'm a size six. Buying these would be like admitting I'm fat."

"You're not fat."

"Then why are all the size fours tight?"

"Because you're in petites. Petites always run smaller."

"Only in the length. These are all tight in the ass."

"That's the style this year. You either show your panty lines or buy a bigger size."

"You're just saying that to make me feel better about being fat."

"No, I'm not. I swear it. I just bought a pair of size six pants last week and you know I always wear a size four."

After trying on all the too-tight sixes again and promising myself that next week I would join a new gym and go on a diet, I bought the size eight. They weren't perfect, but they'd do.

In some ways, never being able to find the perfect pair of black pants was a good thing. It forever remained an unfulfilled quest to pursue on boring Sunday afternoons when, after flirting with the idea of going to a museum, you admit to yourself that culture is only something you pursue abroad. It was just bad when you needed something to wear that night.

After the pants purchase, Kaitlyn insisted we have makeovers. She ended up with $200 worth of new cosmetics, and I ended up with a new lipstick that I didn't need but bought out of guilt since the sales lady spent half an hour trying to give me a new look. Kaitlyn and I figured that with all that trying-on and walking back and forth in the mall, we must've burned off at least five hundred calories each. Therefore, we practically owed it to our sugar-deprived bodies to stop at Mrs. Fields cookies on the way out. Besides, I had to eat while I still could. The diet started on Monday.

Ken arrived promptly at 7:30. I opened my front door and stared. It wasn't that Simone's description hadn't been accurate. It was that she'd neglected to mention Ken's most distinguishing feature. The man had a forest growing out of his nose.

It was like looking at a car crash on the side of the road—mesmerizing and repulsing at the same time. After a few seconds of gaping, I forced myself to look away.

I couldn't understand it. Even if he was one of those unpretentious guys that didn't spend a lot of time in front of the mirror, he'd have to be blind to miss those nose hairs. They were practically down to his lip.

Ken led me downstairs to his Lexus and held my car door open despite unlocking it with the remote. I gave him a point for gallantry, then double points when he told me he'd made reservations at several different restaurants so I could choose the type of food I wanted. I chose the Japanese restaurant near the water because I'd been there once years earlier and remembered it being very dark inside. Maybe I could forget the nose hairs if I couldn't see them.

It wasn't until we arrived at Mon Sushi that I discovered it had been completely remodeled. Instead of dark and secluded, it was now bright and airy. I was still hopeful when the hostess led us toward one of the few dimly lit tables in the back, until Ken interrupted.

"I'm sorry," he said, "but when I made this reservation I specifically requested a table with an ocean view."

"I know sir," the hostess replied, "but all the ocean view tables are filled. If you want one, you'll have to wait."

He told her we would and led me toward the bar. "I hope you don't mind," Ken said as he pulled out my barstool. "I thought it would be nice if we could watch the sunset."

Successful, gentlemanly, and romantic. Damn those nose hairs.

When the hostess finally brought us to our ocean view table, all that remained of the sunset was a thin band of orange forcing its way through the clouds. Within minutes, the sky went dark and I could barely make out Ken's face. The nose hairs were reduced to a shadow. All was not lost.

Until the busboy noticed Ken struggling to read the menu in the darkness and rushed over to light the candle in the center of the table. It was amazing how much light one small candle could cast, especially when it was placed directly under Ken's nose. Instantly, the forest was back and my eyes were riveted.

The wine helped. By my second glass of cabernet, I'd discovered that Ken had a small dimple in his left cheek that deepened when he laughed. If I focused on the dimple, the nose hairs almost disappeared. I spent the rest of the meal trying to think of something funny to say.

♡ ♡ ♡

Two hours later Ken walked me to the door of my apartment building. I was contemplating whether there was any polite way to suggest to someone that they buy a nose hair clipper when Ken bent down to kiss me. I closed my eyes as soon as I realized what he was doing, but it was too late. I'd already seen those prickly little monsters coming toward me and the image was branded on my brain. When I felt one brush my lip, I leapt back.

"Sorry," I said, turning my head so Ken wouldn't see me wiping my mouth, "I don't kiss on the first date."

"I didn't mean to offend you." He had a wounded expression on his face.

The guilt was flooding my whole body. He was such a nice guy, so many good qualities. How could I be this superficial?

Then I looked up and saw those nose hairs. There was no way I could get past it. I stopped chastising myself and said good night.

CHAPTER 12

Look Who's Coming to Dinner

The next morning I met Kaitlyn for breakfast at Bread & Porridge, the always crowded café around the corner from her apartment. Since Scumbag had left, Kaitlyn and I had had a standing Sunday morning breakfast date that could be canceled

by either one of us if we were out of town or just found something better to do. We rarely canceled.

"It just seems like such a shame to let a good guy go over nose
hairs," Kaitlyn said, still sipping her Starbucks. The waiter hadn't
yet brought us the coffees we'd ordered.

"You wouldn't say that if they were coming out of Billy's
nose."

"Sure I would. I'd just tell him I loved him, then buy him a
nose hair trimmer for Christmas."

"Easy to say when you've been dating the guy for four years."

"Five," she said. "Next weekend's our anniversary."

"Oooo, that's a big one. Are you thinking ring?"

She answered maybe, but the huge grin on her face told
me yes.

"Does that mean you two have finally agreed on where you're
going to live?" It had been a nonstop debate since Billy had been
promoted and had to move up to San Francisco late last year.

"I've been giving that a lot of thought," she said, "and I've decided it makes more sense for him to relocate. He hates his boss
and was planning on looking for a new job anyway, so it'll be
just as easy for him to find one in L.A."

Somehow I didn't think Billy would see it that way. "And
have you told him that yet?"

"No, I decided it was better to have that conversation in person. I'm flying up next weekend. By the way, what are you doing
Sunday night around nine?"

I mentally flipped through the *TV Guide*. "Watching *Desperate Housewives*. Why?"

"Do you think I could talk you into picking me up at the airport instead? You could tape *Desperate Housewives* and I'll come
over Monday night and watch it with you."

"Sure. Although I'd rather you flew back on Saturday night. Then I'd have an excuse to blow off Scott's birthday party."

"I thought you liked Scott."

"I do. I just hate going to parties alone." It meant I would have to spend the entire evening either interjecting myself into other people's conversations or standing alone in a corner like a complete loser. Neither scenario was appealing. "I suppose I could lie and tell him you're flying in on Saturday night. He'd never know the difference."

"Absolutely not," she said. "Parties are a great place to meet men."

"Not when they're thrown by married couples. I'll probably be the only single person there."

It really was an amazing phenomenon. Whenever a single friend married, the friend instantly acquired an entire set of previously unheard of couple friends. The newlyweds would then spend their weekends with all the other couples and stop socializing on weeknights altogether. We single friends were relegated to the occasional lunch, if convenient. If not, we were completely disowned. Scott worked in the office building next to mine, which was why we were still friends. I was still a convenient lunch date.

"All you need to do," Kaitlyn said, "is call Scott's wife and tell her you're coming alone. I guarantee you she will find at least one eligible bachelor to invite to the party."

"Why would she do that? She hardly knows me."

"Because the last thing a new wife wants is for her husband to spend his entire evening chatting up the only single woman at the party."

♡ ♡ ♡

When I walked into Scott and Emily's recently purchased three-bedroom house in Sherman Oaks, a suburb north of L.A., the following Saturday night, I was surprised to discover that this was a sit-down dinner party. I didn't even know Scott owned a dining room table, let alone twelve matching plates. The last time I'd been to his place he was living in a 500-square-foot studio apartment three blocks from the beach and drinking out of plastic cups.

I hadn't even wished Scott a happy birthday yet when Emily pulled me into the kitchen, handed me a glass of cabernet, and said, "I want to tell you about David."

"Who's David?" I asked.

"Your date. And he'll be here any minute, so we don't have a lot of time."

I didn't know whether I wanted to kill her or thank her. "Emily, you told me there would be other single people at the party. You didn't tell me you were fixing me up."

"Well you knew it was a dinner party."

"I thought that meant buffet." The only people I knew who hosted sit-down dinner parties were my parents' age.

"Too messy," she said. "Have you ever tried to clean lasagna off a chenille sofa?"

I admitted that I hadn't, and Emily assured me it wasn't easy. Then she filled me in on David: thirty-three, divorced, no children, originally from Chicago. Then the doorbell rang. She looked out into the living room and said, "That's him, so the rest you can judge for yourself."

"Wait a minute," I said, temporarily halting her sprint to the front door. "What did you tell him about me?"

"I didn't. David doesn't like setups, so don't be obvious."

I didn't have to. Emily took care of that herself. But what she didn't know was that we'd already met.

CHAPTER 13

Third Times a Charm

Emily orchestrated the table seating with me and David, the ER doctor I'd almost puked on, to her right. The rest of the guests automatically sat down next to each other in pairs.

"Julie, I think you already know Jean and Chuck," Emily said, pointing to the couple holding hands at the far end of the table. Clearly still in the honeymoon phase. "This is Christine and Ted, Bill and Anne, Marshal and Lois, and David."

I was thrilled to see David again when I wasn't vomiting and was actually wearing makeup. It wasn't every day I met single Jewish doctors with thick brown hair and dimpled cheeks. Unfortunately, David didn't appear thrilled to see me. Actually I don't think he even remembered me. I attempted conversation anyway. I had no choice. If I tried to talk to Emily or her friend Christine, who was sitting across from me, they would just ask David a question to draw him into the discussion. It was obvious Christine was in on this too. Every time David and I spoke to each other, she and Emily exchanged meaningful glances.

When I thought neither Emily nor Christine was listening, I asked David how he knew Scott.

"Actually, I don't," he said. "I just met him tonight. I work with Emily."

That made no sense. Emily wasn't a doctor. She was a conference planner for a firm downtown. Hmmm. Perhaps the reason David didn't remember me was because we'd never met. Maybe he just looked like the doctor I'd seen in the ER.

"So you're a conference planner too?" I asked.

"No," he said. "I'm a doctor."

Now I really was confused.

I must've looked it, because he added, "Emily planned a conference for my hospital—emergency medicine in the new millennium. Actually, I was really surprised when she invited me here tonight. I hadn't spoken to her in months."

I wasn't. He was probably the only single guy she knew. Kaitlyn would be so pleased to know she was right. I was just pleased to see him again when I didn't smell like vomit or have an ice pack on my head. And if he didn't remember our previous encounters, so much the better. This way we had a fresh start. Although even after an evening of pleasant, if not scintillating conversation, he still didn't ask for my phone number.

♡ ♡ ♡

With Kaitlyn out of town, I decided to skip the fattening Sunday breakfast and headed to the gym instead. Falling on the treadmill had been embarrassing, but buying size eight pants was traumatic. I'd joined the gym by the office on Monday. This would be my fourth workout of the week.

I'd just stuffed my purse into the locker when my cell phone rang.

"It's me," Kaitlyn said when I answered.

"Where are you? I can barely hear you."

"Boarding the plane. I'll be at LAX in an hour. Can you come and get me?"

"I thought I wasn't supposed to pick you up until ten?"

"I can't explain now, the plane is about to take off and I have to turn off the phone. Will you be there?"

"I'll meet you in baggage claim," I said before the line went dead. Then I turned in my locker key and headed to the airport.

I found Kaitlyn resting on a bench near the luggage carousel. She had dark circles under her eyes and no ring on her finger, but with her red hair swept up off her face and her slightly sunburned nose and cheeks, she still looked beautiful. I watched more than one man take notice of her.

"Billy and I broke up," she said.

"How the hell did that happen? I thought you were getting engaged."

"We did. For about a day."

Her sky-blue eyes welled up with tears that spilled over onto her cheeks. I sat down and put my arm around her shoulder until she stopped crying, then I handed her the pocket pack of tissues from my purse.

"Billy won't move to L.A.," she finally said. "His boss was transferred, and when his boss's boss found out Billy was interviewing, he gave him a huge raise. Now Billy doesn't want to leave."

"Then move up to San Francisco. It's only an hour away by plane." A rare moment of selflessness. It actually felt kinda good.

"I'm not moving to San Francisco! I like my job and all my friends are here. I have a life."

"I pulled out a fresh tissue from the pocket pack and handed it to her. "I know. But is it really worth ending a five-year relationship over?"

She wiped her eyes and said in a surprisingly even tone, "If, after all this time, he's not willing to make a minor sacrifice for the sake of the relationship, then obviously he's not really committed."

"I'm not sure moving to a new city is a minor sacrifice, but if you think it is, then why aren't you willing to?" I couldn't believe that I was actually trying to convince my best friend to leave me.

"It's minor for him. He's lived in San Fran less than a year. I've lived in L.A. for ten years."

I wasn't going to argue with that logic, at least not today. "So how did you leave things?

"We talked about it all last night, and we both agreed the relationship is over. We'll always care about each other, but it's time to move on." Then she blew her nose one more time, forced a smile onto her face, and said, "Let's go."

I offered to do any activity Kaitlyn wanted to take her mind off Billy, but she insisted that she was fine and that all she needed was a big breakfast and a ride home. I was amazed at how well she was handling this. Maybe it helped when your mother was a shrink.

♡ ♡ ♡

After blowing my diet on a stack of blueberry pancakes with Kaitlyn, I headed back to the gym for an hour and a half of penance on the exercise bike. By the time I got back to my apartment all I wanted was a nap, but the blinking red light on my answering machine was insistent. I hit PLAY and the computer voice told me I had three messages.

The next voice I heard was my mother's. "Julia, it's Mommy. I don't know where you are. Call me." How happy am I that I never gave her my cell phone number.

The second message was from Simone. "I found a great way

for you to meet a bunch of new men. Call me." I had given Simone my cell phone number, but she never remembered it.

The third voice I didn't recognize. "Hi, Julie, it's Joe, the bartender, from the casino party. I was just wondering if you figured out who I am yet. Call me at (310) 555-0196. I have something of yours I'd like to return."

I listened to Joe's message again, and this time I wrote down the phone number. How did he find me? How did he even know my name? And why was I so excited? When my heart no longer felt like it was going to burst out of my chest, I dialed. His answering machine picked up on the fourth ring. "Hi, it's Joe." I hung up before it could finish.

This was stupid. I was a grown-up. Or at least I was supposed to be a grown-up. I should act like one. My hands were still shaking when I hit the redial button. This time the machine picked up on the second ring. "Hi, it's Joe. If you want me to call you back, leave your message at the beep. If not, then hang up now."

"Hi, Joe," I said after the machine beeped. "It's Julie. Julie Burns. From the party. You left me—"

"Hi, Julie. I was hoping you'd call me back. Did you just try me a few minutes ago?"

"No," I lied.

"Sorry, it's just that someone called and hung up about two seconds before you did. I thought it might've been you."

"Nope." That's the problem with lying. Once you start, you have to see it through to the end. Hopefully he didn't have caller ID. I decided to deflect with an offensive maneuver. "Do you always screen your calls?"

"Not usually. But with four bags of groceries and a container of water in my arms, it was just easier."

"I see," I said. Then silence. "So how did you get my number?"

"You gave it to me."

"No I didn't." This time I wasn't lying.

"Yes you did. You even wrote it down for me. (310) 555-2139."

That was my number. But of course he knew that. He had called me. This was too weird. "Listen, I don't know what your deal is, but—"

"You still haven't figured out who I am yet, have you?"

"Of course I have. That's why I called you back. You're the bartender from my boss's party."

"No, I mean where we *first* met."

I ignored the remark. Never admit defeat. At least not if you still have an opening. "I really just called because you said in your message that you had something of mine you wanted to return. I thought maybe you found my earring. I lost one at the party." More lies.

"No," he said, "It's not an earring. But I still think you're going to want this back."

"What?"

"I'd rather show it to you in person. I was about to start dinner. Why don't you come over and have dinner with me, and I'll give it to you then."

"I'm not coming to your house for dinner!"

"Why not? I'm a great cook."

Modest, too. "Are you insane? I don't even know you. I don't even know your last name. You could be an ax murderer for all I know."

"My last name is Stein and I'm not an ax murderer. Have you ever heard of a Jewish ax murderer?"

"What about that Berkowitz guy in New York?"

"He was a serial killer, not an ax murderer. But no, I'm not a serial killer either."

"Are you a lawyer?" He certainly sparred like one.

"No," he said "but my dad was a lawyer, so I know how to play."

Smart for a wannabe.

"Julie, I'm really hungry. Is there any chance I'm going to be able to convince you to come over here tonight?"

"Nope."

"What about meeting me somewhere else for dinner?"

"I have plans tonight." That wasn't really a lie, because now that I'd already picked up Kaitlyn, I planned to stay home and watch *Deperate Housewives*.

"Then how about lunch one day next week? Broad daylight, public place. I'll even let you choose the restaurant."

"That way I can have my bodyguards waiting to jump you in case you try anything?"

"Exactly."

"I guess that would be okay." I was dying to know what he had of mine, and it looked like meeting him was the only way I was going to find out. Besides, he was really cute.

"Great. You tell me where and when."

"How's Wednesday, one o'clock, P.F. Changs on Wilshire?" I'd been craving Chinese food all week.

"Sounds perfect. Have a good night, Julie."

"You too, Joe." I could hardly wait.

CHAPTER 14

Bad Chinese Food

I woke up Wednesday morning feeling nauseous. I knew it was just nerves. The same thing happens on days when I have to go to court.

I was twenty minutes late to work because I couldn't decide what to wear. Since I couldn't wear my date outfit to the office, I ended up choosing a black pantsuit and a white silk tank top. Business attire, but still sexy, or so I hoped.

I spent the morning reading discovery responses, the opposing side's responses to my side's questions, but I couldn't concentrate. After two hours I gave up and doodled on my legal pad until it was time to leave for lunch. I knew I would pay for this later with a very late night at the office, but it couldn't be helped.

I calculated that in the middle of the day, I would need at least twenty minutes to get from my office in Century City to the Chinese restaurant four blocks from the beach in Santa Monica. I could've chosen somewhere closer, but I wanted to get far enough away that there would be no chance of me running into anyone from the firm. I didn't want an audience for my date.

At exactly 12:38 (yes, exactly) I put down my pad and retrieved my suit jacket from its hanger on the back of my door.

When I reopened it, Rosenthal was standing in the doorway. Shit, not now!

He looked at his watch. He knew I normally left for lunch at one o'clock. If I was leaving early, it probably meant I was taking longer than an hour. Rosenthal believed no one needed more than hour for lunch. The way he put it, my time was his money.

"Where are you off to?" he asked.

"Lunch," I said. "I'm meeting someone at one so I really need to go. Can this wait?"

"Who are you meeting? A client?"

The only exception to the one-hour-lunch rule was if you were meeting a client—then you could bill it. "Potential client." Not a lie. You never know.

I slid past Rosenthal and out to the hallway. He sniffed the air. "Are you wearing perfume?"

"Yes, I always do." What could be the harm in one more inoffensive little lie?

"I don't think so," he said as he followed me down the corridor toward the elevators.

Why did he have to be so goddamn nosy? "Bruce, I'm running late. Can we talk when I get back?"

Naturally, he ignored my request. "I need to tell you about a new case. It's for Rosebud Productions. Do you have time to take on a new matter?"

"Sure," I said, pushing the elevator call button. Now go away!

"You must've really impressed Mark Parsons. He specifically requested that you work on this."

"That was nice of him." I barely remembered meeting him. Although I did remember his wife. She must've had a hand in this. I'd have to remember to call her and thank her.

"I've set up a conference call with him at three."

I stepped into the elevator and turned to face Rosenthal. "Then how about I come down to your office at two-thirty and you can bring me up to speed."

"I guess it can wait until then," he said and frowned.

"Good," I said as the elevator door began to close.

"And Julia . . ."

What now? I pushed the DOOR OPEN button.

"Have fun on your date." He gave me a wide grin.

"Goodbye, Bruce." I hit the DOOR CLOSE button and looked at my watch. 12:46. Now I really was going to be late. I raced down to the car and out to Olympic Boulevard. The traffic wasn't as bad as it could've been. I only had to run two yellow lights to make it to the restaurant close to on time.

I fluffed my hair and reapplied lipstick while waiting for the lights I didn't run. My stomach was doing flip-flops. I hadn't felt this nervous before my other dates. The last time I remembered feeling this way about a guy was with Scumbag. I didn't know if that was a good omen or a bad one.

Joe was waiting for me at the entrance. God he looked good. He was wearing black jeans and a slate-gray button-down shirt. Those blue eyes glowed even more in the daytime. I stared at him for half a minute before I even noticed his Banana Republic shopping bag.

"Sorry if I kept you waiting. I was hung up at work."

"No problem," he said. "I just got here."

I gave the host my name and he brought us to a booth in the back of the restaurant. When the waitress came by, Joe ordered a beer and I ordered an iced tea.

"What, no vodka and 7-Up?"

"No, I have to go back to work. But I'm impressed that you remember."

"I'm a bartender. It's my job to remember."

I wanted to follow-up on that with some career-related questions, but I had more pressing concerns. "What's in the bag? Is it the mystery item you wanted to return to me, but only in person?"

"Yup," he said, but didn't make a move toward the shopping bag sitting next to him.

"Well? Aren't you going to give it to me?"

"I thought I'd save it for dessert."

"There is no way I'm going to sit here for the next hour wondering what's in that bag. You've strung this out long enough."

He pondered the idea for a moment, then said, "I guess you're right. Besides, I can't wait to see the look on your face when you open it."

He set the shopping bag on the table and slid it toward me. I reached inside and pulled out a dark blue Gap bag. Inside was something wrapped in a white plastic grocery bag. I gave Joe a nasty look.

He smiled back. "In case you peeked."

I unfurled the grocery bag and pulled out a beige water bra. "What the hell is this?"

"It's your bra." He folded his arms across his chest with a self-satisfied grin. "Interesting texture. What's inside that thing? It feels like Jell-o."

"This isn't my bra," I said automatically.

"Really? Then how come it has your name and number in it?" Joe reached for the bra and turned it over. It was my name and phone number in black ink scrawled across the inside of the left cup. I recognized the handwriting as my own.

This was not happening. I had to be dreaming. This had to be a nightmare. I would will myself to wake up. I closed my eyes.

When I opened them Joe was still sitting across from me. Now I remembered where I first saw him. At the bar at the hotel where my cousin Sharon had her wedding.

Think fast. Try offense. It worked the last time. "You could've written that in there yourself. It doesn't mean its mine."

"You think I went out and bought a bra and wrote your name and number in it? Why would I do that?"

"I don't know. You tell me. Maybe you're crazy. Or maybe it's the only way you can get a date."

"I have no problem getting dates."

That I believed.

"Why don't you just admit that it's yours?"

I hated conceding, but I knew I was cornered. "Okay, even if I assume you're not lying and this really is my bra, why would I have given it to you?"

"Because you wanted to prove to me that you could take your bra off without removing your dress first. You told me you could do it, but I didn't believe you, so we bet on it. I lost."

That did sound like something I might do after four or five drinks.

"I was really impressed," he added. "I'd never seen anyone do that before. Do you want me to show you how you did it?"

"No." I knew how it was done. "Assuming you're not making all this up, what happened next?"

"I paid up and bought you two more drinks. Then I went into the stockroom to clean up before closing. When I came back, you had your head on the bar and were sound asleep."

That definitely sounded like me.

"I tried to wake you, but you were out for the night. I ended up carrying you up to your room."

"You carried me?"

"At first I just tried to help you walk on your own, but you kept falling down. Eventually I gave up and carried you the rest of the way."

"How did you know what room I was in?" I was still hoping I could catch him in a lie to prove that he was making all this up.

"You charged your drinks to your room, counselor. The room number was on the receipt."

Damn. "So what happened when you brought me upstairs?" I didn't really want to know, but at this point I had to.

"What do you think happened?" He flashed me a wicked grin.

"I don't know," I said, my voice rising. "That's why I'm asking." It's hard to remain calm when you're being humiliated.

"I was a perfect gentleman. I just laid you down on the bed and left."

I gave him a look that told him I didn't believe him. I knew how I got when I'd had a few drinks. I wouldn't have wanted him to leave.

"I swear," he said and held up his right hand. "I didn't even peek."

"So when did I give you my bra?"

"You didn't exactly give it to me. It was more like you left it for me. I found it the next morning when I opened up. It was lying on the floor next to your bar stool. I tried to return it to you, but you'd already checked out."

"And when did I write my name and number in it?"

"That I don't know. Maybe when I was in the stockroom. All I can tell you for certain is that it had to be some point before you passed out."

The waitress who'd been hovering for the last ten minutes

came to the table and asked for our order. Neither of us had even opened the menu. Joe asked her to give us a few more minutes. Although clearly perturbed, she complied.

Joe scanned the menu. "So what do you want to eat?"

"I'm not hungry." All I wanted to do was get the hell out of there. Fast. I looked at my watch. "I think I may have to cut this short."

"C'mon, you need to eat."

"My stomach's hurting. Whatever I eat now will just make me feel worse." I stuffed the bra and the smaller bags into the shopping bag and pulled my wallet out of my purse. I found a twenty-dollar bill and threw it on the table. "You stay and eat. Lunch is on me."

"Don't do this," he said, and stuffed the twenty back in my purse.

I threw it back on the table. "It's my way of saying thank you for carrying me up to my room." I slid out of the booth and held up the shopping bag. "And for returning my bra."

I walked out of the restaurant and practically ran to the valet stand. I was determined not to burst into tears until I was alone in my car. I heard Joe calling me, but I ignored him and handed the valet my ticket.

"Julie, wait." He was standing next to me. He no longer looked so attractive.

"Joe, I really need to get back to the office. I have a conference call this afternoon, and a meeting with my boss before that, and I really just need to go."

"I'm sorry if I upset you. I honestly thought the whole thing was funny and I thought you would think so too."

"It was. But I need to leave." It was getting harder not to crack with him standing next to me.

"If you don't want to eat, then let's take a walk. We can go down to the pier and play video games and forget this ever happened."

I saw my silver Acura round the corner. "Good-bye, Joe" was all I said before I sped away. I waited until I passed two stop lights before I allowed the tears to roll down my cheeks.

I could picture the scene in my head. It played over and over again, like a tape in an endless loop. I desperately wanted to stop the VCR, but I couldn't. Each time the tape ended, it rewound itself and replayed.

I'd passed out in the hotel bar, my butt still planted on the barstool, my head and arms sprawled out in front of me. Joe walks in and sees me. He calls my name, but I don't answer. He shakes my shoulders, but he can't rouse me. He slaps my face (gently, he's not one of those guys who beats up on women) to try to wake me, but without success. He realizes the inevitable.

He pries me off the bar stool and cradles me in his arms. He carries me out to the elevators, staggering under the weight of both me and my bridesmaid dress. He makes it to the elevators, but just barely. He leans against the wall for support until the car arrives. When the door opens, he steps in and falls to his knees, dropping me on the floor. He pushes the button for the ninth floor. He thanks God for the elevator.

When the car stops at my floor he realizes that there's no way he can make it to the end of the hall with me in his arms. He curses me for having a room so far from the elevators, then picks me up and throws me over his shoulder. When he reaches Room 923 he pulls my matching teal purse out of his jacket pocket with his right hand, balancing me on his shoulder with his left. He fumbles, but eventually finds the key. He swipes the key card and pushes the door open.

He walks inside and flips me onto the bed. I fall onto the blue and gold flowered spread with my arms outstretched, one leg falling to the floor. He pushes the fallen leg onto the bed, then notices the drool dribbling down the side of my face. "Why me?" he mumbles to himself before slamming the door shut behind him and heading back to the elevators.

I could never face this man again.

CHAPTER 15

Postmortem

Simone was walking toward the escalators when I pulled into the parking garage. When she spotted me, she stopped and waited for me to catch up.

"What's wrong?" she asked. "You look like shit."

"Thanks, Simone." I thought I'd fixed my makeup in the rearview mirror, but apparently I was unsuccessful. Why could I never remember to buy waterproof mascara?

"What did he do to you?"

"Nothing. Really." She looked doubtful. "It just didn't go as well as I'd hoped." My voice cracked and the tears started flowing again. We rode the escalator from the garage to the lobby, then I headed toward the elevator bank marked floors twenty-one through thirty-five.

"You're not going to the office looking like that," she said.

"What am I supposed to do? Take the rest of the day off?"

"That's a great idea. Maybe I'll join you. We could go to a spa."

"No," I said through tears.

"It would make you feel better. I guarantee it."

I didn't doubt her, but there was no way. "I have a meeting with Rosenthal at two-thirty and a conference call at three."

"So cancel. Tell him you're sick."

I shook my head. "He knows I had a lunch date. He'd probably just think I got lucky and I'm off in a hotel somewhere getting laid."

"Not a chance. We all know how virginal you are."

"Thanks, Simone." She has a lot of admirable qualities, but diplomacy isn't one of them.

She looked at her watch. "It's only two o'clock. Take a walk with me and I'll buy you a cup of chamomile tea."

"I don't want any tea."

"Well, I need caffeine, and I don't want to go alone, so you're coming."

Simone led me to the Coffee Bean in the lobby of our office building and ordered a latte for her and tea and a giant chocolate chip cookie for me. We sat down at a table for two with our sugar and steaming cups. I spilled my guts and Simone laughed out loud.

"You are totally overreacting."

"No, I'm not. I was completely humiliated."

"Someday you're going to look back on this and laugh." This just started her on another wave of giggles.

I told her I doubted it, but she was laughing so hard she didn't hear me.

"Are you going to see him again?" she asked when her laughing fit had finally subsided.

"Weren't you listening to a word I said? That was the most humiliating experience of my life." A slight exaggeration, but I was on a roll. "Every time I see him I will have to relive that nightmare. No, I'm definitely not seeing him again."

"We'll see." She looked at her watch. "C'mon, let's go fix your makeup. You don't want to go upstairs looking like that. You know how nosy Rosenthal is. Although I'm sure he would get a kick out of this one." This launched her into a whole new cycle of hysterics.

I kept telling Simone it wasn't funny, but that just made her laugh harder. By the time we reached the thirty-second floor, even I was laughing, although not as much as she was.

♡ ♡ ♡

I sank into Rosenthal's black leather couch. He had the corner suite with views of both the mountains and the city.

"Did you have a nice lunch?" he asked.

"Yes," I lied for both our benefits. I was sure he didn't really care how my date went and I didn't want to share. "How was yours?"

Rosenthal proceeded to tell me every minute detail of his lunch hour. I nodded and occasionally commented just so he would think I was listening. After the lunch story, Rosenthal opined about lawyer-client relationships in general, the qualities needed for a successful television show, and the prospects for the Lakers in the upcoming season. There is no area in which Rosenthal does not consider himself an expert.

At five minutes to three, Rosenthal finally told me about the

Rosebud Productions case. At three o'clock, he called Mark Parsons, Rosebud's general counsel.

Mark's voice boomed through the speakerphone. "Julie," he asked, "has Bruce brought you up to speed?"

"I think so," I said. "One of your production executives fired his assistant and she's claiming sexual harassment."

"You've got the facts right, but the genders wrong. The executive is Rita Levin and her former assistant is Jared Kinelli."

"That's a new twist."

"Unfortunately, not for Rita. She was involved in a similar suit when she worked at Worldwide. It settled out of court."

"Confidentially, I hope."

"Yes, but not before a complaint was filed, so it's all public record."

Not good. "If it's all right with you, I'd like to come in and interview Ms. Levin." It was always best to get the facts in person. Besides, it was a good excuse to get out of the office for a few hours.

"I'll have her assistant call you to set up a meeting."

"She has a new assistant already?"

"He's a temp."

♡　♡　♡

This case didn't sound particularly exciting, but a new case I could throw myself into was just what I needed to forget about my date with Joe. I went back to my office and checked my voice mail. The first message was from my mother wanting to know if I was still alive. The second was from Kaitlyn wanting to know about the date. And the third was from Joe: "I just wanted to say again that I'm really sorry about this afternoon.

I'd love to make it up to you. No surprises this time. I promise. Call me."

I called my mother back first, before I forgot again. Luckily she wasn't home, so I got away with just leaving a message that I'd talk to her over the weekend. Although that might seem like I merely put off the inevitable one more week, I'd actually accomplished something. My parents and I normally spoke once a week. By pushing off the conversation to the following weekend, I'd reduced the number of "When are you going to get married/You're not getting any younger you know" phone calls per year from fifty-two (plus birthdays) to fifty-one (plus birthdays). When it comes to preserving sanity, every little bit helps.

Next I returned Kaitlyn's call.

"I can't believe you waited this long to call me back," Kaitlyn shouted when she picked up the phone.

"I had a meeting right after lunch," I said in my defense. "I do have to do some work you know."

"All right, stop your whining and just tell me who he is already."

I told her the whole story.

"Look at it this way," Kaitlyn said, "at least you got your bra back."

Only Kaitlyn could find the upside in that date.

"So when are you gonna call him back?"

"I'm not calling him back. He completely humiliated me." Why did no one understand this?

"No, he didn't. Perhaps wrapping your bra up like a present and giving it to you in the middle of a restaurant wasn't the best idea he ever had, but he apologized. Besides, you have to call him back. There are too many unanswered questions."

"Such as?"

"Such as does he live in Los Angeles? If you're assuming he does, then why was he bartending in New Jersey? If not, then what's he doing in L.A.?"

Good points, but not worth calling him back for. "I think he lives here. When I told him where to meet for lunch he didn't ask for directions."

"That doesn't mean anything—guys never ask for directions. You also forgot to get his work story."

That answer I already knew. "I'm sure he's a wannabe. He's good-looking, so he's probably an actor. They're the worst. Although he's smart, so he could be a writer too."

"What if he's just a bartender?"

"Nobody in L.A. is just a bartender. They're all wannabe somethings."

"He could be the exception to the rule. The one bartender who's just a bartender."

"Then that's just as bad."

"Why?"

I couldn't believe I had to explain this. "Bartenders aren't husband material. Besides the fact that they work nights and weekends, the only time I'm free, what would I do with a bartender at all those ridiculous lawyer functions I have to go to?"

"He could mix drinks and get everyone drunk. He'd be a big hit."

"Like you would ever marry a bartender. You won't even go out with a guy if he doesn't have a master's degree."

"That's not true. When I started dating Billy he only had a bachelor's."

I was glad she'd brought Billy up. I wanted to ask, but I didn't want to be the one to broach the subject. "Have you talked to him since you got back?"

"Briefly," she said. "Last night."

"And?"

"And nothing. He said he called to see how I was doing. I told him I missed him, but I was doing fine. He said the same, then his call waiting clicked in and we hung up."

"Are you really fine?"

"Yes, I really am."

She sounded okay, but I was still having a hard time believing it. "When Scumbag left I cried for three days."

"I remember. But this is different. Billy and I have mutually agreed to end the relationship."

Scumbag and I had mutually agreed to end the relationship. Of course, that was after I found him in our bed with the actress from his TV show. I should've known the date with Joe wouldn't work out. Me and wannabes never do.

CHAPTER 16

Tough All Over

The next morning I decided to treat myself to a few hours in the firm's law library. As a junior lawyer, I'd spent so many hours in the library that the senior partners used to tease that they were going to make it my office. Unlike most of my counterparts, I love legal research. I've always thought of it as a treasure hunt for the perfect case. Similar to dating, but better. When you found a case you didn't like, you just closed the book and moved on. Bad dates lasted longer and were harder to get rid of.

I'd just settled into a comfy chair with a casebook and my coffee, when I heard what sounded like an underwater chain saw coming from the other side of the room. Past the bookshelves, and on the other side of the partition, I found Greg. He was lying on Rosenthal's worn, stained, former living room couch, snoring. His black lace-up shoes and yellow tie were lying on the floor next to him. His head was resting on a soft covered book and he was using his suit jacket for a blanket.

I called his name, but he didn't answer. When I shook his shoulder, he opened his eyes, but stared at me without recognition. "What time is it?"

"Almost nine-thirty," I said. "You better get up. Rosenthal's going to be in any minute."

He sat up and reached for his tie. "What's today?"

"Thursday."

He laid back down. "Then I've got time. Rosenthal goes for acupuncture treatments at nine. He won't be in before ten."

"How long has this been going on?" And why was I always the last to know?

"Just a few weeks. I overheard Rosenthal and Parker talking about it in the men's room. Parker told him he'd read somewhere that acupuncture prevented hair loss."

"Is that true?" If it was, I wanted to tell my dad.

"I doubt it. Actually, I think Parker made it up just to get Rosenthal out of the office more. But it worked, so I'm not complaining."

"And when were you going to share this information with your comrades?"

"Sorry, I forgot. I've been a little preoccupied lately."

I wanted to know if it had anything to do with why he was sleeping on the couch in the library, but I didn't want to pry. That was Rosenthal's territory.

I had turned to leave when Greg blurted out, "Samantha left me."

I sat down on the edge of the couch. "I'm so sorry, Greg." I knew that was a lame response, but I didn't know what else to say. Divorce was new for me. "Maybe it's just temporary," I added. "Maybe the two of you can work it out."

"No, it's permanent. I went home last night and all her stuff was gone. That's why I came back here. I couldn't stand to be alone in the house."

"That's awful." I knew it was. I'd felt the same way when Scumbag left. Although I'd spent the night at Kaitlyn's, not the office.

"Fucking bitch didn't even have the guts to tell me in person. She left me a goddamn message on the answering machine."

"Did you call her back?"

"She said not to, that she'd be in touch. I'm supposed to just sit home and wait for my fucking wife to call me and tell me my marriage is over."

"I'm really sorry, Greg."

"Don't be sorry. It's not your fault."

"Well, it's your wife's loss."

I'd planned on extolling Greg's virtues, but before I could begin, Greg said, "I completely agree." At least the breakup of his marriage hadn't altered his personality.

When I asked Greg if he needed anything, he told me just a

shower and a change of clothes. "Will you cover for me if Rosenthal starts nosing around?"

"What do you want me to say?"

"I don't know, make something up."

"How about I tell him that I saw you this morning and you were just leaving for a court appearance downtown. That should buy you a couple of hours."

Greg tied his shoes and stood up. "That's what I love about you, Burns—you can lie with the best of them."

"Only when necessary, and even then I don't really like it."

"You're too good at it not to like it."

"What's that supposed to mean?" I'm trying to be nice to the guy and this is the gratitude I get.

"You're a lawyer, Burns. You're paid to lie." Then he put his hand on my shoulder. For a moment I thought he was going to hug me. Instead, he just gave me that reptilian smile again and left.

Despite what Greg thought, I am not a good liar and I don't particularly like doing it. Nor do I agree with Greg's view of lawyers. Representing clients doesn't mean lying for them. They do that on their own.

CHAPTER 17

Clients, the Joy of Every Lawyer's Life

On Friday afternoon I drove out to Rosebud Productions' offices to meet with Rita Levin. I was waiting for her in the reception area when Mark Parsons arrived. He told me Rita was running late and asked me to come down to his office to talk. I was hoping that meant he wanted to tell me about a new case. I wasn't up for partnership until the following year, but as Rosenthal constantly reminded me, it was never too early to start bringing in business. Not that I wanted to spend the rest of my life working for Rosenthal; I didn't. I just wanted to make partner so I could leave with the title and get a better job somewhere else.

I followed Mark up the stairs and down the hall to his cavernous office. I sat down on the short side of the L-shaped sofa with my pad and pen in hand. Mark shut the door and sat down next to me in the corner of the *L*. Our knees were practically touching.

"You're not going to need that," he said, motioning to my pad and pen.

"No, I do. I have a terrible memory."

"This isn't about the case. I just wanted to talk to you."

The general counsel just wants to chat? "About what?"

"About you. I like to get to know my lawyers."

I shifted my sitting position so it wasn't as obvious that I was moving farther away. "What would you like to know?"

"Just tell me a little bit about yourself."

I hated questions like that. I never knew the right answer. "Like what? Where I went to law school?"

"I don't give a shit where you went to school. I want to know if you're married. Single? Do you have any kids?"

"Good thing this isn't an interview," I said, trying to keep my tone light. "You know you're not allowed to ask those questions."

"I know."

I didn't see any diplomatic way out of it, so I answered, "Single, no children."

"Boyfriend?"

It was no wonder their executives were being sued for sexual harassment. Even their general counsel was doing it.

"Just dating," I told him. Then I asked him about his wife. If we were going to get personal, I preferred to be asking the questions rather than answering them. I also wanted to remind him that he was married.

"She's fine," he said.

"Did she have the baby yet?"

"No, not yet. But she's due any minute."

I continued hammering away at him with questions about his wife and future child until his assistant opened the door and said, "It's Ron on line one." Mark picked up the phone and instantly started schmoozing.

I listened to him talk about his plans for the weekend until his assistant returned a few minutes later and told me Ms. Levin was ready to see me. When Mark saw me stand up, he put his hand over the mouthpiece and whispered, "Call me Monday."

I mouthed back that I would, but he'd already turned away.

♡ ♡ ♡

I followed Mark's assistant down the hall to Rita Levin's office. I'd assumed that any woman who resorted to sexually harassing (or allegedly sexually harassing) her male assistant wouldn't be that attractive. I was wrong. She was gorgeous. Tall and thin, with long blond hair and striking green eyes. She wore a short, tight, charcoal gray skirt, matching high-heeled, pointy-toed shoes, and a hot-pink sleeveless sweater. She didn't need a water bra. Or maybe she was wearing one.

She motioned to a chair across from her desk, and I sat down.

"So you're here about that little prick Jared," she said.

"If you mean Jared Kinelli," I said, "then yes."

"He's just a money-grubbing little bastard."

This should be entertaining. I pulled my pad and pen out of my briefcase. "Why don't you tell me what happened."

"Nothing happened. He's just doing this for the money."

"But you did fire him, right?"

"Of course I did. The bastard tried to blackmail me."

"With what?"

She lit a cigarette and walked to her file cabinet. She unlocked it, pulled out a file, then locked it again. "With this," she said, throwing the file onto my lap.

I opened it and saw that it contained a copy of a Complaint against Worldwide Pictures for wrongful termination and sexual harassment. It also contained a copy of a confidential settlement agreement. I presumed this was the case Mark had told me about.

"I didn't used to lock my file cabinet, but I do now. Jared found those in my office. He said if I didn't promote him he would sue."

"So you fired him instead, and now he thinks that Rosebud will settle just like Worldwide did?"

"Rosebud and me. He's threatening to sue me personally. He thinks he can get more money that way."

"But even if you did settle, wouldn't that hurt his career? No one would ever hire him again after a stunt like that."

"He told me the settlement would be confidential. If it ever leaked out, whether he could prove it was from me or not, then he would get additional payments. The little shit thought of everything."

"Maybe not," I said. I had some ideas, but I wanted to research the issues first before I shared them with Mark or Rita.

As I walked to my car, I saw Mark Parsons at the other end of the parking lot. I didn't think he saw me, so I put my head down and picked up my pace. I'd just inserted my key into the lock when his silver Jaguar pulled up behind me.

"How did it go with Rita?" he asked.

"Good. I want to go back to the office and look up a few cases, then I can call you with an analysis."

"I hope Rita wasn't too rough on you. She can be a real bitch sometimes, especially since Jared left."

Since Jared left? "I would think she'd be happier now that he's gone."

"I guess she hasn't found a replacement boy toy. I warned her if she started sleeping with any more assistants I'd fire her myself."

"She and Jared were sleeping together?"

"Of course. Didn't she tell you?"

No! "When I asked her what happened between them, she said nothing, that he was just blackmailing her for a promotion."

"And you believed her?"

"She told me that Jared had found the Complaint in her files and saw an opportunity."

"Jared's not that smart. Rita told him about the Worldwide lawsuit."

"Why would she do that?"

"Who knows," he said, then his cell phone rang and he was gone.

♡ ♡ ♡

Why did clients lie to their lawyers? I'd never understand it. But on the upside, thanks to Mark's revelation, I no longer had to look up any cases. If Rita was sleeping with Jared while he worked for her, then there was only one option. I had to settle the case.

CHAPTER 18

Bosses. What's Not to Love?

When I got back to the office, I checked in with Rosenthal's secretary, Diane, to find out if I'd missed any crises. My own secretary, Lucy, had called in sick. It was Friday, after all.

"He's been looking for you," Diane said.

"I was at a meeting."

"I know. Simone told me. He said he wanted to see you as soon as you got back."

"Why?"

"I don't know, but he's on the warpath."

♡ ♡ ♡

I admired the view from Rosenthal's corner window while I waited for him to get off the phone. Even the sky looked ominous.

"So, how did it go?" he asked as soon as he hung up.

"With Parsons you mean?"

"Of course Parsons. Who else?"

"Actually, I went down to Rosebud to meet with Rita Levin. The only reason I saw Mark at all was because Rita was running late."

"Rita Levin doesn't send us business. Mark Parsons does."

"Why are you yelling at me?"

"I shouldn't have to tell you who the client is, Julia, you should know."

"The client is Rosebud Productions," I said, raising my own voice. "That includes all of its employees."

"No," he said, and slammed his glass of water down on the desk. "The client is Mark Parsons. At least as long as he's Rosebud's general counsel. He's the one who pays our bills, which pays your salary. Now how did it go?"

"It went fine." This was definitely not the time to complain to Rosenthal about Mark's and Rita's behavior. "I told Mark I would call him on Monday with an update."

"Call him tonight."

"He's already left for the day. He's probably home with his wife. She's about to have a baby, remember?"

"Then leave him a message. And not just on his voice mail. Make friends with his secretary and tell her to call you when the baby's born."

"Why?"

"So we can send him a gift! Christ, Julia, you've got a lot to learn about client relations. You'd better learn quick if you want to make partner here someday."

Actually, Bruce, you can take your fucking partnership and shove it up your ass! "Fine, Bruce," was what I really said. But I did stomp out of his office.

♥　♥　♥

After spending Friday evening downing margaritas with Kaitlyn, I spent Saturday afternoon downing aspirin and Coke from my living room couch. The last thing I felt like doing on Saturday night was going to a bar, but I'd promised Emily. She, Scott, and their friends Christine and Ted were going to listen to

David's band, and she'd invited me to join them. I was pretty sure David wasn't interested (since he'd never even asked for my phone number) and this was just Emily playing matchmaker again. But she swore he'd asked about me after the birthday party and, more importantly, she wouldn't let me off the phone until I said yes.

I arrived at the Love Lounge ten minutes before David's band, the Scalpels, began their fifty-minute set. I was an hour too soon. They were awful. Truly awful. David and the other guitarist sang off-key, the keyboard player's voice kept cracking, and the drummer had no rhythm. When the band finished its set, David came out front and sat with us. This time Emily kept her word and made an early exit with Scott, dragging Christine and Ted after them.

"I guess I should be going too," I said when it was just the two of us.

"It's still early," David said. "Let me buy you a drink."

"No offense, David, but the last thing I want is another drink." I was barely able to drink the one I'd ordered.

He paused for a moment with a quizzical look, then said, "How about some food? Are you hungry?"

"Not really."

"What about dessert?" he offered. "I know a great place on Beverly. There's always room for dessert."

I couldn't argue with that.

♡ ♡ ♡

I followed David in his Mercedes to the great dessert place, but it was closed. We ended up at Norms on La Cienega—the L.A. version of a greasy-spoon diner. David studied the menu until the waitress took our order.

"So how are you feeling?" he asked after she left.

Strange question, even if he was a doctor. Wasn't this supposed to be a date? "Fine. And you?"

"Good," he said. "But I've never had food poisoning."

I was too startled to respond.

After a few seconds of silence he said, "That was you a few weeks ago, wasn't it?"

There was no point in lying. He knew my name. All he'd have to do is look up my chart. I admitted it was, and he admitted that he didn't make the connection until tonight.

"It was something about the way you looked when you were sipping your drink."

"Like I was about to throw up?"

"Yes," he said and laughed.

I explained about my hangover, and he offered to track down our waitress to switch my order from coffee and apple pie à la mode to ginger ale and toast. Then things got easier. David told me about his job and his ex-wife, and I told him about Rosenthal and my new case.

"No ex-husbands?" he asked.

"Just ex-boyfriends."

"Anybody serious?"

"There was one. We broke up about a year ago."

His mouth was filled with strawberry shortcake, but he motioned with his fork for me to continue.

"It's that old Hollywood story. He was a screenwriter who was gonna make it big someday and I was young and stupid and completely in love."

He gulped down his cake and said, "Should I get out my violin?"

Sarcasm. I liked that. "I'll give you the short version. I met him when I was still in law school. After I graduated, we started living together. A year later he quit his job and I supported him so he could write full-time. Two years later he got his big break. His career took off and so did his ego. Then one day I flew back early from a business trip and found him in bed with someone else."

"That hurts."

"Yeah, well, whatever. I learned my lesson. No more wannabes."

"Well you don't have to worry about me," he said. "My band is just a hobby. I seem to have a lot of them now that I'm single again."

Maybe that's what my life was missing: a hobby. Did shopping count?

David spent the next half hour telling me about his newest passion, flying planes. He'd only been taking lessons for six months, but he was just four flight hours away from being instrument-rated.

"Maybe you could come with me sometime," he said. "You're not afraid of small planes, are you?"

"No." I'd flown on commuter planes before.

"Good, I'll set something up."

CHAPTER 19

Flying Lessons

David called two days later and asked me if I wanted to go flying with him the following Saturday. He suggested we wing up the coast and have dinner somewhere, then fly back the same evening. How romantic! A flight to Santa Barbara just to have a meal at a fabulous restaurant on the water, followed by a moonlit walk on the beach. Of course I said yes.

After a half-hour consultation with Kaitlyn Saturday morning, we decided I should wear my black linen sheath dress and black sandals with a hot-pink rayon sweater thrown over my shoulders both for style (according to Kaitlyn, it looked chic) and practicality (in case I got cold).

David arrived at my door at four o'clock wearing khaki shorts and a blue T-shirt. I told him to give me a minute to change. After switching to tan pants, a white tank top, and a denim shirt, I returned to the living room and found Elmo lying facedown on the floor where David must've tossed him, and David sitting in Elmo's spot on the couch. He was reading my old copy of *Modern Woman*.

"I didn't know there were 10 million more single women over thirty-five then men," he said.

I'd have to remember to throw that magazine away.

♡ ♡ ♡

When we arrived at the Santa Monica Airport, David went into the rental office to fill out paperwork and I walked around to the back of the building where the planes were parked. They were mostly four- six-and eight-seaters. The largest of them was still considerably smaller than even the smallest commuter jet I'd flown on. Maybe this hadn't been such a great idea after all.

Ten minutes later David escorted me to the tiniest plane I'd ever seen—a two-seater Cessna. I didn't even know they made planes that small. David opened the passenger door and helped me climb in. I must've looked as scared as I felt.

"Don't worry, it's completely safe."

I just nodded. Be brave.

David sat in the pilot's seat and started checking instruments. When we were taxiing down the runway and David still hadn't mentioned where we were going, I finally asked.

"San Luis Obispo."

The name sounded familiar, but I had no idea where it was. "Is that near Santa Barbara?"

"About 30 miles north."

I'd never heard of any five-star restaurants on the water in San Luis Obispo. Then I remembered why it sounded familiar. "Don't they have a prison up there?"

"According to my guide," David said, "the San Luis Obispo Airport is only a few blocks from the ocean. I figured we could fly up and watch the sunset, and then grab some dinner."

This still might work. Wrong city, but otherwise we were on the same page.

David calculated that it would take about two and a half hours to reach San Luis Obispo. It took over three. By the time we landed, the sun had already set. We walked the few blocks to the beach, but with the sun down, the air had turned cold and the sky was completely dark. No moon, no stars, no romance.

We left the beach and walked around the neighborhood looking for a place to eat. The choice for dinner was easy. There was only one restaurant.

We had the best table available at Mama's Fish & Chips—Formica, with a view of the kitchen. The waitress set our places with plastic cups and utensils, and I added napkins from the metal dispenser. This definitely was not the fine-dining experience I'd imagined. I don't even think it was the restaurant David had envisioned. But it was warm and open, and we were cold and hungry. At least until I saw the roach crawling on the wall above our table. After that, I just drank the iced tea.

♡ ♡ ♡

The first hour of the flight back to L.A. was wonderful. The moon and stars were shining and we could see the coastline below. David even let me fly the plane for a few minutes.

The second hour I spent wishing for a bathroom.

We were just entering the third hour when David told me we were passing Malibu. I looked out the window and searched for the lights from the Ferris wheel at the Santa Monica Pier. All I saw was black. Then the moon came out from behind the clouds and all I saw was white. David picked up the radio and contacted the Santa Monica Airport control tower. The air traffic controller confirmed that the airport was completely fogged in.

I looked over at David. "So what does that mean?"

He looked at me with his killer smile. "That means if we want to land, then we have to find another airport."

"Are you serious?" He couldn't be.

"Oh, yes."

He was still smiling. Why was he still smiling? I had two choices. I could either completely lose it, which would probably increase our chances of crashing. Or I could remain calm, or at least pretend to remain calm, which might increase our chances of landing safely. I chose calm.

"Is there anything I can do?" I asked.

"You can find us a new airport."

I decided he wasn't being sarcastic. "How do I do that?"

"Reach behind you and pull out the loose-leaf binder."

I pulled a three-inch notebook out from behind my seat. "What is this?"

"It's the airplane version of the Thomas Guide."

"What am I supposed to do with it?"

"Just flip through it and see if you can find us another airport."

I started turning loose-leaf pages, looking for names I recognized. "How about Ontario?" An inland airport was probably less likely to be fogged in.

"Too far," he said. "We only have an hour's worth of fuel."

A chill rippled through my body. Calm, calm, calm, I intoned and flipped more pages. "How about Burbank Airport?"

David contacted the control tower and asked for the weather conditions at Burbank Airport. Silence. More silence. Damn you, radio, say something! When it finally spoke, it told us that Burbank was also fogged in.

I felt my denim shirt sticking to my underarms. Calm, calm, calm, I whispered to myself as I flipped more pages. "Van Nuys Airport?" I asked without confidence.

David contacted the control tower again. More silence. When the air traffic controller finally came back on, he said, "Van Nuys has partly cloudy skies. You might be able to make it. What are your coordinates?" David told the controller our location and they plotted our course. The last thing the controller said to David before signing off was, "Watch out for those mountains on your left."

I looked at David. "Is he serious?"

"Oh, yes."

I looked out the window to my left. I didn't see any mountains. All I could see was black. I looked at David again. He was still smiling. Why the hell was he still smiling? Didn't he know we could actually crash and die? Calm, calm, calm wasn't working anymore. Now it was pray, pray, pray.

I looked out into the darkness and wondered how long it would take them to find our bodies. It was too bad no one I knew still spoke to Scumbag. He was the only one I'd told that I wanted to be buried in a mausoleum. Less bugs.

Why wasn't my life passing before my eyes like it was supposed to? All I could think about was what everyone else would think when they found out how I'd died. I was sure Scumbag would think it served me right for going out with someone else—even though he was the one who left me. Emily would probably feel guilty since she set David and I up. My parents, or at least my mother, would probably be happy that at least I died while on a date, and with a Jewish doctor no less. Everyone else would just think I was a complete idiot for going up in a two-seater plane with a guy I hardly knew who wasn't even instrument-rated.

As we crested the hill, we flew out of the fog and I saw the mountains off to our left. That controller wasn't kidding: Those mountains really were close. But that could be a good thing. This way, when we crashed, we wouldn't have far to drop and we might actually survive the impact. Then it would be just like that old TV movie I saw where the couple survived the plane crash and lived for seventy-eight days in the wilderness by eating snow and toothpaste.

As we flew past the mountains, I noticed all the trees and shrubs covering the landscape. That was even better. They would really cushion our fall. Then all the foliage disappeared and we were following the path of red and white lights from the traffic on the freeway below.

"Is that the airport?" I asked, pointing to a long row of white lights off to our right.

"It looks like it," David said, and veered off in that direction.

The plane had started to descend when the controller's voice boomed from the radio, "Alpha charlie four nine three zero, come in alpha charlie four nine three zero."

David picked up the handset and acknowledged.

"It looks like you're headed towards Whiteman Airport. You're not cleared to land at Whiteman Airport. Repeat, you are not cleared to land at Whiteman Airport."

There was an incredibly loud roar above us, and a few seconds later a jet five times bigger than our prop plane dropped down in front of us. My heart nearly stopped. I looked over at David. He had finally stopped smiling.

He picked up the radio and told the controller he acknowledged, but that we were low on fuel. The controller told him he would check with the airport to see if we could be cleared for an emergency landing. While we were waiting, the runway lights disappeared.

"David, what happened to the runway?"

We both looked down at the blanket of white below us. "Fog," he said. David picked up the radio again and told the controller we had no choice but to try to make it to Van Nuys

Airport. The controller gave David the coordinates and wished us good luck.

Once we veered north, the fog disappeared and we could see the street lights below us. This time David spotted the runway before I did. I was too busy looking for an empty street or some soft trees.

The tires hit the runway and bounced once before settling back down to the ground. We were on our way to an empty space at the end of the row of parked airplanes when the engine choked and then died. David didn't even attempt to restart it. We both climbed out of the plane and I followed him across the tarmac.

"Evening folks," the terminal attendant said when we were close enough to hear. "Are you spending the night?"

"The plane is," David told him. "I'll pick it up in the morning."

"No problem," the attendant replied. "What space are you in?"

"We're not," David said. "We ran out of fuel on the runway."

The attendant pointed me in the direction of the ladies' room and I ran inside for the longest, most satisfying pee of my life. My mind was racing, but I couldn't focus. All I kept thinking was the next time I go up in a two-seater plane with a guy who isn't even instrument-rated, I was definitely bringing toothpaste.

CHAPTER 20

Never Say Never

By the time I unlocked my office door Monday morning, I was deep into my depression. I had a conference call with Mark Parsons at eleven, which meant that not only did I have to start working right away, but I would also miss the Monday morning bitch session which I sorely needed. Rosenthal had been on a tear lately, and I had a lot of venting to do.

I finished looking over my notes at 10:55, but I was feeling rebellious, so I waited until 11:03 to call Mark's office. I congratulated Mark on the birth of his son, then we quickly got down to business.

"So what's your analysis," he asked.

"Although Rita maintains that the sex was consensual—"

"I'm sure that's true."

Having seen Rita, I agreed. "Unless we can prove that Jared is lying, my recommendation would be to settle the case. With Rita's track record, we wouldn't want to go to trial. It's too great a risk."

No response.

"Unless you object, I'm going to call Jared's lawyer and set up an informal meeting. I want to get a sense of how strong they think their case is and what kind of money they're looking for."

"Good. Call me after the meeting." He hung up before I could even say good-bye.

Since the conference was so short, I was able to catch the tail
end of the Monday morning bitch session. When I walked into
Simone's office, Greg was already sitting on one of her two guest
chairs. This was a new development. Greg didn't normally join
our bitch sessions. I moved Simone's stack of files off the other
guest chair and sat down.

"What'd I miss?" I asked.

"The usual," Simone said. "Rosenthal's being a prick to
everyone." She gestured to Greg. "Even golden boy."

"It's not possible." I was only half joking. Greg had earned his
nickname.

" 'Tis true," Greg said. "My sheen must've dulled. He ripped
me a new asshole this morning for—"

Greg's secretary opened the door and said, "Parker's looking
for you. He said he needs to talk to you before Mr. Rosenthal
gets back."

Greg stood up and bowed slightly. "Ladies, it's been a pleasure,
as always."

I waited until Greg closed the door behind him before I
asked, "What's up with that?"

"I guess now that he's single again, he's decided to be more
social," Simone replied. "Why? Don't you want to let him in the
gang?"

"Of course I do. You're the one who didn't like him. I'm just
surprised, that's all."

"I like him better now that he's getting a divorce. He's not so
uptight."

"He must not be if he doesn't mind being called golden boy."

She laughed. "That one sort of slipped out. But he took it
pretty well."

"Probably because he knows it's true."

After Simone told me about her weekend adventures with her fiancé, Todd, I filled her in on my disastrous date.

"I just have one question for you," she said. "What the hell were you thinking?"

"I was thinking it would be romantic. I didn't know he couldn't land the plane if the airport was fogged in."

"Clearly trolling emergency rooms isn't working out for you. I think you need to find a new source for men."

I agreed. Even a Jewish doctor wasn't worth dying for. "Got any ideas?"

"Actually, yes. Remember that company I told you about—Just A Date?"

"Isn't that the dating service?"

"Yes, and don't make it sound so suspicious."

"I told you, I'm not joining a dating service."

"Why not?"

"Because it's for desperate people, and I'm not desperate." Not yet anyway.

"Why do you keep saying that? Joining a dating service doesn't mean you're desperate. It just means you're a busy professional who's having trouble meeting quality people on her own."

"You sound like a brochure."

"As a matter of fact," she said, and reached into her bottom desk drawer. She handed me a glossy purple pamphlet folded in thirds. Instead of ripping it up and throwing the pieces at her, I opened it. I'd hit a new low.

The following Friday afternoon it was Kaitlyn who called me looking for a drinking partner. Of course I obliged. When I arrived at El Cholo, a loud, always crowded Mexican restaurant on Wilshire, she was waiting for me at the entrance.

"No table?" I asked.

She shook her head. "And it's three-deep at the bar."

If El Cholo didn't have the best margaritas and fajitas in Los Angeles, we would've found a new favorite long ago. We split up and each made several laps around the lounge until Kaitlyn spotted a couple paying their check. Kaitlyn hovered next to them and I grabbed their seats on the couch as soon as they stood up. It wasn't roomy, but at least we had a place to sit and someone to take our drink order.

"Have I told you lately how much I love my job," Kaitlyn said after our waiter had left. "My assistant brought me home-baked cookies this morning and my boss has to go out of town next week and is giving me his *Producers* tickets."

If I'd had my margarita, I would've dumped it over her head. "Let me know when you're hiring; I'll send my résumé."

"You should," she said. "You know in-house is the way to go."

Kaitlyn left her firm job after only two years and had been at KRLA-TV ever since. "Eventually, but not yet. I want to make partner first."

"You're not up for partnership for another year and a half."

"It could be shorter. Brian Reynolds made partner at the end of his sixth year. Of course, he's a guy and he kisses Rosenthal's ass."

"Which I'm sure you're not doing."

"No, I just don't have it in me. I'm not an ass-kisser. Besides, right now I need to concentrate on finding my soulmate. I can only focus on one major life-changing event at a time."

"Any new developments?"

"I'm considering a new plan of attack."

I waited for the waiter to set down our margaritas before I pulled the Just A Date brochure from my purse. I handed it to Kaitlyn and inhaled chips and salsa while she read.

"So what do you think?" I asked after she'd set it down on the table.

She paused for a moment before she said, "I can't believe you're really thinking about doing this."

Not the answer I expected. Usually, Kaitlyn was incredibly supportive. "Why are you being so negative."

"Why do you feel you need to do this?" she said in her best pseudopsychologist voice. She'd definitely picked that one up from her mother.

"I don't *need* to do this," I responded in full defensive mode. "I'm not even sure I *want* to do this. I'm just *thinking* about doing this." I'd been thinking about it nonstop all week.

That was when the woman sitting next to Kaitlyn picked up the brochure. "Is this yours?" she asked Kaitlyn.

Kaitlyn leaned back as if the woman were trying to hand her a snake. "No, it's hers."

The woman reached across Kaitlyn and gave it back to me. "Sorry, my sister joined one of these a few weeks ago. I think that was the one."

"How does she like it?" I asked.

"She's only had one date," the woman said, "but she liked the guy, so I guess it's working." The woman turned back to her friends and I put the brochure back in my purse.

"See," I told Kaitlyn. "You've been with Billy too long. You don't know what it's like to date."

"Past tense," Kaitlyn said. "We broke up, remember."

"Yes, but you haven't started looking again. It's not so easy. Once you're out of school and past the singles bar stage, it's really hard to meet people."

"How can you say that? You've had tons of dates."

"But none of them worked out. I need to find a new source for men."

"What about David?"

"Besides the fact that he almost killed us, there's no chemistry. I've decided to stop wasting time with people I know aren't The One. My new rule is three dates max. If I'm not convinced there's a chance in hell that I might want to spend the rest of my life with someone after three dates, then they're out."

"You only had two dates with David."

"Three if you count the dinner party—"

"That doesn't count."

"Fine, then we only had two. But it doesn't matter, because three is the maximum, not the minimum."

"Well, if that's the rule, then you're definitely going to need to expand your horizons."

"Exactly my point. Everyone keeps telling me it's a numbers game, so all I need to do is increase my numbers."

I'd stumbled halfway across the living room before I noticed the blinking red light on my answering machine. "Yaaay," I said to Elmo, who was dutifully waiting for me on the couch. "Somebody loves me—besides you, I mean."

I gave Elmo a squeeze, and he responded with "Elmo's not ticklish there." Obviously he was mad at me for leaving him alone so long. I pushed PLAY and the answering machine told me I had one new message. "Well at least one person loves me," I told Elmo.

The machine beeped again and my mother's voice came on the line. "Julia, it's Mommy. Call me when you get this. Daddy and I are coming to visit."

Sometimes it's better when nobody loves you.

CHAPTER 21

Parental Crisis

I called my parents the next morning before I'd even had my coffee. My mom picked up on the second ring. "Hello, Julia. We were wondering when you were going to call us back."

"What are you talking about? I just got your message last night. By the time I got home it was too late to call you back."

Her voice brightened. "Oh, did you have a date?"

"No, I was out with Kaitlyn."

The critical tone returned. "You're never going to meet anyone if you spend all your time with Kaitlyn."

"Mother, I'm not discussing this with you. I called because you said you and Daddy were coming for a visit."

"Right," she said. "Your father has a business trip to San Diego at the end of next month. Since it's Labor Day, we thought we'd stay over the weekend and visit you in L.A."

Another holiday weekend shot to hell.

"We figured we'd drive up on Friday afternoon and spend the weekend at your house. Then you can take us to the airport Monday morning. We have an 8 a.m. flight, so you'll have the rest of the day to yourself."

"Won't you need to drive yourself to the airport so you can return the rental car?" I didn't want to have to get up at 5 a.m. on a vacation day.

"Your father thought we'd drop it off on Friday night. No sense having two cars all weekend."

"What if you two want to go off and do something on your own? Spend the day at Disney or something?" In other words, save my sanity.

"I guess either you'll come with us or we won't go."

I made a final attempt. "Are you sure you wouldn't be more comfortable in a hotel? My apartment only has one bedroom."

"We can sleep in the living room. You still have the pull-out couch, don't you?"

A ray of hope. "No, I replaced it with a futon."

"Oh, let me tell your father."

In the background I could hear their yelling to each other from opposite ends of the house. Having lived with them for the first eighteen years of my life, I knew exactly where they were and what they were doing.

"Phil," my mother yelled from the phone in the kitchen.

"What?" my father yelled back from the couch in the den. The TV was so loud I could hear the announcer's play-by-play.

"Julia's on the phone. She says she got rid of the sleeper sofa and now she has a futon."

"So?" he yelled back. At this point he would be rolling his eyes and muttering to himself.

"So do you want to sleep on the futon?" she said with an edge to her voice, "or do you want to stay in a hotel? I know you don't like futons."

"What are you talking about? I never said I didn't like futons."

"The last time we slept on one at Deborah's house, you did nothing but complain about it the—"

"Mom, can't you argue with Dad later?"

"We're not arguing, we're just talking."

"Then can you talk to Dad later? In the meantime I'll assume you're staying with me." Maybe Kaitlyn could get her mom to write me a prescription for a weekend supply of Prozac.

"Hold on a minute and I'll put your father on the phone."

I could hear more yelling in the background, then my father came on the line.

"Hello?"

"Hi, Dad."

"Hi, baby. How are you?"

"Fine, Dad. How are you?"

"As well as can be expected for someone my age."

"What are you talking about? You're only sixty."

"That's old. But it's better than the alternative."

After we discussed what he would be having for dinner, what I would be having for dinner, and the weather, we hung up.

I immediately dialed Kaitlyn's number, and she convinced me that all I needed was some ice cream and a little retail therapy. We agreed to meet at the mall at noon.

♡ ♡ ♡

"It's too bad your parents told you so far in advance," Kaitlyn said between bites of waffle cone.

"Why?" I asked, swallowing another spoonful of hazelnut gelato.

"Because now you're going to spend the next six weeks stressing about your parents' visit. If they'd waited to call you until the week before they came, you'd only have one week to stress about it. That would be five less weeks I'd have to deal with you like this."

"I told you my mother was selfish."

"Jules, don't say that. She's your mother."

"I know she's my mother. And I'm not saying she doesn't love me and that I don't love her. I'm just stating facts."

"As seen through your own filter."

"Spare me the psychobabble and help me figure out what the hell I'm going to do with my parents for three days and nights."

"We live in L.A. There's tons of things to do with out-of-town relatives."

"Yes, but we've done them all. We've already been to Disneyland and Universal, and taken all the studio tours. We've walked the Santa Monica Pier, Third Street Promenade, the Venice Boardwalk, and Hollywood Boulevard. We've day-tripped to San Diego, Santa Barbara, Solvang, and Tijuana. What's left?"

"You could fly up to San Francisco for the weekend."

"They've already been. Twice."

"How about museums?"

"My dad hates museums. He won't go."

"Well, what do they like to do?"

"Argue with each other."

"I'm serious," she said.

"So am I."

"What do they do when they go on vacation?"

"They go somewhere warm and lay on the beach and talk about what they're going to have for dinner. Then they go out to dinner."

She considered that for a moment. "Actually, we do a fair amount of that ourselves."

"That's the scary part. We're both turning into my parents."

We finished our ice cream and headed to Bloomingdale's. Our first stop was the men's department so Kaitlyn could buy a birthday present for her brother. I left her searching through men's wallets, while I wandered over to watches. I don't know how I could've been so oblivious for so many years, but this was the first time I ever noticed how many cute guys shopped in the Bloomingdale's men's department. I was glad I'd bothered to put on makeup and blow-dry my hair. Some were clearly coupled, either with other men or women, but I was hoping at least one or two might be available.

I was headed toward an attractive brunet shopping for a dress shirt when I froze. Standing on the other side of my prospective date was a couple with their arms around each other. The male half of the couple was Joe.

I hadn't heard from Joe since the day of our disastrous lunch. He'd left me a message saying he'd called to apologize. I might've returned his call eventually if he'd kept calling, but he hadn't. Now I knew why. He'd already moved on.

I turned and sped through jewelry, zigzagged through hand-bags, and circled back to men's wallets.

"We need to leave," I told Kaitlyn. "Now."

"Why?"

"Because I just spotted Joe."

"The bartender?"

"Yes."

She started scanning the store. "Where is he? I want to see what he looks like."

I pointed in his direction. "The one in jeans with the woman holding a shirt up to his chest."

"I can't see," she said. "We need to move closer."

I told her no, but it was too late. She was already deep into belts. I caught up with her in ties and pulled her behind a bank of acrylic cubes filled with dress shirts. We pulled out the top few packages so she could peer through, and I kneeled on the floor out of sight.

"Which one is he? The one in Polos or the one looking at the Calvin Kleins?"

"I don't know. He's the one in the black T-shirt."

"They're both wearing black T-shirts."

I stood up, took a quick glance, and ducked back down. "The one on the right."

"He's cute. You should say hello."

"I'm not going over there."

"You don't have to. He's coming this way."

I grabbed Kaitlyn's arm and ran. We were six stores away before we finally stopped laughing. I felt like we were in junior high. At Kaitlyn's suggestion, we continued on to Macy's, where Kaitlyn managed to purchase a pair of black Enzo heels, a DKNY T-shirt, and two new lipsticks in under an hour, while I was still undecided between two pairs of Kenneth Cole earrings. Kaitlyn convinced me to buy them both, and we headed back to Bloomingdale's. This time I sent Kaitlyn to the men's department alone while I went upstairs and shopped for shoes. I didn't really believe that Joe would still be down there, but I wasn't taking any chances.

An hour later we were both hungry again. We settled on a late lunch at Houston's, the only restaurant in the mall we could both agree on. I was just about to reach for the handle on the smoky glass door, when it opened from the inside. The four of us stood in the entranceway. Me, Kaitlyn, Joe's girlfriend, and Joe.

CHAPTER 22

The Story of Joe

"**T**his is a surprise," Joe said.

"Yes," I said and silently thanked God that he hadn't spotted me running away from him in Bloomingdale's.

"How are you?" he asked.

"Fine," I responded. "And you?"

"I'm good," he said.

"Good," I said back.

After a few seconds of awkward silence, the girlfriend extended her hand to me. "Hi, I'm Cheryl."

"Julie," I said as we shook hands. That was when I noticed her diamond engagement ring. Either Joe moved really quick or he was stepping out on her when he went out with me. Goddamn wannabes! They're all alike. You couldn't trust any of them. Now I was glad I never called him back.

I introduced Kaitlyn to Cheryl and Joe, and after a few more seconds of awkward silence, they left.

The restaurant door hadn't even closed behind us before Kaitlyn laid into me. "What did you do that for?"

"What?" I said, pretending I didn't know exactly what she meant.

"You totally blew him off."

"No I didn't."

"Yes you did."

"Well, what did you want me to do? Didn't you notice the girl he was with was wearing an engagement ring?"

"That doesn't mean anything. She could be a friend."

"I don't go shopping with my male friends. At least not the straight ones."

"Why would he have gone out with you if he was engaged to her?"

"Obviously because he's just another two-timing wannabe."

"I don't understand you. You'll join a dating service to meet men, but you blow off the cute guy standing right in front of you that's clearly interested."

"First, he wasn't clearly interested. Second, he was with his fiancèe. Third, I didn't say I was joining a dating service, I just said I was thinking about it."

"You're ridiculous."

"We've established that. Now do you want to eat or not?"

♡ ♡ ♡

Kaitlyn and I studied our menus in silence until a waitress set down a glass with clear liquid, a stirrer, and a slice of lime.

"I think you've got the wrong table," I told her. "We didn't order any drinks."

"It's from the guy at the bar," the waitress said. "He asked me to bring it to you with this." She handed me a folded cocktail napkin, which I opened immediately. CAN I JOIN YOU? NO SURPRISES. I showed the note to Kaitlyn, and she motioned for Joe to join us.

"Be nice," she whispered as he walked toward us, sans fiancée.

"May I?" he asked.

I moved closer to the partition and Joe slid into the booth next to me.

"Thanks for the drink," I said.

"No problem," he replied.

"Where's your friend?" Kaitlyn asked.

"Cheryl, my sister, went back to the hotel. She and her fiancé are staying at the Century Plaza across the street."

Kaitlyn gave me a self-satisfied "I told you so" smile, then spent the next hour interrogating Joe. He told us that he'd lived in L.A. for ten years and that he moved out here after college to pursue an acting career. (I knew it!) He'd gotten some commercial work and guest spots on a few TV shows, he said, but that was it. The last few years he'd spent working for his aunt's catering business, Food For Thought. He said he started out serving hors d'oeuvres and tending bar, but discovered that he loved to cook. Now he was splitting his time between bartending and cooking.

Although I was loathe to bring up the night we met, I had to know. "Then what were you doing working at that bar in New Jersey? It's not the kind of job you would commute across the country for."

"I went back home for a few months when my dad died," he said.

Now I was sorry I'd asked.

"We, my sisters and I, were all concerned about my mom. She'd never lived alone before. My sisters all had their own families to take care of, so, according to them anyway, I was the logical choice. I took the job at the Montrose to cover my expenses and to give me something to do. I never realized how boring New Jersey was until I moved back. Who was it who said 'You can't go home again'?"

"Thomas Wolfe," Kaitlyn and I answered in unison.

"Is that why you came back to L.A.?" Kaitlyn asked.

"I always intended to come back. I only agreed to stay for a couple of months until my mom adjusted. When she decided to spend the summer at the Shore with one of my sisters, I hopped the next plane to L.A. I think my mom realized I was itching to get back here and just wanted to give me an excuse to leave."

Kaitlyn looked satisfied.

"So is there anything else you'd like to know?" he asked. "Birth date? Shoe size? My favorite color?"

"I think we're satisfied," I said, "for the moment."

"But we reserve the right to redirect at a later time," Kaitlyn added.

"You're not a lawyer too, are you?"

"I am," Kaitlyn said.

"You're surrounded," I told him. "Next time bring your attorney."

"Does that mean there's going to be a next time?" he asked.

I walked into that one. "I guess you'll have to wait and see."

CHAPTER 23

Just Friends

The three of us split the check and left the restaurant. Joe said good-bye at the entrance and disappeared into the late after-noon shopping throng.

Once he was out of sight, I turned to Kaitlyn. "So? What did you think?"

"I think he's a good guy, and you shouldn't rule him out just because he's a caterer."

"I'm not ruling him out because he's a caterer. You know I love it when a guy can cook."

"Then why are you ruling him out?" she asked.

"Who said I'm ruling him out?"

"Because if you weren't, you would've told him you wanted to see him again."

She knew me too well. "I have to. He's a wannabe."

"No, he's not. He's a caterer."

"That's his day job, or half of it, but he hasn't given up the dream."

"Who cares as long as he has a day job?"

"I do. Scumbag used to have a day job too."

"One that you let him quit."

"Yes, and I've learned my lesson. No more wannabes, and that includes Joe. Even if he's cute and he can cook."

When I arrived home from work Wednesday night, I found a message from Joe. I checked the time stamp on my answering machine and discovered that he'd called at four o'clock. He had to know I'd still be at the office in the middle of the afternoon. He was testing me to see if I'd call him back. I called Kaitlyn instead.

"Why do you always assume the worst?" she said. "Maybe he's working tonight and that was the only time he could call you."

"Then why didn't he call me in the office?"

"Maybe he didn't have the number."

"Yes he does. He called me at the office after our lunch date."

"Then maybe he lost it," she said, clearly exasperated. "Why do you care? You've ruled him out anyway."

"I know. But I've been thinking maybe we could be friends. It'd be nice to have a friend who could cook."

"I'm pretty sure he wants to be more than just your friend, Jules."

"Maybe so. But it's friendship or nothing."

"And you're going to call him back to tell him that?"

"No, I don't want to do it over the phone. I'd rather tell him in person. Soften the blow."

"Good thinking. Otherwise he'd really be devastated."

"Ha, ha."

♡ ♡ ♡

Joe arrived at my house Sunday morning wearing dark blue Levi's and a spotless white T-shirt. He looked great. I'd dressed in white jeans and a mint green tank top in a vain attempt to show off my slightly muscled arms. I'd started working out with five-pound weights at the gym, and although I was still a long way from buff, I wanted recognition for the small amount

of definition I'd suffered to acquire. Just because we were only
going to be friends didn't mean that I wanted him to stop
looking.

"So where are we going?" I asked as we climbed into Joe's
black Jeep. Not an SUV, but a real Jeep with a vinyl roof and
plastic, zip-out windows.

"The best breakfast place I know," he said.

"Which is?"

"My house. Assuming that's okay with you. I figured now that
you knew my whole life story it would be okay for us to meet
in private."

"You did, huh?"

"Yes. If I was going to murder you, I wouldn't do it at my
house. Too obvious."

"But maybe that's just what you would want people to think.
Then they wouldn't suspect you."

"No, they still would. I'd be the last person to have seen you
alive."

"But how would the police know that?"

"I'm sure your friend Kaitlyn would tell them. Don't tell me
you didn't tell her about our plans?"

"No, I told her. But maybe you were planning on killing her
too—to keep her quiet."

"That's a great idea. Where does she live? We can stop and
pick her up on the way."

"She's not home."

He snapped his fingers. "Too bad. I guess I'll have to be satisfied with just breakfast. We'll save the double homicide for another day."

It was eighty-five degrees and sunny. A perfect day for a drive
with the top down. We wound our way west along Sunset

Boulevard with the radio tuned to *Breakfast with the Beatles*. I'd just glimpsed the Pacific Ocean when Joe turned off Sunset onto a tree-lined side street. After a succession of lefts and rights, I quickly lost my bearings. I'd never driven through the Pacific Palisades before and had no idea where we were.

Joe pulled into a circular driveway at the end of a cul-de-sac and parked in front of a huge peach stucco house with white shutters and a red-tiled roof.

"You live here?" I didn't think bartender/caterers made that much money.

"It's my aunt's house; I live in the guesthouse out back."

Joe led me down a gray flagstone path, around the house, and out to the backyard. I followed him past the patio and the Olympic-size swimming pool to a cottage in the corner of the yard. It was the same color and style as the main house, but a quarter of the size. Joe led me inside and gave me the tour. The living room, kitchen, bedroom, and bath were all decorated in cream and beige with occasional splashes of color in peach or pink.

"My aunt decorated this place years ago," he said.

"I assumed. You didn't strike me as a peach and pink kind of guy."

He flashed me his perfect smile and led me back to the kitchen. "So what do you want for breakfast?"

"What are my choices?"

"Just about anything. Eggs, an omelet, pancakes—you name it."

"How about a bagel?" I asked.

"Sorry," he said. "No bagels. But I have English muffins."

"Do you have blueberry muffins?"

He opened the refrigerator and scoured every shelf. "I'm out of blueberries. How about banana muffins?"

"I hate bananas."

"You're not gonna make this easy, are you?"

"Nope."

"Wait here," he said and grabbed his keys from the counter. "I'll go check my aunt's house."

Now I felt bad. "You don't have to do that. An English muffin is fine. Or pancakes. Whatever you feel like making."

"No, I promised you the best breakfast in town and I intend to deliver. I'll be right back."

I settled into the overstuffed living room chair and read the travel section of the Sunday paper, careful to make sure the newsprint didn't stain the cream cushions. Joe returned a few minutes later with a pint of blueberries.

From my perch on the high-backed kitchen counter stool, I watched Joe measure, mix, pour, and fold. Then I licked the batter bowl while he squeezed orange juice and ground coffee. Half an hour later we were sitting at a wrought-iron bistro table on his aunt's patio eating warm blueberry muffins and cold strawberries with cream. I could get used to this.

When we finished eating, Joe brought out two towels and we moved down to the lounge chairs near the deep end of the pool.

"Do you want to go for a swim?" he asked after we'd settled in.

"I didn't bring my bathing suit."

He turned on his side to face me. "You don't need one," he said with a wicked grin. "It's a private pool."

I hadn't intended to have the "just friends" discussion until the end of the day, but if he was planning on us getting naked, then I needed to move it up. "Listen, Joe, I think we should talk."

"Uh-oh. I don't like the sound of that."

"It's nothing bad. I just think it would be better if we didn't get romantically involved."

"It's just a swim, Julie. Don't make more of it than it is."

Typical man. "Joe, I'm past the fling stage. I'm looking for a relationship. Something potentially long-term."

"Well I'm not making any promises, but I don't have any commitment phobias, if that's what you're worried about."

He wasn't making this easy. "No, that's not it. I just think it would be better if we kept this platonic."

"Why?"

"Because I don't see this relationship going anywhere."

"How come?"

"We're not compatible." It was the first thing that popped into my head.

"You don't know that. We just met."

"Trust me," I said. "I know."

"How?"

Most guys would've let it go by this point. Either he was incredibly inquisitive, unbelievably horny, or he really liked me. I didn't know him well enough to know which one.

I ran through my options. I could only think of two plausible lies. I could tell him I was getting back together with my ex-boyfriend, or I could tell him we didn't have any chemistry. The problem with the second lie was that he'd probably try to prove me wrong and I didn't think I was strong enough to pass the test. Since he didn't know about Scumbag, the first lie might work. But then if we did become friends, he would ultimately find out the truth, and then he'd hate me for lying to him.

I didn't see any alternative. I was going to have to be honest. "Please don't take this the wrong way, Joe, but you're just not husband material."

He sat up in his lounge chair and faced me. "Really. Why is that?"

"Because you're a wannabe."

"I'm a what?"

"You're a wannabe. A want-to-be actor."

"I'm not a wannabe actor!" he said in an octave higher than his normal voice. "I *was* an actor. Now I'm a chef. If I'm a wannabe anything, it's a wannabe restaurateur."

There was no point in arguing. I laid back down. "Fine, Joe. Whatever. But all we're ever going to be is just friends."

"Let me see if I understand this," he said, even louder this time. "You don't want to go out with me because you think I want to be an actor, even though I told you that I *was* an actor and *now* I'm a chef."

"You're telling me that if someone offered you a role in a movie right now you would turn it down?"

"I don't know," he said. "I might. It would depend on the role."

"Exactly. You haven't given up the dream. You're still a wannabe."

"And you've got something against wannabes?"

"Let's just say I've been burned before."

"We've all been burned before. It doesn't mean you stop living."

Now my voice rose too. "I haven't stopped living! I just don't want to date you." What an ego!

"But you want us to be friends?"

This was not going as planned. "I thought it might be nice, but not if you don't want to."

He stood up and told me to stand up too.

"Why?"

"Can't you do one simple thing without an argument?"

I stood up.

In a romantic gesture worthy of a Harlequin Romance novel,

he put one arm around my back, the other under my knees, and lifted me up in his arms. "Are you sure you want to be my friend?" he asked.

I wasn't so sure anymore. "Why?"

He walked over to the edge of the pool and threw me in.

CHAPTER 24

Swimming Without a Suit

The water was freezing and tasted like chlorine. When my butt hit the bottom of the deep end, I kicked back up to the surface. After I stopped choking, I swam to the side of the pool and hauled myself out.

The goose bumps on my arms made me look like a plucked chicken. My clothes were clinging to me and I was only wearing one shoe. Its mate was somewhere at the bottom of the deep end. It wasn't worth retrieving. The tan sandal on my right foot was clearly ruined.

"What the fuck did you do that for?" I screamed.

"We're friends, aren't we?" he said. "That's just the kind of thing I do with my friends." He was trying hard to keep the smile from his face, but he couldn't quite pull it off.

"You're a real prick."

"Does that mean you don't want to be my friend anymore?" This time he let the smile shine through.

I could've killed him. Instead, I grabbed him by the T-shirt and attempted to push him into the water. He managed to disentangle himself from my grip, and in the process I lost my balance and fell back into the pool. This time I lost the other shoe.

I heard his laughter as soon as I broke the surface. "Would you like me to help you get out of those wet clothes?" he asked after I'd hauled myself out for the second time.

"Is that what you do for your friends?"

He ignored my sarcasm. "Not usually, but for you I'll make an exception."

I looked down at my now see-through tank top. My nipples were standing at attention. I pulled the towel off the lounge chair and wrapped it around my shoulders, covering my chest. "Just take me home."

"Are you sure? We could lay here and sunbathe while we wait for your clothes to dry?"

"I want to leave. Now!"

"Whatever you say," he said. "I'll go get my keys."

I sat on the edge of the lounge chair and steamed. He returned five minutes later jangling a ring of keys in his hand. "Ready?" he asked.

"I need my shoes. They're at the bottom of the pool."

"I can wait."

"I thought maybe you could get something to fish them out. Don't you have one of those things people use to clean the pool?"

"I don't know, my aunt has a pool service." He must've caught my glare. "But I'll look."

He dropped his keys onto the other lounge chair and disappeared into the shed near the shallow end. After some clanking and cursing, he returned with a skimmer attached to a ten-foot pole. I watched Joe plunge the silver rod into the water and attempt to scoop up the shoes. Every time he'd catch them, they'd slip off the net and he'd have to start all over again.

I sat and waited in my wet clothes and my bare feet, getting angrier by the second. How dare he throw me in the pool just because I didn't want to go out with him. Who the hell did he think he was?

I wiped my eye makeup off onto his white towel, hoping it would stain. When I looked up, I noticed that he'd switched tactics. He was now trying to push my shoes up the slope into the shallow end. He wasn't having much success, but it gave me an idea.

I reached over and grabbed Joe's keys from his lounge chair and slipped them into my purse. Then I waited until he was precariously perched at the edge of the pool, and when his back was toward me, I pushed him in. Then I ran.

With his keys in my hand, I sprinted as fast as I could around the house and out to the driveway. I jumped in his Jeep and took off, lunging and lurching down the street. I hadn't driven a stick shift since college.

I didn't know where I was going, but I knew I didn't want to be there when Joe got out of the water. I drove to the end of the block, made a right, a left, another right, and somehow managed to end up back on the same street. Luckily, I recognized Joe's aunt's house before I reached it and had started my U-turn when I was still three houses away. Unfortunately, I couldn't cut the turn tight enough to clear the parked cars. When I put the jeep in reverse and turned around, I saw Joe running toward me in his dripping-wet T-shirt and jeans.

I turned forward and shifted the Jeep into first gear. It stalled. Shit! I started it up again, pushed the stick shift into first gear, and slowly eased up on the clutch. It stalled again. By the time I started it for the third time, Joe was standing next to me with one hand on the windshield and the other hand on the roll bar. I guess he thought he could physically stop the car from moving forward.

"Enough," he said. "Give me the keys."

"No way."

"Julie, I'm not kidding around. Give me the goddamn keys."

"If I give you the keys how am I going to get home?"

"I'll drive you."

"Yeah, right."

"If you don't give me the keys, we're going to be here all night. I'm not letting you leave with my car."

I believed him. "How about I drive us both to my house and then you can drive yourself home?"

"No."

"Why not?"

"Because by the time we get to your house I'm not going to have a clutch left."

He had a point. But I didn't trust him. I was afraid that if I gave him the keys he would take off and leave me standing in the middle of the street. Scumbag had done that to me once. We'd had an argument in the grocery store parking lot and he drove home without me. Luckily, I only lived six blocks away, so it was an easy walk. Joe's house was at least ten miles from mine. Too far for an afternoon stroll, especially without shoes.

I shut the ignition and twisted the car key off its ring. I

stood up and stepped into the passenger seat. With my seat belt buckled and the rest of Joe's keys buried at the bottom of my purse, I handed Joe the ignition key. "Okay," I said, "you drive."

"Am I going to get the rest of my keys back?"

"As soon as I arrive safely at my doorstep."

He climbed into the driver's seat and smoothly shifted the Jeep into first gear. We took off down the street. About halfway through the silent thirty-minute drive to my house, I caught him glancing at me when he thought I wasn't looking. I only noticed because I was stealing glimpses of him. I still had the towel wrapped around my shoulders. All he had on were his wet clothes. His clinging T-shirt revealed great pecs and a six-pack stomach. I looked away. Too bad that body was wasted on a wannabe.

Joe pulled up in front of my apartment building and left the engine running. I unbuckled my seat belt and opened the passenger side door. I'd only managed to maneuver one leg outside the Jeep when he grabbed my arm.

"Aren't you forgetting something?" he asked.

I picked up my purse and fished out his key ring, but held it outside his reach. "You're going to let me get out before you drive away, aren't you?"

"Don't worry," he said. "You're the last person I want to be with right now."

"Good," I said. "Then we're agreed. As soon as both my feet are on the ground I'll give you the keys." Before he could object, I wrenched my arm free and jumped out of the Jeep. Then I tossed his key ring onto the passenger seat and slammed the door shut.

He smiled at me for the first time in hours. "You're one crazy girl, Jules."

"You can't call me that."

"Why not?"

"You haven't known me long enough."

CHAPTER 25

Just a Date

After the Joe fiasco, Just A Date started looking like a better alternative. After all, I really was a busy professional having trouble meeting quality people on her own. But it still took me another two dateless weekends with Elmo before I worked up the nerve to call. The woman on the phone told me they were having a $50 off special that was ending on July 31st. I made an appointment to meet with one of their "dating specialists" on the 30th. Love on sale is still love.

♡ ♡ ♡

I snuck out of work early on the 30th to make my six o'clock appointment. When I pulled into the parking garage of the nondescript glass office building, I was stopped at the gate by an attendant.

"Where are you going?" he asked.

I wasn't expecting this. I pulled a piece of paper out of my

purse and pretended to read it. "A company called Just A Date,"
I said. Maybe he would think I was just making a sales call.

He snickered and told me to park on level C.

I felt like I was in a doctor's office. I gave the receptionist my
name and was told to have a seat in the waiting area. Five minutes later another woman showed me to a small, windowless
room containing two white sofa chairs and a television on a
stand. "The program director will be with you shortly," she said,
then shut the door behind her.

I wished I'd brought my magazine from the waiting area. I
tried my cell phone, but I couldn't get any reception, so I tucked
my phone back in my purse and started counting ceiling tiles. I
was up to twenty-three when the door opened and a tall, thin,
stunning woman with long black hair and caramel skin walked
in. She introduced herself as Celia Barker, a "dating specialist"
and director of the L.A. office of Just A Date.

Celia explained how the program worked. Each client had to
fill out a questionnaire describing themselves, their interests, and
the qualities they were looking for in a potential date. Celia told
me that once a week she and the four other dating specialists in
the L.A. office met to discuss their respective clients and
whether any of them could be matched up.

"When I find you a match," Celia said, "I'll call you up and
describe him to you on the phone. If you want to meet him,
then I'll set the two of you up on a date. Are you interested?"

Maybe. "How much is this again?"

"It's normally $350 for six dates, but right now we're offering
an introductory special of $50 off or two extra dates. But the
special ends tomorrow. Would you like to join?"

It sounded like the service my friends had been providing, except that my friends did it for free. Of course my track record with my friends' blind dates hadn't been too good. And my track record with the men I met on my own was even worse. I thought of Joe and The Doctor–Pilot and Nose Hairs and John the Annoying Cheapskate and the fact that I had no prospects for any future dates. I heard my mother's voice reminding me that I wasn't getting any younger. I imagined the inside of my vagina covered in cobwebs from lack of use, and my ovaries shriveling up and dying, still enclosed in their cellophane wrappers.

I handed Celia my Visa card and told her to sign me up. I couldn't even buy a good suit for $300. Surely a potential mate was worth that much.

Celia called me a week later and said, "I found you a match. His name is Michael. He's thirty-four years old, lives in Hermosa Beach, and he's a director."

"What kind of a director? Movies? Television? Commercials?" I figured if she said he was a movie director, then he was really a wannabe. If he described himself as a television or commercials director, then he was probably for real.

"I don't know, the form just says director."

So much for the personal touch.

"He's 5'10"," Celia continued, "has blond hair, and he likes to ski, play tennis, go to movies, restaurants, and the beach, play baseball, softball, basketball, and cook gourmet meals."

Except for the blond hair (I preferred brunets unless the guy looked like Brad Pitt) and that he was geographically undesirable (Hermosa Beach was at least a thirty-minute drive without traffic, and there was always traffic), he sounded perfect.

"Would you like to meet him?" she asked.

"Sure, he sounds great."

"Good. Just give me some dates you're available and I'll call you back with the time and place."

I never knew finding a husband could be this easy. I should've called this place months ago!

♡ ♡ ♡

Celia called me back the next day. "I spoke to Michael. Unfortunately he's not available on any of the days you gave me and he's leaving town on Monday for two weeks. Can you make it next weekend?"

"I thought you don't set up dates for weekends."

"Normally we don't. We've found that weeknights work better. But since the two of you have such conflicting schedules, I thought maybe a weekend would be easier. Are you available for lunch on Saturday?"

"Sure," I said. "Where?"

"How about The Range in Beverly Hills? I'll make a reservation for one o'clock."

Normally I didn't go to snooty, overpriced restaurants like The Range. But in this case, it was a good choice. I didn't want to run into anyone I knew, and I was sure that I wouldn't at The Range.

"Whose name will it be under?" I just realized that Celia had never told me Michael's last name.

"The reservation will be in both your first names. We don't give out last names in order to protect everyone's privacy."

I liked that.

"I'll call you on Friday to remind you about the date."

It was already Wednesday. "I don't think I'm going to forget between now and Friday."

She laughed. "I know. But it's our policy to call and remind both clients the day before, just in case."

I wasn't concerned when I left the office on Friday night without having heard from Celia. I was sure she'd left me a message on my home machine. I'd told her I preferred she not call me at work. I didn't want to risk my secretary, Lucy, finding out and blabbing to the rest of the office that I was so desperate that I had to join a service just to get a date.

When I walked through the living room and didn't see a blinking red light, I was only slightly concerned. The window on my answering machine showed "0" messages, but I pushed the PLAY button anyway. No messages. I looked at my watch. It was 6:45. I was now mildly concerned.

Since it was at least possible that Celia was still in the office, I called. Her voice mail picked up on the fourth ring. "Hi, Celia," I said after the beep. "It's Julie Burns. You didn't call to remind me about my date with Michael tomorrow. I don't know if that means we're still on for tomorrow and you just forgot to call, or that the date is canceled. Please call me back and let me know."

I didn't start to really worry until eleven o'clock. By that point, even if Celia picked up my message, she would think it was too late to return the call. But it wasn't too late for me to call Kaitlyn. Her solution was for me to phone Celia again in the morning, but if I didn't hear back from her, to go anyway. Kaitlyn was sure if the date was canceled Celia would've called and told me. This time I was praying she was right.

I called Celia three times on Saturday morning, but she never returned my call. At noon I showered, dressed in the outfit of black pants and turquoise sleeveless shirt I'd carefully planned the night before, and headed out to The Range.

A parking spot opened up right before I reached the restaurant's valet stand. Normally a good omen, but if my parking karma and my love life really were inversely related, then it was actually bad. Only one way to find out. I filled the meter with two hours' worth of quarters and headed inside.

The hostess was a woman in her mid-forties who was clearly used to sucking up to celebrities and was not at all interested in me. I told her I had a reservation for Michael and Julie at one o'clock, and she peered at me over the rim of her Armani frames.

"We don't normally make reservations in first names. What's the last name?"

"My secretary assured me that she made the reservation in our first names," I said in my angry lawyer voice.

She reluctantly checked her book. "No, there's no reservation for a Michael or a Julie. What was the last name again?"

Had this woman been even the slightest bit warm and fuzzy I might've told her the truth—that I was so pathetic I had resorted to a dating service that didn't give out last names, and even they had stood me up. Instead I mumbled, "We must've had our signals crossed," and ran out of the restaurant.

Obviously my parking karma theory was right! From now on I wasn't even going to look for street parking. I would only valet. At least when I was on a date.

By the time I made it home, my mortification had turned to anger. I called Celia's voice mail and left her my fifth and final message of the day. Then I changed into shorts and a T-shirt and ate a bag of potato chips with Elmo.

Celia finally returned my calls on Monday morning. She apologized profusely and told me it was all just a horrible mix-up. I didn't care what her excuse was, all I wanted was a refund. Celia swore it would never happen again and attempted to placate me with an extra date for free. After ten minutes of cajoling, I relented. The worst was over. The only place to go was up, right?

CHAPTER 26

Helping Others

I waited until 11:05 before I went next door to Simone's office. "Where's Greg?" Since his wife had left him, Greg had become a regular fixture at our Monday morning bitch sessions.

Simone looked up from her desk with dark circles under her eyes. "He had a court appearance this morning. He must not be back yet."

"What's wrong? Is Rosenthal on your case again?"

"No, I had a fight with Todd."

"About what?" I always thought Simone and Todd had a great relationship. According to Simone, they never argued.

"About the wedding. What else?"

"I thought you'd settled that. Big wedding, New Year's Eve, the Four Seasons Hotel."

"That's only the beginning. Now it's bands, flowers, menus, guest lists, and rehearsal dinners, just to name a few."

"I thought the grooms left all those boring details up to the brides."

"Maybe guys without mothers, but Todd's mother is alive and well and she's driving me crazy."

"Can't you have Todd tell her to back off?"

"He's telling me to back off. Apparently, my twenty-eight-year-old fiancé is a mama's boy. I'm about ready to give him back to his mama."

This was serious. Simone almost never complained about Todd. "You don't mean that. You're just going through a rough time. Planning a wedding always puts a strain on a relationship."

"How would you know? You've never even been engaged."

Ouch. That hurt. I reminded myself that Simone was under a lot of stress and said, "True. But I've been a bridesmaid seven times, and every single time the bride wanted to call it off at least once. But after the wedding, they all said it was worth it."

"The wedding maybe, but not the groom."

"Don't you think you're just pissed at him right now because he's taking his mother's side?"

"Yes, but if this is the way he's going to act after we're married, then I'm not sure I want to be married to him."

Uh-oh. "Did you tell him that?"

"At about three o'clock this morning at the top of my lungs. That's when he left."

I'd known Simone six years and this was the first time I'd ever seen her cry. I handed her the box of tissues she kept next to her computer.

"Thanks," she said and blew her nose.

"No problem. They're your tissues."

She smiled for a moment, then started crying again.

I returned to my office and rummaged through the bottom drawer of my desk. Buried under three back issues of *California Lawyer* magazine, half a dozen take-out menus, and a rubber stress ball, I found my mini dartboard. The picture of Scumbag was still attached. I could barely make out his face through all the dart holes. I threw the picture in the trash and carried my board and all the darts I could find next door to Simone's office.

"What's this?" she asked when I set them down on her desk.

"Call it an early wedding present."

I picked up her pad and pen and drew two stick figures side by side. I labeled one Todd and the other Todd's Mother. I added long curly hair and fangs to Todd's Mother, then tore the drawing off the pad and handed it to Simone.

"You can start with these," I said, "and replace them with real pictures later."

She studied my drawing for at least ten seconds. "Did anyone ever tell you that you have real artistic ability?"

"No."

"Good. Then you know you haven't been lied to."

"Thanks, Simone." Sometimes it was hard to remember why we were friends.

"Although this actually looks a little like Todd's mother. It must be the fangs."

I tacked the drawing onto the dartboard, and propped the board on top of the file cabinet. I handed Simone the black darts and kept the red ones for myself.

♡   ♡   ♡

By the time Simone's alarm rang warning us of Rosenthal's impending return, our aim had really improved. Simone had hit Todd twice in the chest and his mother three times in the head. I'd concentrated on the mother and had managed to hit her once each in the head and chest, and had practically severed her right arm.

"What are you doing after work tonight?" I asked as I gathered the stray darts.

"No plans," Simone said. "I figured I would just go home and feel sorry for myself. Why?"

"We haven't had an associates dinner in a long time. I think we're due for one."

"I don't remember us ever having one."

"Then we're definitely due for one. I'll ask Greg if he wants to join us."

♡ ♡ ♡

At a quarter to eight, Greg and Simone walked into my office with their suit jackets on and their briefcases in hand. "Come on, Burns," Greg said. "You organized this dinner. You don't want to be late."

Greg, Simone, and I walked through the lobby, an army of three in dark suits. Simone was the first to notice the huge bouquet of long-stem red roses on the security desk.

"Hi, Bobby," Simone said to the seventy-two-year-old security guard. "You must be really good if the women are sending you flowers." She really was a shameless flirt.

Bobby blushed. "They arrived an hour ago, but it was after hours so I couldn't let the delivery man upstairs. I was going to bring them up to you myself when I took my dinner break."

"They're for me?" she cooed as she snatched the card from its plastic fork. Bobby was the only one of us who believed she hadn't already read her name scrawled in big black letters on the outside of the envelope. She opened the card and a huge grin spread across her face.

"Well?" I asked.

"Baby, I'm sorry," she read to us in a soft voice. "Let me make it up to you. Dinner tonight at eight. Our place. I'll have the Champagne on ice. Love, Todd."

"I didn't know Todd could cook," Greg said.

"He can't," Simone replied.

"Then what's he going to do?" Greg said. "Order a pizza to go with the Champagne?"

"Our place isn't our *house*," Simone said in a tone that made it clear that it was incredibly obvious and Greg was the only idiot who didn't get it. "It's Patina. Our favorite restaurant."

Patina was rated one of the top ten restaurants in Los Angeles. It was also one of the most expensive. I'd never been.

Simone pulled her cell phone out of her purse and turned toward the windows. "Hi, honey," she said into the receiver. After a pause she said, "I just got them." Another pause. "I'm on my way. Love you." She shut her phone off and turned back to me and Greg.

"Sorry guys, you understand."

"Sure, Simone," I said, and handed her the vase of flowers. "See you tomorrow."

She took off in the direction of the parking garage escalators, her black pumps clicking against the marble tiles. I watched Greg stare after her until she disappeared around the corner.

"She's got great legs, doesn't she?" I said to Greg.

"She's got a lot more than that," he replied.

"She's a real looker," Bobby chimed in.

"All right," I told them. "I'm not one of the boys, ya know."

"Sorry," Bobby said and looked down, pretending to study the security camera images on his television screens.

"You're cute too," Greg said. "It's just different."

"Yeah, I know. I'm attractive in an approachable way. Simone's a goddess."

"Exactly."

"Thanks, Greg."

"You know I'm just kidding with you."

"I do?"

"Of course you do. Come on, I'll buy you dinner."

"At Patina?" I asked hopefully.

"No, at Il Paio, where you made a reservation when you thought you were paying."

♡ ♡ ♡

Fifteen minutes later I found Greg in the bar, sipping a martini and talking to an attractive Asian woman. He certainly didn't waste any time.

We shared a pizza and a pasta and our best dating horror stories. My near-death experience trumped Greg's worst date, but he shocked me by telling me he'd already slept with two different women. He'd only been separated from his wife for six weeks.

"How many times did you go out with them before you slept with them?"

"The first one, I think her name was Nancy, was a one-night stand. The second one, Carol, I actually went out with a few times."

"How do you get these women to sleep with you so fast?"

He put down his fork and spread his arms out. "Well look at me. They can't resist."

"C'mon, I'm serious."

"They know the rule just like I do."

"What rule?"

"The three-date rule," he said. "You either get some by the third date or it's over. Surely you've heard this before?"

Of course I had. "I thought that meant fool around, not sleep together."

"What do you think fooling around is at this stage. Second base?"

"I don't know. But I know I've gone out with guys more than three times before I've slept with them."

"Well there are exceptions to every rule."

"You mean you'll give them four dates if you think they're really hot?"

"I'll actually go up to six dates for a really hot woman. Especially if I'm dating multiple women at the same time. That sort of takes the pressure off any one relationship."

I used to think Greg was a nice guy. It's not the first time I've made that mistake. "Were you like this before you were married?"

"No," he said. "I dated my wife for four years and I was faithful the entire time. And that includes the three years after the wedding before she moved in with her jogging buddy. I have a lot of lost time to make up for."

"I kind of feel the same way. Except for me it's about dating men, not sleeping with them."

"What's the point of dating them if you're not going to sleep with them?"

"It's not like I've set out *not* to sleep with them. I'm just only interested in sleeping with the right guy."

"Which is what? The guy you're going to marry?"

"Not necessarily. But it has to be a guy I would at least consider marrying."

"Those don't come along every day, Julie. You're going to have to go through an awfully long dry spell."

"Tell me about it!"

"Well if you change your mind, I'd be happy to oblige."

"Thanks for the offer. You're really sweeping me off my feet."

"Don't knock it till you try it."

"I'll wait for the movie."

CHAPTER 27

The Opposition

I waited for Jared Kinelli's attorney in the offices of Carr, Geary, & Rogers. It looked like most law firm conference rooms—a long, narrow table with a dozen low-backed swivel chairs atop industrial gray carpet. The only item that ever varied even slightly was the furniture. This one had a black Formica table with black leather chairs. Not very original, but the seats were comfortable. Plus the offices were convenient—only eight floors below mine on the south side of the building.

A few minutes later, a stocky man in his mid-thirties with dirty-blond hair and tortoiseshell, horn-rimmed glasses walked in. I gave him a seven and a half on a scale of one to ten, but only because of the flattering suit. Without it, he wouldn't be higher than a six and a half. Seven at the most. A good suit can do that for a man. I suspected he knew that.

He extended his hand and introduced himself as Steve Rogers. Once he started talking, I detected a slight Midwest twang. After a few minutes of chitchat about lawyering and the weather, I brought the conversation around to Rosebud.

"We have a very strong case," Steve Rogers said in an authoritative voice.

"Really," I replied, casually sipping from the Pellegrino his secretary had brought me. "From our perspective, it's a classic he said/she said. Very difficult to prove."

"Usually that's true, but in this case it's a repeat performance for your client. That will make it a lot easier."

I knew he was referring to the case filed against Rita Levin when she was at Worldwide. "The allegations in the complaint were never proven and you know the settlement is inadmissible."

"Yes, but you know that most people think where there's smoke, there's fire."

A cliché, but no less correct.

We continued the debate in gracious tones for another ten minutes until Steve told me he'd consider settling the case for half a million dollars. That's when I packed up my briefcase and walked out. I went as far as the reception area before I allowed Steve to cajole me back into the conference room. I knew the next settlement figure he proposed would be much more reasonable. I'd learned that trick from Rosenthal.

After another five minutes of debate and a promise to speak again soon, I took the elevator back to the thirty-second floor. When I got back to my office I checked my messages and was surprised to find one from Celia at Just A Date. Luckily, she'd only left her name and number and not the name of the company. Hers was the first call I returned.

"I have great news," she said. "Michael called me this morning. His business trip was cut short and he'll be back in town from Thursday to Sunday and would love to meet you. Are you available?"

"I need to check my calendar." The guy had stood me up once already. I didn't know if I wanted to give him another chance.

"I almost forgot," she added. "He asked me to tell you that he went to The Range on Saturday looking for you too. You must've just missed each other. He wanted me to make sure you knew that he didn't stand you up."

I assumed Celia was not a mind reader, so this was probably the truth. "Okay. But I think this time we should do a weekday and a different restaurant."

"Just tell me where and when, and I'll make the reservation as soon as we hang up."

"Let's say Friday at one o'clock. It will need to be a restaurant near my office."

"You're in Century City, right? How about Il Paio?"

"I was there last night. How about Il Toro instead?" It was another trendy Italian restaurant, but one I'd never been to. I wanted to meet someplace where they didn't know my last name.

"I'll call you Thursday to confirm."

"Promise?" I hoped it sounded like I was joking, even though I wasn't.

"I promise," Celia said. "And you need to promise to call me after the date and tell me how it went."

I figured she was still trying to make it up to me for her screw-up last time, but I wasn't going to let her off that easy. "Do you take such a personal interest in all your clients' love lives?"

"Yes, we ask all our clients to call us after the date to tell us how it went. We use the feedback to help us find your next match."

Wasn't a dating specialist supposed to be more optimistic than that?

I arrived at Il Toro five minutes late. I rushed inside and waited impatiently while the nineteen-year-old hostess/actress (she was beautiful and this was L.A.) talked on the phone. When she hung up, I gave her my first name and held my breath.

"What's the last name?" she asked.

Not again! "I'm sure it's under my first name," I said and peered down at the reservation book. When I found the entry for Julie and Michael, I pointed it out to her. The words JUST A DATE were in parentheses next to our names. Was that really necessary?

"Oh, right," the hostess said and smiled at me.

I was sure she was thinking this is the pathetic girl that can't get a date on her own. I wanted to say "Just wait until you're thirty-two, miss perky breasts." Instead, I kept my mouth shut and followed her to a table for two in the center of the restaurant and, not coincidentally, directly in her line of sight.

According to the *L.A. Restaurant Guide,* Il Toro boasted a European ambience. I now understood that this meant the tables were so close together, you couldn't help but overhear the conversation of the person sitting next to you. In the future I needed to remember to choose a larger restaurant.

I hid behind my menu while I waited for Michael. At first I just skimmed it. Then I read it from cover to cover. When the waiter refilled my water glass for the third time I ordered an iced tea. Then I started nibbling on the bread he'd left in the center of the table. After I'd finished two slices of focaccia and a bread-stick, I pulled out my cell phone and checked my messages. I looked at my watch again. It was 1:20 p.m. I decided I would wait until 1:30 and then leave.

Michael arrived at 1:25. He looked like what I always imag-ined someone who grew up in Southern California would look like. His hair was golden and his skin was deeply tanned. All that was missing was the surfboard. He wore khakis, a white button-down Polo shirt, and a blue blazer, which came off the minute he sat down.

"I'm so sorry," he said when the hostess brought him to my table. "I drove up from Hermosa and the traffic was awful."

"That's okay," I said. "I was late too." I'd already waited, so there was no point in being a bitch about it.

"Especially after the last time," he continued. "I didn't even know if you would still be here. But I'm so glad you are."

I didn't mention that if he hadn't shown up in the next five minutes I was planning on leaving.

"I'm sure by now you've probably memorized the menu. Just tell me what's good here and we can order."

"I don't know," I said. "I've never been here before."

"Oh, I thought you picked this restaurant. Never mind, I'll ask the waiter." Michael stopped talking just long enough for me to order, then resumed the conversation. "So I'll ask you the stan-dard first question. Why did you join Just A Date?"

"Is that the standard first question?"

"You haven't been asked that before?"

"This is my first date."

He clapped his hands together. "A novice, how wonderful."

If I hadn't met Michael through a dating service I would've

sworn he was gay. He was the most effeminate straight man I'd ever met. He was also completely self-absorbed, which in this instance was a good thing. Between the hostess constantly glancing our way and the mother and daughter at the next table listening to our every word, I was having trouble initiating conversation.

Michael made it easy on me. He would ask me a question and I would get maybe one or two sentences in, then he would interrupt me and talk for the next fifteen minutes. The only down side was that I finished my meal before he did because he did all the talking and didn't have time to eat.

Michael had such a good time chatting that he even ordered dessert. This pleased the hostess immensely. I guess she figured if we didn't like each other, we would've left after the entrée. She seemed to have a vested interest in the outcome. Maybe that happens when you seat people together.

By the time we'd finished the tiramisu, I'd learned that Michael was the director of marketing for Adidas (not a director of movies, television or commercials), he was an only child, he had a house in Hermosa Beach, he loved to entertain and often invited friends over to watch sporting events on his fifty-inch plasma-screen TV, and he'd joined Just A Date because he was having trouble meeting women, supposedly because he traveled so much. I told him I was a lawyer and I didn't cook.

When Michael excused himself to use the men's room, the sixty-something mother at the next table seized the opportunity. "Excuse me," she said, "I don't mean to pry, but did I hear you say you met this fellow through a dating service?"

Before I could answer, her clearly mortified, fortyish daughter leaned over and said, "Please ignore my mother." Then she turned back to her mother and said, "If you keep this up I'm going to diagnose you with Alzheimer's and put you in a home."

"What am I doing that's so terrible?" the mother asked.

"You're embarrassing her," the daughter said, "and me."

"I'm not embarrassing anyone. I waited until her boyfriend left, didn't I."

"He's not my boyfriend," I said. "It's our first date."

"See Beverly," the mother said to her daughter. "I told you they were on a date. When's the last time you had a date?"

The daughter didn't answer, but looked like she was about to explode.

"So did I hear right?" the mother asked me. "Did you meet through a dating service?"

"Mom, if you don't stop this right now I'm leaving."

"You career girls are all the same. If you spent half as much time looking for a husband as you do worrying about your job, you'd be married by now."

The daughter threw some money on the table and walked out.

The mother turned to me. "She thinks because she's a doctor she doesn't need a husband. I don't know what I'm going to do with her." Then she shook her head, wished me good luck, and left before Michael returned.

I felt like the Ghost of Christmas Future had just given me a glimpse of what my life was to become. It was too horrible to contemplate.

When Michael came back, I offered to split the check per the Just A Date rules, but he refused. When he walked me outside and asked me for my phone number I gave it to him. I was pretty sure he wasn't The One, but after the scene I'd just witnessed, I needed to be absolutely sure.

CHAPTER 28

strategic Dating

"**W**hat movie are you going to?" Kaitlyn asked as we both pedaled our respective exercise bikes. I'd talked Kaitlyn into joining me at the gym Sunday morning. No easy task. She only agreed because I promised to buy her a spinach and cheese breakfast burrito afterwards.

"I don't remember the name of it," I said. "It's the new Tom Cruise action flick. I told Michael I'd see whatever he wanted, so long as he drove up to the west side. The traffic down to Hermosa on the weekend's a nightmare."

"What if he said no?"

"Then I would have canceled. I don't like him enough to drive an hour on the 405."

"Then why are you going out with him again?"

"Because I'm only ninety percent sure he's not The One."

"Are you even attracted to him?"

"Not really. Not yet, anyway. But sometimes when you get to know someone they become more attractive. And objectively, he is attractive. He's just not my type."

She took a swig from her water bottle and asked, "Is he *my* type?"

"No, he's too skinny for you. I know you have that thing about not dating guys with butts smaller than your own."

"Too bad. I wouldn't mind dating someone who had a house by the beach."

"You're ready to start dating again?" I would've thought after a five-year relationship, she would've needed more than a month to recover. Between her and Greg, I was starting to think I really was the only idiot who believed in mourning periods.

"Sure," she said. "I already have a lead. He's a good friend of my friend Marie's husband. Marie gave him my number and he told her he'd call me next week."

"What's his deal?"

"His name is Adam, he's thirty-two, he runs marathons, and he works at E-Cards."

"Sounds promising. What does he do at E-Cards?"

"I'm not sure. I know it has something to do with their website. Marie explained it to me, but I didn't really understand."

"Just as well. This will give you two something to talk about on the date. Guys love it when you show an interest in their career."

Kaitlyn stopped pedaling and stared at me. "Where did you come up with that one?"

"I think it was *The Smart Woman's Guide to Finding a Husband.*"

"You read that? I'm way more traditional than you are and even I wouldn't read that book."

"I didn't actually read it," I said. "I found it in the bargain bin at Borders and skimmed it a little. I made it to the chapter where it said if you're playing a game with a man you should purposely lose so that he can feel more powerful. Then I tossed it back."

"So you're willing to spend $300 on a dating service, but you're not willing to throw a game of Monopoly?"

"Not even if it only costs $1.99."

CHAPTER 29

Second Dates

I met Michael at the Regent Theater in Westwood Village for a twilight movie. I showed up on time. He was ten minutes late. But this time it was my fault. I accidentally gave him the wrong address. Really, it was an accident. There are ten movie theaters in Westwood within a six-block radius. It could've happened to anyone. Luckily, Michael didn't seem too perturbed. He scored points for that.

I handed him a movie ticket that I'd already purchased and he bought the popcorn. I didn't think that when the lights went down he would try the old arm-around-the-shoulder trick, but I was surprised he didn't at least try to hold my hand. By the middle of the film I decided he was either: (a) a gentleman, (b) gay, or (c) completely not attracted to me either.

When the movie ended, Michael walked me to my car. "That was fun," he said. "We'll have to do it again when I get back from New York."

What, no dinner? Not even coffee or a drink?

"Do you have my cell phone number?" he asked.

"No, just your home number."

"You should have my cell number."

I didn't ask why.

Michael pulled a business card out of his wallet and I handed him a pen from my purse. He passed me the card and said, "If you want to talk, call me on my cell. My mother hates it when she has to pick up my messages."

"Why would your mother have to pick up your messages?" Even my $30 answering machine allowed me to dial in to retrieve messages.

"Didn't I tell you my mother lived with me?"

"No," I said. I definitely would've remembered if I was dating Norman Bates.

"It's great for me because I travel so much. This way, there's always someone around to water the plants and feed the cat."

The second date worked. I was now 100 percent sure that Michael was not The One.

♡ ♡ ♡

I called Celia Monday morning to let her know I'd be needing a new match. She wanted to know why, but I dodged the question. I knew the feedback was supposed to be confidential, but mistakes happen and policies change. After she assured me for the third time that there was no way Michael would ever find out what I said about him, I told her, "He's a little too effeminate for me. I like guys who are a bit more masculine. Preferably one who doesn't live with his mother."

"Not a problem. I've got the perfect guy for you. Hang on a second while I pull his file."

I stayed on the phone until the silence switched to a message from the operator telling me to make a call or hang up. Celia called me back two hours later. "Sorry about that," she said. "We're having problems with our phones. But I can't wait to tell you about Ronald. He's thirty-three years old, 5'11", and has dark brown hair. He lives in Marina del Rey and works for a major credit-card company. It says here he likes to swim, sail, water-ski, go to the beach, and go fishing, hiking and white-water rafting. What do you think?"

"He sounds great." A little too outdoorsy maybe with the fishing and hiking, but I liked the rest of the water sports. And I'd always wanted to try white-water rafting. I gave Celia my availability, and she promised to call me back the next day.

When I walked into the Carriage Grill the following Wednesday, I knew that Ronald would not be effeminate. If this dark, brooding steak house, with its heavy wood paneling and deep leather booths was his favorite restaurant as Celia had said, then he had to be a manly man. Or at least one who wasn't concerned about calories, fat grams, or cholesterol. I glanced at the menu on the way in. It contained only one entrée that wasn't red meat.

I told the hostess my name and prayed that I wouldn't have to explain why the reservation was only in my first name.

"Julie, we're so glad to have you here at the Carriage Grill," the forty-something woman said with a smile. You would have thought we were old friends. It was a little disconcerting, but a nice change of pace. "Ronald just called and said to tell you he was running a few minutes late. He asked if you wouldn't mind waiting for him in the bar."

Before I could even ask where it was, she told me the bar was down the steps and on the right. It contained the same wood and leather decor as the dining room, but took the masculine theme a bit farther with a stone fireplace and a stuffed moose head on the wall.

I felt extremely out of place in my lavender, floral print silk dress. (All of my black pants were at the dry cleaner's.) I would've felt more comfortable in the navy pant suit I'd worn to work. Then I could have blended in with half the men in the room. The other half were wearing black or gray suits.

I ordered a vodka and 7-Up at the bar and took the drink with me to a red leather chair with a view of both the television and the entrance. I pretended to watch CNN with rapt attention when I wasn't glancing at the door every few seconds, hoping to spot someone who fit Ronald's description.

The first tall, dark-haired man who walked in headed straight for the bar. When he started talking to another man, I concluded he wasn't Ronald. Too bad. He had a great smile.

The second dark-haired man who walked in wasn't that tall, but he was walking toward me. I looked up and smiled, but at the last minute he swerved and headed in the direction of a party a few chairs away from me. No great loss. He was too short anyway.

The third man was tall and what little hair he had was dark, but there wasn't much left. Wouldn't Celia have mentioned if he was balding? He sat down near me and looked around the room. I was close enough to see his cigarette-stained teeth and acne-scarred skin. Please, please, please let it not be him.

While I debated whether to ask the third man his name, a fourth dark-haired man walked in and headed in my direction.

"Hi, Julie," he said and extended his hand. "I'm Ronald. Sorry to keep you waiting."

CHAPTER 30

Financial Planning for Lovers

I was so happy that Ronald wasn't the third man, I didn't really care that he wasn't anything like the Ken doll I'd imagined. He had a full head of black curly hair, olive skin, and a huge nose. His shoulders were narrow and his charcoal gray suit hung loosely on his thin frame.

We followed the hostess to a half-moon booth set for four people. I sat down on the end. Ronald walked around to the other side and slid into the middle of the booth. I was happy he hadn't asked me to slide over so we could sit side by side. I like to look at the person I'm talking to, which I've always found difficult when our sides are touching. Not enough personal space.

The waiter came over to our table as soon as we sat down.

"The usual, Mr. Tarakian?"

"Yes," Ronald told him. "Thank you."

"Would you like something else?" the waiter asked me.

I had barely touched my vodka and 7-Up, which turned out to be mostly vodka. "No, I'm fine."

I waited for the waiter to leave before I asked, "How often do you come here that you have a 'usual'?"

Ronald smiled. "Not that often. Well, maybe once a week. It's been more often lately because I've been working late and this place is only a few blocks from my office. Sometimes I come here for dinner and then go back."

"You have my sympathy." I hated working late.

"It's normally not this bad. It's just been incredibly busy lately because we're launching a new product next month. I think my hours will calm down after that."

"What kind of product?"

"Financial planning services."

"Like what?" I realized I was treading dangerously close to *The Smart Woman Guide's* conniving female zone, but it was the next logical question.

"Advising customers on their portfolios, estate planning, retirement, that sort of thing."

Boring! My dad was always after me to start investing and trading online. He'd even sent me an *Investing for Dummies* book for Hanukkah last year. I tried to read it, but I could never make it more than five or six pages before I fell asleep.

Ronald must've mistaken my nodding for interest. He was now explaining in detail all the different services his company offered. I kept shifting my position and adding a "really" every now and then just to stay awake. I didn't know anyone could get this excited about financial planning.

I stared at his face and let my mind wander. I noticed the spittle forming in the corner of his mouth. I also noticed how wet and mushy his lips were. He was probably a terrible kisser. My eighth-grade boyfriend had lips like that. It was like kissing a wet mop. Once, during one of our make-out sessions, I was so disgusted I almost vomited. I broke up with him the next day.

The waiter interrupted my reverie. He placed Ronald's scotch on the rocks in front of him and waited for a few seconds. When Ronald didn't acknowledge him, he left. After the waiter walked by our table for the third time, I put my hand on Ronald's arm (Chapter Four from *The Smart Woman's Guide*— "Touching"). "I think he needs our order," I said, nodding in the waiter's direction.

Ronald asked for a medium-rare porterhouse without even opening the menu and I requested a petite filet and salad. As soon as we were alone again, Ronald pulled a mini calculator out from his inside breast pocket and started to crunch the numbers for me with various hypotheticals. I was grateful when my salad arrived. Eating gave me something to do.

The lecture continued through the entrée. "This steak is delicious," I said after my first bite. I was desperate to change the subject. I didn't care what we talked about, as long as it wasn't financial planning.

"Yes," he said. "They're always good. Now you're a lawyer, right?"

"Right. I work for an entertainment litigation firm." I usually preferred not to talk about my job with new acquaintances. All anyone ever wanted to know was how many movie stars I'd met. When I'd tell them the truth—none—they were always disappointed. But even my dull job was a more interesting topic of conversation than financial planning.

"Do they offer pension or profit sharing?" he asked.

"No, just 401(k)."

"With company matching?"

"Nope." Maybe if I gave him one-word answers he would take the hint.

"Too bad," he said. "But most women end up relying on their husband's savings for retirement anyway, so it's not as bad for you as it is for the men in your firm."

I thought my eyes were going to bug out of my head. He

must've noticed, because he quickly added, "I know you career women don't like to hear that, but statistically, it's true."

"I'm sure that was true in my grandmother's generation. It's probably even true for my mother's generation. But that can't be true for my generation."

"No, it's true. We've done a lot of research in this area. Most of you career women get married and have babies, then you either cut back your hours or quit your jobs altogether. In either case, you're not saving for retirement as much as your male counterparts and end up relying on your spouse's savings."

"What about women who never get married and have kids on their own?"

"That phenomenon is too new for us to have viable statistical data. But don't worry," he added. "I'm sure that won't be your situation."

"Really, why?"

"Because you're too pretty to end up alone."

I knew he meant it as a compliment, but I still wanted to pick up my plate and shove it in his face. "So you think only ugly women have babies on their own?"

"No, but I just don't see you as one of those women who never gets married."

"You're basing that on what exactly?" Didn't he realize he'd been the only one talking for the last forty-five minutes? He knew absolutely nothing about me except that I had a 401(k) plan with no company match.

"Well, you joined Just A Date, so you must be looking."

"Of course I'd like to meet someone," I said. "But that doesn't mean I will. And even if I do, and I have a kid some day, I still wouldn't quit my job."

"That's what all the women say until they actually have a child. Then all they want to do is stay home with them."

"That's not true. I know plenty of women who have kids and still work." Actually, I only knew two. But that's just because most of my friends hadn't had children yet.

"Well, many women do continue working because they need the money. But polls show that if they could afford not to work, they wouldn't."

"I'm sure if you polled men and told them to assume money was no object and then asked them if they'd rather stay home or work, they'd all rather stay home too."

"I don't think anyone's ever taken that poll, but I doubt that's true. As a whole, men are much more competitive and career-oriented than women. Women can be satisfied just taking care of their families. Most men need something more. Outside validation."

There was no point in continuing the argument. "I guess we'll just have to agree to disagree on this one," I said and changed the subject to sailing. I needed a noncontroversial topic upon which Ronald could opine and that would require no input from me. I didn't know if I could be civil any more.

I wolfed down the rest of my steak and begged off on coffee and dessert. I wanted the evening to end as soon as possible. Ronald paid the check and walked me to my car.

"So what are the odds of me getting your phone number?" he asked.

Zero! But I didn't say it. I'd recovered my composure and didn't want to be that rude. "I'm surprised you even want it."

"Of course I want it. I love feisty women. They're so much fun to tame." He was smiling, but I didn't think he was joking.

"Ronald, you're one of a kind." Or at least I hoped he was. But he definitely wasn't the one for me.

CHAPTER 31

An Exceptionally Bad Start

I didn't have much time to fret about Ronald. My parents were arriving the next day, I had no food in the house, and I was desperately trying to settle the Rosebud case before Mark Parsons left for a three-week photo safari in Kenya.

"Mark, I've got them down to $25,000 from half a million. I really think you should take it."

"Why should we pay anything?" He was shouting again. "The sex was consensual, and Rita got him on tape practically admitting that he made the whole thing up just to bribe her into a promotion. I think we should send it to the D.A. and file criminal charges."

I sighed. Since Rita's postfiring sex tape had surfaced, we'd had this conversation nearly every other day. "Mark, you're thinking like a defendant again. I need you to think like a lawyer. Jared didn't actually admit that he lied. He merely implied it."

"You're splitting hairs, Julie."

"Yes, and so will the D.A. They're not going to prosecute, which means that the tape is inadmissible in the civil trial. Based on the evidence, it's still a he said/she said, and Rita's got a bad track record."

"I know." He was calmer now. "It just pisses me off that we

have to pay this guy anything. I'd really love to take it to trial and see him get nothing."

"It will cost you half a million dollars to go to trial. You can settle it for $25,000."

"It just irks me, that's all."

"If it will make you feel any better, his attorney told me that his costs and fees are already up to $15,000. Jared will only get $10,000, and that's before taxes. In the end, he'll clear maybe $6,000."

"Yeah, that makes me feel a little bit better."

"Good. Then you'll agree to settle for $25,000?" Please, please, please say yes.

"I guess so. Just draw up the papers fast before I change my mind. If we're going to settle, then I want it taken care of before I leave for vacation. I doubt there will be a fax machine out in the bush."

"Consider it done."

♡   ♡   ♡

So I thought. I sent Steve Rogers a standard settlement agreement, which he insisted on revising. We spent Thursday evening and Friday morning hammering out the language. By one o'clock Friday afternoon, I'd made copies of the final version and called a messenger service.

The plan was that the messenger would pick up the documents from my office and take them to Mark Parsons' home in Malibu. The messenger would wait while Mark signed the agreements and Mark would give him the $25,000 check. Then the messenger would return the signed agreements and the check to me that afternoon.

At the same time, Steve Rogers would have his client sign a

second set of documents. Then Steve and I would meet later that afternoon to exchange signed copies and I would give him the check. The case would be closed by the end of the day.

When the messenger picked up the package at 1:30 p.m., I was already the last person in the office. It was the Friday before Labor Day weekend, and Rosenthal had announced at noon that we could all leave at one o'clock. It figured the one time he decided to be a nice guy I got stuck working anyway. With any luck, I'd be out by three-thirty, maybe four o'clock at the latest. Which would give me just enough time to get home, clean up the apartment and pick up some groceries before my parents arrived that evening.

The phone interrupted my planning.

"Julia, it's Mommy."

"Where are you?" It sounded like she was calling from inside a tunnel.

"We're on the 405 Freeway. We just passed La Jolla."

"What are you doing in La Jolla?" They were supposed to be at the San Diego Zoo all afternoon.

"We decided to skip the zoo. We went the last time we were here and figured the traffic would be bad, so we should get an early start."

"But I thought you weren't coming until tonight. I told you I had to work today."

"I'm sure we won't be up there before five. You'll be home by then won't you?"

"I don't know, Mom. I don't usually get home before seven at the earliest."

"Well can't you leave a little early? We're driving all the way up just for you."

"I don't know, Mom. I'll see what I can do."

This was all I needed today! I called the messenger service to check on their progress. The receptionist told me the messenger was stuck in traffic too. I called again at two-thirty and three o'clock. He was still stuck in traffic. Apparently there'd been an accident, and Pacific Coast Highway was down to one lane, which was being used alternately for both directions.

Mark Parsons called me at 3:15 p.m.

"Julie, the messenger just got here and I'm signing the papers."

Thank you, God.

"But I have some bad news. I left the settlement check back at the office. I asked my assistant to copy it and she must've forgotten to put it back in my briefcase."

Don't panic. Stay calm. This could still work out. "That's okay. Just call her and have her messenger it over to me."

"I tried, but she's already left for the day. We closed early for the holiday weekend."

Now would be a good time to panic.

"But there's still one thing we can try," he said. "The security guard will be there until six o'clock. I can call him and tell him to let someone from your office in to pick up the check. But it can't be a messenger. It has to be someone you trust. Whoever it is will need to go through my desk."

"Everyone here is gone for the day. I'm the only one left."

"Can you do it then?"

Like I had a choice. "Sure, Mark. Just put the signed agreements in an envelope with my name on it. Tell the messenger if he makes it back to my office before I do, to leave the envelope downstairs with our security guard."

"Great. I'll call Christian and tell him to be on the lookout for a cute brunette."

"Who's Christian?"

"Our security guard. You'll like him. He looks like the guy in the Calvin Klein ads."

♡ ♡ ♡

I ran downstairs and pulled my car into Friday afternoon gridlock. It should've taken me twenty minutes to get to Rosebud's offices. It took me almost an hour. When I got there, the entrance doors were locked. I put my face up to the tinted glass and peeked inside. The security desk was empty. I pounded on the door for ten minutes until someone emerged.

"Christian, right?" I asked the twenty-two-year-old model look-alike when he cracked open the door. He wasn't wearing a badge on his white T-shirt, but those hideous blue polyester pants had to be part of a uniform. He had a waffle pattern rubbed into one side of his face and crusty yellow gunk in the corner of his eye. I must've interrupted his afternoon nap.

"Yeah," he said and yawned. "What do you want?"

"I'm Julie Burns. The one Mark Parsons told you to look out for."

"I don't know what you're talking about, lady, everyone's gone for the day."

This was not happening. "Mark Parsons, the general counsel of Rosebud. You know who he is, right?"

"Yeah."

"Didn't he call you earlier and tell you that he would be sending someone down here to pick up a check from his office?"

"No," he said. "I haven't seen him all week."

This had to be a bad dream. I pulled out my cell phone to call Mark and realized that I hadn't taken his home phone number with me. There was no one to call at my office, so I dialed directory assistance. The operator told me there was no listing for a Mark Parsons in Malibu. He must have an unlisted phone number.

I wanted to slit my wrists, but instead I said, "Do you have a contact list for Rosebud?"

"A what?"

"A list of home phone numbers for all of the employees."

"No."

Okay. Remain calm. "Christian, I have to pick up a check from Mark Parson's office. It is extremely important that I get this check today. I understand that you can't let me do that without Mr. Parsons' authorization." I stopped for a breath and continued. "I know he's at home because I spoke to him an hour ago. Unfortunately, I don't have his home phone number with me, but I'm sure his secretary must have it in her Rolodex." Another breath. "Why don't we go up to his office together. I'll find the number, call Mr. Parsons, and he can give you authorization. Then I'll leave with the check and I promise never to bother you again."

"I can't do that," he said.

"Why not?"

"Because I can't let anyone inside without authorization."

If he wasn't twice my size, I would've had my hands around his throat. "I understand that, Christian. I really do. But can't we make an exception this one time?"

"I'm sorry, I just can't do it. I could lose my job for something like that."

Still a no, but he was softening. "Do you know which office is Mr. Parsons'?"

"Yeah."

"Do you know where his secretary's desk is at?"

"Yeah."

"Do you think you could go up there and look in his Rolodex yourself? You can lock the door and I'll wait outside." I gave him the pleading, wide-eyed innocent look.

He thought about it for a few seconds and agreed. He locked the door and disappeared into the cool air-conditioned building. I sat down on the 110-degree sidewalk in front of the door and waited.

I looked at my watch. It was now 4:30 p.m. I pulled out my cell phone and dialed my office voice mail. I had three messages.

"Julia, it's Mommy. It's about 3:30 and we just passed Newport Beach. Call us back on Dad's cell phone."

The recording beeped and I heard a second voice. "Julie, it's Steve Rogers. Jared signed the agreement and we're both very anxious to wrap this up today. Call me as soon as you get this message."

The recording beeped again and a third voice came on the line. "Hi, Julie, it's Mark. I've been trying to reach Christian but he's not answering the phone. When you get there, tell him to call me at home. You know the number."

"Grrrrr! Do you think I have it memorized!"

Christian unlocked the door. "Are you okay? I thought I heard someone scream."

"I'm fine. Did you find the number?"

"No. I looked under 'P' for Parsons and 'M' for Mark and it wasn't in there."

I had no alternative. It was my only option. I started to cry.

"Oh, c'mon," he said. "Don't do that. Please don't do that."

I let the tears roll down my cheeks unabated.

He sighed. "Come inside. I'm sure we can figure something out."

I played Mark's voice mail message for Christian. That and the tears were enough to get me up to Mark's office. I checked his secretary's Rolodex myself, but Christian was right. There was no listing under *M or* P. I tried *B* for boss and *E* for employees, but no success.

I looked around the office. I didn't see any phone or address books. Even people who used electronic organizers kept a paper copy for backup. Mark's secretary was too efficient not to have all of his numbers somewhere.

I opened the top drawer of the desk and pulled out a stack of papers. I'd been hoping to find an employee phone list. There wasn't one. But taped to the bottom of the drawer was an index card with all of Mark's phone and fax numbers.

"Julie, where are you?" Mark asked when he picked up the line. "I've been trying to reach you."

"I know, I got your message. I'm in your office with Christian. I'm going to put him on the phone."

Christian nodded a few times and said, "Okay, sir." Then he handed the phone back to me.

"You're set," Mark said. "Thanks for going down there and taking care of this."

"No problem. Have a good trip." What else could I say? He was still a client.

Christian unlocked the door to Mark's inner office. I found the check sitting on top of a stack of papers in his in-box. I stuffed it in my purse, thanked Christian, and left. I tried to call my parents and Steve Rogers from the car, but my cell phone battery was now dead.

By the time I got back to my office at 5:30 p.m. I had six new messages on my voice mail. Three were from Steve Rogers. The other three were from my mother. Both of them wanted to know where I was and why I hadn't called them back.

I called Steve first. He picked up on the first ring.

"Where the hell have you been? I've been trying to reach you for two hours."

"I'm sorry," I said. "I had to drive over to Rosebud's offices to pick up the check, and the place was locked, and the security guard didn't want to let me in, and . . . just trust me, it was a nightmare."

"But you have the check now, right?"

"Yes. Why don't you come up to my office so we can exchange documents and then we can both get the hell out of here."

"I'll be right there," he said.

♡ ♡ ♡

Five minutes later Steve Rogers was sitting in my guest chair. He handed me two copies of the settlement agreement signed by his client and I handed him two copies signed by Mark, plus the check. "We're done," I said.

"Yes," he replied with obvious relief. "Not that it hasn't been a pleasure working with you."

"Same here." Normally I hated opposing counsel by the end of a case, but these negotiations had been shorter and less contentious than most. There'd even been moments over the last couple of weeks when I thought Steve Rogers was a nice guy.

"Maybe we can grab a beer some time," he added. "Exchange war stories."

"Sure." I assumed it was one of those "let's do lunch" lines that people say but never really mean.

"Great. How about one night next week? Maybe Friday?"

Hold on a second. Was this a date? I looked at Steve Rogers in his casual-Friday outfit—khakis, deck shoes, and a plaid short-sleeve shirt with a white T-shirt underneath. Way too preppie for me. And he definitely needed to update those horn-rimmed glasses. But I was too tired to come up with an excuse. What little energy I had left I needed to save for my parents. "Sure, Steve, Friday sounds good."

"Then I'll see you next week." He smiled at me and stood up. "Have a great weekend."

"You too." I knew my weekend would be anything but great.

CHAPTER 32

Fun With Mom and Dad

When I was alone again, I called my parents back.

"Well it's about time," my mother said. "Where have you been? I've been trying to reach you for hours."

"I was working Mom. I told you I had to work today."

"You don't answer your phone?"

"I had to go to a meeting outside the office which took longer than expected. I just got back."

"Why didn't you check your messages? You knew we'd be calling."

Deep cleansing breaths. "This is the first chance I've had, Mom," I said in a voice I reserved for difficult children and childish adults. "Where are you?"

"We're parked outside your apartment building. We've been

here for twenty minutes waiting for you to call us back. Were you planning on coming home soon or should we just fly out tonight?"

Please do. "I'm leaving now but I won't be home for at least half an hour. Probably longer with traffic. Why don't you and Dad go to the mall for an hour and come back." I live in the shopping mecca of the world. Surely she could find something she liked.

"I don't feel like shopping."

I counted to five backwards. "Well, you could always take a walk. I know you and Daddy do a lot of walking at home."

I could hear her ask my father if he wanted to take a walk and his sleepy "no" in response. He must've been napping in the car. "Your father doesn't want to take a walk."

"Fine, then sit in the car and wait." Now I was the childish one.

"Don't you have an extra key somewhere?" my mother asked.

"Where, Mom? Under the mat? This isn't Mayberry."

"Don't get angry, I'm just trying to be helpful."

Her standard routine. She pushes me over the edge then tries to pull me back from the abyss. It worked. "I can call my landlady and see if she's home. Maybe she can let you in."

♡ ♡ ♡

Luckily, Mrs. Klein, my always helpful, seventy-six-year-old landlady answered the phone and agreed to let my parents into my apartment. I'd driven halfway home before I realized that I'd forgotten to warn my mother that my apartment was a mess and I had no food in the refrigerator. I thought of calling her back, but it was already too late. Thank God I'd at least remembered to put Elmo away. My parents just wouldn't understand.

♡ ♡ ♡

When I unlocked my front door, I found my father lying on the couch watching television and my mother making noise in the kitchen. My father stood up long enough to give me a hug, then returned to CNN. My mother came out to the living room and also gave me a hug. She then waited a whole ten seconds before she nodded toward last Sunday's newspaper strewn across the living room floor and said, "I really like what you've done to the place."

That was a new record, even for her. My father sighed. He knew where we were headed.

"Nice to see you too, Mom," I said, picking up the newspapers and throwing them in the kitchen trash. I noticed that my dirty spoon and coffee mug were no longer in the sink. My mother must've put them in the dishwasher. I would've thanked her if she hadn't made that crack about the newspapers.

"Aren't you going to thank me?" my mom said, standing in the entrance to my galley-style kitchen.

"For what?"

"I cleaned your kitchen."

I looked around. Except for the empty sink, it looked the same. Okay, maybe the chrome on the faucet was a little bit shinier, but otherwise it really did look exactly the same. The kitchen was the one room in the apartment I always kept clean. I was afraid if I didn't, I'd get bugs.

"It looks the same, Mom."

Instead of answering me, she turned around and stomped back into the living room to pout.

My father had no choice but to get involved. "So what do you ladies want for dinner?"

For a few seconds, neither of us answered, then my mother

said, "We'll have to go out somewhere. You know your daughter doesn't cook." Now I was *his* daughter.

"I can cook," my father said. The man barbecues steaks and cooks turkey on Thanksgiving and he thinks he's a seasoned chef.

"Well then you'll have to go to the grocery store first," my mother said, "because she doesn't have any food either."

"That's not true." I walked into the kitchen and opened my freezer. "I have two Lean Cuisines and a box of popsicles."

"Gourmet all the way," my mother said.

"Well some of us have jobs and are too busy to cook."

Silence. I'd played my trump card. My mother hadn't worked since the day she found out she was pregnant with my sister. My father had been pushing her to get a job for the last twenty-five years, but without success. She was content staying home, with or without children in the house.

I played this card often; usually when my mother was criticizing my domestic skills. It always worked. But just as inevitably, afterward I was contrite and would say something to make amends. Total annihilation of the opposition was more fun in court than it was with family.

"If you had come later," I said to my mother, "when you were supposed to, I would've stopped at the grocery store on the way home. I planned on buying you both orange juice and raisin bran. And if I thought you were going to be nice, I might've even bought you skim milk for your coffee instead of the two-percent kind that I like."

"Well why do you always have to leave everything for the last minute?" She couldn't accept the olive branch without one more dig.

"So the food will be fresh."

My dad laughed and my mom smiled. "Where do you want to go for dinner?" she asked.

♡ ♡ ♡

The next morning over a breakfast of raisin bran, orange juice, and coffee with skim milk, I casually mentioned that I was thinking about buying a new car. It was a fleeting thought, really. I'd spent a considerable amount of time in Kaitlyn's Mustang convertible lately and I thought it might be nice to have one of my own.

My dad seized on the idea. He'd traded in his '62 Karmann Ghia convertible when my sister was born and had been driving family-size sedans ever since. He was eager to test-drive all the new models.

After breakfast, I took my father to Barnes & Noble to buy the latest *Consumer Reports Car Guide* and some automotive magazines. Then my mom and I left him home reading and making notes while we went to Beverly Hills for some power shopping. When we returned three hours later and several hundred dollars poorer, my dad had devised a plan of action.

Early Sunday morning, the three of us set out to visit every convertible car dealership in Southern California. We test-drove Fords, Toyotas, Hondas, Mazdas, Saabs, and BMWs, and just for fun (they were definitely out of my price range) the Mercedes and Jaguars too. My dad liked the Mazdas, my mom liked the BMWs, and I liked the Saabs.

It didn't matter. I had no intention of actually buying a new car for at least a year. Car shopping was just a good family bonding experience. My motto is, a family that shops together is a family that doesn't have to talk to each other about controversial subjects that could lead to arguments. In my family, any topic other than food or the weather could potentially lead to an argument. It worked. For awhile at least.

♡ ♡ ♡

That night my dad went to bed early and I stayed up with my mom while she packed. She was sitting on top of her suitcase and I was kneeling on the floor next to her trying to close the zipper when she sprang on me. "So can I ask you about your love life?"

"I would prefer that you didn't." I'd almost gotten the ends of the zipper together.

"I don't know why you never tell me anything. After all," she added as if the statement had some sort of intrinsic meaning, "I am your mother."

"I don't recall you telling Grandma everything." My mother and grandmother had had a roller coaster relationship. Over the years, they'd been both best friends and mortal enemies.

"I told Grandma plenty. The only time I didn't was when I knew she would judge me. But I don't do that to you."

Could anyone really be that self-deluded? "Since when?"

"I never judge you."

"Mom, you've done nothing but criticize me since you walked in the door."

"That's not true! I just thought you should've cleaned the house before we came."

"I cannot believe you're starting this again. You have no idea what my day was like before you arrived." I gave her the long version of events, with all the details left in, hoping to elicit some sympathy.

"You know," she said after I'd finished, "if you put half as much energy into finding a husband as you put into your job, you'd be married by now."

My future had arrived, only much sooner than I'd expected. "Mother, I cannot believe you would even say that to me. Why are you so desperate for me to get married? How can my being single at age thirty-two possibly be a burden to you?"

"I would just feel better if I knew you were settled."

"I've had the same job and lived in the same apartment for six years. How much more settled could I be?"

At that point, my father piped in from the futon. "Can you two keep it down. I'm trying to sleep."

My mother followed me into my bedroom and closed the door. "I would just feel better if I knew that someone was taking care of you."

"I'm taking care of me. Why isn't that enough?"

"I just think you would be happier if you weren't alone."

"I'm not alone." I was about to say, "I have Elmo," but caught myself in time. "I have friends," I said. "I date. I just haven't met the right guy yet."

"See," she said. (I didn't.) "I had no idea you were dating someone. You never tell me anything."

"I didn't say I was dating someone. I just said I was dating."

"What's the difference?"

I had to think about that one. Instead of telling her the truth, that dating someone means you're sleeping together and just dating means you're interviewing potential sex partners, I said, "Dating someone means you're exclusive, and just dating means you go out with multiple people at the same time."

"Then tell me about the people you've dated."

"There's nothing to tell. They were just guys."

"What was wrong with them?"

"Nothing was wrong with them. They just weren't right for me."

"Why not?"

"I don't know." I knew she wouldn't let up and I would have to tell her something. Since Ronald was as good an example as any, I said, "The last guy I went out with was a complete chauvinist. You would've thought he'd just stepped out of a time machine from the 1950s."

"Why?" she asked. "Because he offered to pay for dinner?"

"No, that part I liked. It was his outdated ideas I had a problem with."

"And the other ones? What was wrong with them?"

"The one before him was too effeminate. Before that, I don't remember." Two should be enough to satisfy her.

"Just line 'em up and shoot 'em."

"I'm sure I'll meet the right one." At least I wanted to believe that. "Just give me some time."

"You're not getting any younger, Julia. Don't you think it's possible that you're a little too fussy?"

I knew it! I knew she would turn this into a criticism about me. And then she wonders why I never tell her anything. "No, Mother, I don't think you can be too fussy when it comes to the person you're going to spend the rest of your life with."

"Well, what if you never meet the perfect person?"

"I didn't say he had to be perfect. I just said he had to be the right one for me."

"What if you never meet the ideal man who is just right for you?"

"Then I'll be single forever. But I'd rather stay single than marry someone I don't want to marry just so you can tell your friends that I'm married."

"Well, let's hope it doesn't come to that."

CHAPTER 33

Freedom Returned

I felt free. True, I was driving to the office. But at least it was a Tuesday morning instead of a Monday morning, the Rosebud case was over, the dreaded parental visit was behind me, and my date with opposing counsel wasn't until Friday night. Life was good.

I was cleaning up the Rosebud files to send to storage when Simone came into my office. She settled herself in one guest chair and stretched her long legs out across the other.

"You don't mind, do you?" she asked.

"I don't, but Rosenthal might."

"Didn't you hear? He went to New York for the weekend and his flight back to L.A. was delayed. He won't be in the office at all today."

This day was getting better and better.

"But enough about Rosenthal. I want to hear about your weekend with Mom and Dad."

I gave Simone the highlights.

"I love it," she said. "You spent all day dealing with annoying car salesmen just so you didn't have to talk to your parents."

"I talked to my parents. We just talked about the cars we were test-driving instead of anything controversial."

"Well, I've got some news for you that ought to make your mother happy."

"What? You found me a husband?"

"Maybe," she said. "If not, he should at least be a good date."

Simone told me how she'd met Dylan. She and her fiancé, Todd, had spent the weekend at Todd's beach club. Todd had left early Sunday morning to play golf with some of his buddies, and Simone stayed. She was lying on a lounge chair by the pool when a man sat down next to her and started flirting. Naturally, Simone flirted back. When he asked for her number, she admitted she was engaged, but told him that she had a friend that she'd love to set him up with.

"I can't believe he agreed to it," I said.

"It took some cajoling, but I convinced him. It really wasn't that difficult. All guys think that attractive women are only friends with other attractive women, so all he really agreed to was to trade one attractive woman's phone number for another. No biggie."

"You gave him my number?" This was getting out of hand.

"Of course not. I would never do that without asking you first. So can I?"

"I don't know Simone. You don't know anything about this guy."

"I know he's tall and very cute. He's personable. He lives in Brentwood. He's a real estate broker. He's single. And he makes enough money to afford a membership at a $6,000-per-month private beach club."

"That doesn't mean he's not a jerk."

"He can't be worse than the last guy. Just go out with him once; you've got nothing to lose."

I drove to Gianni's (yet another Italian restaurant in Beverly Hills with European ambience) on Thursday night straight from the office. I went directly into the bar area and looked for a tall man with a black suit, gray shirt, and no tie, the outfit Dylan told me he'd be wearing.

It wasn't a helpful description. This was Los Angeles. Ten of the fifteen men in the bar were wearing black suits. Four of them wore ties, so now I was down to six. One was short, one was bald, and two were with women. I had it narrowed down to two, but I couldn't figure out which one of them was Dylan. I decided I would wait at the bar and let the right man come to me.

I sat down at the only empty bar stool and ordered a glass of cabernet. Neither man even looked in my direction. I was debating whether I should say something to one of them, and if so which one, when one of the men got up and left. I paid for my wine and was about to walk up to the other man, when someone else walked up to me.

He was tall, cute but not gorgeous, and wore black pants and a gray shirt. I'd noticed him earlier sitting by himself at a table in the corner.

"Julie, right?" he asked.

"Yes," I said.

"Hi, I'm Dylan. Nice to meet you." We shook hands. I must have looked perplexed, because he added, "I left my jacket in the car."

"I wish I knew you were going to do that. I was looking for someone in a black jacket."

"I know. I saw you walk in."

"Then why didn't you come up to me sooner?" I thought he'd say something like "I wasn't sure it was you" or "I was working up my nerve."

He said, "I liked watching you scope the room. It was very entertaining."

Another jerk. Hadn't I met my quota yet? "That's what I'm here for," I said and gave him a fake smile.

"I'm glad to hear that. If the evening goes well, I'll have to call Simone and thank her for setting us up."

If I called Simone right now I wouldn't be thanking her.

How shocked would this guy be if I just got up and walked out? I could. It wasn't like he was a friend of Simone's. He was really a complete stranger. Hmmm. Who was I kidding? I couldn't do it. It was too rude. Even for this guy. I glanced at the clock on the wall above the bar. It was only 8:15. With any luck, I'd be home in time to watch *ER*.

I listened to Dylan's stories about his job, his ex-girlfriend, and his ex-girlfriend's annoying cat. He must have written me off too. Otherwise, why would he spend half the evening talking about his ex-girlfriend?

Around the time our entrées arrived, Dylan must've either run out of stories or gotten tired of the sound of his own voice. I'd bet on the former. Or it's possible he was just hungry and wanted me to do the talking so he could eat. He started asking me questions about my job and my travels.

I was in the middle of a story about a trip to Europe I'd taken with Kaitlyn after we'd graduated from law school when he leaned over to the couple at the next table and said, "It's pronounced 'Title-ist', not 'Tit-list.' "

All three of us just stared at him.

"Sorry," Dylan said to the man, "but I'm a big golfer and I just wanted to let you know the correct pronunciation of the name."

The man at the next table was obviously, and rightfully, annoyed. I was sure he and his dinner companion were on a first date too, because when they were next to me at the bar, I'd heard him ask her how she liked to spend her free time. That was definitely a first-date question.

The man said, "Thanks for the tip," and returned his attention to his dinner partner.

Dylan turned back to me. "I just couldn't listen to that guy massacre the name."

Why were you eavesdropping on the conversation at the next table when you should've been listening to me, your date? I listened to all your boring stories. The least you could do is pretend to listen to my mildly entertaining, if not completely mesmerizing, tale.

"What is Titlist?" I asked, making sure I pronounced the name correctly.

"A company that makes golf equipment. I have a set of their clubs. They're terrific."

"How long have you been playing?" I knew nothing about golf and had no interest in the sport, but I didn't want to keep talking when he made it so obvious that he wasn't listening. I'd let him talk so I could eat. At least the food was good.

I was relieved when we'd both finished our pastas without another incident. I planned on turning down coffee and dessert, so the end of the evening was in sight. Until the busboy came over to clear our plates and accidentally dropped a fork in Dylan's lap.

"You idiot!" Dylan screamed.

The restaurant became momentarily silent as the other diners stared. The busboy grabbed the fork and smiled apologetically.

Dylan continued his tirade. "You think just picking it up makes everything okay?"

The busboy appeared neither to speak nor understand English, but he must've realized from the tone of Dylan's voice that it wasn't good. He quickly cleared the rest of our plates and hurried toward the kitchen. I wished I could go with him.

"Don't you walk away from me," Dylan yelled after him. "I can have you fired for this."

"Dylan, it was an accident."

"Don't defend him. If he can't clear a table without dropping the silverware, then they should send him back where he came from."

The waitress arrived seconds later and the maître d' a few minutes after that. They both apologized to Dylan over and over again in fruitless attempts to calm him down. His anger only subsided when the maître d' agreed to take his entrée off the bill.

I tried to say good-bye to Dylan in front of the restaurant, but he insisted on walking me to my car. As I fumbled for my keys, he shocked me with, "We should go out again."

What was up with this guy? First he bores me, then he ignores me, then he embarrasses me, and now he wants a second date? I knew guys who always asked women for a second date even when they had no intention of ever seeing the woman again, but that was just because, according to them, they were being polite. I was sure that wasn't Dylan's motivation.

"You have my number," I said and prayed he wouldn't use it.

Then he leaned down toward me. I turned my head. No way was I kissing him. What was he thinking? Not only was this a first date, but he ate garlic chicken for dinner.

Dylan kissed my cheek and then moved over to my mouth. I pulled away.

"What's wrong?" he asked.

Take a hint, buddy! "I don't kiss on the first date."

"If your friend told me she was setting me up with a prude, I never would've agreed to this."

"Trust me," I said, "if she had told me what a rude jerk you were, I would've said no, too."

"Your problem is you're just a tight-ass bitch who doesn't know how to have a good time."

I thought of all the nasty things I could've called him in return. But what was the point? Plus it was already five minutes to ten. I needed to get home to watch *ER* and tickle Elmo.

I got off one "drop dead" before I slammed my car door shut and sped away. Even when I took the high road, I still needed to have the last word.

CHAPTER 34

Thank God It's Friday

I loved Fridays. Not only was the weekend mere hours away, but it was the only day of the week I could wear jeans to work and have breakfast waiting for me when I arrived. The firm had a standing order with the bakery on the first floor to deliver two dozen bagels and three varieties of cream cheese to the office every Friday morning. Rosenthal thought this proved to everyone what a generous guy he was. No one was fooled.

By the time I arrived Friday morning, all the popular flavors (i.e., anything with seeds, raisins, or cheese) were gone. I grabbed a plain bagel and a cup of coffee and headed back to my office, where I found Simone waiting for me. She was already halfway through her sesame seed bagel and coffee.

"You're late," she said.

"I know. I tried on five different outfits this morning trying to decide what to wear tonight."

"I almost forgot, tonight's the date with the lawyer. But first I want to hear about last night. What did you think of Dylan?"

I set down my bagel and coffee so I could use both hands for emphasis. "I cannot believe you set me up with that guy!"

"Why? What did he do?"

I told Simone the whole story.

"Sorry about that," she said. "But I can make it up to you."

"How?" With Simone, you never knew.

"Todd told me there's a guy in his office he wants to fix you up with."

"I'm not sure I trust your taste anymore."

"It's not mine, it's Todd's. I've never met the guy. All I know is that he works with Todd and he's good-looking."

"How do you know he's good-looking if you've never met him?"

"Todd told me, so you know he must be. Guys never say that other guys are good-looking unless they're drop-dead gorgeous."

"That's true," Greg said as he walked in with his poppy seed bagel and a container of apple juice. "We're completely clueless." Simone moved her feet off the other guest chair so Greg could sit down.

"Then how do you know when a guy is drop-dead gorgeous?" I asked.

"Because whenever we have one among us, all the women flock to him and tell the rest of us that he's gorgeous. Then we know."

"Do you have any gorgeous friends to set Julie up with?" Simone asked Greg.

"No," he said. "I'm plumb out."

"What good are you?" I asked.

"Very good," Greg said. "I have some information on your new beau that I think you'll want to hear."

"What new beau?" If I had one, it was news to me.

"I told him you had a date with Steve Rogers," Simone said. "I didn't think it was a secret."

I shot Simone a "we're going to have to discuss this later" look, but she'd already fixed her gaze on piece of lint clinging to the hem of her skirt. She and Greg were getting awfully chummy lately. I still thought that Simone could keep a secret, but Greg definitely couldn't. He was the biggest gossip I knew.

"We're just going out for a drink," I said. "It's no big deal."

"Does that mean you're not interested in my information?" Greg asked.

"Of course I'm interested. Spill it."

"According to Carr, Geary, & Rogers' receptionist, your man is thirty-six, divorced, no children, and is a very nice guy. She says he doesn't date a lot, but she thinks he's definitely ready to settle down and get married again."

"He's perfect," Simone said.

"They're all perfect on paper. Let's see how the first date goes before we start planning the wedding. By the way, how did you come by this information?"

"Pillow talk," Greg said and took a huge bite out of his bagel.

I shook my head in disgust. Simone gave him an appreciative glance.

♡　♡　♡

When I arrived in the lobby precisely at seven o'clock, Steve Rogers was already waiting. He was wearing the same casual Friday outfit he'd been sporting the week before, except this time he left out the white T-shirt underneath the short-sleeve, plaid button-down.

"I thought we could go to O'Grady's," he said, "if that's okay with you?"

"Fine," I replied.

O'Grady's was an Irish pub on the first floor of our building. I'd been there a few times when I'd first started at Rosenthal & Leventhal. But that was six years ago. I'd always thought it was too close to the office for true relaxation. I must've been the only person in the building who felt that way. The place was packed.

Steve led me through the throng at the bar and into the restaurant. The hostess, whom I assumed from her accent really was Irish, greeted Steve warmly and led us to a booth. The three other parties waiting ahead of us didn't look pleased.

"I didn't know this place took reservations," I said.

"They don't," he said. "Lori did me a favor."

I guess that meant he was a regular.

When our waitress arrived, Steve ordered a Killian's Irish Red and I ordered a glass of sauvignon blanc.

"Don't you like beer?" he asked.

"I do, I just felt like wine." I wasn't about to tell Steve that although I liked beer, I couldn't make it through half a bottle without belching. I could never figure out how guys trained themselves not to do that. If I got to know Steve better, I would ask. Assuming, of course, he didn't spend the evening belching in my face. I no longer took good manners for granted.

Steve spent the first hour peppering me with the usual first-date questions about my job, my family, and where I was from. He even asked follow-up questions, proving to me that he had actually listened to my answers. I was impressed.

When we ordered the second round, Steve suggested dinner too, and I agreed. Two hours later we were sipping Irish coffees and I still thought he was a nice guy. In the three hours we'd been together, he hadn't said or done anything rude or offensive. This guy was a keeper for someone. I just didn't think that someone was me.

It's not that he was unattractive, I just wasn't attracted to him. But I thought it was a good sign that my opinion of him was improving as the evening wore on. Of course, that might've had something to do with the wine and the spiked coffee.

CHAPTER 35

Beach Blanket Bingo

Although I'd had two dates that week, I still had no plans for the weekend. And neither did Kaitlyn. It was nice when life worked out that way. I picked Kaitlyn up Saturday afternoon and we headed to the beach. Since neither of us could afford a $6,000 per month membership at a private beach club, we had to slum it at the state park with the rest of the working stiffs.

After Kaitlyn had arranged our towels so that we were perfectly aligned with the sun, we lathered up with sunscreen. I applied a thin layer of SPF 15, while Kaitlyn doused her body in SPF 45. After three months of tanning, Kaitlyn was still only one shade past milky white. I was my usual end-of-the-summer golden brown.

"Dylan's clearly history," Kaitlyn said. "But the lawyer sounds like he has potential. What's his name again?"

"Steve Rogers. I'm thinking he's probably not Jewish."

"Why do you say that?"

"He's from Michigan, has five brothers and sisters, and Rogers isn't exactly a Jewish name."

"So? That doesn't mean anything. I'm from a large Midwestern family named La Rue, and I'm part-Jewish."

"Your great-grandmother was half Jewish and you were raised

Roman Catholic. It doesn't count." I don't know why she refused to believe me about this.

"So what if he's not Jewish? You've said before you'd marry someone who wasn't Jewish."

"It's really not about religion. He's just not my type."

"Maybe he could be if you gave him a chance."

She was starting to sound like my mother. "I don't think so. Even without the plaid shirt, he just doesn't have enough edge."

"Then you'd probably like Adam," she said. "He's got lots of edge."

"Is that the E-Cards guy?"

"Yeah."

"What's his last name again?"

"Rosen."

"Jewish, right?"

"Yup. And he's from New York. He's actually back there this weekend for his nephew's bar mitzvah."

"How many times have you gone out now?"

"Three," she said, "if you count the time we just met for coffee."

"That counts. But why are you wasting your time with him when you know you'll only marry someone Christian?"

"I didn't find out he was Jewish until the second date."

"His last name is Rosen and he's from New York. What religion did you think he was?"

"Well, I suspected, but I wasn't sure. Not until he told me about the bar mitzvah."

"Then if you knew on the second date, why go for a third?"

She rolled over onto her stomach and handed me her sunscreen to rub onto her back. "Because he's a lot of fun. But I know I need to break it off. We had the religion conversation before he left, and he told me he would only marry a shiksa—"

"That's a non-Jewish girl."

"Yes, I know. Anyway, he said he would only marry a shiksa if she converted because he wants his kids to be Jewish and just raising them Jewish wouldn't be enough, which I didn't really understand."

"It's because in the Jewish religion, children are considered to be the same religion as their mother. Technically speaking, even if the kids are raised Jewish, if the mother isn't Jewish, then neither are the kids. Although I think the Nazis took a much more inclusive view of Judaism."

"That's not funny."

"Sorry," I said. "But I'm Jewish, so I'm allowed to make those bad jokes. What I think is really funny is that a nice Catholic girl like you is dating a nice Jewish boy from New York and I'm dating a good Christian from Michigan. Too bad we can't switch."

Kaitlyn propped herself up on her elbows and peered at me over the top of her sunglasses. "Why can't we?"

"Because I'm an olive-skinned brunette and you're a freckle-faced redhead. I think they'd notice."

"I don't mean show up for each other's dates, I mean fix each other up."

"Don't you think they might be a little offended if we called them and said 'Hi, I don't want to go out with you anymore, but I'd love to set you up with my girlfriend'?"

"We can't do it like that." I could practically see the gears shifting in her head. "What we need to do is go out with them again and arrange to run into each other somewhere. That way you can meet Adam and I can meet Steve."

"And what? We start flirting with each other's dates?"

"No, they're not going to hit on us. We wouldn't want them if they did."

"True."

"After the next date, we break up with them. Then, after we've waited a respectable amount of time, maybe two or three days, I'll call Steve and tell him I heard about the two of you breaking up and I'll ask him out. Then you call Adam and do the same."

"You've never asked a guy out in your life."

"That doesn't mean I wouldn't," she said.

"What makes you think even if we did ask them out, they'd say yes?"

"They've just been dumped and two days later some cute girl calls them up and asks them for a date. Of course they're going to say yes."

Probably. "Assuming that's true, don't you think it's a little manipulative?"

"You're the one who said if we told them the truth they'd be offended. We're just sparing their feelings."

I loved that about Kaitlyn. She could justify anything.

CHAPTER 36

The Sting

Steve picked me up Saturday night at eight o'clock. This time he wore brown chinos, a tan button-down polo shirt, and penny loafers. Still too preppy for me, but I knew Kaitlyn would love it.

At my request, Steve had made dinner reservations at Ocean Avenue Seafood. Kaitlyn told me she and Adam would be having dinner two doors down at I Cugini. The plan was that after dinner, we'd each suggest to our respective dates that we try The Perfect Cup, a new coffeehouse on Ocean Avenue, where we would accidentally bump into each other. After that, we'd leave it to fate, at least until we reconvened for breakfast the next morning.

Steve held open the door to his dark blue Mercedes, and I sunk into the supple tan leather upholstery. Perhaps I'd been too hasty in agreeing to pass him on to Kaitlyn. I could always tell her I'd changed my mind. It wasn't too late.

♡ ♡ ♡

This time, I peppered Steve with questions. He told me stories about growing up on a farm in rural Michigan as one of six children with his homemaker mother and minister father. He said his passions were religion, politics, and music, preferably classical or Christian rock. His hobbies were golf in the summer, skiing in the winter, and watching sporting events all year round.

He seemed surprised when I told him I was Jewish. He said he thought I might be Italian. I get that a lot. Especially in the summer, when I have a tan.

By the end of the meal, I knew this would be our last date. Our backgrounds could not have been more different, we had few common interests, and after half a bottle of chardonnay, I still didn't want to jump his bones.

After dinner, we walked the length of the Third Street Promenade, a shopping district in Santa Monica known for its great people-watching, before heading to The Perfect Cup. The place was crowded and tiny. After fifteen minutes of standing by the door, a table for four opened up and I wanted to grab it, but the waiter wouldn't allow it. He said it was reserved for parties of three or more. I couldn't mention in front of Steve that we would be a party of four any minute.

Steve and I were seated at the next available table for two. I positioned myself in the chair with the best view of the entrance. If Steve noticed me constantly glancing at the door, he didn't mention it. We ordered two coffees and a slice of chocolate mousse pie. We were still waiting for the pie when Kaitlyn walked in with a man I presumed was Adam.

He looked younger than his thirty-five years. He was tall, with dark brown hair and hazel eyes. He wore blue jeans, a black T-shirt with a black blazer, and those hip, rectangular-framed eye glasses that were showing up all over town. Although Adam didn't quite fit Kaitlyn's description, physically at least, he was my type.

Kaitlyn played her part perfectly. She scanned the restaurant as if searching for an empty table. When she spotted me, she said something to Adam and nodded in my direction. I turned away but kept her in my peripheral vision.

When she was halfway to the dessert counter, I glanced in her direction with what I hoped was a surprised expression. Steve turned around and followed my gaze.

"Who's that?" he asked when Kaitlyn waved.

"A good friend of mine," I said and waved back. "It's so weird that she would turn up here."

Kaitlyn brought Adam over and introduced me, and I presented her to Steve. The quarters were too close for them to stand in the aisle and chat, so they returned to the entrance to wait for a table. Unfortunately, the next seats available were by the front window. They were only ten feet away, but the two tables between us made a group conversation impossible.

When the waiter slipped the check onto the table, I snatched it up and paid the bill. Steve objected, but I ignored him. Buying coffee and dessert was the least I could do for a guy I was about to underhandedly pass off to my girlfriend.

"Do you mind if we say good-bye to my friend before we go?" I asked Steve when we stood up to leave. My plan was for us to sit down at the now vacant table next to Kaitlyn and Adam. I wanted to have at least a short conversation with him before I called him and asked him out.

"You go," he said. "I need to use the restroom. I'll wait for you by the door."

He wasn't making this easy. I couldn't barge into Kaitlyn's and Adam's conversation on my own. I needed Steve to talk to Kaitlyn while I chatted up Adam. Rather than attempting it alone, I waited at the table for Steve to return, then just waved to Kaitlyn and Adam on my way out.

Half an hour later Steve was driving around my block for the second time. I'd told him that my neighborhood was safe and he didn't need to park and walk me to the door, but he insisted. A space on my street opened up on the third pass.

I thought we'd say good night at the entrance to my building, but Steve insisted on seeing me all the way to my apartment door. I hoped he wasn't expecting to be invited in. As far as I was concerned, he was Kaitlyn's guy now. I wasn't going to spend an hour smooching on the couch with my best friend's future date.

I unlocked my door and left my hand on the knob. "I had a nice time tonight," I said. "Thanks for dinner."

"Me too," he said. "And thank you for dessert."

He bent down to kiss me. It seemed mean to give him my cheek when he was clearly aiming for something else, so I gave him a quick kiss on the lips, but no tongue. He just stared at me for a few seconds, then said good night.

The next morning, I waited for Kaitlyn on the bench outside Bread & Porridge.

"So?" I asked before she'd even sat down. "What did you think of Steve?"

"I didn't really get to talk to him," she said. "But I thought he looked darling in that polo shirt."

"I knew you'd love the outfit."

"You, of course, hated it."

"Of course." After we finished dissecting Steve's looks and wardrobe, we moved on to Adam. Kaitlyn thought he was too trendy. I thought he had good taste.

"So what's the next step?" I asked. "Do we wait for them to call again and then blow them off?"

"You mean you didn't break up with him last night?"

"No. Why? Did you break up with Adam?" When it came to men, Kaitlyn was the most nonconfrontational person I knew. She would never have broken up with Adam that night.

"Of course," she said. "I can't believe you didn't."

"What was I supposed to do? Give him the 'just friends' speech over dinner?" Since Joe had thrown me in the pool, I was much more cautious.

"Right before he left your apartment would've worked well."

"Is that when you broke up with Adam?"

"Earlier. I did it on the drive home. I told him I was thinking about what he'd said and that no matter how much I cared about someone, I didn't think I could ever convert to another religion."

"How did he take it?"

"He said he understood. Then I told him I thought he was a great guy, but under the circumstances it would be better if we were just friends."

"I'm really proud of you. Not only did you actually tell someone that you didn't want to date them anymore, but you even did it in person."

"Thank you," she said. "But what I want to know is why you didn't tell Steve. Did you change your mind?"

"No, that was definitely our last date. I just figured that at the end of the night he would say something about us seeing each other again and then I would tell him it wasn't working out. But he never mentioned it. Hopefully, he'll call this week and then I can break up with him over the phone."

"Okay. But you're not calling Adam until you've broken up with Steve."

"Agreed." We didn't discuss what would happen if Steve never called. I didn't even want to think about it.

CHAPTER 37

Just Friends, Again

When Steve hadn't called by Thursday morning, Kaitlyn decided I needed to make the next move. I suggested that we wait. If two weeks passed and Steve still hadn't called, I reasoned, we could safely assume the relationship was over. Kaitlyn thought that was too long of a delay. By then, she declared, her call to Steve and mine to Adam would no longer look impulsive. I promised Kaitlyn that if Steve didn't call me that evening, I'd get in touch with him the following day.

By Friday morning when Steve still hadn't called, I was desperate. I went down to Greg's office to solicit his help.

"Are you still dating the receptionist at Carr, Geary, & Rogers?"

"I wouldn't call it dating," Greg said.

Unbelievable. "Well, are you still sleeping with her?"

"Sometimes, yeah. Why?"

"Do you think you could call her and ask her for a favor?"

"What kind of favor?"

"I need to know if Steve Rogers has lunch plans today and, if not, when he usually leaves for lunch if he's not meeting someone."

"I never really pegged you as a stalker, Burns."

I explained to Greg that I needed to speak to Steve to definitively end the relationship so my friend could ask him out. I left out the part about my friend and I engineering the meeting, the breakup, and the future date. He didn't need to know.

Greg agreed and said he would call me with the information. When an hour had passed with no word, I called him again. He promised that he was working on it, and vowed to call me as soon as he knew something. Forty-five minutes later Greg walked into my office.

"Carly talked to Steve's secretary, and as far as she knew, he didn't have any lunch plans." He held up the legal pad he was carrying and read, "If he's not meeting a client, he either orders in and works through lunch, or sometimes he goes downstairs to O'Grady's. If he's going out, he usually leaves around one."

"Thanks, Greg, I owe you one."

"Yes," he said, "and I intend to collect."

At five minutes to one I took the elevator down to the lobby. If Steve had ordered in, there was nothing I could do, but if he was going to O'Grady's, then I could catch him on his way to the pub and casually suggest that I join him for lunch.

I sat down in a hard-backed lobby chair with a view of the elevators and waited. Fifteen minutes later, Steve still hadn't showed. In a final effort, I went down to O'Grady's myself to look around. It was at least possible that Steve had taken an early lunch. But he wasn't there. This must be one of his work-through-lunch days. Just my luck.

I headed back to the elevators and tried to think of a remotely believable pretext for calling him. Too bad the Rosebud case was over. That would've been perfect. I entered the empty elevator car and pushed the button for the thirty-second floor. It stopped at the twenty-fourth floor. The doors opened and I looked out. Steve Rogers was staring at me from the twenty-fourth-floor landing.

I said hello and so did he, but he didn't move toward the elevator. When the doors started to close, I stopped them. "Aren't you getting on?"

"No. I'm going down. You're going up."

"I'm not going up."

"Well your elevator is." He nodded at the lit green up arrow on the side of the door.

Before I could think of a response, the elevator alarm began to wail. I must've held the DOOR OPEN button past its allotted time. I let go and jumped off, joining Steve on the twenty-fourth floor landing. "I'll take the next one," I said.

Steve pushed the call button and this time the elevator doors opened with the arrow pointing down. We both got in and Steve rang for the lobby.

"So where are you off to?" I asked. I figured wherever he was going, I could just say I was going there too and suggest we eat together.

"The mall," he said. "I need to buy a birthday present for my mom."

"That's so funny," I said, "me too."

Steve just smiled.

♡ ♡ ♡

As we strolled to the mall, which was only a ten minute walk away, Steve asked me about work and I reciprocated. Then I asked him if he had any plans for the weekend. I was hoping if I prompted him, he would ask me out, and then I could tell him I just wanted to be friends.

"I'm going to a Dodgers game tomorrow," he said. "How about you?"

"Dinner, maybe a movie."

Steve changed the subject back to work and I followed him all the way to Macy's. "Well, this is me," he said when we'd reached the entrance. "Thanks for the company."

If I told Kaitlyn I'd blown this again she'd kill me. "Listen, Steve, you haven't said anything about us seeing each other again and—"

He held up a hand to stop me. "Julie, I think you're a great girl, but I just don't see us in a long-term relationship. I think it would be better if we were just friends."

For the second time in my life I was speechless. I knew if I told him that I'd intended to break up with him, he wouldn't believe me. He would just think it was sour grapes. But I had to say something! I wasn't going to let him dump me when I was dumping him.

"Steve, the reason I brought up that you hadn't asked me out again wasn't because I was wrangling for a date. It's because my friend is interested in you and she wanted me to find out if you're available."

"Really," he said, barely concealing his grin. "I didn't know we had any mutual friends."

"We don't. It's Kaitlyn. The girl we ran into Saturday night at the coffeehouse."

He still looked skeptical.

"I met her for breakfast Sunday morning and she asked me about you. I told her I thought you were a great guy, but that I didn't really see us as a couple. Since she was clearly interested, I suggested she ask you out. She said she wanted to, but only if she knew that you felt the same way I did. And that's why I'm here." I took a deep breath. That was a long time to talk without stopping for air.

"Wasn't she with some guy?" he asked.

"Yes, but they broke up."

"How do you know her again?"

"We went to law school together."

He paused, then said, "She was cute."

"Why were you looking at her when you were supposed to be with me?" Then I smiled. "Relax, I'm just kidding. So is it okay if I give her your number?"

"Sure. Why not? It would be nice to have a woman ask me out for a change."

CHAPTER 38

Phase Two

"Guess who I was on the phone with for two and a half hours last night?" Kaitlyn asked a few days later.

"I give up," I said. "Who?"

"Steve Rogers."

"You're kidding."

"Nope."

"That's great. What did you talk about for so long? You don't even know each other."

"I'm not sure. It was just one of those amazing conversations that go on and on. I'm meeting him for dinner tomorrow night."

"You have to call me afterwards and tell me how it went."

"Of course," she said. "Have you called Adam yet?"

"Not yet. But I will." Maybe.

"Don't wait too long. You want it to look spontaneous."

"It's already been a week and a half since we met. I think we're past spontaneous."

"Then just call him already!"

"Okay, I will." Right after I hear about your date with Steve.

And did I! A three-hour candlelit dinner, talking until one in the morning, and they'd already made plans for the weekend. After a twenty-minute monologue on the virtues of Steve

Rogers, Kaitlyn asked me about Adam. She couldn't understand why I hadn't called him yet. I didn't want to admit that I was too embarrassed to call a guy I barely knew and ask him out on a date. Of the two of us, I was supposed to be the bold one. She harangued me until I promised to call him that night.

♡ ♡ ♡

I poured myself a glass of wine from an open bottle of pinot grigio in the fridge, took a few sips to work up my courage, then dialed Adam's number. I was hoping for his answering machine, then I could leave him a message and the next move would be his.

A male voice picked up on the third ring. "Hello?"

"Hi," I said. "Is this Adam?"

"Yes."

"This is Julie. We met a couple of weeks ago at The Perfect Cup. I'm a friend of Kaitlyn's."

"Right," he said. "I remember."

That was a good sign. At least he remembered me. I tried idle chitchat for a few minutes, but it felt forced and I was sure I sounded like an idiot. I decided to get to the point. "The reason I'm calling is, I was just wondering if you'd like to get together sometime."

He didn't say anything, so I continued. "Kaitlyn told me the two of you broke up. I broke up with the person I was with that night too. It must've been something in the air."

Still no response.

"I'm Jewish, by the way, so we won't have that issue."

Silence.

"Hello?" Maybe we'd accidentally been disconnected.

"Sorry," he said. "I'm here. I just didn't know what to say."

"If you'd rather not, that's fine. I just figured I'd give it a try."
This was worse than I'd ever imagined. How did guys do this?
Thank God I didn't have one of those phones with cameras.

"No, I'm glad you did. It's just that I met this other girl last
week and I really like her. I wouldn't want to go out with you
once and then never call again because I'm in a relationship with
someone else. You understand, don't you?"

No. "Of course. No problem. Good luck with the new girl."

"Thanks," he said, then as an afterthought added, "If you
want, I can take your number and give you a call if things don't
work out."

Was that supposed to make me feel better? "No, that's okay."

"All right. Tell Kaitlyn I said hi."

The bastard sounded relieved! "I will," I said and hung up. I
knew I never should've called him.

♡ ♡ ♡

I gulped down the rest of my glass of wine, poured myself a
second, and called Kaitlyn.

"It's not my fault," she said. "You waited too long to call."

"Two weeks is too long?"

"In this case it was. He met someone else."

"I'm not sure I even believe him. Most guys I know would
say yes to the second girl, especially if they had just met the
first."

"Not if they were really interested in the first girl," Kailtyn
said. "I think it shows some maturity on his part that he said no
to you."

The last thing I wanted to hear was any defense of his behavior. "Maturity! How dare he assume that I would be so smitten
with him after one date that I would be completely devastated

if he didn't call me afterward. Most of the time I don't even want to go on a second date with the guy."

"Okay. You're right, he's wrong, and I promise to never speak to him again. Can I go to sleep now?"

"No."

"Why not?"

"Because I'm too angry to sleep."

"So I should stay awake with you in a show of solidarity?"

"Yes," I said. "Because you're the one who made me call him."

"I'm sorry about that. I really am. But I'm exhausted and I'm going to sleep. I'll call you tomorrow and we'll think of some other guy to fix you up with. Okay?"

"Okay," I said. I was still fuming, but not at her. I finished the bottle of wine and passed out in my bed.

♡ ♡ ♡

I awoke the next morning with a throbbing head, a dry mouth, and a sour stomach. I called the office and left a message on Lucy's voice mail that I had the stomach flu and I wouldn't be coming in, then I dragged myself into the kitchen for two aspirin and a glass of water before returning to bed.

Two hours later Rosenthal's secretary, Diane, called looking for me. Lucy hadn't shown up for work yet, so no one knew I'd called in sick. I should've known better than to think that Lucy would actually come in to the office on a Friday.

According to Diane, Rosenthal was gunning for me. I'd forgotten I was supposed to prep him for a court appearance that afternoon and I'd taken all the files home with me. I had to spend the next two hours on the phone with him, first calming him down, then force-feeding him all of my knowledge on the right of publicity and how it pertained to the facts in his case.

He promised to call after the hearing to "fill me up." I knew that he would. He never missed an opportunity to brag about himself and his amazing powers of persuasion.

I checked my voice mail messages and returned the calls that sounded like they couldn't wait. Only two out of nine. Not too bad. When I finished, I was feeling good enough to leave the house, but I knew Rosenthal would be checking in later and I didn't want to miss his call. I decided to make it a phone day.

My next call was to Celia at Just A Date. I hadn't heard from her in weeks and another date was just what I needed to get me over my rejection from Adam. I dialed the number and was connected to a recording that told me the number I'd dialed had been disconnected or was no longer in service.

I must've accidentally rung the wrong number. I tried it again and received the same message. I knew that couldn't be right. I pushed "0" for the operator and listened to one recorded message after another until I pressed enough buttons that I finally reached a live person.

"Operator, can I help you?"

"Yes, when I dial 555-0122 all I get is a recording that the number is no longer in service. I think it must be an error."

"I can check it for you for a $1.50 service fee."

"I have to pay $1.50, so you can correct your own mistake?"

"The service fee is $1.50, ma'am. Would you like me to check that number for you?"

"Fine," I said. I could always argue the point with the phone company when I received my bill. After a minute and a half of listening to commercials about what my phone company could do for me, the operator came back on the line.

"It's not an error message, ma'am. That number was disconnected on September 5th."

It was possible they changed the number. "Is there a new number?"

"No, ma'am. We don't have a listing for a new number."

"Why was the phone disconnected without a new number?"

"I don't have that information, ma'am."

"Well do you know who would have it?"

"No, ma'am, I don't. Is there anything else I can help you with today?"

While I was thinking of what to ask next, I heard, "Thank you for calling the phone company." The operator had hung up on me. I'd have to drop in at Just A Date's offices to figure this out for myself.

CHAPTER 39

Follow Up

I drove over to Just A Date on my lunch hour Monday. Again I was stopped by the parking attendant. I couldn't be sure, but I thought it was the same man. If he was, he didn't appear to recognize me.

"I'm going to Just A Date," I said.

"They're no more," he said.

"What do you mean they're no more? Did they move?"

"Don't know. The men came and locked up the offices. No one been up there since."

"What men?"

"Don't know," he said. "But they're no more."

The attendant agreed to let me park for a few minutes so I could go upstairs and check for myself. He was right. Just A Date was no more. The door was locked and an eviction notice dated September 3rd was still taped to the outside.

I drove back to my office and called the Consumer Affairs Bureau. The clerk told me they'd had several complaints about Just A Date in the last few weeks. All they'd been able to discern was that the company had folded and the owners had disappeared.

"What recourse do I have?"

"Our investigation is ongoing," the clerk said. "You can call us back in a month or two and we might have more information for you."

"I don't want information in a couple of months. I want my file and my money back, now."

"Hold on a second," the clerk said. He must've set the phone down on the desk rather than putting me on hold. Instead of music, I heard the clerk ask, "Has anyone seen the lonely hearts club file? It's not in the cabinet."

Nice.

A female voice asked, "Man or woman?"

"Woman," the male clerk replied. "Ten bucks says she's another desperate lawyer."

This was unbelievable.

"You're on," the female voice said.

I could hear more cabinets slamming and papers shuffling, then the clerk came back on the line. "The company was evicted from its offices at the beginning of the month. If the owners didn't take the files with them, then they're in the possession of the building's management company."

"Can you give me their phone number? I'd like to get my file back."

"I imagine it's been destroyed by now. That's usually what happens in cases like these. Whatever can't be auctioned off is dumped."

"That's fine." I would've destroyed the file myself anyway. Although I probably would've peeked first at the comments from Michael and Ronald. "But what about my money? I paid them $300."

"Are you by any chance a lawyer?" he asked.

"Why?" I wasn't about to help him win his bet.

"Because unless you want to sue them, you're out of luck."

"I am a lawyer, but I'm not desperate, so you just lost ten bucks," I said before slamming the phone down.

I wasn't a desperate lawyer, but I was definitely an angry one. How dare they take my $300, set me up with two losers, and then go out of business! I was tired of going on bad dates. I was tired of being manipulated. I was going to make their lives miserable. I was going to sue.

CHAPTER 40

The World Wide Web
of Dating Deceit

I went online and downloaded all the requisite forms and ad-
dresses. By the end of the week, I'd filed my case in small claims
court and served the defendant. Once I calmed down, I realized
that even if I won, I'd probably never be able to collect on the
judgment. But I didn't care. I was fighting back and it felt good.

I had no plans for the weekend until Kaitlyn called me Friday
afternoon and suggested a girls' night—Steve was out of town. I
assumed as much. Kaitlyn and Steve had spent four of the last
five evenings in each other's company. Not that I was jealous.
Well, maybe a little bit. It's just that being single is a lot harder
when your friends aren't.

Kaitlyn met me at my apartment after work. After we'd ordered food—a medium roasted veggie pizza from Johnnie's—I
searched the *TV Guide* for entertainment.

"There's nothing on tonight," I said, "we'll have to rent."

That's when she reached into her purse and pulled out a wad
of paper that looked like it'd been torn from a magazine.

The article was entitled *Finding Love in the New Millennium*. I
read the first two paragraphs. Internet dating was the wave of the
future. . . . I skimmed the rest of it. Nothing I hadn't seen before.
I refolded the pages and handed them back to her.

"Classic or new release?"

"Did you read the last page?"

I was determined not to be so easily manipulated. Distract and evade, that was my new m.o. "Maybe instead of renting we should try pay-per-view?"

"Didn't you see the list of websites? There's one specifically for Jewish singles."

"So?"

"So I thought we could go online tonight and check it out."

"Why would you think I would even consider online dating?"

"Why not?"

"Because I'm not that desperate! Besides, didn't you see that commercial where the teenage girl is talking about this wonderful guy she met on the Internet and he turns out to be a ninety-year-old geezer."

"Yeah," she said. "That was a funny one. But this website has pictures."

"So what. It's all whack jobs and computer geeks anyway."

"No, it's not."

"How do you know?"

"My hairdresser told me he has three clients who met their significant others on the Internet."

"Why were you discussing this with your hairdresser?"

"I read the article last night when he was cutting my hair."

"That doesn't mean anything. Besides, don't you think it seems desperate?"

"More desperate than joining a dating service?"

Kaitlyn had never liked the idea of my joining Just A Date. Considering how it turned out, maybe she'd been right.

After we polished off the pizza and a pint of Cappuccino Commotion ice cream, Kaitlyn and I sprawled on the living room floor with my laptop between us. We logged onto Jews-On-Line and cruised the site. At Kaitlyn's urging, I filled out the visitor's questionnaire, checking boxes for the characteristics I would look for in an ideal mate. Within thirty seconds, I had over five hundred potential matches.

Kaitlyn and I spent the next three hours culling hundreds of online pictures and profiles. I had to admit that most of the men seemed normal, and there were even a handful I would've considered dating.

"Are you convinced?" Kaitlyn asked.

"Maybe," I said. "I need to think about it."

By Sunday night, the maybe had turned into a yes. Somewhere between lying on my living room couch Saturday night watching TV with Elmo and waking up alone in bed on Sunday morning, I decided that online dating wasn't really for desperate people after all.

I logged onto the Jews-On-Line website, filled out a profile, uploaded a photo my dad had e-mailed me after their visit, and hit SEND. Five minutes later I received an e-mail notifying me that I was now officially JOL Member Number 83002. I had the option of e-mailing other members or waiting for other members to e-mail me. I hadn't had much luck lately being forward with men, so I decided to wait and let the men come to me.

And they did. When I checked my e-mail Monday night I had twelve responses. It wasn't anywhere close to the seventy-five e-mails the woman in the testimonial received her first week, but it had only been one day. And I hadn't posted a picture with my boobs busting out of my shirt the way the testimonial girl had. Perhaps I should have.

I rejected five of the twelve candidates outright because their profiles didn't include pictures. Looks weren't the most important criteria, but I had to assume that if the man wasn't posting a picture there was probably a reason. Then I rejected two more based on their photos, one based on his profile, and one because he didn't live in L.A. I figured with twelve responses in one day, I could afford to be choosy.

I e-mailed responses to the three remaining candidates. By the next morning, I'd heard back from all three. Bachelor Number One suggested we meet right away. Either he was pushy or desperate. I deleted him. Bachelor Number Two sent me back a long, boring e-mail. I responded, but my hopes were fading fast. By his third e-mail I decided to drop him. I was focusing my energies on Bachelor Number Three.

His name was Ethan. He was a computer software dealer, but he didn't look like a geek, and he seemed nice and funny online. We'd e-mailed to each other several times a day for three days when he suggested we meet in person. It still seemed too soon, but curiosity was getting the better of me. Besides, as Ethan pointed out, we needed to meet in person to determine whether we had any chemistry. If we had no chemistry, there was no point in continuing.

I told Ethan I'd meet him for brunch on Sunday. He suggested I choose the restaurant, which I liked. I wanted to meet in a crowded public place, just in case Ethan turned out to be a psycho. After all, we had met on the Internet.

I made reservations for noon at The Vine Café, an always crowded outdoor restaurant on Beverly Boulevard. I called Kaitlyn and Simone that morning and told them both where I was meeting Ethan and all the information I knew about him. Kaitlyn took down Ethan's name and phone number, but told me I was being paranoid. Simone said if she didn't hear back from me by the end of the day she'd call the police.

♡ ♡ ♡

When I arrived at The Vine a few minutes after twelve, Ethan was already waiting. Except for the addition of a beard, he looked the same as he did in his photo. Average height, dark brown hair, dark brown eyes, and a bit of a paunch that would surely turn into a beer belly by the time he reached forty.

Once we were seated, we both pored over our menus as if we were cramming for exams. After we ordered and the waiter took the menus away, we had no choice but to talk to each other. I didn't know where to begin. We'd already covered most of the typical first date questions in our e-mails. But in person, we lacked the familiarity we'd developed online.

After a short, uncomfortable silence, I asked Ethan about his weekend. He answered me in two sentences and reciprocated. After I answered, he changed the subject to baseball. I feigned interest in his analysis of the Dodgers' performance this season and surreptitiously looked at my watch. I couldn't believe it had only been ten minutes.

"You know," Ethan said, abruptly changing the subject, "you're much better looking than I thought you'd be."

Had I heard him right? "Excuse me."

He repeated his statement.

"What are you talking about? You saw my picture before you met me."

"Yes, but a lot of women lie about their looks."

I still didn't understand. "How can you lie about your looks when you post a picture?"

"A lot of women post photos that show them from the waist up. Then when you meet them in person, they turn out to be huge from the waist down."

"But the picture I posted was full length."

"Yes, but you were wearing a jacket, so it made me think you had something to hide."

I couldn't believe I was having this conversation on a date. "Ethan, I described myself in my profile as petite. How big could I possibly be?"

"Yeah, you really should change that. Petite could be short and fat. You should describe yourself as firm and toned."

At least going back to the gym had paid off. "Clearly you've been doing this longer than I have, but what would be the point of lying about your appearance when eventually you'll meet the other person and they'll find out the truth?"

"I guess people think that by the time you meet them in person, you'll be so smitten with them from their e-mails that you won't care what they look like."

We both agreed that was unlikely.

I was still processing this information when Ethan added, "It's not just women that lie. Men do too." He must've assumed I was wondering if he was referring to himself, which I was, because he added, "I don't mean me."

Ethan explained that a female friend of his had been a member of JOL for over a year and had met tons of lying men. "The only difference is that women usually just lie about their looks; men lie about other things too."

"Such as?" I had to ask.

"Age is a popular one. They say they're younger than they are and then post photos of themselves from ten years earlier when they still had hair. And then of course there are all the married men."

Married men! "Why would married men join Jews–On–Line?"
"To meet women, of course."

Ethan estimated that at least half of the men on JOL were actually married. He didn't tell me what he based this figure on
and I didn't ask. Instead I asked, "Are you married?" It would explain why he was telling me all this.

"No," he replied. "And this is my real hair. So would you like
to go out again?"

When I got home I called Kaitlyn and Simone to let them
know I was still alive. I also filled them both in on the ugly truth
about JOL. Kaitlyn told me she thought Ethan was crazy and I
shouldn't believe a word he said. Simone said she suspected there
was at least some truth in Ethan's revelations. I agreed with Simone. I would either need to find a new method for meeting
men or concede to spending the rest of my life with Elmo. At
that moment, Elmo was looking like the better alternative.

CHAPTER 41

Matchmaking in the New Millenium

This morning it was Simone's turn to play hooky. She had her first fitting for her wedding gown at ten o'clock. She figured she could make it in to the office by noon, so there was no point in wasting a vacation day. Since Simone's secretary was on vacation this week, I was assigned the task of turning on her lights and computer. If anyone asked where she was, I was supposed to tell them that she'd left for a doctor's appointment and that she'd be back by lunchtime.

Thankfully, Rosenthal left for his therapy session without asking me Simone's whereabouts, but Greg appeared in my office five minutes later.

"Where's Simone?" he asked.

"At a doctor's appointment," I said without looking up from my desk.

"Yeah, right. Where is she really? Job interview?"

I stared at him with my lips pressed together. I knew the story was for Rosenthal's benefit, but Greg had a big mouth.

"Oh, fine," he said. "I'll ask her myself when she gets back. Actually, I'm glad she's not here. I wanted to talk to you."

"Shoot."

He sat down in my guest chair and put his feet up on the corner of my desk. "What are you doing Wednesday night?"

"Watching *Law & Order.* It's the special two-hour season premiere."

"You're pathetic."

"Yeah, I know. But I can't help it. I'm addicted to lawyer shows. They're so much more interesting than actually being a lawyer. I keep hoping I'll pick up some pointers on how to make my life more exciting."

"That's easy," he said. "Condense six weeks of work into an hour, then spend the rest of your time screwing the other lawyers in the firm."

"That was the plot line for *Ally McBeal,* not *Law & Order.* But I'll take it under advisement."

"You should. In the meantime, how about going SpeedDating with me on Wednesday night?"

"What's SpeedDating?"

"I'm surprised an avid dater such as yourself hasn't heard about it. It was dreamed up by some rabbi to promote Jewish marriages. Basically, it's an introduction service for Jewish singles."

"What is it? A singles party?"

"No, you're actually paired up with seven different people for seven minutes each. The only rules are that you have to talk to each person for the full seven minutes, and you can't talk about your job or where you live. At the end of the night, you decide whether you want to see any of the seven people again. If both parties say yes, then they match you up."

"Are you serious?"

"Absolutely. I read an article about it in the *Times* last week. I called the number and asked if it was for real. They said it was and the next event was Wednesday night at Starbucks. Do you want to go?"

"Not really." I could just imagine all the nerdy Jewish guys that would go to something like that. "Why don't you go first and tell me how it is? If you like it, I'll go to the next one."

"I think it would be more fun if we went together. Besides, you owe me one for getting you the lowdown on Steve Rogers."

"You're going to call in your favor for this?"

"Why not?"

He probably thought he'd look like more of a stud if he walked in with another woman. "Okay, it's a date."

♡ ♡ ♡

When we arrived at Starbucks, the place was already packed. Greg and I each paid our $10 registration fee and filled out the top portion of a questionnaire with our name, address, and phone number. The lower portion of the form was broken into seven sections with a blank line for a name and one question underneath: WOULD YOU LIKE TO SEE THIS PERSON AGAIN? YES OR NO (CIRCLE ONE).

We'd just handed in our forms when the organizer of the event rang the bell and introduced himself. He placed me and the other twenty-one women at small tables spread throughout the room. On the center of each table was a plastic number. I was seated at table number thirteen.

He then assigned each man a number from one to twenty-two. I never did figure out how they managed to come up with an equal amount of men and women. The organizer told the men that when he rang the bell, they should go to the table that matched their number. After seven minutes, he said, he would ring the bell again, and all of the men would move to the next odd-numbered table if they'd been assigned an odd number, or the next even-numbered table if they'd been assigned an even number. This way, no one would be staring at the table on either side of them looking for their next date.

That seemed fair. Completely random, but fair. A combination matchmaking and musical chairs, except only the men played. At the end of seven rounds, the organizer told us, we could socialize and talk to whomever we pleased. That way, if fate didn't match us with the person we wanted, we could introduce ourselves at the end of the night.

The organizer waited until everyone was seated before he shouted, "Ready, set, date." And we were off. Match Number One was named Richard. He was tall and stocky with black hair. His nose was too large for his face, but he was cute in spite of it.

Richard told me he'd grown up on the East Coast and had just moved to Southern California last year. I told him I'd been living in Los Angeles almost ten years and couldn't imagine ever moving back. He said since L.A. was now his home, he felt he should learn to surf. I told him I tried boogie boarding a few times, but preferred scuba diving. He said he wasn't scuba-certified, but that he liked to snorkel. We were still talking about our favorite snorkeling spots when the bell rang.

I waited for Richard to leave, then pulled the questionnaire out of my purse. I wrote down his name and number on the blank line and circled YES. I wasn't smitten, but he was attractive and could hold up his end of a conversation. I returned the questionnaire to my bag and another man sat down.

Match Number Two was named Josh. Based on looks alone, he would've been a seven. Cute enough to date. But his incessant whining about Los Angeles' lack of culture, combined with his nasal voice, reduced him to a five. Before SpeedDating, I hadn't thought seven minutes was enough time to spend with someone to know whether you wanted to date them. I was wrong. After two minutes with Josh, I knew I never wanted to see him again. I just had to wait another five minutes for the bell to ring.

Match Number Three was named Seth. He was probably 5'5" in his work boots, but 5'3" without them. We talked about our hobbies and how hard it was to meet people in L.A. He seemed nice and normal. When the bell rang, I pulled out my questionnaire and considered it for a full ten seconds before I circled NO. I knew I could never get past the height issue.

Match Number Four was named Ira. He was tall, but about fifty pounds overweight. Despite the rules of the program, he spent the entire seven minutes talking about his career as a stockbroker. He told me how much money he'd made last year, and how much more money he intended to make in the future.

I asked him for a stock tip so the seven minutes wouldn't be a total waste, but by the time the bell rang and I had a pen in my hand, I'd forgotten the name of the company whose stock I was supposed to buy. I pulled out my questionnaire and circled NO. Even a lucrative stock tip wasn't worth an entire evening with Ira.

Match Number Five was named Barry. He was the reason I was afraid to go to singles events. I couldn't accurately guess his height because he sat with his shoulders slumped over the table and his head bent down. This position did, however, afford me a great view of his few remaining strands of hair, which he'd coiled into a bird's nest on the top of his head.

After thirty seconds of post-bell silence watching Barry finger the grooves in the table, I started asking questions. I knew he was an unequivocal No, but we had seven minutes to kill. His re-sponses were either monosyllabic or "I don't know," and were al-ways directed to the tabletop.

The highlight of our mini-date came at the end of minute five when Barry removed the hearing aid from his left ear to check the battery. It was still working, but the sudden movement caused the bird's nest to fall and I was afforded the rare pleasure of watching Barry coil it back into place. I spent the last two minutes staring out the window.

Match Number Six was named Evan. He was short with red hair, freckles, and wire-framed glasses. I wasn't attracted to him, but at least he talked and wasn't afraid to look at me.

Evan also ignored the guidelines and opened the conversation by telling me that he was a plastic surgeon and had just joined a practice in Beverly Hills with a large celebrity clientele. I told him I didn't think it was possible to be a plastic surgeon in Los Angeles without celebrity clients. He told me that even though I wasn't a celebrity, he would be happy to help me with those little lines around my eyes. I had no hesitation circling the NO under his name.

Match Number Seven was named Danny. Danny was a sweater. By this point in the evening, the wet rings under his armpits had seeped out onto his chest and were creeping down toward his waist. Danny made a real effort at conversation, but I was distracted by his constantly wiping the perspiration off his face with his shirt sleeve.

After the third time, I handed him my pocket pack of tissues. They helped to soak up the sweat, but shredded in his beard. By the end of seven minutes, Danny looked like he'd had a terrible shaving accident. When I gently pointed this out, he quickly brushed the tissue particles off his face, but they just landed on his chest and shoulders, giving him the worst case of dandruff I'd ever seen.

When the bell rang, I circled the last NO and beelined across the room to Greg. I was ready to leave, but Greg wasn't. He'd spied two women he hadn't been matched with, but wanted to meet and said he wasn't leaving without at least one phone number. I braced myself for a long night.

CHAPTER 42

Coffee Buzz

I wished Greg happy hunting and went to the counter to order a grande café au lait. I waited for my coffee at an empty table in the corner while I perused an abandoned copy of *Daily Variety*. I was only halfway through the lead story when I heard, "I'm sorry, but that's my paper."

The first thing that registered about the man standing before me were his warm hazel eyes outlined by long, thick, dark lashes. The rest of his features, his average height and build and dark brown hair, were unremarkable.

"Sorry," I said. "I didn't know anyone was sitting here." I got up and handed him the paper.

"You don't need to get up." He sat down in the empty chair across from me, still holding his steaming *venti*-size cup with the name "NOAH" scrawled in black marker under the lip.

The counterman called, "Julie," and I said, "That's me."

"Nice to meet you, Julie, I'm Noah."

The counterman called my name again. I released my hand from Noah's handshake and said, "I better go get that."

"Why don't you join me?" he said. "I'm almost done with the paper. You can have it when I'm finished."

I looked around the room and spotted Greg pretending to listen to every word being uttered by a buxom blonde. "Sure, I'll be right back."

I picked up my coffee, stopped at the condiment bar for a Sweet 'N Low and a sprinkle of cinnamon, and returned to Noah. When I sat down, he handed me the paper. I read the portion of the address label that hadn't been torn off: NOAH GREEN, CAPITOL STUDIOS, BUILDING 9, ROOM 214, 1600 CAPIT.

"So how do you like working at Capitol?"

"How did you know I—"

I held up the paper and pointed to the mangled address label.

He smiled. "It's as good a place to work at as any, I guess. How about you? Are you in the business?"

"Tangentially. I'm an entertainment litigator."

"That's close enough for me. I'm in business affairs."

I knew a few people from law school who had left law firms for studio business and legal affairs jobs. The general consensus was that the hours were better, the pay was worse, and it was the closest a lawyer could get to making movies without quitting the law altogether and becoming a producer.

"So you're a lawyer who isn't a lawyer anymore?" I asked.

"Exactly."

We talked about his job, my job, and current movies. We both liked intelligent, mainstream pictures—which we both estimated was less than 20 percent of the pictures released by the studios in any given year—and art house films that contained stories as well as angst. Compatible taste in film was always a plus for a movie fan like me.

I hadn't even realized we'd been talking for almost forty minutes when Greg came over and put his hand on my shoulder. "Are you ready to leave?"

"Sure," I said. "Whenever you are."

Greg and Noah exchanged a look and Greg said, "I'll wait for you at the door."

I picked up my purse and stood up. "It was really nice meeting you."

"You too," Noah replied.

I waited a few more seconds, hoping he would ask me for my phone number. When he didn't, I turned to leave.

"We should get together and see a movie sometime," Noah said when I was two feet from the table.

Yes! I turned back. "I'd like that."

Noah didn't move, so rather than wait for him to figure out the next step, I pulled my pen out of my purse, wrote down my name and number on the front page of his *Variety*, and handed it back to him. He promised to call and said good night.

Greg was waiting for me at the entrance. "It looks like you found yourself a match."

"We'll see," I said, and looked away before my smile betrayed me. I hoped Greg was right.

CHAPTER 43

It Had Been Too Long

By the time I got back to my apartment it was almost eleven o'clock. I went through my nightly routine—removing my makeup, washing my face, and brushing my teeth—and climbed into bed. I fluffed pillows, rearranged blankets, and switched sides of the mattress, but nothing worked. All I could think about was Noah. I'd talked to him for less than an hour, and I was already fantasizing about waking up with him on Sunday mornings.

By four o'clock that afternoon, I was debating whether anyone would notice if I locked my office door and took a nap. Having had less than five hours of sleep the night before, I'd been dragging all day. I had a narrow panel of frosted glass in my door frame, and I didn't think it was clear enough for anyone to see through. I had just put my head down on the desk when the phone rang.

"Hi," the caller said in an exceptionally perky voice. "Is this Julie Burns?"

"Yes," I said. "Who is this?"

"My name is Sarah. I'm calling from Aish HaTorah."

"Where?"

"We organized the SpeedDating event you attended last night."

"Oh, right." I was a little embarrassed that I'd already forgotten their name.

"I wanted to let you know that you had one match."

"What?" How could she know about Noah?

"You circled YES next to Richard's name on your questionnaire. He circled YES next to your name too."

"Great," I said, without much enthusiasm. In the afterglow of meeting Noah, I'd completely forgotten about Richard.

"I've already called Richard and given him your phone number. He was very excited. I'll give you his phone number, and the two of you can take it from here."

I took down Richard's number on a Post-it and stuck it on top of the pile next to the phone on my desk. Phone numbers I saved but would never use.

♡ ♡ ♡

I arrived home that evening to a flashing red light on my answering machine. I pushed PLAY before I'd even set down my briefcase and kicked off my shoes. "Hi, Julie, it's Richard. We met last night at SpeedDating. I'd really like to see you again. Give me a call when you have a chance. I'll be home the rest of the evening."

Damn. It wasn't that I didn't want to see Richard, I was just disappointed that it wasn't Noah. I waited two more hours hoping Noah would call. When he didn't, I called Richard back. We were on the phone less than five minutes before he asked me if I'd like to get together over the weekend.

"What did you have in mind?" Maybe he would wow me with something completely unexpected.

"How about dinner Saturday night?" he asked.

Or not.

We made plans to meet at La Mer, one of those ridiculously expensive restaurants I'd always wanted to try, but only when someone else was paying. I figured if he was asking, that meant he was paying.

When I arrived at La Mer Saturday night, promptly at seven-thirty, Richard was already waiting. I was glad I'd worn my long black skirt instead of my usual black pants. Richard was wearing a gray pin-striped suit complete with white cuff-linked shirt and yellow tie. If he hadn't already told me on the phone that he worked for his father's shipping company, I would've thought he was a banker.

The maître d' greeted Richard as if he were an old friend and seated us at a table for two in the corner. As we walked through the restaurant, I was surprised to see that almost all of the tables were filled. It was the quietest crowded restaurant I'd ever been in.

Richard ordered a bottle of wine with dinner and immediately began telling me the story of his life. I learned about the boarding school in Boston he'd attended from the time he was eight years old, his Ivy League college, and his family's home in Charleston, which was actually a twenty-room mansion on ten acres of land complete with swimming pool, tennis courts, and a stable out back where he and his three brothers learned to ride.

The other family residences were a six-bedroom apartment on Park Avenue in Manhattan and a vacation home in Antigua where they spent the winter holidays.

"What, no summer home?" I asked as a joke.

"No," Richard replied in all seriousness, "it wasn't practical. Every summer my parents would take my brothers and me to a different country in Europe so we could learn the language and soak up the culture. It made more sense for us to rent a villa for the season rather than buy a home in every country we traveled to."

At Richard's urging, I told him about my family's annual winter vacation. It began with a twenty-three-hour drive from my house in New Jersey to Pompano Beach, Florida, where my parents, sister, and I would descend upon my grandparents in their two-bedroom condo. Our daily activities consisted of lying on the beach in the morning, the pool in the afternoon, and going out to dinner and watching TV at night. All my family wanted to soak up was a tan. If we all came home a shade darker than when we'd left and no one ended up in the emergency room, my parents considered it a successful vacation.

Richard seemed unfazed by the differences in our backgrounds. I wasn't. By the time we'd finished coffee and dessert, I knew it would never work out.

CHAPTER 44

Too Rich

"How can anyone be too rich?" Kaitlyn asked over breakfast Sunday morning, which was an unusual occurrence now that she and Steve were an item.

"I'm not comfortable with him. Our lives are just too different."

"Well how did you manage to have a five-hour date with someone you're not comfortable with?"

"Easy," I said. "I was fascinated. I've never met anyone like him before. I didn't even think people like that existed outside of books and movies."

"I think you're overreacting. I'm sure you could get used to the money if you tried. You'd probably even like it."

Maybe, but . . . no.

She shook her head. "So how did you leave it?"

"He said he'd call. I think he will."

After breakfast, Kaitlyn and I went to the Santa Monica Mall, then the Century City Shopping Center, and finally Beverly Hills. I spent the afternoon searching for black suede boots and Kaitlyn spent the afternoon persuading me to give Richard another chance. By five o'clock I was convinced that there was not one pair of comfortable suede boots in all of Los Angeles, and that Kaitlyn was right.

I could get used to the money if I tried. It wasn't fair of me to rule out Richard, or "Richie Rich," as we were now calling him, just because he was wealthy. It wasn't his fault he was a member of the lucky sperm club and had everything handed to him on a silver platter since the day he was born.

And it wasn't like I had anything against money. In fact, I'd even fantasized about being rich myself someday. Since I hadn't had much luck playing the lottery, and I knew I'd never get rich working for Rosenthal, the next best alternative would be to marry someone rich. I just needed to keep an open mind.

I tried to remember my new policy when Richie Rich called me Tuesday night. I listened intently when he told me about the new yacht his father had just purchased, and I even remembered to ask him if he'd solved his problems with his decorator. I was doing pretty well until he mentioned that he had season tickets to the opera.

"You're kidding me."

"No, why?"

I didn't even know anyone who had actually been to the opera, and he had season tickets. I reminded myself to keep an open mind. "I'm just surprised, that's all. I didn't think people our age had season tickets."

"This is the first year I've had them in L.A. My family's had season tickets at the Met for years."

"I thought your family lives in Charleston?" Even I knew the Met was in New York.

"They do," he said. "My parents used to take the corporate jet up to New York the day of the performance. My dad would fly back the next morning. My mom usually stayed and shopped for a few days. Depending on our school schedules, my brothers and I would fly in from Boston to meet them. Or sometimes we'd take the train."

Open mind, open mind, open mind. After all, he did say they sometimes took the train. When Richard told me he'd like to take me to the opera sometime, I changed the subject. I wasn't ready to make plans for our future beyond a second date.

Richard told me he had a business dinner on Saturday night, and since I had an arbitration brief due Friday and knew it would be a hellish day, I agreed to meet Richard for brunch on Sunday at Ivy at the Shore. It was another one of those expensive restaurants I'd never been to before. If I was going to date Richard, I'd have to learn to take the good with the bad.

♡ ♡ ♡

Just as I was about to climb into bed, the phone rang again.

"Hi, Julie," the caller said, "it's Noah. We met last week at Star-bucks. Remember?"

I was so focused on trying to make myself like Richard, I hadn't thought about Noah in days. Actually, I had thought about him a few times, but I'd been trying not to because I was afraid he'd never call. "Of course I remember."

We talked for two hours—one of those great late-night phone conversations where every statement leads to another tangent and you hang up because you can't keep your eyes open rather than because you have nothing left to say.

Around one in the morning, Noah finally suggested that we get together over the weekend. We made plans for an early movie followed by a late dinner on Saturday night.

CHAPTER 45

Two for Two

I met Noah in Westwood Village. I was glad he'd purchased the movie tickets in advance, since the line at the theater was already winding its way around the block. It hadn't been too difficult to choose a film: There was only one playing that we both were interested in and hadn't already seen.

After the movie, Noah suggested we walk around the Village and have dinner in the neighborhood. We made a left out of the theater and stopped at the first restaurant we came to. It was a small Italian place with black booths, red and white checkered table cloths, and a short wine list. Noah said he'd eaten there once before and the food was good.

I followed Noah inside and we settled into a booth with two glasses of Chianti. The wine was awful, even for cheap stuff, but the pasta was good. We talked about the movie and our favorite restaurants, then the conversation hit an unexpected lull. I wanted to fill the void quickly, so I asked Noah the first question that popped into my head.

"Was last week your first time SpeedDating?"

"What are you talking about?" he said. "What's SpeedDating?"

What was this, *The Twilight Zone*? "You know. The event we met at last week. At Starbucks."

"What event? I just went there to pick up a bag of coffee beans and a cappuccino. Actually, I was surprised at how crowded it was. It's usually empty at that hour on a weeknight."

I wished I could crinkle my nose and disappear like Samantha on *Bewitched*. I'd assumed that the only people at Starbucks that night were other SpeedDaters. Obviously, I was wrong.

"What's SpeedDating?" he asked again.

At this point, there was no way I could lie my way out of it, so I explained the program to Noah. He responded with hysterical laughter. I tried to be a good sport, but when the tears started rolling down his cheeks . . . "It's not *that* funny."

He quieted down and took a sip of his wine. "You're right, I'm sorry. I'm not laughing at you, I'm laughing at the situation. All this time you thought I was there SpeedDating, and I'm not even Jewish."

This last part sent him off on another laughing binge, which started me laughing too. I supposed from his perspective it was pretty funny. For the rest of the evening, every time he smiled at me I imagined he was thinking about our misunderstanding, then I would start laughing, which would start him laughing too. It made for a fun date.

As Noah walked me to my car, I thought about inviting him back to my house for coffee, but decided against it. It was already past midnight, and I didn't want him to get the wrong idea.

When we reached my Acura, Noah grabbed my hand. "I had a lot of fun tonight," he said.

"Me too," I replied.

"We should do this again soon."

"I'd like that."

We sounded like we were reading from a bad script. Then Noah went off the script and kissed the palm of my hand. He held it to his face and, to my surprise, my fingers began stroking his neck and the tip of his earlobe. His skin was warm and incredibly soft.

Then he bent down and kissed me. First he just brushed my lips with his. Then he softly pushed down and I responded. His lips were warm and his mouth tasted like the mint chocolate chip ice cream he'd had for dessert. It was delicious. I was just starting to feel the tingle spread through my body when Noah pulled away.

"You'd better go," he said.

I was a little startled by the sudden change. But once the moment passed, I realized he'd been right. It was only a first date. We shouldn't let things go too far.

I climbed into the driver's seat and drove home, alone, as usual. But that night I dreamed about Noah. And we weren't just kissing.

♡ ♡ ♡

I woke up the next morning and looked at the clock: 9:18 a.m. Too early for a Sunday. I rolled over and went back to sleep. The next time I looked at the clock it was 10:42 a.m. I jumped out of bed. I'd almost forgotten about my date with Richie Rich. I was meeting him for brunch at noon. If the traffic was light I might still be able to make it on time. But the traffic was never light.

I hopped into the shower without even letting the water warm up first and was out of the house in under an hour. That was fast for me. Especially without coffee.

Half an hour later I pulled up in front of Ivy at the Shore and handed the valet my keys. I was only eight minutes late. Not terrible, but bad enough to go inside armed with an apology and complaints about L.A. traffic. It turned out they weren't necessary. Richard was late too. I wish I knew beforehand—I could've looked for street parking.

Richard showed up five minutes later with an apology and his own complaints about L.A. traffic. I sympathized. The maître d' seated us on the enclosed patio, and Richard told me about the dinner party he'd attended the night before. I told him I went to the movies with a friend. It was only our second date: I didn't owe him full disclosure.

I was happy to let Richard do most of the talking. I was having trouble concentrating on the conversation. I kept thinking about Noah and imagining it was him sitting across from me instead of Richard. Maybe the mimosa had something to do with it.

I switched to water and tried to fulfill my promise to keep an open mind. If I could keep the date short I might be able to pull it off. It was just brunch, how long could it last?

When we left the restaurant, I headed toward the valet stand, but Richard suggested we take a walk. I suppose I could've said no, but I didn't. I felt guilty for fantasizing about Noah. Mental cheating.

We picked up two lattes to go at the Coffee Bean around the corner and headed out to the park that ran along the beach side of Ocean Avenue. The benches were filled with tourists enjoying the sunshine and homeless people happy to have a place to crash.

By the time we'd walked the six blocks to the Pacific Coast Highway incline, my nerves were fraying. I didn't want to ask or answer any more questions about careers, goals, hobbies, or families. Two dates in less than twenty-four hours was too much for me. I just wanted to go home.

It was a slow walk back to the restaurant. We stopped several times to snap pictures for tourists and enjoy the view. We must've been strolling in the park for close to an hour before Richard noticed the homeless people.

"Is that guy taking a nap?" he asked, pointing to a man lying on the grass wearing army fatigues, no shirt, and a threadbare blazer.

If anyone else had said that to me I would've thought they were kidding. But Richard didn't kid. In the eight hours and seven minutes I'd spent with Richard, he'd never even attempted to crack a joke.

"Sort of," I said. "He's homeless. A lot of homeless people sleep in this park because the cops don't kick them out."

Richard went silent and we continued walking. Five minutes later he said, "I don't understand why all these homeless people don't just get jobs. Surely there must be something they're qualified to do."

I knew he wasn't just being callous; he really didn't get it. "Well, it's kind of hard to go on a job interview when you haven't showered in three days and you have no clean clothes and no address or phone number to put on an application."

Of course Richie Rich wouldn't know any of this because he'd never once in his entire life had to fill out a job application or even submit a résumé. I knew I needed to end the date quickly before I said something I'd really regret.

"I spoke to my decorator yesterday," Richard said, clumsily changing the subject. "She said my apartment will be finished in a few weeks. I'm hoping you'll come over and give me your opinion."

I could lie and say yes. Or I could be brutally honest. I chose the third option—I pretended I hadn't heard him and pointed out the crowds waiting in line for the roller coaster at the Santa Monica Pier.

He pushed on undeterred. "What are you doing two weeks from Friday?"

"I don't know," I said. "Why?"

"I have tickets for the opera. I'd like to take you."

"I can't. I don't have anything to wear." Lame, but I was on the spot.

"You don't need a formal gown. A cocktail dress would be fine."

"I don't own a cocktail dress." Of course I did, but he didn't know that. Although he should've suspected.

"We don't have to go to the opera if you don't want to," he said with real disappointment, "but I hope we'll be spending more time together."

Obviously, we were going to have to do this the hard way. "I'm surprised to hear you say that. Aren't I too plebeian for you?"

"What do you mean?"

Surely with his Ivy League education he knew the definition

of the word "plebeian." "Richard, you must've noticed the differences between us. I didn't go to boarding school, my family doesn't own any vacation homes, and I've never been to the opera. Aren't you a little out of my league?"

"I can't believe you would even think that." He seemed genuinely surprised. "You're smart and beautiful and someone I enjoy spending time with. I find the differences in our backgrounds refreshing. I haven't met a lot of women like you."

Now that was the "A" answer. I was just starting to feel bad about what I'd said when he continued.

"Besides, I'm really looking forward to showing you some of the things you've missed, like the opera."

The nerve of this guy! This wasn't *My Fair Lady*. I wasn't Eliza Doolittle, and he was no Henry Higgins. If only he'd quit while he was ahead.

While we waited for the valet to bring us our cars, Richard told me that he was leaving for Charleston in the morning, but that he'd call me when he got back. He could call all he wanted, this was still our last date.

♡ ♡ ♡

The next day a dozen long-stem red roses arrived at my office. I was reading the card when Kaitlyn called.

"Guess who just sent me flowers?" I said.

"Noah."

"I wish. They're from Richie Rich. Does this mean I have to go out with him again?"

"Yup."

"Are you sure?" I whined.

"Yes," she said, "and you also have to call him and thank him for the roses."

"Of course I was going to do that. I do have some manners you know."

I called Richard's office and left him a message on his voice mail. I hoped that since he was out of town, that would be the end of it. He called me from Charleston later that night and asked me if I would see him again when he returned. He was trying so hard, how could I say no? The flowers had bought him one more date.

Noah, however, didn't need to send roses. When he called the next night and asked me if I wanted to go with him to the premiere of Capitol Studios' new picture, I didn't need to be persuaded to say yes. I would've gone even if I didn't want to see the movie.

CHAPTER 46

Movies & Stars

I left work early Thursday night so Noah could pick me up at my house on the way to the premiere. He buzzed my apartment at six o'clock and told me to meet him downstairs. I found him standing next to a black BMW in the driveway of my building's parking garage. He was trying to calm the old lady who lived on the first floor. She was threatening to have his car towed.

"Are you excited?" he asked when we were ensconced in the black leather interior.

"Of course," I said. "I've never been to a movie premiere before."

"Enjoy it. After the first one, the thrill is gone. Then it's just another hassle to be endured."

"If you don't like them, then why do you still go?"

"Because I'm expected to. They're also great opportunities to network, since everyone's there."

I didn't ask who "everyone" was. I wasn't interested in networking. I just wanted to see movie stars. Rosenthal would shoot me if he heard me say that.

"Isn't Robert De Niro in this movie?"

"Yeah. Why?"

"I'd love to meet him." Then I could call everyone I know and tell them I'd met Robert De Niro.

Noah laughed. "You're not going to meet him. I doubt you'll even see him."

♡ ♡ ♡

We parked the car in a garage south of Hollywood Boulevard and walked up to Grauman's Chinese Theatre. It was a jumble of police barricades, camera crews, and screaming fans. It took us fifteen minutes winding through the crowd just to find the entrance to the red carpet. I didn't see any movie stars, but it was still exciting.

It was almost as chaotic inside the theater as it was outside, and just as crowded. Luckily, Noah knew one of the ushers, who found us two seats together in the reserved section. Otherwise we would've been sitting at opposite ends of the theater. He brought me popcorn and a Diet Coke, and left me holding the seats while he went out to the lobby to schmooze.

When he returned forty-five minutes later, I'd eaten half the popcorn, finished the soda, and was rummaging through my purse looking for something to read. "I thought you were going to miss the movie," I said when he'd sat down. "It's almost seven-thirty."

"Are you kidding? These things never start on time. We'll be lucky if it starts by eight."

Noah finished my popcorn and pointed out a few people in the crowd. Their names sounded familiar, probably people I'd read about in the trades, but I didn't recognize any faces. The guests fell into two distinct groups—the "Suits," comprised of agents, lawyers, and studio executives, and the "Artistic Types," which consisted of a handful of working actors, directors, and producers, and a whole bunch of hangers-on and wannabes.

It was easy to distinguish between them. The "Suits" were dressed in suits, hence the name, and were generally older, flabbier, and ninety-five-percent white male. The "Artistic Types" were younger, hipper, and more evenly split among paper-thin wannabe actresses displaying their silicone breasts and gym-maintained wannabe actors with high cheekbones and chiseled jaws.

When the movie ended, we retrieved Noah's car and followed the crowd to the afterparty at a trendy Japanese restaurant six blocks away. Between the traffic on Hollywood Boulevard and the line in front of the valet, it would've been quicker to walk. But no one did.

Once our names were checked off the list by a security guard at the entrance, we were allowed inside the restaurant. Noah handed me a drink, and I accompanied him as he walked around the party looking for people he knew. After a few minutes of searching, he introduced me to another lawyer from one of the A-list talent firms. I recognized the name. Rosenthal used to brag about playing golf with the guy. When I mentioned to the talent lawyer that I worked for Bruce Rosenthal, he said he didn't know him. I'd have to remember to tell Simone about that.

After half an hour, I was completely bored. I left Noah chatting with an agent while I went in search of food. I was waiting in line at the buffet table when someone put their hand on my shoulder. I turned and saw Mark Parsons and gave him an enthusiastic hello. I was happy to see a familiar face, any familiar face.

"Julie, I'm surprised to see you here. It's not like Bruce to give his premiere tickets to one of his associates."

"My invitation didn't come from Bruce," I said. "I'm here with a date."

He raised his eyebrows and I could see that I'd just moved up one notch in his estimation. "Anyone I know?"

"Noah Green. He works at Capitol Studios."

"Don't know the name," he said, and began scanning the room.

I was sure I'd lost half a point for that. I was about to inquire after his wife and baby when Mark spotted someone more important by the sushi bar and abruptly excused himself.

After I'd managed to score a few tempura shrimp and a spoonful of noodles, I headed back into the crowd to search for Noah. It took me ten minutes to find him in the sea of dark suits. I told him I was ready to leave and he said he was too. That meant he only stopped to chat with one more Artistic Type and two more Suits on the way to the door. I never did see Robert De Niro.

CHAPTER 47

Then There's TV

As soon as I arrived at the office the next day I went looking for Simone. I couldn't wait to tell her about the premiere. I found her in the conference room with Greg's secretary, Marlene. They were standing in front of the television, but the screen was black.

"What are you guys doing?" I asked.

"Come in quick and close the door," Simone said. Then she pushed a button on the remote and I heard the whir of a tape rewinding in the VCR.

"What are you watching?" I asked.

"Greg was on *First Date* last night. Marlene taped it."

"What's *First Date*?" We all turned around and stared at Rosenthal standing in the doorway. I hadn't even heard him open the door.

"It's one of those reality television shows," Simone said, "where they follow couples around with a camera on their first date."

The tape clicked to a stop in the VCR, but nobody moved.

"What are you waiting for?" Rosenthal said. "Let's watch it."

Simone pushed PLAY and Greg appeared on the screen with his arm around an attractive blonde named Susie. We watched two-minute snippets of Greg and Susie playing miniature golf, talking about their sex lives over dinner at a Greek restaurant, and engaging in some heavy petting on the dance floor at a

Hollywood nightclub. When the next couple appeared on the screen, Marlene popped the tape out and left the room.

"It's too bad Greg didn't spend more time talking about his job," Rosenthal said. "It would've been good publicity for the firm."

Simone and I glanced at each other, but neither of us replied.

Rosenthal was almost out the door when he turned to face me. I could practically see the lightbulb go off above his head. "Julie, you're single. Why don't you go on *First Date*?"

The man never ceased to amaze me. "No thanks," I replied.

"Why not?" he asked. "It would be good for you to get out more and network."

"Bruce, I'm not going to humiliate myself on national television just so you can get some free publicity for the firm."

"You don't have to decide now, just think about it."

"I don't need to think about it," I shouted after he'd shut the door behind him. I looked at Simone. I could see her wheels turning too. "No," I said before she even asked. "Absolutely, positively, not going to happen."

♡ ♡ ♡

Simone and I walked down to Greg's office and stood in his doorway until he finished his phone call.

"What?" he asked before the receiver even reached the cradle.

"Tell us about Susie," Simone said coyly.

Greg blushed. "It was her idea. She's an actress and she wanted some exposure."

"What's your excuse?" I asked.

"The show pays for everything," he said. "You women don't realize how expensive dating can be for a guy. Besides, it's kinda cool to be on TV."

"Rosenthal thinks you should've hyped the firm more," I said.

"I did," he responded. "But the editors cut our thirteen-hour date down to six minutes. I guess they thought work talk wasn't sexy enough to air."

"Unlike all that footage of the two of you on the dance floor," Simone cooed.

Greg blushed again.

"Did you get lucky?" she asked.

"A gentleman doesn't kiss and tell," he said.

"A gentleman doesn't tape his date and broadcast it on national television," I said.

"Let's just say it was a worthwhile experience."

Simone followed me back to my office and told me about her latest wedding planning fiasco, and I told her about the premiere. She wasn't impressed. Todd's cousin was a film director, so she'd been to a few herself. I guess Noah was right. After the first one, everyone's jaded. I needed to find someone who hadn't already experienced a movie premiere, so I called Kaitlyn.

"Wow, that's so cool," she said. "Did you see any movie stars?"

"No," I admitted. "Noah said he saw a couple of those guys from the WB, but I don't watch those shows, so I didn't recognize them."

"Too bad," she replied, crunching potato chips in my ear. "So when are you seeing him again?"

"I don't know. There was nowhere to park by my apartment when he drove me home last night, so he just dropped me off and said he'd talk to me soon."

"Did he at least walk you to the door?"

"No, but he did wait until I was inside the building before he pulled away." Even I realized how pathetic that sounded.

"Well, there's always Richie Rich. I'm sure he'd be thrilled to take you out this weekend. Maybe you two can go to the opera."

"Ha," I said. "A lot you know. The season doesn't even start for two more weeks. But it doesn't matter, because he's in Charleston anyway. Two men in my life and I'm still dateless on Saturday night."

After fifteen minutes discussing Kaitlyn's plans for Steve's surprise birthday weekend in Palm Springs, Kaitlyn made me promise I wouldn't spend the next two days sitting home waiting for the phone to ring. I kept my promise. I spent all day Saturday running errands and all day Sunday in the office. I'd had a lot of early evenings lately and I needed to catch up on work. Or at least that's what I told myself.

The highlight of my weekend came when I received my letter from small claims court notifying me of my trial date. With the exception of this weekend, my love life had been so active lately I'd completely forgotten about my lawsuit against Just A Date.

CHAPTER 48

Round Three

I'd just shut down my computer for the night when the phone rang. It rang two more times while I debated whether to answer it. I finally picked it up on the fourth ring because I thought it might be Richie Rich. He'd called me last night from the plane on his way home from Charleston and I'd agreed to meet him tonight for an early movie. But the voice on the other end of the line wasn't Richie Rich.

"Hi," Noah said. "Did I catch you at a bad time?"

I paused to recover from the surprise and said, "Actually, yes. I'm on my way out the door. Can I call you tomorrow?" Maybe he'll think I'm going out on a hot date. He would be half right.

"Sure. I just called to see if you were free for dinner Saturday night."

Hmmm. I could say yes now or I could wait and let him worry. "Let me get back to you tomorrow." He left me hanging all weekend, let him suffer a little.

"Okay. I'll talk to you then."

He sounded disappointed—exactly what I was hoping for.

My phone call with Noah lasted just long enough to make me late for my date with Richie Rich. I arrived at the theater and found him pacing in front of the box office. I apologized for being late and blamed it on the traffic. That was the good thing about L.A. traffic, always a believable excuse.

"Expecting rain?" I asked, nodding to the tan trench coat he wore over his suit.

"The weather report this morning predicted a twenty percent chance of precipitation," he said. "I like to be prepared."

I'd heard that report too, but a twenty percent chance of rain wasn't high enough for me to lug my umbrella around all day. I needed at least a fifty percent chance of rain accompanied by menacing clouds. I hadn't seen any yet.

Richard bought our tickets and I saved our seats while he waited in line for popcorn. By the time he joined me in the theater, the trailers were already running. I couldn't have planned it better. We didn't even have to talk to each other.

My euphoria didn't last long. The opening credits were still rolling when Richard reached for my hand. His skin was warm and smooth, yet it still repelled me. Probably because it wasn't Noah's. I pulled my hand away and wiped it on a napkin, then whispered "the popcorn's greasy." After his third failed attempt at physical contact, he gave up.

But that didn't stop him from talking to me. Maybe if he'd attended more movies and less operas he would know that "Silence is Golden." Goddamn rich people. They have no respect for the art form of the masses.

Every time Richard leaned over and whispered in my ear, I winced. At first I tried to discourage his talking by suggesting that if he didn't watch the screen he'd miss the best part. Then I tried ignoring him. Finally, I shushed him. But it wasn't until the man sitting in front of us turned around and told him to "shut the fuck up" that he finally stopped chattering. Instead, he wrote me a note on his Palm Pilot suggesting we leave.

This was only the second time in my life that I walked out of a theater in the middle of a movie. The first time was during *Judge Dredd,* and that was because the movie was bad instead of the company.

As soon as we stepped outside the theater, Richard suggested dinner. I was hungry too, but I couldn't imagine spending another two hours with this man. I probably should've just gone home, but instead I proposed coffee. At least coffee would be quick.

Richard and I set off on foot for the Coffee Bean on the next block. We were only ten feet from the theater when it started to rain. Just drizzle really, but Richard offered me his coat anyway. I politely declined. Ignoring my protests, Richard removed his raincoat and draped it over my shoulders.

Maybe it was his having been right about the rain. Or maybe it was his constant reaching for my hand. Or his incessant chatter. Or asking me to leave in the middle of a movie. Or maybe I was just PMS-ing. But I snapped.

I tore Richard's raincoat from my shoulders and threw it at him. "I told you, I don't want your goddamn coat." When you didn't even want the man's clothing touching you, clearly it was time to end the relationship.

Richard put his raincoat back on and we walked the rest of the way in silence. By the time we reached Coffee Bean, the drizzle had turned into a downpour, my hair and suit were soaked, and I felt like a raving bitch. I apologized to Richard for snapping at him and forced myself to pay penance by spending the next hour listening intently to all his boring stories.

After the rain stopped, we walked back to the parking lot where we'd both left our cars. I looked wistfully at Richard's brand-new Mercedes convertible, which I would now never get to ride in. Then I thanked him and gave him a peck on the cheek. He said he would call. I was skeptical, but it didn't matter. This was our last date, no matter how many flowers he sent me.

On the drive home, I rolled down the car windows and blared the stereo. It felt good. With Richie Rich out of the way, I could really concentrate on Noah. Wouldn't it be great if he was The One? Julie Burns-Green. It had a nice ring to it.

CHAPTER 49

Party Time

I spent Saturday afternoon with Kaitlyn, shopping for a new outfit for my date with Noah.

"Poor Richie Rich," Kaitlyn said when I told her what I'd done.

"I know. I feel bad. But he just wasn't The One."

"Do you really think you gave him a fair chance?"

"Of course I did. I went out with him three times."

"Yes, but you'd already met Noah. I wonder if you would've been so quick to dump him if Noah wasn't in the picture."

"Noah wasn't the problem," I said. "It was the money."

"I thought you wanted to be with someone who had money."

"I want to be with someone who earns money, not someone who inherited it."

"I'll add that to the list."

After two and a half hours at the Beverly Center mall, I came home with charcoal gray pants, a low-cut black sweater, and a new black lace bra. This was our third date. I wanted to be prepared.

I tickled Elmo while I listened to the one message on my answering machine: "Julie, it's Noah. Call me when you get in."

"I'll kill him if he cancels on me after I just spent $200 on a new date outfit." Elmo just laughed, but I knew he agreed with me.

"What's wrong?" I asked when Noah picked up the phone.

"Nothing major," he said. "My car's in the shop. Would you mind driving tonight?"

"No, that's fine." It would save me the trouble of having to clean up my apartment and change my sheets.

"Great," he said. "Pick me up at eight."

I pulled into the driveway of Noah's small, Mediterranean-style house, but before I could get out of the car, he came out to greet me. I was disappointed. I wanted to see the inside of his home so I could complete my mental picture of the two of us living together. Maybe he was saving it for later.

Noah directed me to Le Champaigne, an upscale French restaurant in Hollywood. The night was warm and the patio had heat lamps, so we dined al fresco. I'm sure there were stars, but they weren't visible through the smog.

As I was finishing the last of our shared chocolate soufflé, Noah mentioned that he'd like to stop by a party after dinner. "If you don't mind," he added.

"Sure," I said. It was still early. Too early just to go back to his place for the rest of the evening. "Where is it?"

"Not too far from here, in the Hollywood Hills. My friend Ron's house."

"Is he the one you told me about? The one who opened his own talent agency?"

"Right," he said. "One of the few openly gay agents in Hollywood."

"I don't understand why you say that. You think the rest of them are in the closet?"

"A lot of them," he said. "I heard one of the big agencies actually told its employees that if they want to keep their jobs they need to get married and conduct their extracurricular activities in private."

"I don't believe that. This is Hollywood. It's acceptable to be gay in Hollywood."

"Hollywood is owned by corporate America, where it's never acceptable to be gay."

"I guess I'll have to take your word for it. You seem to know a lot more gay men than I do."

"It's the job," he said, and reached for the check.

Noah directed me to a house buried deep in Beachwood Canyon that I never would've found on my own. We parked the car at the end of the block and followed the noise to the party.

Noah led me into a large living room with whitewashed wood floors, black ultra-suede furniture, and forty to fifty expensively dressed drunk people. It was a small-scale version of the same industry crowd that had been at the premiere.

The Suits weren't wearing their suits, but you could still pick them out from their merino wool sweaters and Armani jackets. The rest of the guests, mainly Artistic Types, included a few actors whose faces I recognized but whose names I didn't know, and a handful of nonindustry people wearing jeans and sneakers, who needed to lose twenty to thirty pounds each. Noah told me they were someone's out-of-town relatives. From the accents, I assumed Chicago.

Noah pushed his way to the bar and returned with two margaritas on the rocks. He handed me one, took my other hand, and led me down a flight of steps, through a den, and out to the backyard. It was large by L.A. standards. It comfortably held another thirty people, a bar, and a set of wood patio furniture.

Noah walked us toward a tall, thin man in his early forties wearing a pale blue sweater. He was attractive despite his mostly bald head. When the man spotted Noah, he excused himself from the couple he was talking to and headed in our direction.

The man hugged Noah as if he hadn't seen him in years. When he released his grip, Noah introduced me.

"It's so nice to finally meet you," Ron said, and gave me the same bear hug. "I've heard a lot about you."

"You too," I said. Noah had told him about me. That was a good sign.

Ron and Noah gossiped about work and their mutual friends, then Ron led us back into the house so he could show Noah a new painting he'd just purchased. They were discussing the perfect wall space for the picture when I left them in search of a bathroom. Ron told me the downstairs bathroom was still being remodeled and suggested I try one of the upstairs bathrooms.

I attempted to follow Ron's directions, but the living room was still filled to capacity and I couldn't find the hallway he'd told me to follow. When I thought my bladder was about to burst, I asked a group of women standing near me if they knew where the bathroom was. They didn't, but one of them suggested I check with the caterer.

I headed toward the kitchen and found two women in black pants and white shirts scooping hors d' oeuvres from baking sheets onto silver trays.

"Excuse me," I said to the redhead, "would you by any chance know where the bathroom is?"

"Down that hall," she said, pointing toward an archway on the far side of the living room. "Second door on the left."

I thanked her and turned around, smashing into a tall man similarly dressed in black pants and a white jacket. I started to apologize as I looked up into radiant blue eyes.

"Julie, this is a surprise."

"Hi, Joe. How are you?"

"Good," he said. "Really good. And you?"

"Great," I said.

We stood in the entranceway of the kitchen, neither of us knowing what to say next, until the redhead interrupted. I was blocking her way. I stepped aside so she could exit the kitchen with her silver tray.

"It was good seeing you, Joe," I said when the redhead was out of earshot. I wanted to get away from him and I really did have to pee. I left my drink on the counter and pushed through the crowd toward the archway and the second door on the left. Luckily, there wasn't a line.

I stayed in there a long time. In the mirror, I pulled up on the roots of my hair in a futile attempt to make it look full and thick, reapplied my dusty-rose lipstick then wiped half of it off with a tissue so it would look natural, and thought about Noah and Joe.

It had been months since Joe had thrown me in the pool and I stole his car. He'd been a good sport about that, all things considered. And he looked great, as always. But I was with Noah. Noah was the one I wanted.

Noah was good-looking too, I reminded myself, just different from Joe. Polished rather than merely sexy, but no less attractive. More importantly, Noah was a grown-up. He had a good career, a nice car, and a house with a lawn. Noah was stable and knew what he wanted. Joe was still finding himself. I wanted to be with someone who was already found. I wanted to be with Noah. Or at least I wanted to marry Noah. I still wanted to sleep with Joe.

My reverie was interrupted by pounding on the door. I relinquished the bathroom to two twentysomethings in stiletto heels, one of whom looked like she was about to be sick. I headed back to the living room and back to Noah.

"Where have you been?" he asked when I found him by the fireplace.

"Searching for the bathroom. Then waiting in line."

"I better go take my place," he said, and heading toward the archway.

"I'd try a different one if I were you. The girl behind me didn't look too good."

"Thanks," he said and walked off in the opposite direction.

I wandered around looking for someone I knew or an empty chair. I didn't find either. But Joe found me.

"You left your drink in the kitchen," he said, and handed me a fresh margarita.

"I know. I wasn't planning on drinking it."

"On the wagon?"

"No, just driving."

He nodded. Driving drunk was always a bad idea, but on dark, twisty canyon roads it was suicidal.

"Are you a friend of Ron?" he asked.

"No," I said. "But my date is."

His eyebrows raised. "Serious?"

"Potentially."

"That must mean he's not a wannabe?"

Apparently he hadn't forgotten our last date either. "No, he's a lawyer too."

"How nice for you. The two of you can argue together all night long."

His sarcasm made him less appealing. Maybe that was a good thing. "How about you? Are you seeing anyone?"

"You know me. I just like to pick up drunk women and carry them home."

"I'm sure that's not too difficult in your line of work."

"Slightly more difficult lately," he said. "Now I'm just cooking and organizing."

A small improvement, but an improvement nonetheless. "Are you still working for your aunt?"

"Yes, but she's decided she wants to semiretire, so I'm running a lot of the events now. At least the smaller parties like this one."

Noah came up behind me and kissed the top of my head. He wrapped his arms around my shoulders and asked, "Ready to go, honey?"

That was the most demonstrative he'd been all evening and the first time he'd ever called me "honey." What was going on here? Could he be jealous of Joe? How much had he had to drink?

"Noah, this is Joe Stein. He's catering the party. Joe, this is Noah Green." They shook hands, but neither seemed pleased to meet the other.

"We should really be heading out," Noah said.

I couldn't imagine why he was in such a hurry to leave, but I had no great desire to stay either.

"I really need to get back to work," Joe said. "It was good seeing you, Julie." He bent down as if he was kissing my cheek, and whispered "call me" in my ear.

♡ ♡ ♡

At first I was a little annoyed with both of them. It wouldn't have surprised me if one of them had peed a circle around me to mark his territory. But then I realized I should be flattered. If Noah was jealous because he saw me talking to Joe, then that was a good thing. That had to mean he really liked me. What else could it mean?

"Earth to Julie," Noah yelled in my ear.

"What?"

"I asked you how you knew that caterer guy?"

"I met him a few months ago at a party."

"Was he catering that one too?"

I didn't like his snide tone. "Bartending," I said, and changed the subject. "Why were you in such a hurry to leave?"

He smiled and his whole demeanor changed. "I just couldn't wait to get you all to myself."

That was exactly what I wanted to hear.

CHAPTER 50

Score

Noah directed me out of Beachwood Canyon and back to his house in West Hollywood. He spent the whole ride back droning on about some important guy he'd met at the party. I didn't care what we talked about, as long as it wasn't Joe.

I pulled into Noah's driveway and left the engine running. I expected to be invited in, but I didn't want to seem presumptuous.

"Would you like to come in for a drink?" he asked.

"I don't know if I should," I said coyly. "I'm driving."

"I promise if you get too drunk I'll make you spend the night." Then he kissed me. It was like the first time again, long and slow and warm, except he tasted like margarita instead of mint chocolate chip ice cream.

Noah gave me the grand tour. Living room, dining room, kitchen, master bedroom, bath, and home office. It was tastefully decorated with leather couches and heavy wood furniture. It wasn't my style, it was way too dark, but that would be easy to remedy. The house had potential, and I already loved the remodeled kitchen.

Noah poured us each a glass of cabernet and popped a CD onto the stereo. Diana Krall's *Love Scenes* hummed from the surround sound speakers. I sat down on the couch and Noah followed, picking up where he'd left off in the car.

Before long, both of our shirts were off and he was massaging my nipples through my bra. They didn't need much encouragement to stand up straight. But I was distracted by my urgent need to pee again. I would have to stop drinking so much water, no matter how good it was supposed to be for my skin. When Noah reached for my zipper, I knew I couldn't put it off any longer. I excused myself and headed to the bathroom.

I tried to be quick this time. I didn't even bother to fix my hair and makeup. But I did check my breath. I didn't think the margaritas and the wine were a good combination, so I opened Noah's medicine cabinet looking for some mouthwash. I found a bottle of Scope, along with the usual aspirin and Band-Aids, and an unusually extensive assortment of hair-care products. No wonder his hair always looked so good.

After I gargled and returned the mouthwash to Noah's medicine cabinet in what I hoped was exactly the same position, I headed back to the living room. I found Noah lying on the couch with his head resting on a throw pillow and his eyes closed. I shut the lamp and laid down next to him. He didn't move.

"Noah," I whispered, and rubbed up against him.

All he said was "Hmmm" and rolled over on his other side with his back toward me.

I got up and put the light back on. "Noah," I yelled.

He opened his eyes, smiled at me, and closed them again with his forearm shielding them from the light.

I grabbed my purse and slammed the front door on my way out of the house. Then I sat in my car and fumed. I was hoping the noise would've woken him and he would come outside looking for me. After two minutes of waiting, I gave up and drove home.

I suppose it could've been worse. He could've fallen asleep *while* we were fooling around. At least this way I could tell myself he'd just had too much to drink. But at this rate, I was never gonna get laid!

CHAPTER 51

The Morning After

Noah called the next morning.

"How are you doing on this beautiful morning?" he asked, sounding refreshed and revived. Ten hours of sleep will do that for a person.

"I've been better." I was tired and cranky from my sleepless night. I should've taken a cold shower before I went to bed.

"I wish you were here with me," he said.

"I didn't think there was room for both of us on your couch." A tad bitchy, but I didn't care.

"Sorry about that. I had a lot of late nights last week and a few too many margaritas at the party. I guess I just needed to catch up on my sleep."

"Apparently." I wasn't going to let him off so easy. He was saying all the right things, but my bruised ego still needed some massaging.

"I'd like to make it up to you."

"I'm listening."

"I thought I could start by taking you out to breakfast. Then maybe a drive along PCH or a museum. Whatever you want."

I was softening. "I suppose I could do that."

"Great. Why don't you pick me up and we'll go from here."

♡ ♡ ♡

I showered, blew-dry my hair, and applied my makeup, then I climbed into a pair of jeans that weren't particularly comfortable but, according to Kaitlyn, made my ass look great. I was debating between the plum V-neck sweater and the burgundy cotton shirt when the phone rang. I assumed it was Noah wondering where the hell I was. I hadn't even left the house yet, and I was already ten minutes late.

"I'll be right there," I said when I picked up the phone.

"Julie?" the caller said. It wasn't Noah.

"Who is this?"

"It's Joe. From last night. Who did you think it was?"

"Just a friend." I don't know why I lied to him.

"The same friend you were with last night?"

We were not having that conversation. "What do you want, Joe?"

"You didn't answer my question."

"Yes, his name is Noah. Is that what you called to talk about?"

"As a matter of fact, it is."

"Listen Joe, I'm flattered, I really am. But I'm with Noah now and—"

"You think I called to ask you out?"

"Well, didn't you?" Why else would he be calling?

"Geez, and people think *I* have an ego. They obviously haven't met you."

"Then why did you call? Looking for some free legal advice?"

"No, I know what that's worth. I called to give *you* some advice."

"Really. About what? How to make the perfect crab cake?"

"How to stay away from two-timing assholes."

"And you would be referring to?" Probably himself.

"Your new friend."

"Noah? You called to tell me Noah's cheating on me?"

"I called to tell you that if you think you're exclusive, you're not. Your boyfriend's seeing someone else."

This was low, even for Joe. "Assuming that's true, and I don't think it is, how would you even know? You just met the guy last night."

"I overheard him talking to Ron in the kitchen. It was after you took off. Your boyfriend's so arrogant, he didn't think twice about speaking in front of the hired help."

"And he just happened to tell Ron, 'By the way, I'm cheating on Julie.' How convenient."

"No," he said, straining to keep his voice even. "Ron asked him if you, or someone named Julie, I didn't know it was you at the time, knew about Jean. Your boyfriend told him no. Then Ron said something about him playing a dangerous game, and I left."

"Do you always eavesdrop on other people's private conversations?"

"When they have them right in front of me, yes."

"And you decided to share this with me, why?"

"Because when you introduced me to him and I knew you were the Julie he was talking about, I thought you'd want to know. Especially since the two of you looked so close."

Now I was the one fighting to keep my voice steady. "I don't know why you would make something like this up, Joe, and I don't care. Just do me a favor and lose my number."

"Consider it done," he said, and slammed the phone down in my ear.

I didn't believe him. But I also didn't think he would stoop to lying just to split us up. What would be the point? He clearly had no interest in going out with me again—he'd told me that much. The incident with his car was months ago and I didn't think he was the type to hold a grudge. Not for this long anyway. But maybe I didn't know him as well as I thought I did.

The phone rang again. This time it was Noah.

Noah came to the door holding a bouquet of Stargazer lilies. Not my favorite, but he was trying. "Where did you get the flowers? I thought your car was out of commission."

"It is," he said. "I rode my bike down to the florist."

"Wow, all that effort for me. I'm impressed."

"You should be. I haven't ridden my bike in years." Then he kissed me, short and sweet, and said, "I've decided that today is going to be all about you."

I liked the sound of that.

CHAPTER 52

Sweet & Sour

Noah directed me to a café on Santa Monica Boulevard. We sat on the outdoor patio and ate Belgian waffles and sugary French toast. It would've been very romantic were it not for the screaming two-year-old at the table next to us. But that wasn't Noah's fault.

By the time we finished breakfast at a quarter to two, we decided to skip the museum and the scenic drive in favor of a walk up to Sunset Plaza. After an hour of window-shopping at stores I couldn't afford, Noah suggested we go back to his place so I could sample his self-proclaimed world-famous cappuccino.

Soon I followed Noah into the kitchen and watched him measure the coffee, add the water, and push the button on his cappuccino-espresso coffeemaker. I didn't need Joe. I had Noah. He could cook, or at least make coffee, and he had a real job.

After Noah steamed the milk, he listened to the messages on his answering machine. This proved Joe was lying. Noah would never play his answering machine messages in front of me if he was cheating. His other girlfriend could've called.

The first message was from someone named Bill asking Noah to call him when he got a chance. "My brother," Noah mouthed, as if Bill were actually on the line. The second message was a voice I recognized. "Hey, it's Ron. I just called to let you know I have to pick Chris up in Glendale tonight. I can either come get you beforehand, or you can catch a ride with Jean. Let me know what you decide. Ciao."

"Who's Jean?" I asked. I hoped it came off sounding casual. My heart had nearly stopped when I heard the name.

If Noah thought it was weird that I'd asked, he didn't let on. "A friend of mine and Ron's," he replied. "We're all going to a Lakers game tonight." He must've thought I wanted to go, because he added, "If they were my tickets, I would've invited you, but they're not. Jean got them from his boss. They're great seats—center court, five rows up, practically celebrity alley."

Noah said *his* boss. That meant Jean was really Gene. That also meant Joe wasn't lying about what he'd overheard. He just misunderstood. I should've realized it was something ridiculous like this. Joe wasn't that vindictive.

Although if Jean was really Gene, why wouldn't Noah want

me to know about him? It didn't make sense. Maybe Noah knows I'm on to him and he just said *his* boss instead of *her* boss to throw me off the scent. That would also explain why he'd been so nice to me today. He felt guilty for being a lying, cheating snake. I was dating Scumbag all over again.

Noah handed me my cappuccino and I followed him into the living room. He turned on the stereo and sat down on the couch. This time it was Sting. He must've changed the CD this morning. Maybe Jean had stopped by for a quickie before Noah called me. That's something Scumbag would've done.

I sat down on the chair across from him.

"Don't you want to join me on the couch?" he asked. "I promise not to fall asleep."

"No thanks," I said. "The chair's more comfortable." Should I confront him before or after I throw the cappuccino in his face? Probably before.

"Really? I never noticed." Noah got up from the couch and squeezed himself into my chair. He was practically sitting on my lap. "It doesn't feel more comfortable to me," he said.

I slid out from under him and stood up. "I think I'm gonna go." I needed proof before I confronted him. Otherwise he'd just deny it and I'd end up looking like a raving lunatic.

"Why? Is something wrong?"

"I'm just not feeling that great. It must've been all the powdered sugar and syrup on the French toast."

"I think I have a bottle of the pink stuff in the bathroom. Do you want me to go look for it?"

"No, I just need to go home and lie down for awhile."

I retrieved my purse and walked out to the car. Noah followed. When I opened the car door, he bent down to kiss me, but I pulled away.

"I'll call you tomorrow," he said.

"Sure," I said before I put the car in reverse and drove away.

As soon as I turned the corner at the end of Noah's street, I reached for my cell phone and dialed Kaitlyn's number. She picked up on the second ring.

"Are you alone?" I asked.

"Yeah. Why?"

"Can I come over?" I was really trying, but my voice cracked anyway.

"Of course. What's wrong?"

"I'll explain when I get there."

When Kaitlyn saw me she gave me a hug and handed me a box of tissues. Then I filled her in on my last twenty-four hours.

"You're completely overreacting."

"How can you say that? Noah's cheating on me!"

"He's not cheating on you. You're not even exclusive. You've only gone out what, three times?"

"Four including today."

"Okay, four dates," she said. "That's not many. Why would you assume that he wasn't seeing other people?"

"Because I'm not."

"You are too. You just went out with Richie Rich a few days ago."

"I told you, that's over."

"So because you decided three days ago to make your relationship with Noah exclusive, you think that means he decided the same thing?"

"Why are you taking his side? You're my friend, you're supposed to be on my side."

"I'm on your side. That's why I'm telling you this. I know you really like Noah and I don't want to see you blow it with him over something stupid like him going to a basketball game with another woman. For all you know, this could be their last date too. Or maybe she's just a friend."

"If she was just a friend, he wouldn't have said she was a guy."

"The point is you don't know and it could be nothing. You need to relax."

"If he's seeing someone else, I have a right to know."

"Why?"

"Because I'm not going to sleep with him if he's sleeping with someone else."

"But you're not sleeping with him."

"I would have if he hadn't fallen asleep!"

Kaitlyn threw up her arms in disgust. "What are you going to do? Ask him if he's seeing someone else?"

"I would if I thought he would tell me the truth. But he lied about Jean. Now I can't trust him."

"Then what? Hire a private detective to follow him around like some suspicious wife?"

"No, you know I can't afford that. I'll have to do it myself."

"You're not going to start stalking Noah!"

"Of course not," I said. "We're dating. I'm just going to casually bump into him at the Lakers game tonight. Then I can judge his relationship with Jean for myself."

"You don't have a ticket," she said.

"Then I'll buy one."

"I'm sure the game's sold out."

"Then I'll get one off a scalper.

"You're going to spend $300 just to spy on him at a basketball game?"

"Do tickets really cost that much?" I had no idea.

"For a good game."

Hmmm. I hadn't anticipated that.

"I have a better idea," Kaitlyn said. "Why don't you come with me and Steve to the movies tonight. Then tomorrow, when you've calmed down, if you still feel like you need to you can call Noah and ask him if he's seeing anyone else. I'm sure if you explain to him how important it is to you, he'll tell you the truth."

Kaitlyn had a point. I couldn't think rationally on four hours sleep. I should go to bed early tonight, get lots of sleep, and confront Noah in the morning when my head was clear. Then I could really nail him to the wall.

CHAPTER 53

Surprise

I'd already seen the movie that Kaitlyn and Steve wanted to see, so I went home and took a nap. I awoke an hour later feeling groggy and disoriented. I brushed my teeth and splashed water on my face before returning to the couch to watch TV.

I caught the end of *Suspicion* on Channel 11, then clicked up the dial. I was into stations I never watched like the Golf Channel and the Soap Network when I passed a basketball game. I clicked back. It wasn't the Lakers game, but it gave me an idea.

I called Greg. "You're a Lakers fan, right?" I asked. I could hear people talking in the background.

"Yeah," he said. "Why?"

"Do they broadcast the home games too?"

"On cable. Which must mean you're not already watching the pregame show."

"No. What channel is it on?"

"Thirty-eight."

I clicked over to Channel 38. "We must have different cable systems. My channel thirty-eight is Spanish language news."

"Look for Fox Sports West."

I pulled out my cable guide. "I don't think I have that one."

"Too bad. You're welcome to come over here and watch it if you want."

I desperately wanted to, but I didn't want to intrude. "It sounds like you've already got some people with you."

"Just my buddy Mike and his girlfriend. There's always room for one more."

That was all the encouragement I needed.

I stopped at the grocery store on my way to Greg's house and picked up a six-pack of Sam Adams. I knew I'd be welcome if I brought along beer. My timing was perfect. I reached Greg's door just as the pizza delivery man was leaving.

The four of us ate pizza, drank beer, and watched the game. At half-time, Mike and his girlfriend went out for more refreshments and I stayed behind with Greg.

"So why the sudden interest in basketball?" he asked. "I didn't think you were a sports fan."

"I'm not, but I'm seeing a guy who is. He's actually at the game tonight."

"So what's the plan? You pretend to like basketball to reel him in?"

"Something like that." Greg didn't need the whole story.

To my surprise, I caught a glimpse of Noah in the stands at

the end of the third quarter. Of course I'd been hoping to see him. That's why I was watching. But I didn't really think I would. The gods were smiling on me tonight.

He was exactly where he said he'd be—five rows up and a little to the left of Jack Nicholson. He was sitting between Ron and some guy I didn't recognize. I didn't see a woman, but they were only on camera for a second. I could've missed her.

The next time the camera panned Noah's seats, I pointed him out to Greg.

"How did he score those seats?" he asked.

"They're not his, they belong to a friend of a friend."

"Well tell him to introduce me."

♡ ♡ ♡

The game was in the fourth quarter with only three minutes left when I saw the woman two seats away from Noah. If that was Jean, he sure wasn't paying much attention to her. Maybe Kaitlyn was right. Maybe they were just friends and I'd blown the whole thing out of proportion. It wouldn't be the first time.

Two seconds before the buzzer, Kobe scored the winning basket. The camera panned the cheering crowd, then froze on two men kissing.

"Only in L.A." one of the announcers said.

"You got that right," the other one agreed.

The two men stopped kissing and looked up. One of them pointed to the overhead television screen and waved. The other one looked embarrassed and sat down.

Greg turned to face me. "Isn't that your boyfriend?"

CHAPTER 54

Coulda, Woulda, Shoulda

I could not believe my eyes. At least Noah was the one who looked embarrassed. Although not as embarrassed as I was.

I told Greg I needed to leave and ran out without even saying good-bye to Mike and his girlfriend. I tried both Kaitlyn and Simone from my cell, but I couldn't reach either one of them. I was debating who to call next when I passed the twenty-four-hour grocery store. I made a fast U-turn and screeched to a stop in the parking lot. The fruit popsicles in my freezer weren't going to cut it tonight.

♡ ♡ ♡

I was two-thirds of the way through the pint of Ben & Jerry's Coffee Heathbar Crunch before I started feeling sick, but all I could think was how could I not have known Noah was gay? I missed all the signs—gay friends, extensive assortment of hair-care products, not wanting to sleep with me. How could I be such an idiot!

But if he's gay, why is he still dating women? Is it just about appearances? Is he really that insecure? I had to know.

I dialed his number and was debating whether I should leave a message on his answering machine when he picked up the line.

"I was about to call you," he said breathlessly. "I just walked in."

"How was the game?" I asked.

"Good. Very exciting."

"I know. I saw it on TV."

Silence.

"I especially liked the close-up of you at the end. I've never seen you kiss from that angle before. But then again, I've never seen you kiss a man before either."

"It's not what it looked like."

"Really? You mean me and the other ten million people watching the Lakers game only thought we saw two guys kissing? We all had some sort of collective delusion?"

"Gene was excited and he kissed me. That's all. It was no big deal."

"No big deal! Noah, you kissed him back."

"He caught me off guard. I didn't know what to do. After all, he was the one who invited me."

"So what are you saying? You only kissed him because you didn't want to offend him?"

"Exactly."

Talk about denial. He made my mother look positively self-aware. "Noah, you're thirty-six years old. Don't you think it's time you admitted you're gay?"

"I'm not gay!"

I hung up. Dating was hard enough without adding closet homosexuals to the mix. Five seconds later the phone rang. I let the answering machine pick up. As soon as I heard Noah's voice, I unplugged the machine and the phone and went straight to bed. Even with all the sugar and caffeine I'd just consumed, I fell right to sleep.

CHAPTER 55

Moving on, Again

I was actually happy to go to work Monday morning. It would be a good distraction. I needed to think about something other than Noah. I planned on spending the entire morning researching right of publicity claims. Simone had other plans. She didn't even wait for Rosenthal to leave for his therapy session before she came into my office.

"I'm so sorry," she said.

"About what?" I hadn't even told her about Noah yet.

"About Noah. Greg told me."

That big mouth. "Who else knows?"

"No one, as far as I know."

I hoped she was right.

We both heard Rosenthal coming down the hallway. He was yelling to Diane to tell whomever was on the phone that he'd call them back. It was too late for Simone to sneak back to her own office unnoticed, so I handed her some papers and picked up a pad and pen in the hopes that when Rosenthal walked by he would think we were discussing a case.

Ten seconds later, Rosenthal was standing in my doorway. "What are you two up to?"

"The Kirby case. The reply brief is due tomorrow and I wanted Simone's opinion on the procedural issues."

She handed the papers back to me and said, "I think you're right on target. Let me know if you want me to read through the final draft."

Simone stood up to leave when Rosenthal said, "Write it up as research. Clients don't like it when they see a lot of lawyer conferences on their bill."

"Sure, Bruce," Simone replied. She waited until he turned his back before she silently growled at him and left.

Rosenthal shut the door behind her and sat down. "So how's everything going?"

"Fine," I said cautiously. A closed-door conference couldn't be good.

"Your personal life, I mean," he added. "Not just work."

What was he up to? Normally, his only concern about my personal life was that it didn't interfere with my billable hours. "That's fine too."

"I heard about your boyfriend."

"What boyfriend?" It was at least possible that he didn't know about Noah.

"I realize that you might think it's none of my business, but as senior partner, I have a right to be concerned about the welfare of my associates."

"Bruce, what are you talking about?"

"Your boyfriend," he said. "The guy from the Lakers game."

I was going to kill Greg. The only person I knew who had a bigger mouth than Greg was Rosenthal. Now the entire firm would know about me and Noah, assuming they didn't already. My only hope was a convincing lie. "Bruce, I appreciate your concern, but he wasn't my boyfriend. He's just a friend. Actually, I've suspected for quite a while that he might be gay. That's why I never dated him."

It must've worked, because Rosenthal looked relieved. "Good," he said. "Glad to hear it. Does that mean you're not seeing anyone?"

None of your damn business. "Why?"

"Because if you're not, I thought you should reconsider my suggestion about *First Date*."

I fought to keep my voice from rising. "Bruce, the answer's no. I'm a very private person and I wouldn't be comfortable appearing on television."

"I understand, but I think it would be a really good opportunity for you."

You mean a good opportunity for you. "I doubt that, and it won't help the firm either. Greg told me he talked about his job for hours, but the editors cut it all out. All they want to air is the sexy stuff."

"I think it would be different this time."

"Why?"

"I played golf with the show's general counsel over the weekend. He thinks we may be able to work out an arrangement. If someone from the firm went on the show again, he said he'd make sure some of the work talk aired in exchange for a break on legal fees."

"Bruce, I'm a lawyer, not a prostitute. I'm not going on *First Date* just so you can get some free publicity."

"It would be publicity for you too, you know. We would all benefit."

I just pressed my lips together and glared at him. I figured whatever came out of my mouth at this point would only get me fired. Which I was starting to think might not be such a bad idea, when Rosenthal looked at his watch and stood up.

"I'm late for a meeting," he said. "Just think about it."

"I've thought about it and my answer is no."

Rosenthal shook his head. "Remember, Julia, it's not good to bite the hand that lays the golden egg."

I wasn't even going to guess at what that was supposed to mean. Instead, I waited for him to leave then counted backwards from ten while taking deep, cleansing breaths. Neither calmed me down, so I walked next door to Simone's office. "You're not going to believe this!"

No matter how much Simone laughed, I didn't see the humor in this one. She finally had to pacify me by telling me about Marty. His full name was Edmund Martin Kale III, but everyone called him Marty. According to Simone, he was thirty-three years old, single, good-looking, and best of all, not gay. He worked with Todd at the stock brokerage firm, and Todd had invited him to Thanksgiving dinner at his mother's house so he could introduce him to me.

"You're still coming, aren't you?" she asked.

"Yes." Since I had just seen my parents in September, I figured I was off the hook to visit them until spring.

"Good. This will be perfect. You'll meet Marty, he'll ask you out, the two of you will start dating, and a year from now we'll be planning your wedding."

If only it were that easy.

The last item on my day's To Do list was to call Joe and apologize. If it wasn't for Joe, I wouldn't have learned the truth about Noah, or at least not so quickly.

"Hi," I said. "It's Julie. Don't hang up."

"Why not?" Joe asked, his voice tinged with anger. "I believe the last thing you said to me was something like you never wanted to speak to me again."

"Actually, what I told you was to lose my number." Before he could respond I added, "But this time I called to apologize."

A short silence, followed by "I'm listening."

"You were right about Noah. Or half right." I relayed the events of Sunday evening.

Joe's response was, "It serves you right for not trusting me."

I could just imagine his self-satisfied grin. I almost objected, but stopped myself. I called to apologize, not to start another argument. "In the future, I'll know better."

"I certainly hope so."

Now he was pushing it. "Thanks again for the warning. I really do appreciate it."

"How much?" he asked.

"Excuse me?"

"How much do you appreciate it?"

"I don't know. I'm not sure how to quantify it."

"Enough to take me out to dinner?"

Hmmm. Looks like we're not done here after all. "I don't know. You were only half right. I don't have my actuarial chart in front of me, but I think a partially correct warning may only entitle you to a lunch."

"I'll take it."

We agreed to meet when Joe returned to L.A. Unlike me, Joe had decided to fly back East to spend Thanksgiving with his family.

CHAPTER 56

Thanksgiving

I was thankful that the grocery store was open on Thanksgiving Day. I stopped to pick up a bottle of wine on my way to Simone's house. I didn't want to arrive at her future mother-in-law's home empty-handed.

The plan was that I would meet Simone at her and Todd's place, then Todd would drive the three of us to his mother's house. Simone said she thought I'd be more comfortable arriving at Todd's mother's house with the two of them rather than alone, which was true. What Simone didn't say was that with me there, she'd have an excuse to leave early. That was also true.

I circled Simone's block three times, but I couldn't find a parking space anywhere. I would've thought that when you pay more than eight-hundred-thousand dollars for a two-bedroom condominium in Brentwood, it would come with a guest parking space. I was wrong.

I called Simone from the car and she came downstairs and waited with me in the red zone. Todd pulled his BMW X5 out of the garage a few minutes later and I pulled into his parking space, Simone and I climbed into his SUV, and we took off in the direction of Bel Air. Poor Simone. Not only was she getting an interfering mother-in-law, she was getting one who only lived ten minutes away.

The security guard stopped us at the entrance to the gated community. The guard checked Todd's name off his list and waved us in. We wound our way along a wide, tree-lined street with a disappointing view. All the houses we passed were set far back on their properties, most behind tall shrubs and fences. When I was lucky, I caught a glimpse of a second-story window. Apparently, this was how the other half lived. Maybe I'd been too hasty with Richie Rich.

Todd turned off the main road onto a long circular driveway. The outer edge was lined with parked cars. They were mostly Mercedes and BMWs, with the occasional Porsche or Jaguar in between. I was glad I'd left my Acura in Simone's garage.

I was surprised the house wasn't bigger. It was large, but not a mansion. The facade was light gray stone with rows of black shuttered windows on either side of the double front door. In most parts of the country, a house like this would probably cost $350,000. In Bel Air, it was worth ten times that much.

The interior was much more impressive. The marble foyer was flanked on the left by a living room about twice the size of my apartment and on the right by a study that was almost as large. A maid disappeared with our coats, and Todd led us into the living room, where a handful of guests were gathered. The three of us were the only ones under fifty.

I hung back near the entrance with Simone while Todd ventured deep into the interior. Simone nodded in the direction of a well-preserved woman wearing diamond earrings large enough to be visible from across the room. "That's his mother," Simone whispered.

She didn't look anything like the drawing I'd tacked to Simone's dartboard. With the botox injections, the perfectly coiffed hair, and her size six figure, she looked like a woman in her early fifties. Simone told me she was actually sixty-four.

Todd hugged his mother and she kissed his cheek, then Todd led her over to where Simone and I were standing.

"Hello, Grace," Simone said to her future mother-in-law. "Happy Thanksgiving."

Todd's mother leaned in and air-kissed Simone. "It's so nice to see you, dear. I'm surprised you remembered how to get here."

"I didn't," Simone said, "Todd drove." Then she introduced me.

Todd's mother gave me a limp handshake and a phony smile. I tried to hand her the bottle of wine I'd brought, but she'd already linked her arm through Todd's. "Just put that in the kitchen, dear," she said, barely glancing at the wine. "Simone can take you there."

"Come with me, honey," she said looking up at Todd. "I have some people I want you to meet." Todd and his mother disappeared into the far corners of the living room and I followed Simone back to the foyer.

"Do you see what I have to deal with?" Simone said.

I sensed a rant coming. "Maybe we should just open the wine."

♡ ♡ ♡

Simone led me down the hallway to the kitchen, where she yanked open drawers and slammed them closed until a bartender appeared with a cork screw. He opened the wine and poured Simone and me each a glass. When he started to walk away with the bottle, Simone pulled it out of his hand. Then she led me and the wine bottle on a tour of the house.

Simone walked me through the dining room and the den and then led me upstairs to the five bedrooms. We stopped in the master bedroom and Simone walked around the room pouring drops of red wine onto the white carpet.

"Oops," she said. "Sometimes I'm just so clumsy."

"You're wasting your time. You know she's just going to call someone to clean the carpet. It's not like your mother-in-law is going to be down on her hands and knees scrubbing out those stains."

"Yeah, you're right," she said and downed the rest of her wine. "Maybe I should steal her jewelry instead."

"Simone!"

"I was just kidding. But I need to do something to get back at her."

"You already have."

"What?"

"You've taken her darling baby boy away from her."

"True," she said with a giant grin, "but that's not enough."

We went back downstairs and Simone walked me around the grounds pointing out the garden, the pool, and the tennis courts. By the time we returned to the house, it had filled up. The kids and their nannies were ensconced in the den, the living room still held the over-fifty crowd, and the younger set was in the study watching football. Someone had finally opened the credenza and uncovered a 35-inch television.

I followed Simone into the study and grabbed the chair across from her when she sat down on the couch next to Todd. She whispered something in his ear and he nodded. At the next commercial, Todd left with his empty glass and returned a few minutes later with a refill and a man with dark blond hair wearing jeans and a burgundy sweater. The man was probably 5'10", but looked short compared to Todd's 6'4" frame.

Todd introduced me to Marty and we shook hands, then Marty

sat down on the couch with Todd and the two of them watched the game. After being ignored for two more commercial breaks, I left for a refill on my wine. Simone had already finished our bottle, and it looked like it was going to be a long, dull afternoon.

Simone followed me out to the bar, and as soon as we were out of hearing range said, "What do you think?"

"I think it's pretty clear he's not interested in me."

"Why would you say that?"

"Because he's been ignoring me for the last half hour."

"No, he hasn't. He's just watching the game."

"He's not watching the game during the commercials."

"That's when they catch up. You know guys don't talk when they're watching football."

"They just saw each other yesterday. What do they have to say?"

"I'm sure Todd's having exactly the same conversation with Marty that I'm having with you. Marty's probably wondering why you're not talking to him."

"I doubt that."

"You'll see," she said. "I'll make sure the two of you sit next to each other at dinner. Then you can get acquainted without distractions."

♡   ♡   ♡

"I hear you're a top-notch litigator," Marty said during the first of our five courses.

Flattery was always a good start. "I try. And you're a financial wizard, right?"

"As a matter of fact, I am. Which works out really well for me, because I have no other skills."

"None?" I asked with a suggestive look. I really needed to stop drinking the wine.

Marty leaned in a little closer. I was mesmerized by his perfectly aligned white teeth. "Actually, I have a few, but they can't be discussed in mixed company." Then he nodded toward the older woman and her ten-year-old grandson whom Simone had seated on his right.

I don't know if it was the sexual innuendo or the lack of interesting alternative dinner companions, but Marty spent the entire meal chatting me up. He was actually very funny and had a great laugh. His sense of humor made him more attractive. Or it could've been the wine.

After coffee and dessert, Simone decided that I'd had long enough to get to know Marty. She grabbed Todd and me for a post-meal getaway. When Marty saw us with our coats on, he said he needed to leave too.

The four of us walked out together, but once we were outside, Simone made sure she and Todd stayed ten paces behind.

"I had a great time tonight," Marty said.

"Me too," I replied. "If this stockbroker thing doesn't work out for you, you could always try stand-up comedy."

"You really think so?"

"Absolutely." In my inebriated state, I really did.

"I'm leaving for Colorado tomorrow, skiing with some buddies, but I'd love to see you again when I get back."

I agreed, and Marty pulled out his Palm Pilot and entered my name and number into his electronic black book. When we arrived at Todd's SUV, Marty said good-bye and continued down the driveway to his Porsche.

Simone didn't even wait for me to close my car door before she began interrogating me. "So? What did you think? Do you like him?

"Maybe," I said. "He certainly kept me amused."

"I know. I could tell."

"Simone, you promised you wouldn't spy on us."

"I didn't. I could hear the two of you laughing from the other end of the table."

"Were we really that loud?"

"Not really. I was sort of listening. I know Marty can be really funny when he turns on the charm. So when are you seeing him again?"

"I don't know. All he did was ask for my number."

"I'm sure he'll call you. Don't you think so, Todd?"

"Sure," Todd said, and switched on the car stereo.

If he didn't meet someone better on the ski slopes first. Marty was amusing and very charming, but definitely a player. I figured the odds were 50-50 that I'd ever hear from him again.

CHAPTER 57

Played

It's amazing how quickly the weekend passes. Even a four-day weekend. It was already Monday again and I was back at the office. I wasn't feeling particularly motivated to work, so I flipped through my desk calendar hoping to find some inspiration. Maybe a looming deadline or a hearing I'd forgotten about. What I found was my trial date against Just A Date, which was only three days away!

It was personal, and it was only small claims court, but it was still a trial. I pulled the file out of my desk drawer where it lived under a pile of take-out menus. I wasn't going to leave this one in my file cabinet where anyone might discover it. Simone was the only one in the office who knew I'd joined Just A Date, and I wanted to keep it that way.

Small claims court was much less intimidating than state and federal court, the only other courts I'd argued in. Instead of days or weeks, a small claims court trial lasts half an hour at most. But I still had to prove my case. So far, all I had for evidence was my contract with Just A Date and my sworn statement that I'd only had two dates before the company folded. I needed more.

I called Just A Date's former phone number and reached the same recording telling me that the number had been disconnected. I called the phone company and asked the customer service representative if they would put that information in writing. After being transferred to five different departments and agreeing to pay a $15 service fee, the phone company agreed to fax me a letter stating that Just A Date's phone number had been disconnected.

Next I called the management company for Just A Date's former office building. I wanted a similar letter from them stating that Just A Date had been evicted from its office space. They were less cooperative. Their leasing agent told me it was their policy not to provide any information about their past or present clients without a court order. No exceptions.

If I hadn't waited until the last minute to prepare, I could've mailed a letter to Just A Date's offices. Then, if the post office did its job, the letter would've been returned to me marked "Addressee Unknown." Now I was going to have to do this the hard way.

I left the office at noon for an early lunch and drove to the drugstore. I purchased a Polaroid camera and a packet of film (I still hadn't gotten around to purchasing that digital camera I'd been planning on buying for the last year and a half) and headed over to Just A Date's former offices. I parked on a side street and walked the three blocks to the building just to avoid having to explain myself to the parking attendant.

I rode the elevator up to the fifth floor and followed the hallway to Suite 504. The eviction notice was no longer posted, but it didn't look like a new tenant had moved in yet. All that remained of Just A Date was a dirt outline on the office door. No one had bothered to clean the spot where their gold lettering had been removed.

I loaded the film into the Polaroid and took three pictures of the door from different angles. While I waited for the pictures to develop, another woman, who looked like she was in her early twenties, strode purposefully down the hall. I was surprised when she stopped in front of Just A Date's office. She tried the handle, but it was locked.

"Do you know if they're closed for lunch?" she asked.

"They're closed permanently," I said. "They're out of business"

"Are you sure?"

"Pretty sure." I pointed to the dirt outline on the door.

The woman introduced herself as Molly Truitt. She told me she was a journalist working on a story about dating in Los Angeles.

"Who do you work for?" I asked.

"Actually, I'm freelance."

"Which magazine is this for?" Maybe when the article came out, I could pick up a few pointers.

"I don't know yet," she said. "I'm writing the article first, then I'm going to submit it for publication."

"I thought magazines commissioned people to write articles they wanted to print, not the other way around."

"Only when you're established. When you're starting out, you write the articles first and then hope to get them published later."

I looked down at my pictures. All three of them had developed and the outline of the words JUST A DATE were clearly visible in two of them. "Well, good luck," I said, and turned to leave.

"Wait," Molly said. "Why did you come down here if you knew they were out of business? Are you a client?"

"No, I'm just helping out a friend." I wasn't about to explain my situation to a reporter. The last thing I needed was my name in the paper. "Julie Burns, disgruntled dater." No thanks. I stuck the pictures in my purse and started walking toward the elevator.

Molly followed. "Why are you taking pictures of the place if they're out of business?"

I pushed the elevator call button and looked at my watch. "Sorry, I really have to get back to work. Good luck with your story."

When the elevator arrived, I stepped inside and pushed the button marked LOBBY. Molly jumped in as the doors were closing.

"Just tell me why you were taking pictures," she said.

I looked straight ahead at the closed doors and tried to ignore her.

"Then just tell me who you're taking them for."

I stared at my fingernails and picked at the chipped paint. When the elevator doors opened, Molly followed me through the lobby shouting her same two questions. People were starting to stare.

"Please," I hissed, "just leave me alone."

"As soon as you answer my questions I will."

"No," I said, and started walking again. Molly followed me through the building's entrance and out onto the street.

I pulled my cell phone out of my purse and held it in front of her. "If you don't stop following me I'm going to call the police and have you arrested."

"For what?"

"Harassment." I didn't think police actually arrested people for harassment, but Molly must have. Her big brown eyes filled up with tears that quickly spilled onto her cheeks. She sat down on the curb with her head in her arms and sobbed.

"Oh, for God's sake, stop crying. I'm not going to have you arrested. I just want you to leave me alone." I fished through my purse for a clean tissue and handed it to her.

"I'm sorry," she said and stood up. "It's just that I can't get anyone to talk to me, and I can't sell a story, and my boyfriend moved out without paying his half of the rent, and I can't ask my parents for the money because they didn't even know I was living with my boyfriend, and. . . ."

Did I need this? "Okay, I get that you're having a bad day. But you're wasting your time. There's no story here."

"Then why won't you tell me why you were taking those pictures?" She said, wiping her eyes.

"If I tell you, will you promise to leave me alone?"

"Yes." She sniffed loudly for emphasis.

"I was taking the pictures for a friend. She's suing Just A Date and needs proof that the company's out of business."

"How does taking a picture of the door prove that they're out of business?"

"It doesn't by itself. It's just one piece of evidence."

"Are you a lawyer?"

"Why?"

"Because you sound like a lawyer. And you're dressed like one too."

I looked down at my gray pin-striped pantsuit. I suppose I did look like a lawyer. No point in denying it. "Yes, and now we're done." I started walking toward my car again.

Molly followed. "Are you suing the company? For your friend, I mean."

"No." I crossed the street to the side where my car was parked.

Molly crossed the street too. "Then who's her lawyer?"

"She doesn't have one."

"Why not?"

"Because its small claims court. They don't allow lawyers."

"Really?"

"Really," I replied, and unlocked my car door.

"How come?"

What was this, twenty questions? "I don't know. You'll have to ask them that."

"Can I get your name and number so I can call you if I have more questions?"

"No!"

"How about your friend's?"

"Molly, you promised if I told you why I was taking the pictures you'd leave me alone. I told you why. Now go away."

"I can't. I smell a story."

"There's no story."

"Then why is your friend suing them?"

"Because they breached their contract."

"How?"

I shook my head and climbed into the car. I'd already said too much. Molly was still standing in the street shouting questions when I pulled away.

I should've kept my mouth shut. Even when she started crying, I should've kept on walking. She probably faked the tears and the whole story about her boyfriend just to play me. I must have the word "sucker" written across my forehead. Thank God at least I hadn't given her my name.

CHAPTER 58

The Trial

I arrived at the courthouse Wednesday morning with the usual nausea that accompanied me whenever I went to court. Those were the days I always wondered why I went to law school. I hate public speaking. Fortunately for me, I don't go to court very often.

When I walked into Courtroom 3, the judge was hearing another case. My trial was scheduled for 10 a.m. I still had another fifteen minutes, so I sat down in the gallery and listened.

The judge was in her early sixties and maintained an all-business demeanor. She probably wished she could just retire instead of listening to people's petty disputes all day. I know I would if I were her.

The judge rapped her gavel, and the clerk called the next case. The parties for Hills v. Sparkling Dry Cleaners took their places. The judge allowed each party a few minutes to tell their side of the story, asked one question, then told both parties they would receive her ruling by mail.

The judge rapped her gavel again and the clerk called out, "Burns v. Just A Date, Docket Number 62397N."

I stood up and walked to the table on the right behind the sign marked PLAINTIFF. The clerk collected my documents and handed them to the judge. She skimmed them for maybe thirty seconds before she looked up. The table marked DEFENDANT was still empty. The judge glanced at the wall clock. It was already five minutes after ten.

The judge told the clerk to check the hallway. I turned and watched the clerk walk to the back of the courtroom and stick his head out the door. That was when I noticed Molly Truitt sitting in the last row of the gallery. What was she doing here? The last thing I wanted was an audience.

Molly looked older today. When I'd met her on Monday in her jeans and T-shirt and her hair pulled back in a pony tail, I'd guessed her age as twenty-two. Today, in her black pin-striped pant suit, high-heeled shoes, and full hair and makeup, she could've passed for thirty-five.

The clerk returned to his seat next to the bench sans defendant.

"Well, Ms. Burns," the judge said, "today's your lucky day. Since the defendant has not seen fit to join our gathering, I'm entering a default judgment in your favor. You'll receive written notification of my ruling by mail."

The judge rapped her gavel, and the clerk called the next case. I never even had to open my mouth. I wish I could win all my cases so easily. I gathered my notes and extra set of documents and headed out to the hallway. Molly and the two men sitting next to her followed me outside. The younger man was carrying a large black case. When he reached the hallway, he opened it and pulled out a video camera, which he handed to the older man, and a microphone, which he handed to Molly.

I kept on walking. Molly and her entourage followed.

"So tell me, Ms. Burns," Molly shouted at my back, "do you feel vindicated by this judgment?"

I ignored her and picked up my pace.

"You're an attractive woman," she shouted again. "Why did you feel the need to join a dating service?"

I could feel my blood pressure rising, but I kept moving.

"Do you believe all those statistics that say a woman over thirty-five has a greater chance of being hit by a bus than getting married?"

She had to be making that one up!

"Tell us, Ms. Burns, do you agree that women who join dating services are desperate?"

I stopped to turn and look at her. Then I looked at the camera. Don't go there, Julie, you'll regret it. I turned back and continued walking down the seemingly endless hallway.

"You must admit," she said, "it's certainly a sign of desperation when you have to pay someone to get a date."

That got me.

I turned and faced her, ignoring the camera eight inches from my face. "First of all, I'm not desperate. Second of all, I'm only thirty-two. And third, I've got plenty of dates, with or without Just A Date."

"How many dates?"

"Lots," I said, and started walking again.

"How many? One? Two? Maybe three in the last three years?"

"I've probably had twenty-five dates in the last six months." I hadn't actually counted, but it certainly felt like that many. Of course it wasn't twenty-five different men, just twenty-five dates. I'd probably only dated ten or twelve men.

"That is a lot. I guess I had you all wrong."

"Yeah," I said without thinking, "I'm not desperate, I'm just romantically challenged."

She paused a moment and then smiled. "You're right."

Oh, shit. I smiled at Molly for the first time that morning. "You know I was just kidding, right? There's no such thing as romantically challenged. I made it up."

"Of course there is," she replied. "A woman who dates tons of men but never has a relationship with any of them. No one man is ever good enough. They all have something wrong with them. It's a great story."

"No," I said, this time without the smile. "There won't be any story because I'm not romantically challenged." That's when I noticed the other people in the hallway staring at us. I decided to cut my losses and sprint to the exit.

Molly and her camera crew followed me down the stairs and out to the parking lot, Molly shouting all the way. "Then why can't you find just one?"

"What are you, my mother?"

"Just a hardworking reporter trying to get a story."

"You told me the other day you were a freelance journalist."

"I am," she said. "I'm on assignment."

"For who?"

"*Hollywood Tonight.*"

"Why would *Hollywood Tonight* be interested in me? I'm not a celebrity."

"They run human interest stories too. Especially during the holidays. Don't you want to be on television?"

"No, what I want is to be left alone!" I hurried across the parking lot in the direction of my car. This time Molly didn't follow.

As I pulled out onto the street, I caught a glimpse of Molly and her camera crew setting up their gear in front of the courthouse sign. She was wasting her time. *Hollywood Tonight* would never air this. There was no story to air.

♡   ♡   ♡

I slipped into my office only an hour and twenty minutes late and immediately called Kaitlyn.

"How did it go this morning?" she asked. "Did you win?"

I told her about my default judgment and the appearance of Molly Truitt. "You don't really think *Hollywood Tonight* would air it do you?"

"Of course not. There's nothing to air. It's not like you talked to the woman."

"Well, not really. I mean, I did deny some of the allegations."

"Yeah, but you didn't give her any information."

"No. Except that I went on twenty-five dates in the last six months."

"That's not a story. That's just dating when you're over thirty."

"True. But the complaint I filed with the court is a public record."

"Yes, but all that says is you joined a dating service, you were promised six dates, you had two, and the company went out of business. No story there. Companies go out of business every day."

"Keep going. You've almost got me convinced that my entire life is not about to be revealed on national television."

"Jules, you know I love you, but you have to trust me on this, your life just isn't interesting enough to be the basis for national news."

"Not even seedy tabloid news?"

"Not even *The National Enquirer*. Now just forget about it and concentrate on your date with Joe. When is it again? Saturday?"

"Yes, but it's not a date. I'm just taking him to lunch to say thank you."

"Uh, huh."

"It's true!"

"Have it your way," she said. "Just call me afterward with an update."

I promised I would and hung up.

It really wasn't a date. Joe might not be a bartender anymore, but he was still a wannabe.

CHAPTER 59

The Non-Date

I called Joe Friday afternoon to confirm our lunch plans for Saturday. We agreed to meet at Johnnie's in Santa Monica at one o'clock for the closest thing to New York pizza either of us had found in L.A. Since this wasn't a date, I decided I could wear jeans rather than my usual black pants. It was just coincidence that the first pair I pulled out of the closet were the jeans that made me look thin.

When I arrived at the restaurant at two minutes to one, Joe was already waiting. He was wearing blue jeans and a navy sweatshirt. Obviously he didn't think it was a date either.

"You're prompt," I said.

"I was afraid if I was late, you might not wait."

"I'd have given you ten minutes."

"I'll have to remember that."

After a heated debate over whether good pizza actually needed toppings and if so, which ones, Joe and I compromised by ordering a half-pepperoni, half-cheese pizza. After we polished off most of the pie, the waiter cleared our dishes and placed the check on the table next to Joe. I reached across and grabbed it before Joe even had a chance to look at it.

"I'll take that," I said.

"Don't worry," he said, "I wasn't going to pay."

"You're really enjoying this, aren't you?"

He folded his arms across his chest and grinned. "As a matter of fact, I am."

"Just for that, you're not getting any ice cream."

"Ice cream? I didn't know you were buying me dessert too."

"I was going to, but not anymore."

"Pleeeease," he said. "I promise to be good."

"Sorry, you blew it." I left the money on the table and walked outside. Joe followed.

"Surely there must be something I can say to change your mind."

"Nope."

"How about a challenge?"

Hmmm. "What kind of a challenge?"

"A game," he said. "Loser pays for dessert."

"That's fair, as long as I can choose the sport."

I led Joe down to the video arcade at the Santa Monica Pier.

"You want to play a video game?" he asked.

"Skee-Ball," I said. It was one of my hidden talents. I'd won a

Skee-Ball championship when I was in the third grade. Skee-Ball machines are hard to find, but I knew they had them at the Santa Monica Pier. Or at least they did five years ago, which was the last time I'd played.

"What's Skee-Ball?" he asked.

"You've never played Skee-Ball before?"

"I'm not sure. What is it?"

"A cross between bowling and archery."

"This I gotta see."

♡ ♡ ♡

I led Joe to the back of the arcade. Luckily, the Skee-Ball machines were still there. It was the only spot in the building that wasn't crawling with teenage boys. Skee-Ball was way too low-tech for anyone under twenty-five.

I inserted my quarters into the slot, and eight small wooden balls whooshed down the chute. "You score points by rolling the ball up the hill and into the numbered circles. The higher the number, the better."

"Wouldn't it be easier just to throw the ball into the circles?" Joe asked.

"This isn't baseball. You have to roll it." I picked up a wooden ball and demonstrated the proper Skee-Ball technique. Then I handed Joe a ball so he could try it. He wasn't as bad as I thought he'd be for a first-timer. We both took a few more practice shots, then I started a new game.

I won the first match 180 to 120.

"Best two out of three," Joe said.

He won the second two matches 190 to 160 and 200 to 180.

"Want to play best three out of five?" he asked.

"No," I said. "You're getting too good."

"Beginner's luck."

I wasn't so sure. "Tell me the truth. I promise I won't get mad. Have you ever played this game before?"

"Well, once you showed it to me it did seem a little familiar."

"You liar! You knew how to play all along, didn't you?"

"I'm taking the Fifth."

"Too late. I already know you're guilty. Since you cheated, I win by default."

"That's not fair. You picked the game."

"That was when I thought you didn't know how to play."

"No, you picked it before I told you I didn't know how to play."

I was hoping he wouldn't remember that detail. "Yes, but I won the first match. I never would've agreed to best two out of three if I knew you were scamming me."

Joe considered that for a moment. "Okay. I'll buy the ice cream, but only if you take me on the roller coaster." The Santa Monica Pier had rides as well as video games.

"Done," I said, and we shook hands on it. I would've gone on the roller coaster anyway.

♡ ♡ ♡

By the time we left the Pier, the sun had begun to set and the air was getting chilly. I was wearing a long-sleeve shirt, but I was still freezing. Joe must've noticed me rubbing my arms.

"Do you want my sweatshirt?" he asked.

God, yes. I'd been eyeing it jealously for the last hour. "No, I can't take your shirt."

"Sure you can. I have a T-shirt underneath."

"Won't you be cold in just a T-shirt?"

"I'll be fine. I've been hot all day." Joe pulled off his sweatshirt and handed it to me. I caught a quick glimpse of his stomach before he pulled his T-shirt back down. Even after half a pizza, it was still flat as a board.

I yanked the sweatshirt over my head. It was just as warm as I'd imagined, and it smelled good, too—a combination of laundry detergent, sea air, and Joe.

We walked back to the car in comfortable silence. Usually by this point in a date I couldn't wait to get home. But then again, this wasn't a date.

"Thanks for lunch," Joe said when we reached my car. "I had a really good time today."

"Me too," I replied, and meant it. I wasn't ready for the day to end, so on impulse I asked, "Do you have any interest in going to the movies tonight? The new Harrison Ford film just opened and I'm dying to see it."

"I'd love to, but I can't. I have plans tonight."

"Hot date?" I asked without thinking. I really needed to work on that.

"I should probably take the Fifth for this one too."

I agreed. I'd already been deflated. I didn't want to know any more.

"Maybe we could see it one night next week," he added. "I'm off Thursday and Friday."

"That's okay," I said. "I'm sure I can rustle up another movie partner."

As soon as I could no longer see Joe in my car's rearview mirror, I pulled out my cell phone and called Kaitlyn. As I'd suspected, she and Steve were going to see the new Harrison Ford movie tonight. Steve was almost as big a fan as I was. We agreed to meet in front of the Century City multiplex at seven o'clock.

♥   ♥   ♥

Aaaaah Harrison! The one man who never disappoints. By the time the movie ended, I'd recovered most of the good mood I'd had before Joe blew me off. Steve, Kaitlyn, and I walked the hundred yards from the theater to Houston's to add our name to the waiting list, then we headed to the bookstore to kill forty to fifty minutes until our table became available.

Brentano's bookstore was packed. Unfortunately, it had a lot less to do with Los Angelenos' being avid readers (most weren't) and a lot more to do with Brentanos being the only store in the mall that was still open at ten o'clock at night. It was too crowded to browse comfortably, so I bought a magazine with Harrison on the cover and told Kaitlyn to meet me outside when she was finished.

I settled in at an empty table at the edge of the food court. From that vantage point, I had enough light to read by, and if the line at the box office ever shortened, I would be able to see the entrance to the bookstore.

The line at the box office never did shorten. I couldn't see the entrance to the bookstore, but to my astonishment, I did see Joe. He was waiting in front of the will call window. He'd traded in his blue jeans and T-shirt for black jeans and a gray sweater. It must be his date outfit. He'd worn something similar on our first date.

The woman standing next to him was tall, thin, and blond. She wore a black miniskirt, black stilleto heels, and a low-cut blouse. What she lacked in natural assets she made up for with a push-up bra. I hated her already.

I wanted to walk up to Joe and say hello so I could see the bimbo up close and he'd be forced to introduce me and explain our relationship. That would be interesting. I could even make his life really difficult by offering to return his sweatshirt, which I was still wearing. But then Joe would see me at Century City alone on a Saturday night. That would be humiliating.

I was still concealing myself behind my magazine when Kaitlyn interrupted.

"Why are you holding the magazine over to your face? I only knew it was you because Harrison Ford was on the cover."

"Sit down and be quiet," I whispered. "I'm trying to hide."

"From who?" she asked in her normal 'loud' speaking voice.

I yanked her down into a chair and shushed her. "From Joe. He's here with a woman who's definitely not his sister."

"Where?" she said, standing up.

I pulled her down again and described what both of them were wearing. She sat up in her chair and scanned the line at the box office until she found them.

"She's definitely a date," Kaitlyn said.

"Thanks a lot."

"Why do you care? You don't want him."

"That doesn't mean I don't want him to want me. Besides, we had a really good time today. I was actually reconsidering the whole wannabe thing."

"Did you tell him that?"

"No, and I'm glad I didn't, since he's obviously dating someone else."

She stood up and refastened her red hair into its clip. "You're hopeless. I'm going to find Steve. Why don't you go to the restaurant and check on our status and we'll meet you over there."

I waited until I saw Joe and his date pick up their movie tickets and move off in the other direction before I went back to Houston's. The hostess told me there were still five parties ahead of us. I was walking back to the bookstore to tell Kaitlyn and Steve that they didn't need to rush when I saw Joe and his date walking toward me. There was nowhere to hide. And there was no point. Joe had already seen me.

"I didn't expect to see you tonight," he said.

"Me neither," I replied. It could've been worse. At least he didn't have his arm around her.

Joe introduced me to the bimbo, whose name was Barbara. "But everyone calls me Barbie," she said. I didn't need to wonder why. Although all of my Barbie dolls had been real blondes. This Barbie definitely wasn't. She was long overdue for a touch-up.

"So you decided to see Harrison tonight after all."

He didn't say "by yourself," but I knew that was the implication. I didn't look like I was on a date. Besides being alone, I was still wearing my jeans and his sweatshirt. But that didn't stop me from lying. "I told you I'd rustle up a date."

"I never doubted you," he said.

"He's in the bookstore," I added before Joe could ask. "I was checking on dinner. You know what the wait at Houston's is like on a Saturday night. It's always an hour no matter what they say."

"That's where we're headed," Barbie said. She was either oblivious to the tension or chose to ignore it.

"If the wait's not too long," Joe chimed in. "But it looks like it is. So maybe we should try someplace else."

"That would probably be best." I spotted Steve and Kaitlyn leaving the bookstore and added, "There's my date. I should go."

Joe turned and followed my gaze. "Isn't that your friend Kaitlyn?"

I couldn't believe he remembered her. "Yeah, she tagged along with us tonight." I waved to Kaitlyn, who waved back and whispered something to Steve. When they reached the three of us, Steve put his arm around my shoulder and gave it a squeeze.

"Hi, honey," Steve said. "Did you miss me?"

"More than you could imagine," I replied. At that moment I could've kissed him and Kaitlyn.

CHAPTER 60

The Beginning of the End

When I arrived home Saturday night I had a message from Marty. He said he was back from his ski trip and was wondering if we could get together that night. If only I'd checked my messages earlier in the day.

I played phone tag with him for the next three days. When we finally spoke he said he wanted to tell me all about his ski trip over dinner. He promised that both he and his stories would be much more entertaining over a bottle of wine. I suspected he was right.

We made plans for Saturday night. Since he was a good friend of Todd's, I thought it was safe to have him pick me up at my house. Besides, I wanted to ride in the Porsche. Even if we only lasted one date, at least I'd have that.

♡ ♡ ♡

The next afternoon I was in Simone's office discussing a fraud case we were both working on when my secretary, Lucy, stuck her head in the door. "Your mother's on the phone. She didn't want to leave a message."

If my mother was calling me at the office in the middle of the week then there had to be a problem. I just hoped it wasn't serious. I went back to my office, closed the door, and picked up the receiver.

"What's wrong?" I asked.

"I can't believe you didn't tell me you joined a dating service," my mother said.

"What?"

"And you might've mentioned when I spoke to you on Sunday that you were going to be on TV. I'm your mother, Julia, didn't you think I'd want to know?"

"Mom, what are you talking about?"

"What am I talking about? Your interview on *Hollywood Tonight!*"

This was not happening. Someone please tell me this was not happening. It had to be a bad dream. Kaitlyn swore *Hollywood Tonight* wouldn't run the story, that there was no story to run. I'd even taped the show for a few days, just in case. But it had been over a week. I thought I was in the clear.

I noticed that my mother was still talking and heard my sister's name. "You mean Deborah saw it too?"

"Yes, Julia. I just told you, she's the one who saw it first and called your father and me. You know we don't watch those celebrity gossip shows."

"Tell me exactly what they said in the story."

"I don't know about the rest of it. We only caught the last few minutes."

"Then just tell me what they said in the last few minutes."

"Don't yell at me, Julia. I'm still your mother and I don't appreciate your tone."

I took a deep breath and counted to five, backwards. "Okay, Mom, I'm sorry. You just caught me by surprise here."

"You mean you didn't know you were going to be on TV?"

Duh! "No, Mom, I didn't."

"Can they do that?"

"Apparently they can. Now will you please just tell me what they said."

"Well, like I told you, we only caught the last part. You told the reporter that you'd dated twenty-five men in the last six months and that you were romantically challenged."

"I'm not romantically challenged!"

"Well, that's not what you said on TV. You have to admit, Julia, twenty-five men in six months is a lot. That's one a week."

"It wasn't twenty-five different men, it was twenty-five dates. It was probably only ten men."

"Still, I hope you're being careful."

Careful? "What do you mean 'careful'?"

"You know," she said, and lowered her voice. "It's not just about pregnancy anymore. These days you have to worry about diseases, too."

I'm thirty-two years old and now she wants to give me the sex talk! "I didn't sleep with them, Mother, I just dated them."

"I didn't say you did. But I'm sure you will someday, and I just want you to be prepared."

"I didn't say I was a virgin. I just didn't sleep with any of those men. But I promise, if I ever have sex again I'll use protection."

"I'm not telling you not to have sex, I just—"

"Listen, Mom, I gotta go. I'll call you back later."

"Wait a minute," she said and put the phone down before I could hang up. I could hear my father's voice in the background shouting over Alex Trebek from *Jeopardy*. My mother picked up the receiver a few seconds later. "Your father just checked the *TV Guide*. *Hollywood Tonight* is on again at one in the morning. He wants to know if you want him to tape it for you."

"No! Do not tape it." I could just imagine us all watching it together at the next family gathering.

"Are you sure?"

"Positive."

"All right. If you change your mind, you can always get a copy from your sister. I know she taped it."

Just shoot me.

CHAPTER 61

Hooray for Hollywood

I hid in my office for the rest of the afternoon and left work early to make sure I was home in time to catch *Hollywood Tonight*. As soon as I heard the "Hooray for Hollywood" theme song, I planted my butt in the living room chair across from the television and determined not to move for the next half hour, not even during the commercials.

I watched celebrity interviews from the red carpet at last night's movie premiere, found out who was sleeping with whom, who was marrying whom, who was divorcing whom, and who was going into and out of rehab. My story was last. It came right after the troubled love life of the latest "It" Girl.

The screen filled with a shot of former male model turned host Rod Light, sitting at the anchor desk. "And it's not just celebrities who have problems with their love lives," Rod said. "As every single woman in America knows, it's not easy finding the right man. Rebecca."

The camera cut to cohost and former beauty queen Rebecca

Quinn, standing in front of a matte painting of the Hollywood sign with the words REEL LIFE sprawled across it in red letters. "That's right, Rod," Rebecca said. "The search for love affects us all. For more on a growing trend, we go to our newest on-the-spot correspondent, Molly Truitt, for this week's 'Reel Life' story. Welcome aboard, Molly."

The screen showed Molly Truitt standing in front of a Starbucks. "Thanks, Rebecca," Molly said. "Times may change, but the search for love continues. In this week's 'Reel Life' story, we've discovered a disturbing new trend in America, romantically challenged singles."

The camera panned the crowd at the outdoor tables while Molly's voice-over continued. "Coffeehouses like these across the nation have become the spot of choice for first dates. But are we dating too much? Have we forsaken true love in our quest for the perfect mate?"

The camera returned to Molly, who walked over to a couple drinking coffee at a table for two. The woman was a beautiful brunette in her mid-thirties. She was much better looking than the man sitting across from her with the receding hairline. Although he actually looked a little familiar. Could I have dated him?

Molly introduced herself to the couple, who gave their names as Eric and Susan. "Is this your first date?" Molly asked Eric.

"Yes, it is," Eric said, and smiled into the camera.

"Going well?" Molly asked.

"Very well," Eric said. "I'm very pleased."

Molly placed the microphone in front of Susan. "How about you, Susan? Do you think it's going well?"

The very uncomfortable-looking Susan responded, "It's going fine."

Molly stayed on Susan. "Would you say that most of your first dates take place at coffeehouses?"

"Sometimes," Susan said. "More often I meet the man at a restaurant for lunch or dinner. But Eric wanted to meet for coffee first, so that's why we're here."

Molly turned back to Eric. "Why coffee, Eric? Why not take your date out for a fabulous dinner and sweep her off her feet?"

"If I'd met Susan in person," Eric said, "then I probably would've suggested dinner. Until recently, I always took a woman to dinner on a first date. But when I started going on blind dates and meeting people on the Internet, I switched to coffee. There's no sense sitting through an entire meal with someone you're not attracted to."

Molly turned back to Susan. "Do you agree?"

"Sure," Susan said. "No sense wasting time and money on someone who might turn out to be a dog."

Molly raised her eyebrows. She hadn't missed Susan's sarcasm, but Eric evidently had. He continued smiling into the camera.

"How did the two of you meet?" Molly asked.

Susan said "blind date," at the same time Eric said "on the Internet." The camera panned down to Susan kicking Eric under the table. "I mean blind date," Eric said. "I met my last girlfriend on the Internet."

"Do you do a lot of dating?" Molly asked Eric.

"Yeah," he said. "I usually go out with two or three women a month."

Susan choked on her coffee.

"How about you, Susan?" Molly asked. "How many men do you date in a typical month?"

"About the same," Susan said.

"And do either of you see this as a problem?" Molly asked.

"No," both Susan and Eric responded in unison. "I'm going to keep dating until I meet the right person," Susan added. "No matter how long it takes."

"I agree," Eric said. "I'm thirty-six years old and I have no intention of settling. I'll date for as long as it takes to meet Ms. Right."

The camera cut to a close-up of Molly wearing an earnest expression. "And that's the problem," Molly said. "In our quest for the perfect mate, we've become a nation of romantically challenged serial daters, which sometimes leads to disastrous results."

The camera cut to a shot of the complaint form I'd filed in small claims court. "These court documents obtained by *Hollywood Tonight* reveal one such story."

The camera then cut to a shot of me walking down the hallway. "Local entertainment attorney and self-proclaimed romantically challenged single, Julia Burns was so desperate to meet Mr. Right that she paid a company called Just A Date three hundred dollars for an introduction. When Just A Date didn't deliver, Burns sued."

The camera cut to Molly asking me, "Do you feel vindicated by this judgment?" and me ignoring her. Molly's voice-over continued. "Burns is savvy enough to win her lawsuit, but still won't admit that it's her desperation that has led her down this jagged path."

The camera then cut to me saying, "I'm not desperate, I'm just romantically challenged. I've got plenty of dates, with or without Just A Date."

Then it cut to Molly asking, "How many dates?"

Then it cut to me replying, "Twenty-five dates in the last six months."

Then it cut to Molly standing in the hallway. "Like most romantically challenged singles, Burns dates three, four, even five men a month in her constant quest for the perfect man. But when asked why, Burns just gets defensive."

The camera cut to me asking, "What are you, my mother?"

Then it cut back to Molly standing in front of the courthouse. "No, Ms. Burns, we're not your mother. But we certainly hope your mother's watching and gets you the help you need. This is Molly Truitt reporting from West Los Angeles for *Hollywood Tonight.*"

The screen switched back to Rod and Rebecca at the anchor desk in the studio. "Thanks, Molly," Rebecca said, "for that insightful report." The camera zoomed in for a close-up on Rebecca, who added, "If you're romantically challenged or know someone who is, please log on to our website for a list of licensed therapists that can help."

The theme music began to swell and I shut the television off.

"My life is over, Elmo."

Then the phone rang.

CHAPTER 62

Out of the Woodwork

I picked up the phone on the third ring.

"Oh, my God!" Kaitlyn said. "Did you see it? You were on television."

"Yes, and I haven't forgotten you're the one who told me my life wasn't interesting enough for national TV."

"That was before I knew you were a romantically challenged serial dater."

"I was joking!"

"I know. But you have to admit, it was a pretty flimsy story."

"Is that why you called? To tell me my life story is flimsy?"

"No, I called to tell you that this is a good thing. You looked great and you'll probably get tons more dates out of this."

"I doubt that."

"Don't be so negative," she said as my call waiting started beeping. I told Kaitlyn I'd call her later and clicked over to the other line.

"I can't believe you didn't tell me you were going to be on *Hollywood Tonight,*" Simone shouted in my ear.

When I explained what really happened, Simone told me I should sue.

"Do you think I have a case?"

"No, but it would probably make you feel better."

"I sued Just A Date to make myself feel better, and look where that got me."

The call waiting clicked in again. I left Simone on hold and clicked over to the other line. This time it was Greg.

"It's America's favorite romantically challenged serial dater," Greg said. "Can I get your autograph?"

"Drop dead," I told him and clicked back over to Simone. "That was Greg."

"Did he see it?" Simone asked.

"Yup. He's already calling me America's favorite romantically challenged serial dater."

She laughed.

"I'm glad you're all so amused."

"You'll be too, in time."

"I doubt that."

The call waiting clicked in again. This time it was my Aunt Rose. I hadn't spoken to her since my cousin Sharon's wedding.

"Julia, darling," Aunt Rose said. "We saw you on television. Your Uncle Ed and I just wanted you to know that we think you're doing the right thing, regardless of what those *Hollywood Tonight* people think. You don't need a therapist, you need a husband."

It continued all night. I fielded calls from perverts and wackos looking for a date, and old friends and distant relatives whom I hadn't heard from in years. Apparently everyone I knew or had ever known watched *Hollywood Tonight,* and they all felt the need to call me and share their thoughts about my situation. It was almost worse than actually watching myself on TV.

Almost.

CHAPTER 63

Celebritydom

When I arrived at work the next morning, I sprinted to my office with my head down, avoiding eye contact with everyone I passed along the way. I planned on staying holed up all day. I even skipped the Friday morning bagels so I wouldn't have to talk to anyone in the lunch room.

As soon as my computer booted up, I e-mailed Greg and Simone and begged them not to say anything about my TV appearance. They both agreed, although both e-mailed back that they suspected most of the office had already seen for themselves. Unfortunately, I knew they were right.

Before lunch, Rosenthal's secretary, Diane, sent an e-mail to the entire firm reminding us that the annual Rosenthal & Leventhal holiday party would start promptly at six o'clock. Since the party was at Mr. Rosenthal's house, the e-mail noted, which was only fifteen minutes from the office, Mr. Rosenthal was allowing us all to leave today at 5:45. Dress was Friday casual, so there was no need to go home and change.

Even the e-mail had become an annual event. Unlike every other firm in town, Rosenthal was too cheap to take all of his employees out for dinner at a nice restaurant. He wouldn't even splurge for a lunch at a not-so-nice restaurant.

Instead, each year he invited the entire firm to his house for an evening of hors d'oeuvres and all the wine and beer we could drink. The food wasn't great, but it was plentiful, and so was the alcohol. Everyone partook in the festivities, which inevitably led to at least one embarrassing incident per year, and on a good year, several.

Simone called me after lunch to coordinate.

"Same plan as last year? Leave the office at five, go home and change, and show up at Rosenthal's around seven?"

"Actually, I'm thinking of leaving at five and not showing up at all."

"What! You have to. You know Rosenthal will hold it against you if you don't come to his party."

"Don't you think, under the circumstances, he'll understand?" Even as I said it, I knew he wouldn't.

"No. He thinks he's already taken care of it."

"How?"

"He had Diane send us all an e-mail this morning telling us not to tease you about the *Hollywood Tonight* story. I'm sure the only reason he did that was so you would feel comfortable at the party tonight."

I wasn't so sure. "This is Rosenthal. He's not just being nice, he's up to something."

"Stop being so paranoid."

"I'm not paranoid! I just know Rosenthal."

"If you don't come tonight, he's going to be really angry."

"So he's mad at me. He'll get over it. He's not going to fire me just because I didn't show up to his stupid Christmas party."

"No, but do you really want to piss him off a week before the partnership meeting?"

"Who cares? I'm not up for partner this year. I'm only a sixth-year. He'll never even consider me until next year at the earliest. By then he'll have forgotten."

"Don't be so sure. Besides, Greg's only a sixth-year and he's up for partnership this year."

"I'm not a golden boy." And I don't kiss Rosenthal's ass.

"Well as long as it's still a possibility, don't completely blow your chances by skipping the party."

I knew I'd end up going, but I wasn't ready to concede quite yet. I told Simone I'd go with her to happy hour and then decide.

♡ ♡ ♡

After two vodka 7-Ups with Simone and Greg at O'Grady's, I agreed to go to Rosenthal's party. I was only slightly disappointed when we pulled up to the house and I saw that the catering van in the driveway wasn't Joe's. I hadn't heard from him all week. Not that I was expecting to. It's not like we were dating or anything. I just thought maybe he would've called to explain away his date on Saturday night. But he hadn't.

Greg grabbed a beer, and Simone and I each poured ourselves

a glass of cheap white wine. The three of us headed into the living room, then split up. The plan was that each of us would mingle separately, then reconvene in an hour for a quick getaway.

Rosenthal's e-mail had worked. Not one person mentioned my TV appearance. It wasn't that I wanted anyone to say anything. I didn't. I just couldn't believe that no one would.

At eight o'clock, Rosenthal dimmed the lights and asked us all to take seats in the den for his annual screening of *Rudolph the Red-Nosed Reindeer.* This was Rosenthal's favorite Christmas special, and each year he demanded that we all watch it together "as a family."

I took a seat in the corner of the room and saved two more for Simone and Greg, but they never showed. I couldn't believe those two had ditched me, especially after they'd talked me into coming. The only thing worse than listening to Rosenthal's annual holiday party speech was listening to it alone.

Rosenthal stood in front of his blank television screen until we all quieted down. "I just want to say a few words before we get started, he said. First, I want to thank all of you for your hard work this year. But I also want to remind you that collections are down. So I'm asking all of you whose clients have outstanding bills to call them and ask them to please pay up before Christmas. Otherwise, bonuses will reflect the amount we actually collected, instead of the amount we billed."

There was an audible groan in the room. This speech was another annual event. Rosenthal gave it every year no matter how well the firm had done or how hard we'd all worked.

"But tonight is for celebration," he continued. "Before we start *Rudolph,* I have a surprise for everyone. As most of you may already know, we have a celebrity in our midst. Julia, will you come up here."

"Me?" I mouthed.

"Yes, you," Rosenthal said. "You're the only Julia in the room."

Everyone laughed and I stood up. As I passed Rosenthal's secretary, Diane, on my way to the front of the room, I could see her shaking her head at him. That couldn't be good.

Rosenthal put his arm around my shoulder and hugged me to him. "I always knew you had potential," he said, and gave me another squeeze. I could smell the scotch on his breath.

Rosenthal shut off the lights and pushed PLAY on the VCR. It was my face on his sixty-inch television screen. The zit on my chin that I hadn't quite covered up with makeup was now two inches wide. I watched myself try to ignore Molly Truitt and then have my words twisted and used against me. When the camera cut back to the *Hollywood Tonight* anchors, Rosenthal stopped the tape, turned on the lights, and led the room in an enthusiastic round of applause. I wanted to run, but I stood next to him and vainly attempted to smile.

"We're glad to have you at Rosenthal & Leventhal, Julia, even if you are romantically challenged. But next time, will you please mention the name of the firm? I want us all to get some business out of this, not just you."

Everyone laughed again. Even me. It was either that or cry. I returned to my seat while Rosenthal switched tapes in the VCR. I waited until Rudolph and the elf who wanted to be a dentist left Christmas Town before I escaped to the bathroom.

I let myself wallow in self-pity for a full thirty seconds, then I wiped my eyes, fixed my makeup, and tried to look on the bright side. It could've been worse. A lot worse. Rosenthal actually did me a favor. This way I got all of my humiliation over with in one shot instead of having to have individual conversations with each of my coworkers. Even the timing was perfect. Surely someone would do something tonight that would trump me on the rumor mill Monday morning. Then that would become the story of the week and all this would be forgotten.

I left the bathroom and went upstairs to find my coat. Mrs. Rosenthal told me she had put them all in the guest bedroom. "Third door on the left at the top of the stairs," she'd said with a slight slur. Either I'd misunderstood her or she'd miscounted. When I opened the third door on the left I didn't find any coats, but I did find Greg lying on top of Simone in a four-poster bed.

CHAPTER 64

A New Day

Greg and Simone were both still fully clothed, but he had his hand up her shirt and she was fumbling with his zipper.

I was too startled to say anything, so I just stared.

Simone was the first to react. "It's not what it looks like," she said as she sat up and pushed Greg's hand out from under her blouse.

When Greg turned around and saw me, he practically leapt off the bed. "I'll leave you two alone," he said while simultaneously tucking his shirt back into his pants and sprinting for the door.

I shut it behind him and turned to Simone. "What the hell are you doing! You're getting married in three weeks."

"Three and a half," she said as she got off the bed and straightened her suede miniskirt.

"And you think that extra half week somehow makes it all right?"

"We didn't do anything. We were just kissing."

"Only because I walked in."

"I really don't need a morals lecture from Ms. Romantically Challenged."

And I realized that I didn't need to be giving one. "You're right. It's none of my business."

I found my coat in the bedroom behind the third door on the right and slipped out. It was only eight-thirty and I didn't want to go home, so I pulled out my cell phone and dialed Kaitlyn's number. When I heard her answering machine, I hung up. While the rational side of my brain mentally skimmed my phone book trying to decide who to call next, the irrational side dialed Joe's number.

When he answered, the rational side was too startled to hang up. "Hi. It's me, Julie."

"Hi," he said, sounding surprised. "I didn't think I'd be hearing from you again. Especially not now that you're a celebrity."

"Please don't."

His tone softened. "Actually, I was going to call you. I just figured I'd give you a few days to recover first."

Then I heard a woman's voice in the background complaining that they were going to be late and Joe telling her to give him a minute.

The exchange lasted long enough for my rational side to recover. "The really funny part is that I dialed your number by accident. I thought I was dialing Steve. His number's only two digits away from yours." I knew it was lame, but my rational side was still dazed.

"Well, I'm glad you got me instead. I'm on my way out the door, but I'll call you tomorrow. I want the full story on the life of a romantically challenged serial dater."

We hung up and I drove home. My humiliation was complete. At least until I listened to the fourteen messages on my answering machine. Six were from strange men who wanted to get to know me, four were from former classmates, two were from relatives, one was from a woman who told me my problem was that I was dating the wrong sex, and one was from Marty. They had all seen my story on *Hollywood Tonight,* but Marty was the only one who hadn't asked me to call him back.

He apologized for having to cancel our date on such short notice, but said it couldn't be helped. He neither gave an excuse nor suggested we reschedule. I could only deduce that he didn't want to be seen in public with America's favorite romantically challenged serial dater. After all, what would that make him?

As I had hoped, by Monday morning my foray into celebritydom was forgotten for more juicy gossip. My TV appearance was replaced as the topic du jour by Parker's secretary, who had gotten so drunk at the holiday party that she'd decided to go for a swim in Rosenthal's pool wearing only her underwear. I'd also heard some rumors about Greg and Simone, but no one could substantiate them.

Simone didn't wait for Rosenthal to leave for his therapy session before she snuck into my office and gave me a hug.

"I'm so sorry about the other night," she said.

"No, you were right. It was none of my business. I'm sorry I interrupted."

"Are you kidding? I should be thanking you for interrupting."

Now that we were friends again, I could ask. "What happened?"

Simone told me that she and Greg had gone upstairs to look for the coats and found the four-poster bed instead. "Greg suggested we try out the down comforter, and before I knew it, you were standing there looking horrified. It was just curiosity mixed with alcohol."

I suspected there was a dash of prewedding jitters, too. "So is he any good?"

"I don't know! All we did was kiss." Then she smiled and added, "But he's good at that."

Perhaps I shouldn't have been so quick to dismiss him. Then again, it wasn't too late. "Maybe I'll get to judge for myself. Greg's my date for your wedding."

Simone's eyes widened.

"Not a real date, a pseudo date. Just someone to sit next to at dinner and dance with a few times. You know how awful it is to go to a wedding alone, and yours is on New Year's Eve."

"Sorry, Julie, but I sort of uninvited Greg. We both agreed that under the circumstances it would be better for everyone if he wasn't there."

Everyone but me! "Don't you think it'll look a little suspicious if Greg doesn't show?"

"To who? Besides you and Greg, the only other person from the office I invited to the wedding was Rosenthal, and he's not coming. Todd thought it was weird when I invited Greg in the first place. He won't think it's weird when I tell him Greg can't make it. He'll probably be glad. He never really liked Greg."

Great. Another dateless wedding. And the last one worked out so well.

"What about Marty?" Simone asked. "Didn't you two have a date this weekend?"

I told her about Marty's phone message.

"That's too bad. Although it does explain the one he left at our house asking if he could bring someone to the wedding. I didn't really understand it at the time, since I remembered telling him at Thanksgiving that you didn't have a date."

"Simone, you promised not to interfere."

"I only told him because he asked if there were going to be any other single people at the wedding."

"Well, are there?"

Simone thought about it for a minute. "Todd's cousin Christine. I know she's not bringing anyone."

"Men, I mean."

She shook her head. "Greg and Marty would've been the only ones. Do you want me to tell Marty it's too late to add another guest?"

"No, after the way he blew me off, I don't want him as my date anyway."

"Then you should definitely bring someone else."

"Like who?" At this point, I didn't even have any potential dates.

"How about the bartender?"

"Joe? The guy who went on a date with me in the afternoon and then another woman at night?"

"I thought you said you two weren't on a date."

"We weren't, but that's not the point. He was still on a date with someone else that evening."

"So what?" Simone said. "It was just a date. It doesn't mean she's his girlfriend. You've gone on twenty-five dates and you still don't have a boyfriend."

"Thanks for reminding me."

"Don't be so sensitive. I only meant that just because you saw him out on a date doesn't mean he's not available."

I told Simone about my phone call to Joe Friday night.

"So what? You don't even know if it was the same woman. She could've been some friend of his who stopped by to pick him up."

I stared at her incredulously. I could tell by the smile she was trying to suppress that even she didn't believe that one.

"Did he call you back?" she asked.

"Yeah, but I haven't returned the call yet."

"Well, here's your opportunity. You can call him and ask him to the wedding."

CHAPTER 65

Will He or Won't He

I had just shut my office door when the phone started ringing. I stood in the hallway with my coat on and my briefcase in my hand and debated with myself. It might be Joe. I'd left him a message earlier in the day and I needed to talk to him before I lost my nerve. I unlocked the door and ran to the phone. It wasn't Joe. It was Mark Parsons.

We made small talk while I scanned my list of active cases. If I was working on a matter for Rosebud, I certainly couldn't remember it.

"So the real reason I called," Mark finally said, "was to see if you're free for lunch."

I wasn't expecting that. The last time we'd even spoken was

when we'd bumped into each other at the movie premiere. He'd been cordial, but not effusive. "Sure. Is this business or pleasure?"

"A little of both."

Now I was intrigued. "Care to elaborate?"

"No, I'd rather keep you in suspense."

I agreed to meet Mark Friday afternoon at The Barn, the newest overpriced power restaurant on the west side. I certainly hoped Mark would be paying: Rosenthal would kill me if I tried to expense a $100 lunch, even if it was for his favorite client.

I played out various scenarios in my head on the drive home, but I couldn't come up with a satisfactory explanation for the lunch meeting. After listening to another five messages from assorted psychos on my answering machine, I called Kaitlyn.

Kaitlyn concluded that I needed to switch to an unlisted phone number and that the only reason Mark Parsons could possibly want to have lunch with me was because he was going to offer me a job.

"It's obvious," she said.

It wasn't obvious to me. "Why would you think that?"

"What else could it be? If it was a new case, he would've told you about it over the phone so you could get started right away. Or more likely, he would've called Rosenthal."

"Maybe he just wants to say thank you for my work on the sexual harassment case. I did get a good result."

"No way. That was over three months ago, and he would've invited Rosenthal too. If he wants to meet with you alone, it's definitely about a job."

I wasn't so sure, but I couldn't come up with any other explanation. "I can't change jobs now, I'm up for partnership next year."

"That's ridiculous. You would turn down a great opportunity now because Rosenthal might make you a partner a year from now?"

"The only reason I've stuck it out this long is because I want to be partner. I'm not gonna leave now when I've only got one more year to go." Of course, there were no guarantees that Rosenthal was going to make me a partner. But I had to at least try, didn't I?

"You're making a mistake, but it's your life."

The upside of spending a sleepless night worrying about whether turning down the job that Mark Parsons hadn't offered me yet would be the biggest mistake of my life was that when Joe called me back at work the next day, I was too exhausted to be nervous. I told him the real story behind my *Hollywood Tonight* episode, with minor modifications. I added that I'd only joined Just A Date to appease my mother. Joe had never met my mother, but he knew the type.

I didn't ask Joe about Barbie or if she was the woman at his house Friday night, and he didn't offer any explanation. Nor did he ask me about Steve. Apparently we'd adopted the "don't ask, don't tell" policy. I knew it was better that way, but I was still dying to know.

After we'd exhausted all the safe subjects, I eased into the wedding question by asking him if he was going home for the holidays.

"No," Joe said. "I just went home for Thanksgiving. I'm staying in L.A. for Christmas so I can work. How about you?"

"Same," I said. "It's usually slow around Christmas, so it's a good time to catch up on all those things I never have time to do. Besides, I have a wedding here New Year's Eve, so it seemed silly to fly home for Christmas and then fly back before New Year's."

I was hoping that would prompt him to ask me about the wedding. It didn't. After ten seconds of uncomfortable silence, I dove in. "Do you have any plans for New Year's Eve?"

"I'm working," he said.

"You're catering a party on New Year's Eve?" I guess I should've expected that.

"Actually, I'm bartending."

"I thought you didn't do that anymore?"

"I usually don't, but the money's really good on New Year's, so I couldn't turn it down. Why?"

"No reason." No point in telling the truth now.

"Liar! You wanted to spend New Year's Eve with me, didn't you?"

"I did not."

"You did too. Admit it. What did you have planned?"

"Nothing."

"A night of seduction?"

"You wish."

"Then what?"

I knew he wasn't going to let this one go. "I just needed a date for my friend's wedding, that's all. No big deal."

"Why do you want to bring a date to a wedding? Don't you know weddings are a great place to meet people?"

"Yeah, I met you at the last one."

He laughed, then said, "Touché."

"Maybe it's because it's on New Year's Eve," I added, "but this one's going to be all couples."

"Do you expect me to believe that a romantically challenged serial dater can't get a date?"

I explained to Joe that I had planned on going with Greg until Simone uninvited him, and now it was too late to find someone else. He didn't need to know about Marty.

"I'm really sorry, Julie. I'd love to take you if I wasn't working, but I've already committed."

"No problem, Joe. I understand." Actually, I didn't. But I consoled myself with the knowledge that at least he was blowing me off for work and not another woman. Somehow that made it better.

CHAPTER 66

Partners for Life

I had barely begun to feel sorry for myself when Simone ran into my office and shut the door.

"Guess what?" she said. She didn't wait for a response. "The partners are meeting tonight. You're up for partnership this year, along with me and Greg."

"Are you sure?"

"Absolutely. I heard it straight from Rosenthal's secretary."

Diane was the source for all reliable information. "Why is he considering me now? I'm only a sixth-year. Technically, I'm not up for consideration until next year."

"Greg's only a sixth-year, and you didn't think it was weird that he was up for partnership a year early."

"That's because Greg's a kiss-ass." Now that she and Greg were on the outs, I could say these things to her again.

"True. But you're a celebrity. To Rosenthal, that's even better than a kiss-ass."

I didn't need to work late, but I did anyway. I was hoping the partners' meeting would end while I was still in the office and that someone would tell me the outcome. By eight o'clock, I was tired of waiting. I went next door to Simone's office and told her I was leaving. She said she was going to stick around a little longer and promised to call if there was any news. I stopped by Greg's office too, but he was already gone. No one in the firm doubted that Greg would make partner. Especially not Greg.

Simone, Greg, and I spent most of the day Wednesday going in and out of each other's offices, trying to decide whether no news was good news or bad news. Rosenthal let us squirm until five o'clock, then he called us down to his office for a group meeting.

The three of us lined up on his couch. Greg on one end, Simone on the other, and me sandwiched in the middle. If Rosenthal noticed the tension between Greg and Simone, he didn't mention it. He closed his door, leaned on the edge of his desk, and with his arms folded across his chest said, "I'm sure you know we had a partners' meeting last night. And I'm sure you also know that one of the items on the agenda is whether each of you will make partner this year."

He moved behind his desk and sat down before continuing. "What you may not know is that we didn't finish last night. We're reconvening again tomorrow night, so if all goes well, I should have an answer for you by Friday."

"Why aren't you meeting tonight?" Greg asked what I, and I'm sure Simone, was thinking.

"I have a previous engagement," Rosenthal said, then smiled. He really loved watching us sweat.

I arrived at work Friday morning at 8:15. That was the earliest I'd ever made it to the office. I'd even beat the bagel man. I was surprised when I found Simone sitting at her desk.

"You couldn't sleep either, huh?" I asked.

"No. I figured I might as well come in and get some work done."

"That's what I told myself too."

We spent the next hour drinking coffee and playing darts. This time it was Rosenthal's picture tacked to the board.

At 9:15, I went back to my own office and pretended to work while I waited for Rosenthal to arrive. He walked past my door promptly at 9:30, but didn't say a word.

After half an hour, Rosenthal must've decided he'd tortured us enough for one week. He walked into my office and closed the door behind him. I held my breath.

"Congratulations," he said. "You are now a partner at Rosenthal & Leventhal."

I breathed, but I was still in shock. I never thought he'd do it. Not this year, anyway. It was too soon. I stood up to shake Rosenthal's hand, but he walked around the desk and gave me a hug. I thanked him and he beamed at me like a proud father.

"Just remember," he said, "next time you're on television you need to mention the name of the firm."

"Done." I was too excited to be annoyed.

Rosenthal walked out and turned toward Simone's office. When I heard him shut Simone's door, I put my ear up to our common wall. I could hear voices, but I couldn't make out the words. I didn't have a glass, so I tried holding a paper cup up to the wall, but it didn't help. I waited until I heard Rosenthal's voice in the hallway before I ventured out. He was halfway to Greg's office when I walked into Simone's. She was staring out the window with her back toward the door.

"So?" I asked.

"You first," she said with that inscrutable expression I could never pull off.

"Yes," I said.

"Me too!" she yelled and broke out her best smile. We hugged and congratulated each other and planned how we would spend all that extra money we were sure we would make now that we were partners. Simone said she was going to trade in her old BMW for a Jaguar. I was debating between using the extra money for a down payment on a condo or paying off my student loans.

Greg joined us a few minutes later.

"What's wrong?" I asked. He was the only one of the three of us that didn't look happy.

"Didn't you talk to Rosenthal?" he said.

"Yes, I made partner. Simone too." I didn't dare ask him if he'd made partner.

"Did you ask him what kind of a partner?" Greg said.

"How many kinds are there?" Simone asked before I could.

"Two kinds," Greg said. "Equity partners and income partners. Equity partners actually own a piece of the firm and share in the profits. Income partners are partners in name only. It's really just a glorified title for senior associates so they can tell their clients they're partners."

"That bastard!" I said at the same time as Simone said, "Rosenthal told you this?" Simone was still in denial. I'd already moved into anger.

"Not in those words," Greg said, "but yes."

"How come he didn't tell us?" Simone asked.

"Well, he didn't volunteer the information to me either," Greg replied. "After he congratulated me, I started asking him about the procedure for buying into the partnership. He told me I didn't need to worry about that just yet. When I pushed him on it, he admitted that he'd made the three of us income partners."

"Did he give you an excuse?" Simone asked.

"He started with his usual bullshit about how the firm wasn't as profitable as it used to be and—"

"What does that mean?" I asked. "He only made one million this year instead of two million?"

"Apparently," Greg continued. "He said he couldn't consider any new equity partners before things turned around."

"And did he say how long that would be?" Simone asked.

"He was his usual noncommittal self," Greg said, "but thought it would be at least another year or two."

"And when was he planning on telling us this?" I asked.

"I don't know," Greg said. "You'll have to ask him that."

I didn't need to ask. I knew if I did, he'd come up with some lame excuse and then try to placate me by assuring me that income partnership was just the first step toward equity partnership. Then he'd tell me that, in the meantime, I should be patient and develop business on my own. As if I would stick around working for him if I had lots of my own clients. Fuck that! I would take the Rosebud job and tell Rosenthal to shove his income partnership right up his ass.

CHAPTER 67

Career Crossroads

I tried to calm myself while I perused the menu at The Barn. Mark Parsons showed up ten minutes late in his Friday casual khakis and black turtleneck. I'd changed out of my jeans and into my black pant suit before I'd left the office. Originally, I'd planned on changing in the ladies' room in the lobby, but I was so angry at Rosenthal that I didn't care if everyone in the office saw me in my suit on a Friday and assumed I had a job interview.

We ordered salads and entrées, then Mark opened with personal questions. He asked about Noah, and I told him that was over. When he asked why, I deflected. Then he asked if I'd had any other interesting dates lately. I told him none worth mentioning. I wanted this to be a professional relationship: I didn't want to set bad precedent by sharing personal stories with my future boss. Besides, I had no good stories to tell.

I reciprocated by asking Mark about his wife, his new baby, and his trip to Africa. He told me his wife and child were fine, then regaled me for the rest of the meal with tales from his safari. When we'd finished our entrées and Mark still hadn't mentioned the job, I started to worry. I stopped worrying when he ordered coffee and dessert.

"Did I tell you how great you looked on *Hollywood Tonight*?" Mark said.

"No," I replied. I wasn't sure which part was more disturbing—that he saw me on *Hollywood Tonight* or that he said it like he was hitting on me.

"Not that you don't look great in person," he added.

I gave him a halfhearted smile. "Thanks. Does that conclude the business part of our lunch?" I knew I was being rude, but he was making me uncomfortable.

He continued unruffled. "No, it's just the beginning." He took a bite of the chocolate cake the waiter had left in the center of the table. "You should try the soufflé cake. It's delicious."

He was right. I ate while he talked.

"I have a proposition for you," he said. "As you may know, up to this point Rosebud has primarily been a film production company. But recently we've decided to expand into television."

Here it comes. He wants me to be their television lawyer. I would've preferred film, but I'd take TV. I could always move over to the film side later.

"We're always looking for good material," Mark said, "and we think you're it."

They must really want me. I should milk this. "I'm flattered, Mark. I really am. But before you say anything else, I think you should know that Rosenthal just made me a partner."

"Congratulations! You should've told me sooner, I would've ordered Champagne."

Why was he so happy about it? Didn't he know that meant he would have to pay me more money?

Mark insisted we toast. "To your continued success," he said, and clinked his coffee cup against mine. "I guess you'll be making so much money now that you won't need ours."

Oh, shit, I'd overplayed my hand. Now he thinks I don't want the job. "I wouldn't say that. For me, it's not just about the money. It's about personal satisfaction too."

"I couldn't agree more," he said. "So let's get down to it. What are you looking for?"

"That depends on what you're offering." I knew better than to start the negotiation.

He gave me a knowing smile. "We were thinking $50,000 plus five percent of net."

Was he nuts? I knew his offer would be low, but I didn't think it would be that low. My base salary was more than double that figure. And what was this five percent of net? Company profit-sharing? I tried to keep my expression neutral when I said, "That's kind of low."

"Have you had higher offers?"

"Well, I haven't really been looking."

"Maybe I can get them up to seventy-five thousand, but that's as high as I can go up front. I might be able to work with you on the back end."

Back end? Was that supposed to mean bonus? "Mark, first year lawyers make more than that."

"I'm not hiring a first-year lawyer, Julie, I'm buying the rights to your story."

"What?"

"Haven't you been listening? Rosebud wants to buy your life story rights."

At first I was too stunned to speak. Then I had to laugh. Before long, I was hysterical.

"Are you okay?" Mark asked.

I just shook my head yes and continued laughing. Then he started laughing too. After I'd calmed down enough to speak, I said, "I thought you were offering me a job."

That made Mark laugh even harder, which sobered me up

quick. That part wasn't funny. Corporations hire their outside counsel to be in-house lawyers all the time.

When Mark noticed I wasn't laughing anymore he said, "It's not that I wouldn't offer you a position if I had one, I just don't have an opening right now. But I'll certainly keep you in mind if anything becomes available."

"That's okay." I was still offended that he would laugh at the notion of hiring me.

"So everyone at Rosebud loved you on *Hollywood Tonight*," he continued. "We think your story has real potential."

"As what?"

"A series. Or possibly a made-for-TV movie. We haven't decided yet."

Were they all crazy? "I don't see it. My life is pretty dull."

"On the contrary," he said, raising his hands in the air as if he were placing the words on an imaginary billboard. "Romantically challenged single serial dates L.A." He lowered his arms and reached for his coffee cup. "That's good stuff."

"They exaggerated that part. I'm not romantically challenged, and I'm certainly not a serial dater. I'm just a lawyer who happens to do a fair amount of dating."

"It sounds like a hit to me."

"What are you thinking? *Sex in the City* without the sex?"

"No, we have to have sex."

"Well, there wasn't any. There were only dates."

"Then we'll have to change that part. Otherwise no one would watch."

CHAPTER 68

It's All in the Attitude

I spent the weekend celebrating my partnership. After my initial anger at being duped subsided, I wasn't that upset. I never believed Rosenthal would make me a partner a year early anyway, so I decided to take the income partnership as a compliment. It was at least partial validation. It would do. For now at least.

Greg felt differently. He couldn't get past feeling like he'd been slapped in the face. We went out for drinks Friday night, ostensibly to celebrate, but mainly I just listened to Greg bemoan his fate. Somehow it made me feel better. I just hoped that didn't mean that deep down inside I was a terrible person. It was bad enough being a lawyer, I didn't want to be a terrible person too.

Saturday was better. I met Simone at the bridal store to offer advice on her last fitting. I'd been a bridesmaid seven times. I knew about fittings. Afterward, we treated ourselves to a Champagne lunch. Simone's attitude about partnership was closer to mine than to Greg's. She hadn't expected to be made a full partner, so she wasn't devastated by the idea of income partnership.

"Besides," Simone said after her second glass, "I was planning on having kids soon anyway."

"So what? You can have kids and still be a partner."

"Not if I want to work part-time." In her best Rosenthal imitation, including admiring her reflection in the window and fingering her hair, Simone said, "That's a luxury only afforded lawyers who aren't serious about their profession."

We both knew it was only a matter of time before those words came out of Rosenthal's mouth.

Saturday night I met Kaitlyn and Steve for a celebratory dinner. They came as a package now, at least on weekends. Luckily, I liked Steve. He cracked up laughing when I told him about my lunch with Mark Parsons. Kaitlyn didn't think it was quite as funny, since she was the one who was sure Mark was going to offer me a job.

"So are you going to sell him your life story rights?" Steve asked.

"Of course not." "Do you think I want to be known as a romantically challenged serial dater for the rest of my life?"

"Why not?" Kaitlyn said. "If it will make you rich and famous."

"It's not going to make me rich. They offered me at most seventy-five thousand dollars, which after taxes will be forty thousand."

"Don't forget the five percent of net profits," Steve said, and started laughing again.

Everyone knows there's no such thing as net profits.

"You can still be famous," Kaitlyn offered. "I've never known anyone famous before."

"And you're not going to, so get used to it. I just want this whole *Hollywood Tonight* thing to be forgotten so I can start dating again."

As my mother likes to remind me, I'm not getting any younger.

After drinking all day Saturday, I had to spend all day Sunday lying on the couch with Elmo, recovering from a massive hangover. That's another down side of getting older—the hangovers are worse.

Shockingly, the bright spot of my day was when my parents called. They were ecstatic when I told them that Rosenthal had made me a partner. Even my explanation that I was only an income partner, which wasn't really a partner at all, didn't dampen their enthusiasm. They could still brag to all of their friends that I was a partner in a prestigious Los Angeles law firm. Appearances would be upheld.

"Naturally I would've preferred you called me and told me you were getting married," my mother said. "But this is good too," she added before I could object.

My father just congratulated me and wanted to know how much money I would make. I didn't want to burst his bubble, so I told him I didn't know yet because my new status wouldn't take effect until the following year. After lecturing me about tax consequences and the benefits of saving early for retirement, he put my mother back on the phone. It was the longest phone conversation I'd had with them in years.

Despite my new status, the moment I pulled into the office parking garage Monday morning I was overcome with depression. Nothing had changed. Rosenthal could call me a partner, but I was still a worker bee and he was still the queen.

After checking my e-mail, playing on the Internet, and reading the trades, I made my first call of the day to Mark Parsons. I told him again that I appreciated the offer but my answer was still no. He said he was disappointed, but that he understood. He also told me they were thinking of calling Susan, the other woman from *Hollywood Tonight,* to see if she was interested in selling her story. I wished him luck with a pang of jealousy. I hadn't changed my mind; I just didn't like the idea of being so easily replaced.

I made it through the rest of the week without incident. No dates, no crises, just work. By Friday afternoon I was practically wishing for a minor calamity just to break up the monotony.

My big event for the weekend was taking Kaitlyn and Steve to the airport. Kaitlyn was flying home with Steve for Christmas to meet his family. The first stop on the road to marriage. We both knew the ring was coming. It was only a matter of time.

They'd probably thank me at the wedding. Steve would make a toast and tell everyone that if he'd been interested in another date with me, he never would've met Kaitlyn. All the guests would laugh and I would stand there, embarrassed, in another hideous bridesmaid dress. It would be my eighth. Maybe I should start looking for a date now.

Since our Christmas bonuses were less than everyone had hoped, Rosenthal attempted to placate the troops with extra days off on Christmas Eve and New Year's Eve. I spent my Christmas Eve at home with Elmo. We read back issues of *People* magazine, ate not quite stale Christmas cookies, and watched *How The Grinch Stole Christmas* three times in a row. Actually, I was the only one who ate the cookies. Elmo just read over my shoulder and watched TV.

New Year's Eve day I decided to treat myself to a few hours of pampering at one of those fancy salons in Beverly Hills where all the celebrities go. I wanted to start the New Year looking my best and in better spirits. A day of beauty was the quickest way to a positive attitude, at least according to the brochure at the salon.

I left with manicured nails, pedicured toes, and a new hair style. I wanted a facial too, but all the facialists were booked, so I bought some overpriced creams and scrubs and figured I would try it myself at home.

I came home to one message on my answering machine. "Julia, it's Mommy." I hit STOP. Last New Year's Eve my mother left me a message saying that her New Year's Resolution for me was that next year I wouldn't be alone. I'd just spent $300 improving my attitude; I didn't want it destroyed by a ten-second phone message.

I let my finger hover over the DELETE button, but eventually I hit PLAY again. Even with my new attitude, I wasn't one of those people who could just delete a message without listening to it, no matter how much I wanted to. "I called to wish you a Happy and Healthy New Year," my mother's voice continued, "and to tell you to have a good time at the wedding."

Maybe she'd spent $300 improving her attitude, too. A good omen for the New Year.

That night, after a hundred sit-ups so my stomach would be flat in my gown, I slipped an Andrea Bocelli CD onto the stereo, lit an aromatherapy candle, and soaked myself in a bubble bath. After I'd loofahed every dead skin cell off my body, I started on my face. I wrapped myself in my fuzzy blue moon and stars bathrobe, covered my hair with a shower cap to keep it clean, and lathered on my new facial goo.

The instructions said to massage the cream into the skin and wait ten minutes. When it hardened into a crusty paste, I was supposed to rinse. Under no circumstances was I to leave the cream on my skin for longer than twenty minutes. Piece of cake.

I laid down on the living room floor, face up, with my head resting on a pillow. I checked my watch every two minutes while I flipped through the pages of the January issue of *Vanity Fair*. After ten minutes had passed, I went into the bathroom and checked my face. The goo was pasty, but not crusty. I decided to wait another few minutes.

I'd just repositioned myself on the pillow when the intercom buzzed. I got up, pushed the TALK button, and said hello. No one answered. It was probably just someone who'd accidentally reached the wrong apartment. It happened all the time, but I never buzzed anyone in. This was supposed to be a security building. I wasn't going to buzz someone inside without knowing who it was. I sat back down on the living room floor.

I hadn't even gotten comfortable yet when the intercom buzzed a second time. Again I pushed the TALK button, and again no one answered. When it buzzed the third time, I ignored it and went to check my goo. It was almost crusty, but not quite. I checked my watch. It had only been thirteen minutes. I'd give it two more minutes, then rinse.

I'd just gotten the pillow in exactly the right spot under my neck when I heard someone playing with the lock on my door. At first I was too stunned to move. As far as I knew, I was the only person with a key to my apartment. But when I saw the knob turn, I recovered fast and ran into the kitchen. The person from downstairs must've found someone to buzz them in and now they were breaking into my apartment!

My heart was pounding in my chest so fast I thought I was going to have a heart attack. I wanted to call 911, but the phone was still in the living room. Instead I pulled a steak knife out of the butcher block on my kitchen counter and waited. I might be smaller than the assailant, but at least I would have the element of surprise.

I heard the door open, then someone called out. "Julie, are you home? It's Mrs. Klein."

I breathed. It was only my landlady. I put the knife down and walked back into the living room. The barely five-foot-tall Mrs. Klein was standing in my doorway with a man beside her. The man was Joe.

CHAPTER 69

Looking My Best

"**W**hat are you doing here?" I asked Joe.

It was Mrs. Klein who answered. "Oh, Julie, I'm so glad you're okay. This nice young man said he kept buzzing you but you didn't answer. He thought your intercom might be broken, so he buzzed me."

"I think it is," I said. "It buzzed three times, but every time I picked up, there was no one on the other end."

"I tried calling you," Mrs. Klein said, "but all I got was a message that your number had been disconnected. I started to worry, so I came up to check."

"I just switched to an unlisted phone number. Sorry, I forgot to give it to you." I found a pen and pad by the phone and wrote down the new number for her.

"Well, I won't keep you," she said. "But what's that you've got on your face? You look like your skin's about to crack."

Oh, shit. I touched the goo and it was hard as a rock. I picked up my watch. It had been twenty-two minutes. I ran into the bathroom and splashed cold water on my face, but the crusty stuff wouldn't come off. Shit! Shit! Shit!

I picked up the container and read the warning label. It said not to keep the cream on the skin longer than twenty minutes, but it didn't have instructions for what to do if you didn't follow the instructions. I turned the water to hot, wet my towel under the sink, and began scrubbing my face. Ten minutes later all the crusty stuff was gone. My face was sore from all the rubbing, but I didn't think there was any permanent damage.

I went back out to the living room. My landlady had left, but Joe was sitting on the couch playing with Elmo. Elmo was telling him he loved being tickled.

"All better?" Joe asked.

"What are you doing here?"

He held up a suit bag and a pair of dress shoes. "I came to take you to the wedding. Assuming, that is, you still need a date."

"I thought you had to work?"

"I did. But I got to thinking about it after you called and decided I'd rather spend New Year's Eve at a wedding with you than serving drinks to a bunch of drunk assholes at some Hollywood party."

"Couldn't you have told me this a little sooner?"

"I didn't want to say yes until I knew I could make it. I almost didn't. I just found someone to cover for me this morning. I tried calling you, but. . . ."

I guess I'd forgotten to give Joe the new number too.

"I also left you three messages at your office, but you never called me back. I didn't know what was going on, so I finally decided just to drive over here and talk to you in person."

"I can't believe you did this for me, Joe. This was really nice of you." He just scored big-time points.

"I keep telling you, honey, I'm a good catch." Then he stood up and kissed me. It was long and sweet and I would've stayed there forever if he hadn't pulled the shower cap off my head and said, "What the hell is this?"

I grabbed it out of his hand. "Nothing, I was trying to keep the goo out of my hair."

"You probably should've kept it off your face too. You look a little red."

I put my hands to my cheeks. They felt hot and puffy. I ran to the bathroom mirror and screamed. I looked like a sunburned chipmunk.

Joe ran into the bathroom too. "What's wrong?"

"Look at me," I shouted.

"What? So your cheeks are a little red. You just look like you've been out in the sun too long."

"I look like I fell asleep under a sun lamp for twelve hours and then got stung by a bee!"

"No you don't. Maybe your face is a tiny bit swollen. But if you hadn't pointed it out, I would never have noticed."

I appreciated the effort, but he was lying through his teeth. I looked hideous.

Joe glanced at his watch. "What time is the wedding?"

"Who cares," I said. "I'm not going."

"What do you mean you're not going?"

"I can't go looking like this."

"You look fine," he said. "Just put on a little makeup and no one will ever know."

"Joe, I can't cover this up with makeup."

"Why not?"

What a man! "Because there is no makeup in the world that can unswell my cheeks and turn my skin back to normal. I think I'm having an allergic reaction to something in that face cream."

"Then I'll go to the drugstore and get you some medicine."

It wasn't a bad idea. I certainly didn't have a better one.

"Sit tight," he said. He grabbed his keys, kissed me on the forehead, and was just about to close the door behind him when he stopped. "This time you are going to buzz me in, right?"

I promised I would and he was gone. I laid down on the couch with cold compresses on my face and waited. Joe came back twenty minutes later with a tube of hydrocortisone cream and a package of Benadryl.

I swallowed two pills, rubbed the cream on my face, and then applied my makeup. I didn't look good, but I was presentable enough to leave the house. I gave Joe the bathroom so he could change into his suit, and I went to the bedroom to get dressed. At least this time I wasn't a bridesmaid, which meant I could wear an attractive evening gown.

My dress was long, black, and strapless, with a slit up the back that ended midthigh. I could barely walk in my four-inch heels, but they made my legs look thin, so I bought them anyway. I donned a faux diamond necklace with matching earrings and walked out to the living room.

Joe was wearing a black suit with a gray shirt and tie. The wedding was black-tie, but the suit would do. It would have to.

Joe gave me an appreciative whistle. "You look spectacular."

"Thank you," I said. "You clean up well too." He really did.

CHAPTER 70

Another Wedding

Joe drove us the six blocks to the Four Seasons Hotel. We were fifteen minutes late, but the wedding started half an hour late, so we didn't miss anything.

Simone looked beautiful, the ceremony was mercifully short, and the reception was amazing. Joe and I and the other three hundred guests dined on a seven-course meal while being serenaded by a twelve-piece band in a room filled with thousands of white roses.

Or at least that's how it was described to me the next day. I remembered the ceremony, the flowers, and the cocktail hour. After that it got hazy. I didn't find out until I was on my second vodka and 7-Up that Benadryl is a sedative and shouldn't be mixed with alcohol.

♡ ♡ ♡

I woke up late on New Year's Day. I was alone in my bed, still wearing my bra and underwear. My gown was hanging on the back of the closet door, my shoes and purse on the floor beneath it. I didn't know where my pantyhose were. Knowing me, I'd probably torn them off in the bathroom the night before.

I heard noises coming from the other room so I donned my bathrobe and went to investigate.

"Good morning, sleepyhead," Joe said. He was standing in my kitchen, barefoot, wearing his jeans and T-shirt from the day before. He was stirring something in a mixing bowl I'd forgotten I even owned. He bent down to kiss me, but I turned away.

"Don't," I said. "I haven't brushed my teeth yet."

"That reminds me, I borrowed one of your extra toothbrushes. I hope you don't mind."

"Consider it a gift," I said and headed toward the bathroom. I still had mascara smeared under my eyes, but most of the swelling on my face had gone down and the red had faded to an attractive shade of pink.

I brushed my teeth, washed my face, and combed the bedhead out of my hair. I went into the bedroom and traded my bathrobe for pajama pants and a clean T-shirt, then I joined Joe in the kitchen.

I sat at the table and watched him spoon the batter from the mixing bowl into a muffin tin, then place it in the oven. He pulled an orange juice container from the refrigerator and poured me a glass.

"This seems a little familiar," I said. "Although I believe the last time we dined al fresco."

"I can assure you this time the outcome will be different."

"How do you know?"

"Because I've hidden my car keys someplace you'll never find them."

"We're at my house this time. How do I know you won't steal my car?"

Joe turned off the oven and took the glass of orange juice from my hand.

"Trust me," he said.

Then he kissed me. Slow and seductive.

We had the blueberry muffins for dinner.